"Reading Paul Zerby's novel *The Grass* brought back many memories for me. His description of life at the University of Minnesota reminded me of my college experiences while in ROTC during another controversial 'conflict'—Vietnam. Zerby skillfully explains the history of the Korea conflict and the conflicting opinions about it. He puts a human picture on the horrors of war and forces the reader to experience the unimaginable suffering of boys sent off to combat. This novel, while entertaining, needs to be read by those wishing to understand the brutal nature of war and the incredible sacrifices made by the miniscule percentage of the population who actually fight them."

Dennis W. Schulstad

Air Force Brigadier General, retired

"A well-written, authentic account of the GI experience during the Korean War. At the time pretty much ignored, and then forgotten, historians have recently ascribed to this conflict a more important place in history."

B.G. Schwartzbauer

Twenty-fifth Infantry Division, Korea, 1951-1952

"*The Grass* brings to life the saga of an American Midwesterner, who in his own words, talks about going to Korea as a young boy and coming back as a grown man. Anyone who reads this book will gladly join the young soldier's most remarkable journey, which changed the course of his life entirely. Tom Kelly's journey to war-torn Korea may not be the most exciting subject matter for someone to write about, however, Paul Zerby did an excellent job of weaving many interesting characters' life stories into an impressive novel. The readers will quickly empathize with all the characters in the book, who are all very typical Americans, regardless of their backgrounds. Whether Paul Zerby intended or not, Tom Kelly's story is a tale of acceptance and rejection, of struggle and success, which is unique yet most common among all of us. The novel promises to be a major step forward in our collective understanding of the forgotten war, and how it impacted the lives of young Americans five decades ago."

Woodrow "Wooj" Byun

former President of the Korean Association of Minnesota

"Paul Zerby has created a powerful and captivating volume of writing. Raw in its unexpurgated form. Sometimes shocking. It masterfully and successfully presents a microcosm of the early 1950s U.S.A. during the Korean War. As an infantry veteran of that war, I can personally relate to much of what Zerby wrote. It's not for the faint of heart. Nor does it communicate in lofty words. Rather, it's below the clouds, down to earth, occasionally bloody, but with a satisfying outcome. I heartily recommend it."

Donald E. Montgomery

Edina, Minnesota

The Grass

A NOVEL OF A YOUNG MAN'S JOURNEY TO THE KOREAN WAR

Paul Zerby

North Star Press of St. Cloud, Inc.
St. Cloud, Minnesota

Chapters from *The Grass* were excerpted in *The Best of Northlight 1990*, Edited by W. Scott Olsen; and in *Grounds for Peace, Women Against Military Madness* (1994).

Front Cover: Korean War Veterans Memorial,
Washington, D.C.

ISBN: 0-87839-310-2
ISBN-13: 978-0-87839-310-7

Printed in the United States of America by
Sentinel Printing, St. Cloud, Minnesota.

Published by
North Star Press of St. Cloud, Inc.
P.O. Box 451
St. Cloud, Minnesota 56302
northstarpress.com
info@northstarpress.com

For Betts

Grass

Pile the bodies high at Austerlitz and Waterloo.
Shovel them under and let me work—
I am the grass; I cover all.

And pile them high at Gettysburg
And pile them high at Ypres and Verdun.
Shovel them under and let me work.
Two years, ten years, and passengers ask the conductor,
What place is this?
Where are we now?

I am the grass.
Let me work.

Carl Sandburg   1918

Part I

1
Summer 1950

When the North Koreans invaded South Korea, there weren't thirteen people in Fargo, including me, who knew where Korea was. I was twelve years old when the Second World War, *the* War, ended, and I followed every battle, but I didn't remember a thing about Korea. The caption on the map on the front page of the *Fargo Forum* described it as a peninsula off the Asian continent, pointed "like a dagger at the heart of Japan," although it looked to be aimed a little lower in the anatomy.

At the end of the war, Russia and the United States had divided Korea at the 38th Parallel for purposes of accepting the surrender of the Japanese troops then occupying Korea. The plan had been for a unified Korea, but the Communists in the North created the so-called Democratic People's Republic of Korea, and the South Koreans created the Republic of Korea.

Clashes between the North and the South along the border became common and, on June 25, 1950, the North Korean People's Army attacked South Korea "in force." In three days, the North Koreans captured Seoul, the United Nations condemned the attack, and President Truman ordered in U.S. ground forces to assist the Republic of Korea's reeling army.

When the war broke out, which just so happened to be right before I signed up with Major Goodlittle and Mrs. Brady, Chick Belos didn't know anything more about Korea than I did; he read the box scores, and that was about it. We'd hung the nickname "Chick" on him because he'd been too chicken to tackle a big fullback from Valley City, just fell down in front of him, in a game that cost us the title, and the name stuck. But Chick was the first guy in Fargo to enlist.

"How about that?" Chick said sitting in the Broadway Donut Shop the day the *Fargo Forum* ran the front-page story on his enlistment. He held up the headline with his high school graduation photograph underneath: "George 'Chick' Belos Enlists—First in Fargo."

"Bet you wish it was you. Picture that!" he said, looking up at me from the booth, with that walleye of his making it hard for me to concentrate on the newspaper.

I imagined a story with my name there: "Thomas 'Tom' Kelly Enlists—Second in Fargo," but it didn't quite ring right.

"Aren't you scared, Chick? I mean, they'll be using real guns over there."

"Naw, I'm not scared. My dad was one of the first guys in Fargo to enlist in the last war, you know. Even though he didn't have to."

"I know." Everyone knew. Chick's father had fought in "the war," the Second World War, "WWII," or, as he sometimes called it, the "Big One." Chick showed us pictures of his dad and his army buddies; rifles slung over their shoulders, standing in front of dead Germans and holding up a big Nazi flag. His dad kept his medals in a box he'd made for them. I figured it was because his dad was such a hero that when the Korean War broke out, and Chick got his chance to be a man, he jumped at it.

"My old man says we'd be better off fighting them over there than in the Red River Valley," Chick said. Between the Berlin blockade and the fall of China, there wasn't much doubt the Communists were trying to take over the world. Still, it was hard for me to think of anyone fighting the Communists in the Red River Valley, especially Chick. But when he said that I thought of how only a few weeks earlier he and I and Will had been together down by the river the first time I smelled death.

4

We'd skipped school on a dare—Chick and me from Sacred Heart—Will from Fargo Central, the public high school he went to when his family had moved in from New Germany, after he'd had some mysterious trouble.

We were goofing around down by the Red River on the edge of town, where it flowed between Fargo and Moorhead. It was early May, and there were still gray and white rafts of ice on the river, floating downstream in the dark, slow-moving water.

We talked about when school would be out, about girls. Which ones had the biggest knockers, who'd be the first to go all the way, that stuff.

"Getting any from the blonde, Tom?" Will asked.

"No," I said. "Moira's not that kind of girl."

"She *is* that kind of girl. She just doesn't know it yet," Will grinned at me, his even white teeth flashing in the sun.

I'd met Will the summer before when we were both caddying at the Fargo Country Club. The story was that he was kicked out as a caddy at the Club because the club manager caught Will and some rich girl who was a member in the shower together. He'd denied it, flashing all those white teeth of his.

"She's built, but she's a real pain in the ass about religion. I keep telling Tom he ought to dump her," Chick helped me out.

"You just don't like her because she can read," I said to him.

"Oh," said Will. "She doesn't look all that religious to me. Let me know if you dump her, huh?" He sounded pretty serious.

"How about I punch your teeth out?" I reasoned with him.

"Not me. I'm a coward. She's all yours," he smiled.

A few yards ahead of us a moss-covered oak had plunged into the river, spreading big branches before it like arms to break its fall. Under one of the arms, hooked but bobbing gently in the water, was what first looked like a submerged log, but it was a man. When he bobbed up his face was brown and purple and black, and all puffed up.

"We'd better call the cops," I said.

"We'll get in trouble." Chick looked around like his dad might be peering over his shoulder. "Old man Porter won't do nothing to you, Tom, but I'll get kicked out of school."

"He might have a family wondering where he is, " I said. "We can't just leave him here."

I called the police from a grocery store, but it was the firemen who came. They hauled him onto a heavy canvas tarp, cinched it tight around him with webbed belts, and winched him up a ladder with a hook under one of the belts, his heavy work boots bumping on every rung. Even when we stood back, like they yelled at us to, the smell—putrid, like sewer gas—got to us.

We talked about him as we walked home, smoking right out on the street where anyone could see us.

"He looked dark, like a Mexican," said Chick.

"He was so rotten I thought his feet might fall right off banging up that ladder," said Will.

"He could have been one of those people who come in at harvest time," I said.

"So, if he was a Mexican, he'd be a Catholic, and in heaven," Chick said, "unless he committed suicide." Then Chick said this weird thing, "If his feet fell off, do you suppose he'd be just stumping around up there in heaven?"

"This is the dumbest conversation I've ever heard," said Will.

We never did find out who he was. The *Fargo Forum* ran a story that mentioned our names, but the news that Mr. Porter jerked me from consideration for the National Honor Society for skipping class didn't make it into the paper. Chick told me that he dreamed about him the night afterward, waking up in a sweat.

I had to admire Chick's guts for enlisting. I knew we were right to go into Korea and defend our way of life, and I even worried about missing "my" war the way my dad had missed his. But I wondered, deep down, whether I'd have the courage to risk death for what I believed in.

Not to mention my mother and father were counting on my going to college. To be the first in our family. "I'm trying to get a scholarship to the University of Minnesota," I said to Chick, looking again at his picture in the paper. "It's an ROTC scholarship," I added. Pretty stupid sounding, compared to "First in Fargo."

It was Dad who culled the Terrance Brady Scholarship from the catalog, and he took time off from the packing plant to drive with me in our 1935 Chevy to Minneapolis to meet Major Goodlittle and Mrs. Brady.

When I saw a chance to go away to the University of Minnesota down in the Twin Cities, I grabbed at it. Since the invention of the printing press and the wireless and all, it wasn't as far from Fargo to Minneapolis, or anywhere else, as some people liked to think. The city mothers in Fargo, at least mine, got as worked up by *Forever Amber* as they did in Boston; and Alger Hiss looked as "upstanding and elegant" and Whittaker Chambers as "fat and perspiring," as my mother put it, on the screen at the Fargo Theater as on any screen in New York City. Still, I'd never been farther from Fargo than Detroit Lakes, and I wanted to start seeing the rest of the world.

Minneapolis was a lot bigger town than Fargo, but the downtown buildings rose out of it gray and ugly. One skyscraper that towered over thirty stories, and dominated the whole skyline, Dad said was supposed to be like the Washington Monument, but it looked more like a giant gray dink.

Mrs. Brady's home overlooked all of downtown. It was a regular mansion, sitting way back on a hill guarded by a low stone fence. Parked in the driveway was a block-long Packard with wire wheel caps that by themselves cost more than our old bucket of bolts, washed and shined as it was.

Before he rang the doorbell, Dad held me out at arms length and imitated my mother giving me the once over before leaving for a holiday dinner at the relatives. "Just be yourself, Tom, and look them right straight in the eyes, and you'll get the scholarship. But remember, if you don't have anything to say, it doesn't hurt not to say it."

A ramrod of a guy, with graying brown hair, all decked out in uniform with ribbons and brass, opened the door. "I'm Major Goodlittle, the commandant of the Reserve Officers Training Corps at the university," he announced, as he pumped our hands.

"Bill," said my dad, "and this is Tom."

The major led us into the huge living room, introduced us to Mrs. Brady, and explained that he was acting as advisor to Mrs. Brady in awarding the Terrance Brady Scholarship.

I liked Mrs. Brady, with her lined face and sad eyes, and her chest like a lumpy sofa. But Major Goodlittle wasn't the friendliest, and wouldn't you know, right away he mentioned how it was odd, that I, being first in my class, wasn't in the National Honor Society.

"I did something stupid and cut classes right before graduation." I looked him square in the eyes, and then Mrs. Brady. "It won't happen again."

"I'm sure it won't," said Mrs. Brady; she looked at me pretty hard as she said it. She had sharper eyes than I had first noticed.

My dad brought up Korea. Things still weren't going too well over there. We were taking heavy casualties. My dad told the major that my mother was worried about me and this ROTC business and me being an only child.

Mrs. Brady said she could well understand that. Major Goodlittle explained I would be deferred the whole time I was in college. Besides, even if it took a little longer than we expected, the Korean War would be over by the time I finished college.

"But Tom will do his duty if he is called," said my dad.

Dad and the major hit it off. The next thing you know they were shooting the bull about the Civil War. You might not expect a guy who spent all day on the line in a packing plant to be a Civil War expert, but my dad was a surprising guy, especially for someone so quiet. Dad had been too young for the First World War—although his favorite older brother died from influenza in training camp—and too old for the Second World War. He sort of made up for that with the major by his interest in the Civil War.

Dad's trip to Gettysburg was a high point of his life. He had started saving for it before he and my mother married, but postponed it until they married and my mother was carrying me. He barely made it back in time, and my mother never fully forgave him.

Dad and the major had common memories of tramping over Cemetery Hill and Seminary Ridge and Little Round Top, and looking across the rolling open plain where Lee sent General George Pickett's 15,000 proud Virginians right into the blazing Union rifles.

My dad marveled that for the right of the South to hold black men as pieces of property, "Ten thousand Rebs were slaughtered by their Northern brothers."

"Nobody knew how to kill Americans like Americans," agreed Major Goodlittle.

My dad shook his head. At home he had a bushel basket of photos he took with a box Kodak, the pictures so small and dark you could hardly tell what you were supposed to be seeing, except for the ones of all the white tombstones. I asked if they were all for white soldiers, or if black soldiers had died at Gettysburg, too, but despite all they knew about the battle neither of them knew.

Mrs. Brady said again she understood my mother's worries about the war and me. It had been the sorrow of her husband's life he'd outlived their son, Terrance, killed in the Second World War. "He was a beautiful boy, beautiful. Like you, Tom."

But Terrance had died fighting for the country he loved, and Mr. Brady had chosen to honor his memory with a modest scholarship for a lad who felt the same way. "And," she said, first smiling at Major Goodlittle and then at me, "we would like you to have it."

"Thank you," I said. "This means an awful lot to me, Mrs. Brady, being able to go to college. I won't let you down."

"I'm sure you won't," said the major.

The next morning, while Dad did some errands for my mother in the big city, I bummed around the campus on my own. It was everything I had dreamed of. The wide, slow-moving Mississippi flowed behind the

Coffman Student Union. In front of the union, across Washington Avenue, a broad, tree-shaded mall stretched to the front steps of Northrop Auditorium, flanked along the way by buildings on either side. Giant oaks and elms, looking a hundred years old, towered above, their huge roots burrowed deep into the ground. Modern buildings had been built over the years but even those had been there long enough to lose that raw brick appearance. Even the optimistically named "Temporary" North of Mines and South of Folwell buildings, thrown up like barracks to handle the overflow of returning veterans from World War II, had begun to weather into the landscape.

Gardens of marigolds and zinnias and snapdragons were scattered here and there on the campus, as if carelessly sown by the wind, but were as carefully tended as my mother's. On University Avenue, there were bookstores with sidewalk tables heaped high with books. On one stall over in Dinkytown a girl with dark-brown hair and an open-necked blouse was standing in the warm sunshine looking at a book. It lay there open to her, with her bending over it. After she left, as I turned its pages, an annotated copy of Shakespeare for a dollar and a quarter, the thought passed through my mind there might be life at the University even without Moira.

2

oira Stacey was a year behind me in school, and she'd followed me around ever since we were little kids. Even though she lived across town with the other rich people, she used to tag along after me on my paper route on 13th Street uninvited, chattering at me all the while. When Moira first came to Sacred Heart, she wasn't that much of a looker. Her nose was high-bridged; her eyes an odd green; her mouth a little full. She wore braces on her teeth and, for a while after that, one of those removable retainers with a plastic hump. But by the time she was a sophomore, her braces came off and her breasts were coming out, and by her junior year she was built something like Marilyn Monroe, not quite so big, but firmer looking, and a lot of guys were sniffing around after her.

No doubt that all had something to do with why I began to be seriously interested in her. But only something. It wasn't just Moira's body. It was the way her mind worked. Moira read faster than anyone I knew. She had a photographic memory, but very selective and limited to what she really wanted to remember, like her part as Emily Webb in Sacred Heart High's production of *Our Town*, so she wasn't cluttered up with irrelevant crap, as far as she was concerned.

I enjoyed reading, but I didn't noise it around with my friends, who didn't get past the sports page. I could talk about books with Moira, and often she knew more about them than I did. It always bugged me to read a book with foreign phrases I couldn't understand. When I complained about that in *Tender is the Night*, which I liked otherwise, Moira had said "Give it to me, Tom," and walked off with my book.

A couple of days later in school she'd handed it to me, inscribed "Translated by M.S. *pour mon tres cher ami*, Tom," and when I thumbed through the pages, beside a passage where Tommy says to Nicole: "*Mais pour nous heros il nous faut du temps, Nicole. Nous ne pouvons pas faire de petits exercises d'heroisme—il faut faire les grandes compositions*," now, inked in Moira's flowing, controlled handwriting in the margin was: "But as for us heroes, we take time. We cannot do small exercises of heroism—we have to do the great feats."

"That one's not quite English yet," she'd said, frowning.

"I couldn't do it at all," I'd said, turning the pages, and seeing she'd done all of it. It had made the whole book mean more.

Moira read stuff I'd never even thought of reading. We'd had to recite in high school "O Captain! My Captain! Our fearful trip is done" and so forth, but when Moira lent me her copy of *Leaves of Grass*, I read it all nearly non-stop. She gave me Carl Sandburg's *Complete Poems*, which worked hard at being Whitman, and I agreed with a lot of Sandburg's stuff, but the hell of it was, Sandburg just couldn't write as well as Whitman, so it wasn't a fair fight.

The one who really caught me unawares was T.S. Eliot, a guy you practically needed one of those old Captain Midnight Decoder Rings that I'd had as a little kid to understand sometimes. But then he'd come out with lines like "I grow old . . . I grow old. I shall wear the bottoms of my trousers rolled" that just made you see the homeless old guys walking along Broadway in downtown Fargo; of course, measuring out their lives with belts of Thunderbird instead of coffee spoons.

Moira didn't like it that the homeless guys were there, though sometimes I wasn't sure it was from her concern about them like Dorothy Day, as she said, or whether she just thought they messed up Broadway. Moira was the closest thing there was to a student radical at Sacred Heart

High, though that didn't take a whole lot. She was always trying to slip social messages into her stories in the school paper about the stamp club. Her social views came strictly by way of Christ and Dorothy Day.

Dorothy Day had been one of about three people in the whole USA against America fighting in World War Two, and when the Korean War broke out, right away she and her pacifist friends were picketing against it around New York City. The *Fargo Forum* ran a picture of her standing in Central Park along side some anarchist who was holding a picket sign:

> ALL THEY
> THAT TAKETH
> THE SWORD
> SHALL PERISH
> BY THE SWORD
>   —Jesus

So Moira was against the war, too, even though Cardinal Spellman, who was also in New York, was all for it, not to mention Father Mahoney here in Fargo. Jesus and Dorothy Day counted more than the cardinal and the priest did for Moira. She chose to ignore Jesus' comment about coming not to bring peace but a sword. Not to mention all the things Jesus and Dorothy Day had to say about rich people.

In fact, even though Moira cared so much about God and the poor, every day she wore a different blouse or sweater, from DeLendrecies, and The Store-Without-a-Name and Moodys and Scutts, and every other store in town. She would toss her coat and scarf at a coat tree careless of whether they slid to the floor or not, as a way of saying she was so much more important than the clothes and as an excuse to be continually shopping for new ones. It also gave Mr. Stacey a never-ending way to prove how much money he made, and that he loved her.

Mr. Stacey was always giving presents to Moira's mother, too, as his penance for his screwing the good-looking young women who worked in the office of his Ford dealership. You heard stories about stuff like that, but I knew it was true from caddying for Mr. Stacey out at the Fargo

13

Country Club. That's where I'd met Will when he'd caddied for a real estate guy and I had Mr. Stacey. I'd hauled Mr. Stacey's heavy leather bag, with a place for everything from balls to shaving gear, all over the fairway and into the rough half of the time, and listened to him talk to the real estate guy about the office.

"She knows how to get a raise from me. She must have learned that on the farm, watching the bull have at it!" he laughed. I was just part of his golf gear.

Moira told me once that, like so many kids, she thought she was adopted. She sure didn't get her looks from her dad, except for the eyes. His eyes bored right through you. You could see how he could make a lot of money with those eyes. One reason Moira was interested in me was how she felt about her father. I thought she liked it that I was poor. Maybe the rich-kid poor-kid stuff made us more like a fairy tale. She thought I was smart and hungry enough that I'd make a lot of money like him, but if she got me early she could train me into the money without my turning into an asshole about it. One thing I didn't like was the way she was always telling me how I was too smart to ever end up in a packing plant like my dad. That might have gotten on my nerves so much because I thought so too but it felt disloyal to my dad.

Moira talked a lot about the poor, and she meant it, but she was crazy about hanging around the Fargo Country Club pool wearing one of her dozen different swimming suits and ordering cherry Cokes on Mr. Stacey's number. She had this saying, like a jingle, "You've got to stay with the happy people," and she was always trying to get me to like hanging around there. I liked being in the water on a hot day and I really liked Moira in her swimming suit, but I kept expecting Mr. Stacey to turn up, and, as usual, treat me like I was there to take a leak in the pool or something.

Moira had it all planned out though, right from the beginning. I would go to Harvard Law School, get rich, and join up with the happy people. My getting the Terrance Brady scholarship to the University of Minnesota was just the beginning.

"I don't know, Moira. Maybe I'll do something else."

"What though?"

"I don't know. See the world. Bum around. Maybe write."

"You can do all that. After you get rich."

"Maybe I don't want to get rich."

"Oh you do, Tom. You do."

THE STACEYS WERE RICH. Their big white house was a car salesman's idea of Tara, with a colonnaded porch in front, and a lush green lawn bounded on one side by lilac bushes and on the other by a split rail fence that ran forever. On a July day Moira and I were off to the side of the house with the bushes, the side Mrs. Stacey called "the arboretum." The Staceys were the only people I knew with a "yard boy," John, a student in the horticulture department at the Agricultural College. He had been by earlier, cutting and watering, and the grass was a deep green with lingering drops of water glistening in the sun.

Even for July, it was a sweaty, hot day, and Moira was in one of her swimming suits. The sun came through the dried lilac bushes and the maple trees above them, and we sat on the grass and talked about my getting the scholarship and how I'd be going away to the university down in Minneapolis, and then we made out till our tongues ached and our lips hurt, and made out some more.

Moira decided she would get her dad's camera then, so I could take some cheesecake shots of her to take along in the fall. There she was in this blue-green two-piece suit that barely covered her, wearing her scapular like a saintly necklace, the square with the Sacred Heart of Jesus dangling in her front, and the other square dangling in back. According to a promise by the Blessed Virgin Mary, you were supposed to die in the grace of God if you wore it. It was a little weird seeing her pose wearing the scapular.

She gave me pose after pose. She leaned back on her hands, her legs spread in a v. She lay on her side, her legs cocked together, her hip rounded, and she stared up at me in this real sultry way. She stood up and looked back over her shoulder, with the scapular string in her teeth, and I saw small beads of sweat on her shoulder blades. When she lay with her stomach on the grass, propped up on her elbows, her head tipped to one side, looking up at me, the scapular hanging between her breasts, I wasn't even looking through the viewer as I clicked off the rest of the film.

When she got up there were small blades of grass and tiny white and pink cuttings of clover on her stomach. I reached to pick them off but my hands were sweaty and the grass just moved around on Moira's stomach when I plucked at it. Some of it finally stuck to my fingertips, and I couldn't get it off my own fingers. She smiled and put her hands on the back of my neck, and I saw the fine golden hair on her white arms and delicate beads of sweat gleaming in the sun. I looked down at her, and I knelt down and buried my face against her stomach. I could smell the grass and the clover and her sweat. When my tongue touched her to lick the clover off, she stood so still.

Then she pulled me to my feet and led me past the lilac hedge around front. The oak front door was swollen against the frame in the humidity; the bronze doorknob was slippery under my hand. I banged the door shut behind us with a push from my butt, and Moira's bare feet left their imprint on the cool tile flooring in the entryway. A few blades of grass fell off her feet onto the white carpet that went up the wide stairs to the second floor. She took my hand again, and we went down the white-carpeted hallway to her bedroom. The shades were down but the sun poured through, washing over her bed. She hadn't made her bed and there were pink rosebuds all over the sheets still rumpled from when she woke up that morning.

She said, "We can't do it. I can't. But . . . if you'll promise . . . I'll take off the suit."

I could hardly breathe, but I said, "I promise." I would have said anything.

She pushed out her hands with the palms toward me for me to stay away. I could hardly see any green in her eyes, only the dark of the pupils. She took the top of her suit off with one hand, still holding the

16

other out to keep me away. I didn't move. I wanted to look at her breasts, but I couldn't stop looking in her eyes. I saw her breasts in the edge of my vision though, and they were white with rosebud tips and darker nipples.

When she took off the bottom of the suit, I took a step toward her. Her hands held my shoulders and she said, "You promised." Her hair there was dark, crinkly gold against her white skin and the hidden part below. I stared at her, and I couldn't see anything else, nothing, before she ran out of the room and down the stairs. I got this cramp in my stomach that nearly doubled me over, and, for a moment, I was so mad that I could feel the blood in my eyes.

She called for me to come downstairs, and she sounded scared. She had a towel from the downstairs bathroom, one of those big, white fluffy ones, that she didn't tie or anything, but held between us. I was aching so hard that I reached out toward the towel, but I wasn't going to do anything she wouldn't let me do. She hesitated for a second, looking at me, before she bolted for the stairs and back up to her room.

"No," she yelled over her shoulder, and I knew she meant not to follow, and I just watched her run up the stairs.

It was a good thing because in a minute Mrs. Stacey breezed in. Moira's mother was a blonde too, though her hair was shellacked in place, and she had long, pretty legs. But she was always nervous, like she was expecting someone to yell at her. She was really pleased about being in the Fine Arts Club, along with all the rich ladies from over on Eighth Avenue, and I was grateful she came in gabbing away about that and didn't notice I was dying in front of her due to a swollen pain that didn't go down till I hobbled home.

3

Things continued to be tough for the Americans in Korea. I'd figured we'd kick their butts as soon as we got there, but through the summer we just fought a delaying action down the peninsula. By early August there wasn't much of Korea left in our hands—an area about 100 miles by fifty miles, and the City of Pusan way down on the southeast coast of Korea.

There wasn't much by way of any "Good news tonight!" from H.V. Kaltenborn, like there had been when my dad and I had listened on the radio every night during World War Two, while America fought invincibly to victory on every front. We had a steadily growing, fierce pride, knowing no one could beat America.

Now we had to listen to Fulton Lewis, Jr., talk through his adenoids about the Communists threatening a "new Dunkirk." At the Metro Drug I read a *Newsweek* story that Edward R. Murrow was prevented by censorship from doing a broadcast about our demoralized troops. I told my dad about it that night.

"If that's true, it goes against everything we're fighting for, Tom. It's hard to believe anybody could censor Edward R. Murrow. "

"Yes, but isn't it hard to believe *Newsweek* would print it if it isn't true?" asked my mother, which seemed like a good point. *Newsweek*

18

wasn't as gung-ho as *Time*, but it didn't seem likely to be spreading Communist propaganda.

We didn't take either one, but we took *Life*, and sometimes you really could get a better idea of what was going on from the pictures in there than you could anyplace else. That week *Life* ran a photo of a corpsman carrying a wounded GI from a Jeep to a medical station; the corpsman had his shirt off, and he looked as muscle-bound as Chick Belos, but what you saw was the wounded guy, limp and helpless, in his arms.

THE VERY DAY I SAW that picture, Chick's dad practically pulled me off the street. He wanted to read me part of a letter he'd gotten from Chick. Chick was still in basic training, but he had made squad leader.

"The acorn doesn't fall far from the tree!" Chick's dad said.

"No, sir," I said, feeling guilty for being there.

I didn't mention the picture in *Life*.

That Sunday Father Mahoney offered a special intention for all of our armed forces, particularly our boys in Korea. I wanted to go to communion but with my never-ending "impure thoughts" about Moira, I couldn't.

When Moira and I were together, which was most of the time, I always wanted to touch her. Once when we were holding hands at the movies, a matinee of *Ivanhoe*, I had a hard time concentrating on the movie. I felt Moira's wool skirt against the back of my hand. I untangled my fingers from hers and turned my hand over, and she looked at me like "what's going on?" but she let me put my hand on her lap. After a while, I moved my hand a little, feeling the rough wool under my fingertips, but thinking how soft her white cotton underpants would feel, how smooth her skin would be, and about her golden hair down there, and I started to move my hand some more. After a while she turned to me to be kissed. I kept moving my hand gently while I kissed her, and she shifted her hips. We didn't stop kissing until she grabbed onto me real hard and whimpered and stayed against me.

After the movie we walked for blocks in the rain down Broadway all the way to the river. We watched the rain falling into the water, and the river was high and the current strong as it moved away from us. The rain was sweet on our faces, and we caught some on our tongues. I felt the rain touching both the river and us meant we were strong and free like the river; we were flowing together and Moira was thinking and feeling what I was. But then she began to cry. I'd felt so close to her, but we were apart, and I hadn't even known it. I didn't understand how that could be, and I was angry.

Moira started in about God and Christ and purity. I didn't see how God could be so interested in torturing us. If He was, I said, I didn't have much use for Him. She slapped me, as hard as she could, and split my lip. I walked her home but we didn't touch again the whole way. The lip took a week to heal; it kept reopening. I had to lie to my mom and dad and tell them I'd gotten into a fight with one of the guys, which didn't go over too big.

I went with Moira to confession to Father Mahoney the next Saturday. Father and I knew each other pretty well. In grade school at St. Mary's, Father came over from the rectory every Friday to examine us on the *Baltimore Catechism*, producing jawbreakers and tootsie rolls like loaves and fishes from his mysterious pockets for the right answers, like "To know, love and serve God in this world, and be happy with Him in the next." Father had guided me through my First Confession. Like a scientist peering at a slide, he could see into my soul, a glass plate beneath my ribcage, clear, almost invisible, because Baptism had wiped it free of the stain of original sin.

Father could still see my soul, even through the curtained screen, when Moira and I went to him together, one on either side of the confessional. I knelt with my ear up against the screen, trying with no luck to hear how Moira described our making out. Confession had always been anonymous before, but Father made us tell him who we were and promise to come back together the next week; we were such occasions of sin for one another. How could I argue? It had become the main object of my life

20

for us to be occasions of sin, all the time. I had trouble telling Father I would never again have impure thoughts about Moira, when I knew if she'd let me cop a feel walking her home it wouldn't even be a close call. Not to mention the possibility of entertaining lewd thoughts of her, while I flogged my desperate member to death.

But the Church was the most important thing in Moira's life it seemed. I couldn't understand what she needed from it so intensely. Something that the rest of her life—school, her friends, her parents, me—wasn't giving her. Finally, after we sinned again, and had a big fight, she left a letter at my house. Enclosed in a soft blue envelope, on soft blue paper, with "MS" in darker blue on top, it went on about how she loved me, and that was the problem. I was "destroying" her "sense of purity," and "raising an insurmountable barrier" in her "struggle to get out of the pit of mediocrity and on to the summit of sanctity." So she couldn't go to the University of Minnesota with me. She'd have to go "East" somewhere, like her father wanted her to, which would be her only path back to God.

Well, Christ Almighty. It was such a wuss way to do it, instead of face to face. I was pissed. I felt an empty hole inside me, like I hadn't eaten in three days.

I went over to her house and banged on the door till she answered. She stood in the doorway in the shadow, with the door half-open. She had on a Pendleton plaid shirt of her dad's that made her small and pale.

"Goddamn it, Moira."

"Is that what you've come to tell me? Sometimes I think all you want is to make out with me." She was about to close the door.

"You know that's not all," I said, nudging my foot into the doorway.

"Isn't it? Do you love me, Tom?"

"Sure I do, Moira," I said, feeling the door closing on my foot.

"Sure I do," she mimicked me. "You never say you love me."

"Maybe that's why I'm always trying to make out with you, you know?"

"What's why?" She wanted me to say the words.

"That's why," I said, feeling like it was dragged out of me.

"You sound so angry. Don't be angry. I want us to make love as much as you do."

"Do you?"

"Yes," she said, looking straight into my eyes, till I could hardly breathe.

When I reached my hand toward her face I was afraid she'd pull back. She didn't, but it felt like she did. "But I want you to believe in God with me, Tom."

"I'd like to believe; sometimes I really miss communion, but I'm just being honest with you. If it bothers you so much, I'll keep it to myself."

"Why do you think about it so much? Faith is a mystery. Can't you just accept it? You're such a fine person, Tom."

"I don't know what makes you think that," I said, caught off guard.

"You are. You're so patient with me. And my mother."

"I like your mother," I said.

"And you were so sweet the other night at Roselli's. With little Tony. When he crawled up in your lap and you read to him."

I'd hung out there when she babysat. I'd read the kid *Winnie-the-Pooh*, which was as good a book as I'd remembered, and it had felt good, having him curled up there with me. "He's a neat little kid," I said. "I've got some weird maternal instinct. I like little kids; before they start getting wrecked, you know?"

"I don't think it's any weird maternal instinct at all, Tom," she said, taking my hands in hers. "It's one of the things about you that makes me want to spend my life with you. Everything will be all right when we're married."

"Who knows if we'll ever get married."

"We have to," she said, and my heart bounced around for a couple of beats, while I wondered if I was going to hear about a second Virgin

Birth. "My mother got so angry with me when I told her we were splitting up. She says we make the most beautiful couple she's ever seen."

"That's no reason to get married," I said. "Even if we do, that's a long time away."

"Maybe not so long."

"It might as well be forever."

"And we'll make love all you want. All we want," she said, "you'll see."

We ended up friendly enough that next week when we had to go to confession again Father Mahoney imposed a penance that we not see each other at all for two weeks. Even the temporary separation seemed sadistic, what with my impending departure to the university.

RIGHT BEFORE I WENT OFF TO SCHOOL, it appeared the Korean War might be over before Chick Belos ever had a chance to get there, much less me. In what everyone said was the most brilliant military maneuver since Hannibal crossed the Alps on an elephant, General MacArthur swept behind the North Korean army by sea and landed at Inchon, a hundred and fifty miles behind the front line. Of course, it was the marines who landed at Inchon, while the General watched. In the newsreel, it was like he was at a football game, watching through his big field glasses, as they scrambled ashore.

4

Life at the university, on my own, turned out to be all I'd hoped for. Pep rallies around blazing bonfires that leaped high into the night skies. Football games against Michigan and Ohio State. Foreign students from exotic countries that had only been geography lessons. Coffee places like The Bridge and beer joints like Manning's, where they didn't card anyone unless the police were actually on the premises. All-night poker and beer drinking and bull sessions with guys who'd read every book in Walter Library.

That was the way Will Lindeman and I got to be friends. I lived by myself, with a hundred or so other guys, in Pioneer Hall, the cheapest housing on or off campus. Will stayed with a few other guys in a run-down boarding house north of Dinkytown. It was Will who got me into the weekly game of the NDTSTWPABCADS—North Dakotans to Save the World Poker and Beerdrinking Club and Debating Society. Will was a regular bomb thrower when you got to know what he believed. There were still a lot of old-time radicals out there in New Germany, where he came from.

At my first NDTSTWPABCADS game, we argued about whether we should be in the Korean War and what our purposes should be if we were. Will and his pseudointellectual friends Rick Gunneris and Jack

Byrnes didn't think we should be there at all. When he wasn't busy telling us about his 169 IQ, or about each and every inhabitant of Faulkner's Yoknapatawpha County, Gunneris was busy being the bearded president, and half the membership, of the Young Socialist Alliance. Jack Byrnes, who claimed to understand *Finnegan's Wake*, was the other half of the Young Socialists, also with beard. The Smith Brothers of campus politics.

Will Lindeman was so smooth-skinned and clean-cut looking, it was hard to believe he was a radical. He did take out some sorority girls, who were always after him to join a frat, which I thought he might like if he could afford it. He was a natural born bullshitter, so it fit that he was a philosophy major, the kind of guy who looked comfortable waving his pipe around, which he tried for a while, but gave up for fear chewing on the stem might stain his teeth.

In the dreary kitchen of Will's boarding house, we shuffled and dealt the cards around a yellow enameled table, decorated with ring stains from the bottoms of beer bottles, and brown scars from cigarettes rested on its edges. In a haze of blue smoke, over a couple of cases of "Greasy Dicks," the cheapest beer on seven continents, paid for out of the pots, we debated all night and on into our eight o'clock classes.

I argued our intervention in Korea was necessary to make the United Nations an effective force for international law, more than just a rerun of the League of Nations, which had done nothing to stop the Second World War. But my main point was that Communism was trying to take over the whole damn world and appeasement didn't work.

"We should have learned that last time," I argued. "You know, before the war some British students were debating what to do about Germany, like we're sitting around this table, and they adopted some cockamamie resolution not to fight for king and country, that you guys would have loved, and you know where that bullshit led? Right to Munich, that's where!"

"But Korea's not the same thing at all, Tom," said Will, shoving his glasses up his nose, and leaning toward me. "It's a totally different situation."

"It is the same. It's like when Hitler invaded the Czechs and nobody did squat, and he just kept going into Poland. Only it's Stalin this time, and he's already taken over Czechoslovakia and Poland and half of Germany."

"'Scuse me, but Korea's a civil war, Tom," Will belched some of his last Greasy Dick. "There aren't any Russian troops in Korea."

"And we've got no business butting in," Rick Gunneris helped Will out.

"If the British had come over to America and fought with the South against the North, what would you have thought about that?" Jack Byrnes asked. "That they should get home to Britain, posthaste," he answered for me.

"Civil war, my ass!" I argued. "It's the Russians taking over, with their tanks and North Korean and Chinese bodies, and you guys know it."

Rick and Jack pretty much saw Communism as an effort to treat all men equally. It had just gotten messed up when it had fallen into Papa Joe Stalin's bloody hands. But I argued you had to look at the reality of what happened in Russia with the phony trials and labor camps and what they were doing around the world. "And in Korea they've been just massacring innocent civilians for no damn reason," I said.

"You don't know that," Gunneris said, despite the fact it had been in the newsreels. Instead, Gunneris went off into his usual crap about American blood being spilled for the "venal motives" of our politicians, as part of "a new American imperialism."

"Bullshit! Harry Truman is about as much of an imperialist as me. We're not trying to grab anything in Korea. What the hell do we want with it?"

Of course, he thought I was an imperialist or at least a running-dog lackey.

By dawn, bleary-eyed, belching, and picking through heaping ashtrays in search of half-smoked stale cigarette butts, each of us answered all of the questions for himself. Greasy Dick was the only clear winner for the evening.

At the end of October, my mother wrote me at school that Chick Belos had come back to Fargo on thirty-day leave before he shipped out to Korea. He attended Sunday Mass in uniform, brass polished and shining; his dad marched up the aisle beside him on one side; his mother, red-eyed, on the other, with his little brothers and sisters trailing along. Father Mahoney said from the pulpit that Chick was "a brave young man going to Korea to protect the rest of us, and our way of life from Godless Communism." He "deserved the thoughts and prayers of all of us."

All the while, the Korean "police action," as President Truman kept calling it, had been rolling right along for the good guys, the way it was supposed to. After pushing back the North Koreans and recapturing Seoul, the UN troops crossed the 38th Parallel themselves, headed north. This was more like it. Will argued we were doing the same thing we'd claimed we'd gone into Korea to stop. I said they'd brought it on themselves.

Right about the time Chick went to Korea, we began our final push to the Yalu River, which divided China and Korea. By late November, it was reported the ROKs or the GIs, or both, had pissed in the Yalu, and there was talk of getting the boys home in time for Christmas.

Then the shit hit the fan. Hordes of Chinese Communists came across the Yalu, and it was a whole new war. The Christmas Day issue of *Life* had pictures of dead Marines being hauled back from the frozen Chosin, their boots sticking out over the edge of a truck bed. I wondered where Chick Belos was over there and how things were going for him.

The war yo-yoed back and forth. In January, the Chinese recaptured Seoul for the North, then ran out of gas, and the UN resumed the offensive. In March, we retook Seoul, again, and things were looking up, again, but you had to wonder a little. It puzzled me how we couldn't put these supposedly primitive enemies down for the count.

I DIDN'T SPEND ALL MY TIME drinking beer and playing poker. Besides my two part-time jobs, one as bar boy at the Concord Bar and Fine Dining, and the other handling bills of lading at Shortstop Trucking, that first year, besides the humanities and English courses that I devoured, I took classes in everything from astronomy to political science. In humanities I actually read the old-time economists, like Smith and Marx; and I liked to throw those guys around in arguments with Will and his bombthrower buddies. But you show me someone who says *Das Kapital* isn't boring, and I'll show you a liar.

While I was growing up, President Roosevelt was the president, and that was my working political faith. When he died in 1945, around our house it was like God had passed away. Truman wasn't any Roosevelt, and everyone thought the country would go to hell when he took over, but he was for the common guy. When he ran on his own against Dewey, a guy you could in no way trust, not with that smirk and mustache, all the little kids on our block chanted "Truman's in the White House, waiting to be elected. Dewey's in the garbage can waiting to be collected."

I still couldn't see how regular people could be Republicans.

America was the richest country in the whole history of the world; there was plenty to go around for everybody; we just had to make sure the little guy didn't get screwed. Roosevelt and the Democrats gave us the Securities and Exchange Commission to control the crooks on Wall Street; the National Labor Relations Board so workers like my dad and the other guys down at the meatpacking plant could organize and stand up to the bosses; and Social Security for people who couldn't work any more; and Truman was trying to get health care for everybody. The progressive income taxes and estate taxes worked to give the rest of us a chance in the game with the Rockefeller boys. Meanwhile, the Republicans just whined and fought everything that didn't make the rich richer.

Will was more or less a socialist. His family came from a long line of North Dakota populists, like the Nonpartisan League, men and women who believed the land belonged to those willing to work it, not to the big shots that controlled the banks. From each according to his ability and to each according to his need sounded pretty good to me too, if we could keep the economy going that way. But that wasn't the same as communism. I didn't want any dictatorship, of the proletariat or anything else, telling me what to do, especially not a foreign dictatorship.

For the first time in my life I was free to be what I wanted to be. I wasn't entirely sure what that was, but more than the beer and poker and the arguing, more than any of it, I loved the writers: Hemingway and Fitzgerald and Joyce; and their lives: hanging out with beautiful women in Paris; watching the bullfights in Spain; big game hunting in Africa; strolling the boulevards of Trieste; all the while writing great novels on the side. After *The Sun Also Rises* I spent hours daydreaming of writing in Paris, drinking in smoky cabarets with Brett Ashley, who looked a lot like the brunette I'd seen leaning over the bookstall the first day I'd seen the university, and going home with her. Of course, when we got to her place, I wouldn't have Jake Barnes's terrible wound.

INSTEAD, IT WAS Joan Hendrickson's place I got to.

When I wasn't working at Shortstop Trucking, I was bar boy at the Concord Bar and Fine Dining three nights a week. Compared to Shortstop, the Concord was a great job. After I loaded up the bar, I could study in the basement; empties came slam banging down the chute: *bam, bam, bam, bam*, but I got so I didn't even flinch; I got a free dinner to eat down in my hole and beer from the cooler. It was like a luxury bomb shelter. Blackie Benello, our boss, was supposed to be called as a witness in Senator Kefauver's investigation of organized crime, and he was gone half the time. When Blackie wasn't there, after we closed, the gang would hang around, drinking beer and just kidding around. I got along pretty good with the waitresses, especially Joan Hendrickson.

Joan wasn't fat, but her pale blue denim uniform with brass buttons all the way down the front and Concord Bar and Fine Dining stitched in red scroll over the pocket was stretched tight on her, top and bottom. She was what my mother might have called "pleasingly plump," which was a generally favorable comment since my mother had a bit of a tendency that way herself, not that I ever wanted the two to meet; I was

29

uncomfortable with them even sharing the same thought. Joan was blonde and blue eyed, and had an almost Oriental cast to her face, all flat planes and shadows where you didn't expect them. She had an endless supply of tasteless dirty jokes, for which I had an unending weakness though I could never remember them. I'd kibitz with her when I'd lug the beer upstairs, stock the bar, empty the ashtrays, and otherwise earn my keep before going back down to my study.

One night when we'd had a few beers after work, Joan asked me up to her place for a cup of coffee afterwards. It was a crummy little place that she shared with another girl, who happened to be gone that night. When Joan went into the tiny kitchen to put the coffee on, I followed her and there was barely room for the two of us. When I stood right behind her and just brushed against her, she turned around and pressed against me, and I could feel her big soft breasts and all the way down her belly. When I kissed her, she put her tongue in my mouth and almost vacuumed me right out of my socks.

We came up for air and stumbled together out of the kitchen and onto the couch and kept on kissing. When she let me open the top of her dress the tops of her breasts swelled up from her bra. I reached behind her back under her dress and unsnapped the bra and her breasts bounded free, leaving faint red lines marking where they had strained against the bra. I bent down to bury my face against her and then took one large brown nipple in my mouth and caressed the other with my hand. She put her arms around my neck and held me there. After a while I moved my other hand down between her legs and stroked her rounded thighs and then upward, over her underpants, pushing gently against the cleft beneath them. As I began to try to get my fingers underneath, past the tight band, she said "Just a minute," and I stopped.

She untangled herself and stood up, and we moved into the bedroom. We stood at the foot of the bed in there and I was still trying to kiss her while she unbuttoned the rest of her dress. I struggled to get my clothes off while not taking my eyes off of her and trying to see all of her while she stepped out of her panties. When she lay back on the bed, her breasts splayed off to the sides, and her thick thighs spread from the clump of her hair at their base.

I didn't have a rubber or anything, but "It's okay," she said. "Don't worry about it."

I lay down with her and started kissing her again and touching her all over, and I was so excited that right away I moved over her and between her thighs. She was all wet when I went inside her and she felt so good I just couldn't stop. When I came, her whole body quivered, and I nearly died there on top of her.

I thought I must be one great lover; till she told me she was responding to a sharp pain she sometimes got in her back. But pretty soon we got interested again, and it went a lot better. Joan had a way of being excited but relaxed at the same time, and she slowed me down, and it was nice.

After that Joan used to stop by my basement retreat at the Concord on one pretext or another to sneak up behind me and stick her tongue in my ear while I was studying which I really liked the first couple of times but sometimes it actually got a little annoying. We did what we could down there, but we were always looking over our shoulders, and a couple of times we almost got caught. One night, unexpectedly to me, we did it in the back seat of a car in the parking lot behind the bar. That night I stupidly didn't have a rubber again, and I wasn't going to do it, but she told me again not to worry, and then she said "I want to feel you inside me, Tom," and I had to go ahead and I didn't stop. I sweat tacks afterwards, afraid she'd get pregnant and my life would be ruined. I made sure I always had rubbers in my wallet after that night.

We did it a few times after that. In Joan's apartment when her roommate was home visiting her parents. Once at the Capistrano Motel. When we were able to get a room and she lay on the bed there, she looked a lot like that painting of an opulent naked duchess that was on one of my all-time favorite stamps, but she was real and she was all there for me. When she lay against me, her body was soft and warm and comfortable. That was the thing, she was comfortable.

31

But nice as it was, after a while things just didn't seem right.

One night at her place when we were done and just lying there, I looked over at her, and she was crying, big fat tears rolling down her cheeks.

"What's wrong?" I asked, reaching over and touching her face.

She just kept crying and crying. Then she sighed and shook her head. "You don't love me, not at all, do you?"

"Not, 'not at all,'" I said. As soon as it came out of my mouth I knew how awful it sounded.

Joan got up and started to get dressed. "You'd better leave now," she said.

"Joan, I didn't mean that I don't care about you. I mean I do care."

"Please just leave," she said, and she was right.

The way we ended made it hard to go in to work with her, but next Wednesday when I showed up at the Concord, Joan wasn't there. Wendy, one of the other girls said she'd gotten a better paying job at Murray's Restaurant downtown.

5

It was spring quarter when Will and I took Prof Williams' class. Will talked me into taking it instead of a lit class on contemporary Southern poets. Prof Williams taught "American Democracy in a Changing World" in the Political Science department. He was the first, and only, Negro on the faculty of the university, but taking Prof's course didn't seem like a big deal, one way or the other.

Until he came into the classroom the first day.

Six feet plus tall, lean, bent slightly forward over the podium as he peered down over his students, Theodore R. Williams was one intimidating guy—till his deep-brown-coffee face broke into a smile. When he extended his long arms and turned his palms skyward, welcoming us, he gestured like a priest offering Mass.

Just meeting him was an education for me. He was the first black man I'd actually met, though I'd seen some around the train station; otherwise blacks were long-breasted dark women in the *National Geographic* magazine and black men scampering around in a Tarzan movie. Prof reminded me of a picture I'd seen of a young Theodore Roosevelt: He had the same broad forehead and face, and bushy eyebrows over prominent eyes behind his glasses, except, of course, for the color of his skin and that his nose flared out more than Roosevelt's did.

I wondered if the initial "R" in Prof's name might even stand for Roosevelt, but I didn't ask him.

Prof said right away he didn't like to be called professor. "Mister" was what he wanted you to call him and "mister" was what he called you. That alone made some of the students sure he was a communist or at least a socialist. His reticence about his title, however, ensured the students referred to him as Prof, at least when we weren't talking to him.

He was more entitled to be called Prof than most guys with the title. He was the most exciting teacher I'd ever had. He graced the classroom like a performer on stage. He played his deep voice like a magnificent bass viola and then sent it up high and brought the house down. Even at eight o'clock on a Monday morning it was impossible to sleep through his lecture.

Prof had pungent and profane opinions about most every "in-sti-too-tion." He dragged out the syllables, as if angry at the word itself. I wasn't sure how Prof got there from "American Democracy in a Changing World" the way the class was described in the course bulletin, but he talked about how the First World War was supposed to be the "war to end all wars," and listed all the obscure wars that had been fought since.

And, like everything else he thought we should give thought to, he managed to work in the Korean War. Prof viewed the Korean War as inevitable. Korea was one land, he said, ravaged by wave after wave of foreign armies, notably the Japanese.

"You remember all the a-bom-in-able propaganda about the Japs in the Second World War, don't you, ladies and gentlemen? Yellow-faced, buck-toothed, bandy-legged monkeys!" Prof mugged, and his eyebrows bobbed up and down.

The Japs were no joke to me. They'd stabbed us in the back at Pearl Harbor, starved and beaten prisoners in the Bataan Death March, and killed our guys all the way back across the Pacific. My uncle John, in the Seabees stationed in the New Hebrides, had to be away from my favorite aunt Mary for years because of them. I still had vee-mail letters, white on black, he'd sent me about bloated cows floating in the fields after rainstorms.

Prof said that in Korea we were following in the footsteps of the Japanese we so hated. The Russians and the Chinese and the Japanese had all been involved with Korea for years; a spin of the globe would show the convergence of those three powers at its borders. We ought to be able to understand the way the Russians felt about protecting their interests. It was the American interest that was new.

Six months before the "so-called" invasion, as Prof put it, Secretary of State Dean Acheson, who in the newsreels had a great barroom melodrama mustache, had announced that Korea lay outside the United State's strategic perimeter. Prof thought that meant to North Korea's Kim Il Sung it was okay with us if his army moved south.

President Truman had been under fire from the China lobby and Joe McCarthy, not to mention the *Fargo Forum*, for having "lost" China to Mao Tse-tung because of "pinkos" like General George C. Marshall, who were "soft on communism," and so he went into Korea in large part for domestic political reasons.

Beyond all that, the American presence was "more of the new American hegemony."

I went to see him after class.

His office was the smallest one in the political science department and one of the few on campus with no window. He had a lamp burning, no matter that it was a crisp, bright day outside. The lamp haloed the picture on his desk of his wife, plump and a little solemn, with her arms around two girls who looked like Prof, except with pigtails and no glasses.

Every available inch of his desk but for the picture and an old Remington typewriter was stacked with papers and books and magazines. Prof sat leaning back in a battered wooden captain's chair under a wrinkled red, white and blue poster of a toothy Henry Wallace smiling in the 1948 campaign with "Et tu, Henry?" scrawled across the bottom in handwritten bold black letters. The chair's legs rested in coasters, and, with a thrust of his own powerful legs, Prof glided over the worn floor to get me a cup of the excuse for coffee he kept on a hotplate in the corner. Another captain's chair was squeezed into the room, and a horsehair black couch, straight from Freud's attic.

At Prof's wave I sat down on the couch, and we talked.

I argued that Prof's arguments about the war were paranoid as hell. Maybe the North Koreans thought our government had written South Korea off and that they'd get lucky. That was a far cry from being provoked into invading the South. And whatever Prof or anyone else thought about Harry Truman, Truman was doing what he felt was right. At least he tried to keep the war limited, and he had a hard time doing that.

"Mr. Kelly, I am afraid, ser-i-ous-ly afraid," he said gently, "that you are ser-i-ous-ly naïve. You just don't understand yet the way things work in this world." He went on to argue that the South Korean politicians were American puppets and South Korean President Syngman Rhee was, in a phrase he'd stopped short of sharing in class, the "CIA's prize prick."

I gave him my best shots from our NDTSTWPABCADS discussions on the subject but I didn't make any noticeable progress.

After that, whenever he wanted the warmonger's opinion in class he called on me.

EVERY CLASS HE CHALLENGED the simplest, most deeply embedded assumptions we brought to the classroom, including religion.

"Religion is the opium of the people!" Prof's eyes peered at us from behind his glasses. "Why did Marx say that? Why do I say it?

"Next to the Pope, isn't young Billy Graham's hellfire and damnation one of the best things the system has going for it?" Something to offend everyone. "And aren't we really fighting this a-bom-inable war in Korea to protect the system?"

I wasn't much on Billy Graham. Graham had preached on campus the week before, looking like a refugee from a B movie with his wavy blond pompadour and sweeping gestures. But Prof's diatribe made me uncomfortable.

I went to see him after class again.

With Moira, I argued about the foibles of our Catholicism whose main goal was preventing us from making out. But with Prof I defended it. At worst, I argued, if you couldn't prove God exists, you couldn't disprove it either, so the only intellectually responsible position was agnosticism, not atheism. Prof wasn't overwhelmed by my logic. He argued that, if religion wasn't provable, we should pull it out like a pernicious weed.

"Look at the harm it does," he said softly, sipping his cold coffee. "The wars that have been fought in its name, the op-pres-sion," his quiet voice lingered over the syllables, "it has been a party to. Look at the role of Chris-ti-anity as a tool of the slaveholders in this country, Mister Kelly.

"My own daddy believed it all—dirt poor, and I mean dirt poor, and praying every night for the Lord to swoop down and lift us to the Promised Land! It does nothing but get in the way!"

Prof rummaged through stacks of worn magazines, newspapers and pamphlets piled all over his desk: *New Masses*, *The Crisis*, *The Worker Monthly*, till I lost track of the titles. When he pulled out a dog-eared issue of the *Saturday Evening Post*, I didn't know what I was expecting, but it wasn't Norman Rockwell.

The magazine fell open at the page he wanted. "Listen to this. Listen to Langston Hughes." Prof's big voice boomed out the title, fell as he read:

> "GOODBYE, CHRIST
> Listen, Christ,
> You did all right in your day, I reckon—
> But that day's gone now."

His eye ran down the page and he read again:

> "Beat it on away from here now.
> Make way for a new guy with no religion at all—
> A real guy named
> Marx Communist Lenin Peasant Stalin Worker ME—
> I said, ME!"

"Here!" He thrust it at me. "Read the rest yourself and bring it back! Go read more Langston Hughes and come back and we'll talk more."

As I was backing out the door, I paused and asked him, "But, Prof, I mean Mr. Williams, you did get to college. Did your dad have anything to do with that?"

"Come here!" he said.

I did and he rose up in front of me.

"Yes, he did, young Mister Kelly. Not as much as my wife, Leona," Prof gestured at the picture on his desk. "But, yes, he did, and I honor him for it. Don't you misunderstand me." He leaned so close I could see reddish-brown veins in his eyes.

"I wouldn't," I said. "My father never went to college, but he got me here. He got me the scholarship. That's all I was thinking."

"I see," Prof smiled and gold glinted in the lamplight. He reached out one hand and clamped it on my shoulder, and I could feel the warmth radiate down my back like when my mother put a hot pack on my chest for a cold. He held it there for a second, then turned me back toward the door.

I didn't think Prof was as much of a true believer about his disbelief as he made out. No one could ever say he sought to impose his views on us. He was the only teacher on campus known to give an A to a student paper telling the instructor to go to hell. But Prof was annoyed if not disappointed with me when I went back to discuss Langston Hughes again.

He was willing enough to let me go on babbling about Hughes's use of words and syllables, how they were like notes in the blues that struck chords in me no white poet quite reached. But when he asked me what else struck me about the poems and I started out about Hughes' preoccupation with death, but reverted to the beat in *Drum*, that was too much.

"You're telling me he's got rhythm, and that's about it, ain't that so?" Prof shook his head, removed his gold-rimmed glasses, and rubbed his forehead with his fine, long-fingered hand. "My, my," he said, completing his routine. "Remember this?" he closed his eyes, and recited slowly:

38

"Sure,
A road helps all of us!
White folks ride—-
And I get to see 'em ride."

He paused and his eyes popped open and he looked at me. "That ain't just rhythm, Mister Kelly. That's the whole system in twenty-five words or less!"

If his views had stayed abstract and historical, Prof might have been okay. He was tolerated and even put on display by the university from time to time. After all, there were people from North Dakota and Minnesota and Wisconsin and Nebraska and other reliable places who, like Prof, had proposed doing away with lawyers and judges. Prof's close comparison of the Soviet and American Constitutions, sometimes unfavorably to the American, did evoke shock from some of his students and anger from local politicians, who sought political mileage by attacking the university. But it was all pretty theoretical stuff, and things seemed to bump along okay for Prof, with only minor hassles, except for the Korean War, which, with the Chinese helping the North Koreans, ground along.

IN EARLY APRIL, General MacArthur wrote a letter to crusty Joe Martin, Republican leader in the House, urging use of the Nationalist Chinese forces on Formosa to attack Red China. That did it. Truman fired MacArthur. I watched MacArthur live on television in Coffman Student Union as he addressed Congress after coming home, calling for winning the war against Communism in Asia. "In war there can be no substitute for victory," he intoned, ending, in his deep voice, that he would "just fade away, an old soldier who tried to do his duty as God gave him the light to see that duty." He faded right into a ticker tape parade that seven and a half million New Yorkers gave him the next day.

Meanwhile, I was busy in ROTC, earning my scholarship, being ordered around by student noncoms and officers, and more often than I expected under the watchful eye of Major Goodlittle himself. The other

Regular Army personnel spent a lot of time in the office drinking coffee. It was a cushy assignment but they'd earned it. They didn't talk about it much, but a couple of them had been over in Korea.

One thing about ROTC surprised me. Most days that spring we had to show up in uniform behind the Armory, which looked like a friendly, Grimm's fairy tale vine-covered castle, for close order drill. On a warm, sunny day, we would form in companies and march around the green, grassy drill field, like regular soldiers. I was amazed at how much I got into marching along in cadence with the rest of the company.

I remembered newsreel pictures of Hitler's troops marching past him at night outside Nuremberg, row after row after row, with flags and banners and bands and blazing torches. I'd bet those Krauts felt the hair tingle on the back of their necks. It was a lot bigger deal than Company G hiking in the morning sun, but with the drill going right, and our voices booming out the cadence, in my own small way, I felt that way in Company G. It was scary.

IT WAS IN THE SPRING I heard about what happened to Chick Belos in Korea.

My hand twitched when I held the crummy little article my mother sent me from the *Fargo Forum*, and for a minute it was hard to read it:

> Rites Set Monday
> For Pfc. Belos
> The body of Pfc. George, "Chick," Belos, son of Mr. and Mrs. Warren Belos, will arrive here Friday. Pfc. Belos was the first from Fargo to enlist after the outbreak of the war. Belos, who was 18, was killed in Korea while on duty with the U.S. Army in the Pusan area. He died when he fell from a bridge across the Naktong River. Services will be held at St. Mary's Cathedral at 10 a.m. Monday. Ivers-Landblom Funeral Home is in charge.

It was hard to think of Chick dying in a river in a country that had been only a word to us not long ago. It sounded like he never even got a chance to fight. I thought about the Mexican guy we'd found in the Red River last spring. I hoped they'd gotten Chick out of the river in Korea right away.

I got home for his funeral. In an odd way, the story about how he died somehow took away from Chick's status as a hero. I heard a couple of the guys snicker about it in the vestibule, and I was ready to punch them out if they didn't knock it off. Chick died doing the bravest thing he'd ever done in his life, and it made me mad that how he died should diminish him in the eyes of these assholes. It was a closed casket, underneath the big American flag.

Father Mahoney circled Chick's casket twice: once sprinkling it with the holy water and then incensing it. I'd always loved incense, from the time I was a little boy. It made me think of frankincense and myrrh at Christmas. But at Chick's funeral, the incense was so heavy and sickly sweet in the air I almost had to leave the church before the service ended.

At the cemetery I watched them put Chick into a hole. Afterward, with the icy wind whipping me, I walked by myself down Broadway all the way to the Red River, which was still covered here and there with gray ice. I tried to figure out why Chick had to die in goddamn Korea. I wanted to think the Free World got something out of his death because Chick sure didn't get much, personally, out of dying. With that walleye of his, he could have stayed home eating Bismarcks at the Broadway Donut Shop.

6
Summer 1951

When I wasn't hanging out with Moira, I spent a lot of the summer back in Fargo selling shoes for Kinney Shoes on Broadway. It was an okay job except my boss, George Vincent, had this one-size-fits-all philosophy, which meant we had to tell customers that if the shoes were too small, they'd stretch, or if they were too big, to put them on the radiator and they'd shrink. It was an aggravation to send somebody limping out of there just so George could meet his quota for the week.

Otherwise, it was a golden summer. The Staceys had bought a summer place, a cabin at Detroit Lakes, and a sailboat came with it. For her graduation from Sacred Heart, Mr. Stacey gave Moira a dark-green Ford convertible with a cream-colored top and dual spots. Weekends, if Moira was already out at the lake, I borrowed Dad's old Chevy, put in a half-dollar's worth of gas, and prayed one of the bald tires wouldn't blow. Other times Moira would pick me up in her convertible, and we'd drive with the top down and the wind whistling past us as the radio played Les Paul and Mary Ford, Mitch Miller and Hank Williams at full blast.

At the lake, we went sailing on the Staceys' boat. We came to know every shallow and deep and inlet, where to find a breeze on the stillest days, and where there were quiet eddies so we could anchor even on wind-tossed days. Moira taught me how to handle the small boat, to know when to use

42

the jib sail, how high I could let the high side go, the moment to ease my hold on the mainsail, how to catch the wind and when to let it go free.

Together we learned the lake's moods, shadings, shiftings: smooth, dull, boring on cloudy windless days; rippling, flashing with silvers, pale greens, pure whites and blues on sunny fresh days; peaceful and solid with shimmering golds and blacks and rumpled sheets of silver on the quiet full moon nights; and, when we grew very confident, the nights when the sky and water converged in angry violence and there was a wild joy in being interlopers on that union and conflict. All of nature was there just for us. The rain was lucky and a full moon a bad omen.

And we were alone with it all; as much as we could avoid them, not with Mr. and Mrs. Stacey, not with Moira's rich friends from the Club, not her goofy friends from the theater either, not with anyone else.

Lazy, sultry days we anchored the small boat in one of the half dozen green wooded coves on the other side of the lake. We lay there on the narrow bow, watching the leaf-deflected sunlight make intricate vanishing patterns across the still water. We talked to each other like Moira's crazy happy people from the stage; I'd have been embarrassed if anyone heard us, but it was just us, goofing around.

We swam and sunburned together and I lovingly peeled Moira. She freckled like a trout, slipping through my arms in the water, escaping me when she wanted to tease me, letting me catch her when she wanted to be caught. On land she was a fairy tale princess, spinning gifts and enchantments for me. In her hunter-green Ford convertible, we nosed and sniffed out every cheap place to eat within a hundred miles.

We had king-sized cheeseburgers and onion rings and sat outside eating them in our dripping suits at the Detroit House. We gorged ourselves greasy and happy at Billy's Chicken Shack on all the fried chicken we could eat for a dollar. We found a place without a name off a side road, with a shaggy moose head above a never-used fireplace, a big Wurlitzer with Lena Horne singing our song, "Where or When," for us over and over, and hot succulent barbecued ribs and dark German beer made to wash them down.

Of course there was a worm in the apple in our paradise that Moira didn't know about.

Moira was always asking me if I ever took out any of the girls in my classes at the U. I always said, "No," which was true, but she seemed skeptical. Well, then, she wanted to know, had I wanted to? I told her that was a stupid question to ask. When she persisted, I just told her I hadn't, meaning I hadn't taken them out, but Moira took it as meaning I hadn't wanted to, and I just let it go.

There were times I wanted to tell Moira about Joan Hendrickson, everything, just to be rid of the damn secret and be done with it. Sometimes I wanted to just say to Moira that things could be so much nicer between us if she would only relax like Joan Hendrickson. Moira and I would be talking and, I'd get this crazy urge to tell her. Of course, I knew that was the worst possible thing I could do. It was awful, like that crappy feeling when maybe you need to throw up but you just don't want to. It was hard not to tell Moira about Joan, but it was a lot easier than telling would have been.

Moira and I talked about how great it would be to have a place of our own where we could lie around all the time, do everything we wanted, all the time. She kept back just the one thing for that time. No matter she was sweating and straining as hard against me as I was against her, or touching me while I was touching her, she held back that inviolate seal for when we got married, at least so she said. But our imagination was boundless, and our animal cunning was endless, but for that.

Once, while we were lying together on the bottom of the boat, anchored under overhanging trees, we were touching each other for a long time, touching everything. My knees scraped on the bottom of the boat when I rose up to look at her. I stared down at the patch of dark gold below her white, sunburned stomach. It was almost drawing my head down to her. It was like it wasn't even me, but if she hadn't moved, I was going to kiss her there, where it smelled like sweat and something else. She was whimpering, and she twisted over to one side and opened her thighs, and instead of tensing up, she relaxed her legs, and for a second she let me start to come into her, but suddenly she tensed again and turned away from me, nearly capsizing us. "No!" she said. "Please. Just against my stomach, can't you? It'll be all right."

My parents didn't like it that I was gone all the time, either working or hanging out with Moira. My mother kept telling me it was no sense getting serious with a girl like Moira, but it was hard to pin down what she meant by "a girl like Moira." I sort of thought that it was because Mom overheard Moira making fun of Mom's dyed-red hair at church one Sunday; actually I didn't like Moira doing that either.

Mom talked about the difference in money and how I could end up getting hurt. But she was more concerned about sex and babies and early marriage. She knew somehow there was stuff going on she didn't approve of. Once or twice she asked if I was going to confession that week. I never did if I could avoid it, knowing what grief and aggravation always came out of it, when Moira would get an attack of religion and drag me in. The more passionate she and I got, the more severe her following bout with religion was.

At the end of the summer Moira made theatrical history at the Fargo Little Theater as Essie Carmichael in *You Can't Take It with You*. Essie had been studying to be a dancer for—only—eight years and spent the whole play in ballet shoes, bracing herself against the refrigerator, doing lifts, and passing out the candy she made—"Love Dreams." When Moira tripped down the stairs—in black leotard, red roses tumbling in her blonde hair—stumbling over her own feet, and righted herself with elaborate dignity to address her teacher, Mr. Kolenkhov, even my mother laughed and shook her head.

I HADN'T GIVEN MUCH THOUGHT to the war the whole summer, nobody did; and for most of the summer it looked like anyone who did was ready to end it. Gallup Polls during May had shown only thirty to thirty-five percent of Americans were in favor of the war. Polls might be okay for General Motors to decide whether to put more chrome on next year's cars, but they didn't seem to be the right way for a president to decide to end a war. You could just hear Lincoln saying, "Okay, Gallup says fifty-four percent are for slavery. Pack it up, boys."

But in June, Acheson said the UN might be willing to negotiate a cease-fire at the 38th Parallel. Talks began in July, and there was a pause along the battle line. It took two weeks of bickering at a green table in a teahouse on the outskirts of a devastated town over there named Kaesong to arrive at the agenda for the talks. At the end of the month, both sides said there would be no further cease-fire even though the negotiations would continue. But the talks went nowhere fast, and in August the Communists broke them off.

The UN was determined to keep up the pressure and launched limited offensives against hills named for good reason "Bloody Ridge" where the North Koreans were dug in with deep trenches and hidden bunkers. The Americans and Republic of Korea troops suffered about three thousand casualties to take them, and the North Koreans lost even more, in a slaughter that was compared to the bloody trench warfare of the First World War.

7

In the fall I went down to the university early, to reclaim my jobs at the Concord Bar and Fine Dining and Shortstop Trucking and to wait for Moira. She arrived in September in her dark-green Ford convertible with all her suitcases filled with sweaters.

I'd had these daydreams about how, when we were both at the U, away from home, and parents, and Father Mahoney, we would hang around together, making out all the time. We'd go to school on the side, and paradise would continue. But almost immediately, things started to go wrong. Right after she arrived, Moira went off to freshman orientation camp for a week. No sooner did she get back from that than she was going through "rushing" with the sorority and fraternity types. The next thing I knew, she was joining Kappa Kappa Gamma, along with the rest of the rich girls, and she set about becoming quite the all-campus everything.

She signed up to work for the *Minnesota Daily* her first month on campus. The *Daily* was put out five days a week by a batch of hard-bitten student journalists in the grungy depths of Murphy Hall. The paper billed itself as the "World's Largest College Circulation" paper. It had spawned guys like Max Schulman, Harry Reasoner, Harrison Salisbury, and Eric Severeid, and the kids who worked there saw themselves as removed from *The New York Times* more by geography than anything else.

Moira also continued her theatrical career at the University Theater at Scott Hall. Back home at the Fargo Little Theater, I liked watching her rehearse, but the company she kept at Scott Hall gave me one terrific pain in the ass. After a play they would hang around the green room and sweep down on each other saying things like "We've been drinking martinis!"

IN A WAY IT WAS OKAY she was so busy playing Lois Lane, and Sarah Bernhardt, and sororitying it up, with me having to go to both of my jobs, as well as occasionally show up for classes. I also maintained my membership in the NDTSTWPABCADS, as my answer to Kappa Kappa Gamma. Moira sort of knew Will Lindeman from Fargo too, and she fell right in with his politics, along with everything else she plunged into. In fact, whatever time she wasn't spending with the theater students, or playing reporter at the *Daily* offices, she was hanging around with Will and his radical friends along with me.

The three of us—she and Will and I—had lockers together in the basement of Folwell Hall. Will and I kept a supply of Jack Daniel's there too, in peanut butter jars. Will and I thought that somehow hit the right note of dissipation, though we'd have had a hard time explaining to anyone else what that meant to us. We didn't actually live in Folwell, though sometimes it seemed that way. Will stayed at his dingy rooming house north of Dinkytown. I continued to live in dreary Pioneer Hall with the rest of the brown shoes. Moira lived at revolutionary headquarters at the Kappa house.

With Moira into everything—not that I was jealous—I was impressed, but things between us were changing. Moira told me none of this was going to make any difference to us. But I was beginning to wonder if she was getting friendlier with Lindeman than she let on, or even if there was some frat guy in the picture. Arthur Ramsted was hanging around the U Theater all the time. Moira kept telling me Ramsted was simply a diversion while I was busy working, and it did seem like she didn't take him very seriously. Even Lindeman said Ramsted was way too old for her. We didn't exactly fight about it. But Moira and I started to have a lot of sociological discussions; about Lindeman and his radical friends; about Ramsted and his rich friends; all of them about Moira and me. Whether I was such a brown shoe I would never be one of the in crowd. "In the center instead of on the periphery," was the way she put it. Whether, for all her talk about social justice, she was just another rich bitch, was the way I put it.

WHEN WE WERE HOME OVER THE HOLIDAYS I took her, or I should say she took me, to the Christmas dance at the Fargo Country Club. It wasn't one of our more successful evenings. Moira was always pissing and moaning about our '35 Chevy, and she wanted me to use her dad's big Lincoln, but I wouldn't, so things didn't get off to a very good start.

Then we had the fight about her gold shoes. Moira had very small-boned feet with high arches. There was a thing between us about them ever since I told her that they were really pretty. But for the Christmas dance she'd had to have these fifty-four-dollar gold shoes she was crazy about. I gave her such a hard time about how the damn shoes cost about as much as our Chevy that she took them off and fired them right out the car window into a snow bank. I wanted to stop the car to look for them but she said she'd get out of the car and walk home in her stocking feet if I did.

Naturally, at ten below, the car window she had thrown them out of fell into the door, not to be seen again. We froze the rest of the way over to the club. I carried her in to the club from the parking lot, with her crinolined formal flaring out like an orchid in the snow, and she made a grand entrance to the dance like a wild Grushenka. Moira caused a sensation, which she loved, but failed to give me any credit for carrying her in.

Instead she spent more time than I cared for dancing with Arthur Ramsted, who was home for the holidays too. Arthur's hair was prematurely receding in front, and with couple of brillo pads growing out of the sides of his head, he looked like like one of the Three Stooges, though

Moira disagreed. He was a rich, perpetual graduate student down at the U where he and I had nothing to do with each other.

"Oh, are you there too?" he asked. "I didn't see you during pledge week," he said, but he was right at home at "the club," mentioning several times he had seen me caddying.

He dragged Moira off to do the stupid bunny hop—dada dada dada, dada dada dada da, hop hop hop! over and over—it was a wonder no one hopped on her stocking feet.

All the while she was laughing and dancing up a storm with Ramsted, I was slipping off to the can and nipping at some Old Grand Dad. I got ornerier and ornerier.

Finally, I managed to restart the argument about her shoes. "Not that there's anything wrong with fifty-four-dollar gold shoes, or throwing them in a snow bank, if you have fifty-four dollars to waste, I suppose. I'm sure that would go over big with Dorothy Day."

"Why are you doing this, Tom?" she asked. She sat very straight, her bare shoulders squared, her head high, like a damn princess.

"Doing what?"

"This. Can't you be happy? It's a party."

"You and Arthur be happy. You're the happy people. I'm sure he'd be happy to give you a ride home."

Her green eyes leveled at me, "He would. The way you're acting, I should let him."

"What's he driving? His daddy's Cadillac? I suppose its windows will stay up."

"For your information, he's driving a Plymouth. Not that there's anything wrong with a Cadillac."

"Not for Our Lady of the Cadillac."

"You're being such a jealous ass. We'll go back and find the damn shoes if you care so much about them!"

"Is everything all right here?" It was Ramsted.

"Sure," I said. "God's in his heaven, and all His chil'en got shoes. Let's get out of here, Moira." I headed for the door.

"Tom, that's despicable! I'm not following you." Moira edged over toward Ramsted. "Or calling you."

"Fine," I said. "Maybe I'll give you a ring sometime."

I walked out to the car, the wind biting into me. The old Chevy finally kicked over, and I drove slowly back toward Moira's house, retracing our route to the dance as carefully as I could, leaning out the window on the driver's side for a nice even flow of ten below air when I neared the block where she had chucked the shoes. To my amazement, I found them, lying on their sides, gleaming dully against the snow in the circle of light from the streetlight. I left them neatly beside each other on the front steps of Tara.

We were back at the university a week before Moira talked to me. She didn't even thank me for the shoes, and I didn't exactly apologize for acting like a jerk.

BUT DURING WINTER QUARTER, in a party at the Kappa house, I made a big mistake.

I was the only guy there who wasn't a Greek. I was getting tired of hearing about how Milton Caniff, who drew Terry and the Pirates and Steve Canyon, was going to be coming to dinner to the SAE house.

When I got away from Caniff's fan club, I got cornered by a pimple-headed guy who kept asking me real subtle questions about Moira, like how well did I know her and did we go together and what frat was I in. I kept getting drunker and drunker and finally I said, "Here," pushing him toward her. "You think she's so goddamn smart and be-aut-i-ful. Be my guest."

"Goodnight," I threw at her over my shoulder, and went upstairs to flop out amidst the coats piled on her bed. Like I hoped, even in my angry stupor, Moira came up after me. She started yelling about what a boor I was being, and how I was going to wreck all the coats by lying there in them. But I just looked at her, and she got quiet and looked hard at me.

"Oh, God, this is the fifty-four-dollar gold shoes again. Isn't it?" she said, and she put her arms around me. "Oh, Tom Kelly, my Tom, what am I going to do with you," she said and lay down next to me to talk to me. We were kissing each other, and then moving against each other, and every time I looked up, her green eyes looked down at me and the rest of the world was nothing but a hazy, bleary background to Moira. When I tried to get her to take her clothes off, she said no, but with the knowing, tender way she smiled down at me, I knew, even if I was never going to get her to go all the way, I was going to get some relief.

Till a clown from the Dekes came in and leered at us and spoiled everything. Moira saw him and jumped up like she was just straightening the pile of coats. Instead of getting back down with me when the guy left, she stayed standing, with her cheeks red and her eyes angry, like we'd been fighting instead of making out. I got crazy when she wouldn't lie down with me again. "If I was Arthur Ramsted, you'd close the door," I said, sitting up to drain the last Jack Daniel's from my bottle.

"If you were Arthur Ramsted, you wouldn't be here, trying to make love to me in a pile of coats in front of the whole world. Not all boys are like you."

"Yeah, well, not all girls are like you either."

She got this odd look on her face. "What's that supposed to mean?"

That was when I did it. "Not all girls hang out with rich assholes." Before she could answer, I said it, "And not all girls are prick teasers, some of them actually like to do it."

"Oh," she asked, "what girls?" like she was really interested. I should have stopped right there, when I heard the quavery way her voice was, but I didn't.

"Joan girls. Joan girls from the Concord Bar and Fine Dining."

I was trying to tell Moira things between a guy and a girl didn't have to be such a big deal all the time—full of aggravation and scenes and pain—they could just make love. But drunk or sober I was stupid to say it. Moira wound up and hit me with everything she had and pounded on me all the way down the stairs and out into the cold before slamming the door in my face.

52

I don't think I ever quite got my point across. And it was bullshit. If she hadn't been hanging around with Lindeman almost as much as with me, flitting around with Art Ramsted at the U Theater, and smiling at those asshole frat guys, and I hadn't wanted to get her, I never would have told her. She wouldn't even talk to me for days, and I didn't blame her.

Till one night a week later, I caught up with her on the mall in front of Johnston Hall. With the moonlight pouring down through the dark branches of the trees and over the white snow, the whole world was frozen still, but for Moira.

She was crying and yelling at me and hitting me again and again, all at the same time. Luckily for me, I was wearing my big stormcoat with the fur collar turned up around my cheeks, so I was safe from serious damage. I stood there till she got arm-weary and quit hitting me, and she stood there too, sobbing, her breath curling up like smoke in the cold night air.

She let me walk her home to the Kappa house, and I pleaded my case on the steps there. "If you leave me, I'll lie here in the doorway till you come out and lie down beside me, too." Her nose was red, and she was crying again and at that moment I meant it. "Or the janitor picks me up and puts me in the Dumpster." She went to hit me again but she was laughing too, and she let me kiss her before she went in.

8

eanwhile the war had gone on and the casualties piled up.

After Bloody Ridge there had been another "limited advance" attempted by the UN to "straighten its line." For about a month we threw in artillery fire "such as the world had never seen" against a hill known as Heartbreak Ridge. We finally captured it after about three thousand more American casualties and about ten times as many North Korean.

The Communists called for peace talks again. In October the talks resumed at Panmunjom, a deserted village in no man's land, between the battle lines. In November, each side ratified an agreement on a cease-fire line. But the Communists stalled on an armistice, and the patrols and shelling went on into the winter.

Communist propaganda became more outlandish the longer the war went on. In February the Russians, Chinese, and North Koreans complained the United States was using germ warfare and managed to wring a few "confessions" out of poor guys they had captured. At the same time the Communists managed to brainwash some prisoners into signing peace petitions and pro-Communist statements, which were obviously phony as three-dollar bills.

In March, the UN told the negotiators that many of the prisoners of war we held at Pusan and in a prison camp called Koje-do didn't want to return to North Korea or China. It turned out half of them didn't, which should have told Prof something, but he didn't seem to pay much attention. In May, the Communist prisoners at Koje captured the American general Dodd, who was supposed to be running the place and got him to sign an agreement to stop "mass murdering" the prisoners with everything from germs to poison gas. They churned out propaganda accusing the Americans of running a death camp like Dachau. Most Americans knew this was total bullshit, but Prof seemed to take it seriously.

IT WAS SPRING QUARTER, when Moira took Prof's course on American Democracy.

She was pretty weird when it came to Prof. One day she would come out of his class mad as hell; the next day she was practically in love with him. It was the same way after class. Prof had coffee with us sometimes in his office and now and then at the Bridge or the Varsity. I liked getting Moira to the Bridge. Grungy as it was, the Bridge was nice and quiet so you could talk; not like the Varsity, which was always noisy, and where all the frat and sorority types hung out, and Moira was always running into one ditsy friend or another, wrecking any good conversation, while we listened to planning for the Campus Carnival.

But at the Bridge we had good discussions. Moira and Will and Prof agreed about a lot more things than I did. For a while Moira, like Prof, was convinced Coca Cola and a couple of the big New York banks ran the world, so she and Prof had rapport when it came to economics. Compared to them, I was a dupe for the system. And of course Moira and Will went along with Prof about the war, even his totally paranoid ideas about it.

Prof felt the reporting about the war was unfair. He was especially pissed off about reports after Bloody Ridge that one of the American units that was "wholly colored," contrary to the supposed new policy, had performed poorly, although there were reports "other colored soldiers had done splendidly." After Bloody Ridge, the Army began actually desegregating its units in Korea.

55

Prof was outraged by the whole business: "Splen-did-ly! Splen-did-ly!" he thundered like an Old Testament prophet. "And why should 'col-or-ed' soldiers serve at all? Splen-di-dly or otherwise?"

He took off his glasses and rubbed his face, as he talked about what our country had done to his people. Right from bringing them over as slaves, to counting each one as three-fifths of a person in the Constitution, to "seg-re-gating them and lynch-ing them." He slapped his hand flat on the table, making his coffee cup jump in its saucer. Moira reached across the booth and put her hand on Prof's. I'd gotten so I didn't even notice Prof's skin, but Moira's hand was such a startling white against his it leaped to my eye for a moment. Her cheeks flushed, and she pulled her hand back.

Of course, she had to bring up religion, and there she and Prof totally parted company. He listened to her, and yes, Dorothy Day was doing good work in protesting the war when no one was paying any attention to it, much less protesting it. But, he pointed out, "Car-din-al Spell-man is ready to bless the cannons." Moira had to agree.

But then she went off railing about how the Communists hated religion and how pointless life would be without God. Prof seemed worn out with the whole thing just then. "We all be-lieve what we want to, Miss Stacey. Don't we?" Later Moira told me if he wasn't such a hard-core atheist, Prof might be a great man; but he could do good, or a lot of harm, or both.

PROF CONTINUED TO BE COMPLETELY FRUSTRATED by the way the media presented the war, and the longer the war went on, the more he waged war against it. It all hit the fan when Prof went to a gathering of political scientists at Indiana University and delivered a paper provocatively titled "An Analysis of the National Media's Presentation of War Employing the Principles of Wittgenstein's Tractatus Logico-Philosophicus."

Not much chance of the national media covering that one. But a student stringer assigned to write a couple of paragraphs for the Indianapolis paper did. Smelling a story at Prof's reference to the dialectics of American expansionism, the reporter was able to extract enough from Prof's more colorful departures from his prepared text to write a story headlined: RADICAL PROF SIDES WITH KOREAN REDS. The phrase "jingoist bullshit" didn't make it into the paper intact, but if you knew Prof, you could spot it among the euphemisms.

With its headline and the help of the *Minnesota Daily*'s tireless press clipping service, the story in the Indianapolis paper about Prof found its way back to the university. The *Daily* saw itself as "of the students, by the students and for the students" and as more honest and knowledgeable, certainly about college affairs, than either the Minneapolis or St. Paul papers. Whatever the truth of that modest self-appraisal, Moira took it very seriously, as she did most everything. Her story about Prof was all over the front page of the *Daily*:

INSTRUCTOR BLASTS U.S. ROLE IN KOREA
By Moira Stacey, Staff Reporter
Shock waves set in motion by a speech given by its only Negro instructor, Theodore R. Williams rocked the University today.

In his speech at Indiana University, Dr. Williams sharply criticized American policy as interfering in a domestic civil war in Korea. The UN police action there is only "part of the new American Imperialism," he is reported to have declared.

Dr. Williams, the first Negro instructor in the University's nearly one-hundred-year history has come under fire before for his radical political views and his frequent attacks on religion. He is equally outspoken in opposing the war and in excoriating organized religion.

His students know Dr. Williams as "Prof," even though he does not hold the rank of full Professor. Yet he is highly regarded by his students, who two years in a row have voted him Best Teacher, and cite his unstinting willingness to engage them in dialogue, whether in class or over coffee in his office.

The *Daily* has been informed by knowledgeable sources the University Administration may come under heavy pressure to deny tenure to the controversial Williams. What action, if any,

the popular instructor's students will take is another question.
A petition is being circulated in his support.

From that point, terminal chaos set in.

The state legislators, upon whom the university depended for financing, tended to read the *Daily* from time to time, ever since one issue had playfully suggested doing away with that august body. This time, courtesy of a right wing St. Paul city council member who hated the university in the first place, Moira's story found its way to the desk of each and every legislator. After reading the story from the floor, one member quoted solemnly from the proceedings of the House Un-American Activities Committee that "anybody who allies himself with communists in anything is a fellow traveler."

The *Minneapolis Tribune* and the *St. Paul Pioneer Press* ran ominous editorials. All three television channels carried stories on both the six o'clock and the ten o'clock news. I wished Fargo had TV so my folks could see what was going on, besides having to rely on the *Fargo Forum*. I knew that the *Forum* would label Prof a "pinko" and go after his hide. But if my dad knew what was going on, even if he disagreed with Prof, as I was sure he would, he'd be for Prof having the right to say what he thought.

This time, though, Prof wasn't going to survive with the usual stern talking to from the head of the political science department. The university administration noted that Prof, although on a tenure track, didn't have it yet. It stated he had failed to generate the required quota of "publishable" academic work. A close examination of the papers he had delivered disclosed a sparseness of footnotes that had previously escaped notice.

That his students voted him the Best Teacher award two years running was now seen as the result of pandering. Prof did put an unseemly amount of time and energy into teaching, instead of pursuing more highly esteemed academic endeavors. Some cynical students might even have thought that by the time Moira's story reached the legislators' desks, it was all over but the firing. The administration didn't even wait a week. They thought they could slip it past the students during finals.

They were wrong.

9

"We're not here to listen to this bullshit. We don't need this bullshit," Moira mimicked me, pitching her voice, which naturally had a slight melody to it, up an octave for effect, across the booth in Stub and Herbs. I don't know how many hours Will and I, and Moira, in various combinations, spent in Stub and Herbs; a lot more time than money. Compared even to Mannings, it was a lowbrow hangout. One big dark room with a long bar traversing one wall, pinball machines across the front, a pool table with faded and torn felt in the middle, and a juke box specializing in numbers like Rosemary Clooney's "Come On-a My House." It was not the place you'd expect to find T.S. Eliot if he came to town, but the hamburgers were big, the beer was cold, and we were never carded.

"Just how am I supposed to report that in the *Daily*, Tom? And the rest of it?"

The students had met in the Coffman Student Union to see what we could do about Prof's termination. There'd been a couple hundred students, some faculty and a few guys who looked like they'd never been near the U before.

Rick Gunneris, as exalted president of the Young Socialist Alliance and organizer of the meeting had started off talking about the

Meaning of It All: War and Peace, and Freedom of Speech in Time of War, and, finally, incidentally it seemed, Academic Freedom in Our Society. Rick's words slid endlessly out from under his mustache, slick as half-sucked cough drops, but before he was done, students started shuffling their feet. One or two complained out loud they were here to help Prof, not to listen to "damn commie propaganda."

Next was an old union organizer—wearing a suit straight from J.C. Penney, I could tell because that's where the only suit I owned came from. He spent half his time talking about the big teamsters strike in Minneapolis in the thirties when the Dunn brothers took on the cops. His windup appeal for "worker and student solidarity in the struggle against capitalist oppression" didn't help. The shuffling of feet and scattered coughing in the audience grew into a steady, purposeful scraping of feet and chairs, and even a couple of hisses.

What needed to be said was very simple, but it wasn't being said. I stood up and didn't say anything for what seemed like a long time, and the crowd quieted down a little.

"We're not here to listen to this bullshit. We don't need this bull-shit," I said, my voice coming out a lot louder than I'd expected.

The room fell so silent for a moment that I heard the hand move on the big clock on the wall.

Then a kid who knew me yelled out from the back, "You tell 'em, Tom," and I could hear rising approval sweep around the room and student voices sing out all over the place, "Right! That's right!"

"The issue is simple," I went on. "The issue is whether the university is crapping all over the best teacher on campus because it doesn't have enough integrity to keep a tight asshole when the legislature says squat."

The whole damn place exploded. There was whistling and foot stamping and cheering. For a couple of minutes I was a regular star, and by popular acclaim elected to the Steering Committee of SAFE—Students for Academic Freedom Everywhere, a name straight from Rick Gunneris—an honor, I dimly realized, likely to earn me a mention in J. Edgar Hoover's little black book.

"I loved it! I just loved it!" Will slurped off the head on his beer, gulped down half of the mug in a huge swallow, and wiped the back of his hand across his mouth.

Will had to squint to see me across the table, as the waitress leaned and put a full pitcher in front of him, all but poking him in his big, brown nearsighted eyes with her bosoms. Will wore horn-rimmed glasses, which on most people were conspicuous as hell, but you didn't notice his till he took them off like he did now. He grinned up at the waitress and flashed those goddamn Pepsodent-white, even teeth he brushed three times a day. She giggled and kept them right there for about ten minutes.

"The point is," I said, "where do we go from here?"

"Good point, Tom!" laughed Will.

We decided the Committee had to keep the pressure on the administration. Call a bigger and better meeting and invite the U's big muckety-mucks to smoke out their real reasons for firing Prof. The trick would be not allowing the guys from downtown to take over the meeting.

"And not to get thrown out of school," Moira added.

When I left for the meeting of the Committee, she and Will were still sort of nestled together on the bench.

LATE THAT NIGHT, the Committee finished mimeographing posters and fliers for the meeting the next day, and I went home to the dorm.

I wasn't doing too great this quarter, and I still had to study for the next day's test in Public Health 101, a required class on such mind benders as brucellosis. I hadn't even cracked the book.

I was tired but not sleepy, keyed up from all the coffee at the meeting of the Committee and from having been a star earlier. But now, alone in my room, thinking of Moira and Will together at Sterbs while I had to learn about sick cows, my thoughts began to turn brown like the room. Moira hadn't had anything to do with Will that I knew of, beyond conversation, but I was beginning to wonder just how chummy they were getting.

Brown. That was the color of the whole crummy room: ceiling, walls, carpet. Even the light showed brown through the lampshade. A specialist in monotony must have decorated the place. I walked over to the window and pulled back my grungy shade someone had slobbered all up with foaming brew the other night.

Outside the window, except for a few feeble streetlights, it was dark all the way down to the river flat and on to the Mississippi River. A lone car pulled up along the River Road, glided to a stop, and its lights went out. No doubt a guy and his girl about to settle into serious middle of the night necking.

Before opening the book, I dug out the bottle of Jack Daniel's I had stashed in the bottom drawer of the bureau. It was grounds for instant expulsion if you were caught with booze in the dorm, but it hadn't happened in living memory. In the drawer was a box full of letters from Moira and pictures I'd taken of her in her swimming suit under the dry lilac bushes that hot July day back home. I didn't want to get into that tonight.

Nothing living moved at the bottom of this morning's first coffee cup so I swirled a wash of Daniel's around the bottom to clean it and filled it half full. The first swallow comfortably warmed the pit of my stomach. I sat down in my worn red easy chair from the Salvation Army, avoiding the coils that sprang through the cushions, and settled in to study. But instead I sat there for a long time, feeling horny and terrible. If I was going to feel this bad, I could at least be in Paris, not sitting around in the dormitory for Christ's sake.

Well shit.

With a good part of the night gone, I decided to try to get some shuteye so I'd have a clear head for the test, but I didn't sleep more than a couple of hours, at best. Whenever I managed to forget about Prof or Moira and Will for a few minutes, dead cows lay around in my head.

Usually terror was a good motivator. Last spring I had maxed a test question on the relevance of municipalities in the modern state by a white hot comparison of *The Death of the Ball Turret Gunner* with *War and Peace* that came roaring out of me, Nodoz, and coffee at eight in the morning.

But this morning I'd caught just enough brucellosis to stifle my creativity. My eyes had that scratchy feeling, and even though I'd run the shower needle-hot right on it, my head still felt numb. The damn dead cows just lay there during the whole test. Between them and me, we stunk the joint up.

Afterward, I stopped by our lockers in Folwell Hall, and consoled myself with a few sips of bourbon from the peanut butter jar. It went down warmly and kindled a slow fire in my stomach.

ON THE WAY OVER TO THE MEETING at Burton Hall, on the off chance, I stopped by Wesbrook Hall and looked in on Prof's office. I didn't actually expect to find him, but there he was, packing his stuff.

It was only a few days since the whole flap about him had started, but a weird change had been going on in my thinking about Prof. Until all this ruckus, he was Prof, a terrific teacher, but when you got right down to it, that was it. Now he was on the front page of the newspaper, the big story on the local news at night. There were even rumors Edward R. Murrow was sending a crew to campus. Suddenly Prof had become one of those guys both bigger than life and somehow less than a real person at the same time.

Like a movie star. To me a guy like Gary Cooper was a giant: he became the enormous image on the screen, the Marshall striding down the main street of a dusty cattle town at High Noon. He would outdraw or outlast the bad guys, and, no matter what the odds, he would not die. But he was less than human too; even if the unthinkable happened, and he was gunned down right in front of my eyes, it was just a story, and celluloid had no feelings.

Not only movie stars, but people in real life too: F. Scott Fitzgerald was a drunk and Zelda was crazy, but so what? They couldn't really feel pain through all that fame and glamour, could they? They were Amory and Rosalind, Anthony and Gloria, Dick and Nicole—Scott and Zelda—what was the difference? Or Hemingway. To write *The Sun Also Rises* and *A Farewell to Arms* and *For Whom the Bell Tolls*—to live them—nothing else would matter. Nothing could hurt him after that. Not that Godlike bronzed face.

Prof wasn't one of those guys overnight, but I was beginning to think of him that way, seeing his picture on the front page of the paper, hearing his name on the radio, and on the news on TV. So it was a shock to see him there in his lonely office, bent over a big packing crate, loading books into it, dust flying up from them as they landed. The photograph of his wife and kids wasn't on his desk. That picture being gone made all of them—Prof, his wife, the little girls—real again. It made me sad, and angry, to see him like that.

Prof stopped packing and gave me a try at a smile. "I never," he said, "thought this office was worthy of me."

What popped into my head and out of my mouth was the little kid's plea to Shoeless Joe, "Say it ain't so, Joe."

Prof laughed but not his usual booming whoop, more a grimaced wheeze. "I am afraid, my young friend, it is."

Prof's life was about to be carted out in boxes, but I asked, "Aren't you coming to the meeting?"

"No, you'll do better without me," he said, bending over the stack of books he was boxing, lingering over one as though he was reluctant to toss it in the box. He handed it to me: *Invisible Man*, Ralph Ellison. "Here. Read this. There may be a pop quiz when you least expect it."

"You can't give up this easy, Prof."

Prof straightened up. "Easy? What do you think you know about easy?" He tugged a crisply folded handkerchief out of his back pocket and wiped dust from his hands. "When I was a little boy, I thought I could wash the black off. When my daddy found me trying was the only time I remember seeing him cry, before my mother died." Prof's eyes, behind his gold-rimmed glasses, were dry and opaque. "Well, I couldn't wash myself white and you can't stop what's going on.

"President Werrecker, the man himself, had me into his office this morning for a friendly chat. He tells me, Mr. Kelly, he is doing the honorable thing by failing to grant tenure in my case. If I co-op-er-ate, he will spare my wife and children the embarrassment of opening the file on me to the press. I will be able to find work elsewhere, perhaps at a more suitable in-sti-tu-tion—a Ne-gro in-sti-tu-tion. He will even tell such a school, behind the back of his hand, I am a tolerable teacher, even a favorite among the undergradu-ates. I exercised poor judgment but that may be understandable to those of my race."

I blurted it out. "What's in the file, Prof? Does he have anything?"

"Ah, yes, that is the question, isn't it? And I'm afraid the answer is I don't know."

"You mean that he threatened you. He's blackmailing you."

Prof smiled a small smile, "Precisely."

"He won't show you your own file? For Christ's sake, Prof, you must have some rights."

"Mr. Kelly, you have been following with me the rise of Senator Jo-seph R. Mc-Car-thy, our would-be American Hitler. You know the way the game is played: 'I have in my hands a list—I have in my files the proof.' Now Senator Mc-Car-thy is a shifty-eyed man who needs a shave and a shoeshine. His pants are wrinkled. He reeks of untruth and whiskey. And the American people are so scared of the Red bogey-man that they believe him. Read the polls."

Having breakfasted on Jack Daniel's myself, I tried unsuccessfully not to breathe out. But Prof didn't notice.

He continued talking, his sentences punctuated by the thud of books thrown angrily into the box. "President Werrecker is a clean-shaven man, with his shirt starched and white. His shoes shine and his trousers are creased so sharp you couldn't tell them from a banker's.

"President Werrecker is a man with whom the big boys feel very comfortable. Yet he is a civilized man. He offers me tea, and he speaks so quietly, even sadly, I cannot help but feel how unseemly it is that I am intruding on his morning like dog dung on his Oriental rug. The people will believe President Werrecker, Mr. Kelly. You can bet my black behind on it. But I do appreciate what you and the other students are doing. Please know that." He extended a dismissing handshake. I shifted the book he'd given me to my left hand, and Prof's long fingers closed over my right. I forgot to even thank him for the book.

10

The Burton Hall auditorium was cavernous. Huge, high ceiling, dingy walls, undersized chairs with arm desks reminiscent of grade school. The meeting was due to begin in a few minutes, and students were sauntering in, munching on candy bars and downing bottles of pop.

I hadn't had any lunch other than Jack Daniels, so I plugged a nickel in the vending machine for a Snickers and *clang, bang, thud* it arrived—reminding me of the empty beer bottles coming down the chute at the Concord Bar and Fine Dining. I was due at my job there at five-thirty. I'd been late a lot lately, and Blackie Benello, my boss, was grumbling more than usual.

I fidgeted waiting for the meeting to start. While I chewed, I scanned the house. A couple hundred students. I couldn't spot Moira or Will. Not many union guys. A handful of black guys and a few women clustered in the back of the hall, mostly from the National Association for the Advancement of Colored People.

The only faculty member I recognized was Professor Sonheim of the Philosophy Department. He was somewhere to the right of Senator Wild Bill Knowland in his politics, but he was a neat old guy tooling around in his MG; he also believed teachers were supposed to teach.

I wondered where the rest of the faculty was.

66

I had been part of the herd of students who'd filled this auditorium three times a week for McAndrews, the hotshot young star of the Psych Department, to lecture us on "psychological observation," "perceptual constancy," "measuring intelligence," and "mental diseases." I'd never felt any sense of community among us as we listened, just a shared aloneness.

McAndrews did a real standup piece on Tailgunner Joe's sleazy bag of tricks the week before Senator McCarthy was due to speak on campus, before the university either lost or found its guts and canceled the speech. But, like ninety-nine percent of the faculty, McAndrews had disappeared since it was bombs away on Prof.

My dad, who had never gone through the front door of the university except to bring me down here, would have been here. He was always quoting guys like Oliver Wendell Holmes. Let everybody's ideas compete. Dad had more freedom to speak his mind at the plant than Prof did at the university. Thanks to the packers union.

On stage, Rick Gunneris strode back and forth, arranging a table, sliding chairs a half an inch one direction, then another, checking the podium, and being seen. Now he was impatiently motioning me forward. I heard a few "way to go's" as I went forward.

One kid who could only have been a freshman, his baby face couldn't have ever seen a razor, gave me a high sign and yelled over, "Hey, Tom, just remember we don't need this bullshit!" We laughed like conspirators, and it felt pretty good.

"Full house," I said to Gunneris.

"Yeah," he said. "Werrecker will shit tacks." Werrecker had, surprisingly enough, accepted our invitation to address the students. Chairs for each of us were at a table facing the crowd on one side of the podium; one for Gunneris was on the other side.

"By the way," he added, "I thought it would be appropriate for you to make a response on behalf of SAFE to the Pres's remarks."

"Yeah. Sure," I felt simultaneously pleased and set up.

I glanced out over the crowd again and saw Will and Moira sitting together near the back of the hall. They must have come in the last few minutes. I wondered where they'd been. Her face was pale, and she didn't have any lipstick on. She was nudged over awfully close to Will, but she gave me a wave with her reporter's spiral notebook. Will gave me a big shit-eating grin.

One thing I had to give Werrecker. The moment he arrived he looked and sounded like a president. He was nearly as tall as Prof, slightly stooped, but his dark-gray pinstripe suit fit him like the tailor had measured in his stoop. He had gray hair, closely cropped, and silver-rimmed glasses he extracted from a case in his suit coat pocket and put on in stages, first over one ear and then the other as he joined me at the table.

Gunneris introduced him as though he was presenting him an award. Rick had a future in politics all right. Werrecker strode to the podium with a sheaf of papers in his hand.

"Colleagues, students," Werrecker began, "and others," he added with the slightest pause. The paragraphs marched out of his mouth like well-drilled battalions. "The winds of controversy," it seemed, were "buffeting the Acropolis." He had read the petition presented by the Students for Academic Freedom Everywhere. He wanted to make "one distinction absolutely vital to understanding academic freedom. Mister Williams has not been dismissed," Werrecker put an edge on the mister, as in not professor. "Mister Williams did not have tenure. He simply has not been reappointed."

My hand on the table in front of me fell on the Invisible Man lying there between Werrecker's empty chair and me. I thought about Prof boxing up his books and the picture of his wife and kids. I remembered when my dad was out of work for almost a month before he got the job at the packing plant. He and my mother had been really scared. I got pissed off at what Werrecker had said.

Werrecker went on. "There has been no discrimination against Mister Williams because of his race. Nor are his services being dropped because he is a radical and an atheist. It is true some have expressed concern over Mister Williams' classroom comments. Yet no one from the university has ever presumed to tell him what beliefs he might hold.

"Documentary evidence has raised severe doubts about his scholarship, as well . . ." Werrecker's voice fell slightly, "as other matters too painful for public discussion." Things were quiet for a moment when the winds stopped blowing through the academy, but it was a tense quiet.

When Werrecker scooped up his papers and tapped them on the podium to even out the bottom of the pile, you could hear them crackle through the mike.

Gunneris managed to barely applaud and sneer at the same time, then turned expectantly to me. "Mr. Kelly, I believe you have a response on behalf of SAFE?"

Werrecker and I traded places.

My throat was dry, and there was no water up there.

"President Werrecker says Prof hasn't been fired, he's just not been 'reappointed.'

"There's a word for that kind of distinction." I paused for a second out on the end of the limb, not quite sure where I was going from there, when Werrecker surprised me with that reedy voice of his.

"I've heard that your definition of the issues is more scatological than philosophical, young man. I'll remind you, this once, that this is a university forum, not a barroom brawl, and I'll not tolerate gutter language from you this afternoon."

It felt like a jolt of electricity when it hit me, but not harmful, exciting. The president of the University of Minnesota was arguing with me, or, more accurately, telling me what I could or couldn't say.

"And we know what that word is." I looked out over the crowd and spotted the freshman who'd yelled at me on my way to the stage, but I stopped short of saying it.

"President Werrecker thinks we should sit down and shut up like good little boys and girls and let the university get rid of Prof Williams. Well, the president has been reading too many magazine articles about a 'silent generation.' We won't sit down and shut up, and we won't let this happen!"

From somewhere in the crowd, a lonely voice, it sounded like a girl, echoed, "We won't, Tom. We won't!"

"I remember when my dad was out of work," I went ahead. "Whether Prof Williams is 'simply not reappointed' or is 'dismissed,'" if you're in his shoes you're walking without a job." I thought again of the picture no longer on Prof's desk. "His wife and kids can't eat 'simply has not been reappointed.' There's a word for that kind of distinction," I paused, "and we know what that word is!"

From way in the back of the hall, came a firm, "We do know! We surely do know what that word is!"

"President Werrecker tells us there has been no racial discrimination, but Prof Williams just happens to be the one and only Negro on the faculty and just happens to be the one and only faculty member who 'simply has not been reappointed.' There's a word for that kind of coincidence, and," I paused, and this time students chimed in, "we know what that word is!"

"President Werrecker calls Prof a radical and an atheist. But despite calling Prof those names, the president asserts they have nothing to do with why Prof isn't being reappointed. "There's a word for that kind of assertion, and," this time when I paused, the crowd finished it with me, "we know what that word is!"

I turned sideways and looked straight at Werrecker. His face was red, and he was glaring at me.

"Prof is the only member of the faculty who publicly opposes the Korean War. Prof's speech against the war has angered powerful legislators, legislators who fund this university. President Werrecker states that had nothing to do with Prof 'simply not being reappointed.' Well, there's a word for that statement, and . . ." the whole crowd roared back, "we know what that word is!"

"The university has not dealt squarely with the real issue in this case. The real issue is whether the university has acted for the reasons you state, Mr. President," I put an edge on the "Mr." myself this time. "Or whether the reasons you have given us . . ."

"Young man," Werrecker interrupted, "you are ignoring Mr. Williams's failures as a teacher and scholar which are simply"—there was that goddamn 'simply' again—"beyond the depth of understanding students," Werrecker paused, "undergraduates, can be expected to appreciate."

I was looking straight at Werrecker. He glanced away, then down at the *Invisible Man* where I'd left it on the table, as though noticing it for the first time, and, with a blue-veined hand, shoved it a quarter of an inch away, as contemptuously as if he were giving me the finger, or dismissing Prof.

All my anger overflowed then, and it came out of me. I could feel my voice, strong as I said it, "Or whether those reasons, Mr. President, are simply bullshit. And, Mr. President," I extended my arm out over the auditorium, Billy Graham style, "we say they're bullshit!"

For a moment the only sound I heard was the rush of my blood.

But then "Yeah, bullshit!" "That's right! Bullshit!" the shouts came back from the crowd, at first from scattered voices, but gathering numbers; and then the baby-faced freshman was on his feet, leading the chants from one side of the crowd and then the other: "Bull—-shit! Bull—-shit!" Over and over in rhythmic cadence. As the waves of sound crested, they swept me up, lifting me high above the crowd, and I felt exultant and powerful.

When the roar receded, I looked out over the crowd and saw Will and Moira again and they weren't part of it. I saw her reach up and brush his damn curly locks off his forehead as he leaned forward. As her white hand was falling away, his square brown hand went to hers, and held it, and they looked at each other and were all alone in the middle of the crowd. I might as well not have been there.

I was suddenly very tired, and my gut ached. I turned away from them only to find myself looking squarely into Werrecker's silver-rimmed eyes. He stared back at me, his eyes as impenetrable as ball bearings. Once again I was going to be late for work at the Concord, but when I thought about what the dean of students would have to say to me once Werrecker had gotten hold of him, that didn't seem to matter a whole lot.

11

Overnight I became a celebrity, which did me no good whatsoever. Blackie Benello fired me, claiming he hadn't known I was underage to work there, but he'd heard all about "Joanie" and me.

Major Goodlittle informed me sternly that Mrs. Brady was terribly disappointed in me, and the gentlemanly thing to do was to turn back my Terrance Brady Award.

The dean of students told me I was no longer a student in good standing, to turn in my locker key; and, by the way, I needn't be looking for that peanut butter jar.

I thought it couldn't get any worse, when Moira earnestly told me, her voice quavering, she was really sorry about everything, but she thought it would be a good idea if we gave each other more freedom, for now. She said that garbage like she expected me to believe it.

The final straw: I had my damn patriotism questioned by the *Fargo Forum*, like I was a commie because I stood up for Prof's right to speak his mind about the war, even though I totally disagreed with him about it.

By then it was either try to drown myself in Jack Daniel's or enlist, or both. What the hell, I was fair game for the draft now anyway. There was a storefront recruiting office in Stadium Village right across the street from Stub and Herbs, and I went in and signed up.

Downtown at the armory, after sitting forever in my skivvies on a hard bench with a bunch of scared-looking guys, I got checked out by an old man in a doctor's coat, with "Dr. Mecklen" stitched in red over his pocket, and a dark splotch of ink at the bottom of it. The coat may have started out white but it was as dirty gray as the walls of the post office, with coffee stains all over it. I must have smelled like a vat, with my stomach pleasantly marinating in a fifth of Jack Daniel's, but he didn't ask me any questions about that, though he did ask about my sleeping habits and frustrated sexual urges. The main test was whether I could cough while he played with my testicles with his nicotine-stained fingers.

Delusions of grandeur and paranoia kicked in when I had to sign DD Form 98a, 1 Dec 50. "(Edition of 1 Feb 50 is obsolete)" a line on the bottom advised me. By signing the 1 Dec 50 Edition, I certified I wasn't a member of a couple of hundred groups listed as the "Consolidated List of Organizations Designated by the Attorney General on October 30, 1950, Pursuant to Executive Order No. 9835."

The list was enough to make me pause. I didn't have too much interest in the Hinode Kai (which I learned from the form was the Rising Sun Flag Society—a group of Japanese war veterans) or in the Ku Klux Klan. But I thought the Abraham Lincoln Brigade had some very classy members, and I had consorted with about the entire Socialist Workers Party on campus. I was surprised the Attorney General hadn't kept an eye on the North Dakotans to Save the World Poker and Beerdrinking Club and Debating Society. Maybe he was running out of room on the form, but he at least could have listed our initials. I did nab an extra copy of the form. If that asshole Senator McCarthy came swooping down on me, it might come in handy to know what I'd signed.

But by that time I'd be in the Army.

"Hello?" My mother's voice on the phone sounded tired, not like her usual lively self at all. It would have to be my mother that I got. She wouldn't understand, not in a hundred years. My dad might, but of course he was down at the plant.

73

"Hi, Mom. It's me. How are you?"

"What in heaven's name is going on down there, Tom?"

"It's a long story, Mom, but," I might as well get it over with, "I wrecked everything here, and I've enlisted in the army."

"Oh, my God, Tom!" she wailed, also not the least like her. "Why would you do that? Is it all about that communist professor of yours? It's been all over the *Fargo Forum*."

"I'm sorry, Mom. I just have to get away from everything for a while, you know?"

"No, I don't know, Tom. I don't at all. Aren't you even going to see us?"

"Well, I have to leave for basic training, but maybe if dad could come down and get me and my stuff I could say good-bye and catch a train from Fargo."

"He will, Tom. You wait there, but . . ." she was crying now.

"It'll be for the better, Mom. It will be. I have to get off the phone."

When my father picked me at Pioneer Hall late, he hadn't shaved, his jaw was clamped, and he was so angry that he practically shoved me down the hall, and then slammed his hands into my back when I paused loading my stuff in the trunk of the old Chevie.

The last time we'd made the drive back to Fargo, he and I had been returning from our trip to Mrs. Brady's to get my scholarship. The scholarship that was to put me on the way to being the first one in our family to graduate from college. This time I tried to explain what had happened with Prof and about the meeting and how I'd lost the scholarship.

I said I thought he would have done the same thing I did about Prof.

"Not that way, Tom." he said. "The paper says you led the students in shouting obscenities at the university president. Is that right?"

"Not exactly, Dad, but close enough I suppose. I'm sorry. I guess I just got carried away."

"I guess you did all right," he said. "You threw away your scholarship and all of our plans for you."

I tried to explain how the recruiter had told me that I'd be entitled to the GI Bill when I was done and I'd go back to school somewhere then.

"I'd like your word on that," he said.

"I will," I said, "I promise. I just have to get away from here for a while, Dad, and the army's a good way to do that."

"They'll send you to Korea, Tom," he said.

I said I might not even get sent to Korea. And besides, like we both knew, America and the United Nations were doing the right thing in Korea, defending our way of life.

"The last best hope on earth, like you always say."

"Abraham Lincoln said it, Tom, not me."

"Well, you're the one who says it to me. And we're stopping the spread of communism and backing world law. You've always said I'd do my duty if called, Dad." I rushed to pile on my arguments.

"If *called*, Tom. You weren't called," was all he said. He wasn't interested in my case for international law.

I even tried to hint that part of me just didn't want to miss my war the way Dad had missed his. He got angry then.

"You could get killed over there, Tom," he said. "Your mother is worried sick."

The rest of the drive this time was the longest, quietest drive in the history of the world as the Chevy groaned homeward, following its feeble yellow headlight beams through the dark.

My mother wasn't crying anymore, but her face was pale and drawn and even her hair looked pale when she met us at our door of the duplex. She hung on to me like I was going to try to run away any minute while Dad unloaded the car before he rescued me by handing me a suitcase.

We ate at the kitchen table, but she had made a big dinner like a Sunday dinner with chicken and mashed potatoes and gravy and beans.

"This is a great dinner, Mom, really," I said.

"It's just what I had around," she said.

"Well, it's great."

"None of this would have happened in the first place if you'd gone to school here at the Agricultural College," she said.

"Kate, you know the university is a better school," my dad said. "Tom will get the GI bill when he's done with the army, and he's promised me he'll go back to school somewhere."

"And what does your little girlfriend have to say about all this?" Mom asked. She always avoided Moira's name if she could.

"She's not my little girlfriend, Mom."

"All right, Tom, your girlfriend Moira."

"Nothing, I said. "Moira's not my girlfriend anymore."

"Oh," my mother said, putting one of her pale, freckled hands to her cheek. "Oh." Like that explained everything.

"They'll send you to Korea, Tom," she said a little later.

"It may be over long before Tom ever gets there," my dad said.

"I saw Warren and Dorothy Belos at church last Sunday. She's aged a hundred years," my mother said.

Things were pretty quiet again after that.

Before I went to bed in my old bed, she pulled me aside.

"Your father's just heartsick," she said. "Promise me you'll be careful, Tom."

"I will. I promise," I said.

In the morning it was all a big rush to get to the train station downtown. They were still mad, and she was crying, but we all hugged each other once more, like we'd never see each other again. My dad had left home still unshaven, and I could feel the stubble of his cheek against mine when he hugged me. When they put me on the train, my mother gave me a bag full of enough peanut butter and jelly sandwiches to last me through basic training.

Part II

12
Summer 1952

The heat bullied us awake, even before the phonograph warbled reveille over the camp PA system and Pusgut strode down the aisle reciting poetry.

The summer was one of the hottest in the history of Virginia. At five in the morning, as it had every morning for weeks, the sun was already sending the first waves of heat pounding down on the thin roof of our master-built wooden and tar-papered barracks. According to Walt Manley, an older guy who was a carpenter back home in Fargo, though I'd never met him there, the contractor must have made a fortune on them.

"Drop your cocks and grab your socks!" Pusgut came down the aisle rattling our bunks with a swagger stick the size of a baseball bat, and greeted us with the ever-popular barracks couplet, shouted hoarsely over and over. Sergeant Biller was known as "Pusgut" in honor of his over-hanging gut which, because of the angry red boils on the back of his neck, we liked to think was full of pus.

"That includes you, Kelly!"

It so happened I was innocent, but a couple of bunks away you could hear that slob Schlumberger pounding off as usual, and Pusgut figured any name at random was guilty. If I was sweating just lying there, it must have poured off Schlumberger as he labored.

I sat up and swung my bare feet to the gray, splintery floor. Walt Manley sat on his footlocker across the aisle from my bunk, hunched over a tablet, writing his morning letter to his wife. Walt's hands and haircut were as square as his name. His wife was expecting their first kid, and most mornings he got up even before reveille to write her.

Moira and I wrote each other, but she wasn't my girlfriend anymore. At first her letters were about how foolish I was to enlist when the shit hit the fan for Prof and, as it turned out, for me. She wrote that Prof left campus shortly after I did, leaving behind only rumors: he was still looking for a job; the University of Mexico had hired him; he had an offer from an obscure Negro college in North Carolina; he might even be somewhere around here. With school out, Moira's letters were mostly about her and her girlfriends. Not a lot about her and Will Lindeman.

I tried to tell her what it was like to march in dust so bad it caught in the corners of my lips and the cracks between my teeth like pumice at the dentist's office; to do jumping jacks with sweat trickling down from my forehead and into my eyes, stinging and blinding me while I pushed off leaden legs and swung aching arms over my head; to crawl on the latrine floor with a scrub brush, dipping in and out of the pail of dirty gray water, and into toilet bowls that reeked of piss and shit and jism and vomit, and then with a toothbrush get the studs on the bottom; to fall into my bunk at three a.m. and wake up at four-thirty, with my sweat already dampening the cruddy sheet, and Pusgut yelling in my ear.

I listened to the grunts and groans and mutterings up and down the aisle of the barracks as guys dragged their aching bodies up from sleep. The guys from the South spoke a different language, musical, with different inflections and rhythms, like they were humming gentle songs. After nearly eight weeks on base, it crept into the way the rest of us talked.

Fucking Carl Bergstrom would yell to me in his best impersonation of a Southern gentleman: "Tom! Wait up at the fuckin' the-at-ah, heah now?" He looked sort of like that wimp from *Gone with the Wind*, Ashley Wilkes, or, Leslie Howard, actually. Carl was harder looking, but had that mournful air of carrying around an unspoken burden.

Off in the far corner of the barracks black soldiers woke up and bantered with each other in ways still strange to me: "Hey! Muthah-fuckah! Get your black ass out of that sack, now." "Hey man, wait'll your momma see you. You bald as a cue ball, man, you know that?" "Niggah! What you doin' with that old snake this mornin? Sound like ol' Pusgut caught you."

A bunch of black guys were in the showers as I dragged my sleepy butt in there. At first I had surreptitiously checked out the black guys, to see if it was true they were better hung, like you always heard, and some of them were impressive in that department, and to see whether they got sunburned too, which I couldn't tell.

I turned the water on full blast and cold. I was awake.

Across from me Joe Nash, a black guy from Atlanta, with a face like a pixie, and a quick, nervous smile, showered, his skinny chest covered with foaming white soapsuds.

"Hey, Joe, what's shakin'?" I asked. "Ready for the big weekend pass?"

"What's shakin'? You sound like a fool, man!" Joe grinned in my general direction; without his black horn-rimmed glasses he wasn't too sure exactly where I was.

I'd asked a few times about what Negro colleges were around, hoping I might be able to get a lead on where Prof Williams was. None of the black guys I talked with seemed to know, till I met Joe. He planned on going to college, and he'd even heard of Prof, but Joe didn't want to go to any Negro college. They were impoverished, he said, with inadequate buildings and libraries, and second-rate faculty. It'd be real sad, if Prof ended up in one of them, Joe said, but he'd nose around and let me know if he heard anything about Prof.

"Listen Joe, you want to come with us on pass this weekend?" I asked.

"You are a fool, man!" he said. "Forget it."

"Why? That Jim Crow shit?"

"You think you're a he-ro, Tom? You live down here a while. Then come talk to me."

As he headed out of the shower, I flicked my towel at his skinny black ass, but I missed.

By the time I shaved and legged it over to the mess hall, the Quonset hut was already a big tin oven. Joe'd gone through the line and was sitting at a table with "his own," as the guys from the South put it. I'd tried to make friends with some of "his own" besides Joe. A few would say hi, and even sit next to me at chow now and then, but not many, and we didn't say much.

The only seat open with the other guys from Fargo when I finished the line was next to Schlumberger. Sweat glued his brown, prematurely thinning hair against his scalp and dripped off his forehead. His sweat watered down the creamy consistency of his shit-on-a-shingle making it look even less appetizing than usual.

Morrie Shapiro, the only one of the group not from Fargo, his pudgy face red with sunburn, sat across from Schlumberger. Schlumberger and Shapiro made one weird combination, always together, going to the movies, hanging out at the PX, around the barracks. I didn't know whether Schlumberger was tethered to Shapiro by Morrie's money, that was sort of true of all of us, or whether there was something more. Morrie seemed to have made Schlumberger some kind of personal slave.

"Listen up you a-holes," Shapiro said, "We'll load up the trunk of Old Poppa's Lincoln with booze and look out you Southern belles!" His "Old Poppa's" were particularly grating, since Morrie hated his own father, a big shot in an oil company back in New Brunswick. Morrie firmly believed the last time he got kicked out of Dartmouth, his dad used his pull to be sure Morrie was drafted, "to make a man out of me," so he said.

"What's all the conversation y'all been having with the Ghoul and Pusgut lately, Shapiro? You got them fuckin' pimping for you now?" Fucking Carl Bergstrom asked.

"Just say your Old Dad is negotiating, and our weeks of horniness are about to come to a halt." Morrie poured the last drips of juice into his glass and handed the pitcher to Schlumberger. "Go get this filled up, okay?"

"Yeah, sure, Morrie," Schlumberger began to untangle himself from the table and bench. "Geez, I hope we can get some pussy. I'm really horny," he stood with the pitcher in his hand and hovered over the table, bent at the knees because of the bench behind him, like a supplicant.

"You're supposed to be married and you've got a kid coming too, Schlumberger. For God's sake," Walt shook his head.

"Yeah, but . . ."

"So go fill the pitcher," said Morrie, and Schlumberger lifted his feet over the bench one at a time and trudged off to the end of the chow line again with the pitcher.

"Right," said Gary Kowalski to Schlumberger's departing back. "You get the juice and leave the nookie for me." Gary had played football at the North Dakota Agricultural College till he was caught cheating on a test, lost his scholarship and got drafted. So, though we got kicked out of school for totally different reasons, Gary and I had something in common besides being horny.

Which I was, but I had an idea other than a two-bit hooker. Besides worrying about my cash situation, and a feeling it would be against the Code of the West, a vision from one of our training films of a guy's dink swollen with hammerhead clap lingered in my mind.

"Morrie, what about this supposedly great-looking cousin of yours in Richmond?" I asked.

"Annie Jones. Elizabeth Taylor has nothing on her; I kid you not. You won't see stuff like her in Fargo, trust Ol' Poppa," said Morrie.

Annie Jones was an improbable name for a Jewish lady, but Morrie said she had changed it somewhere along the way. She was "at home" in Richmond recovering from a scandalous affair with a married man where she worked in New York. So it was established that she did it.

"We see Elizabeth Taylor in Fargo the same way you do, Morrie, in the goddamn movies." Where in *A Place in the Sun* you could see why Montgomery Clift would kill to get her.

"Annie's way too old and wise for you, Kelly."

"We'll at least stop by her house though?" Way too old or not.

"My Aunt Rachel's house. Ol' Dad'll take us there to put on the feed bag, but don't get your hopes up about Annie."

"Maybe she'd be more interested in someone who'd know how to take care of her," smiled Gary. You could almost see him flex his biceps under his fatigues.

"Dream on, you guys," said Walt Manley. "But, nobody, repeat nobody," he looked at Schlumberger, who was back with Morrie's juice in hand, "screws up today, and we pass inspection tomorrow. We get off this base this weekend so none of us goes stir crazy. Got that?"

"You know it!" boomed Schlumberger.

WE SAT UNDER THE RELENTLESS SUN, on withered brown grass, and studied war.

"THE THEORY AND PRACTICE OF MODERN WAR— Lecturer Chief Warrant Officer E. Herman" was the description on the training schedule.

But to us he was the Ghoul. The Ghoul had lived through the Big One, and he'd just finished a tour in Korea. Scuttlebutt was, his job in both wars was to retrieve and identify American bodies from battlefields—"Graves Registration."

He'd come back to teach us how to survive and he took it seriously. The Ghoul was in fine form as he lectured us on the theory: His round and freckled face was red under his garrison cap, but his khakis were starched to attention, never mind it was already 100 degrees in the shade.

"Forget everything you see in the newsreels about 'modern warfare' and fancy 'new' weapons. War never changes. War is killing. You men got that?"

"Yessir!" we responded in chorus.

"Tell me!" he barked.

"War is killing! Sir!"

"Louder!"

"WAR IS KILLING! SIR!"

"That's better, but I can't hear you, Schlumberger. Let's hear it from you all by yourself!"

"What sir?"

"WAR IS KILLING!"

"War is killing."

"Louder!"

"WAR IS KILLING!"

"That's better, Schlumberger. Better, but still pitiful. Let me hear you again."

"WAR IS KILLING!" Schlumberger screamed, his face red, the cords on the side of his neck straining.

"SIR!" the Ghoul yelled back at him.

"SIR!"

"Jesus, you'll never get it right, Schlumberger. But I can't hold the whole class up for you. We're moving ahead with the lesson." The Ghoul checked his notes. "Your war is killing the Gooks and the Chinks. Got that?"

"Yessir!"

"Tell me!"

"Our war is killing the Gooks and Chinks! Sir!"

This stuff was simple, but not easy.

"Aw right. Men, this morning you're going to learn how to kill the old-fashioned way. "Mano a mano!" The Ghoul savored the words. "Mano a mano!" His twinkling eyes roamed over the troops.

"What does that mean? Anyone? Schlumberger?"

Schlumberger hesitated for only a second before responding, "Sir! Man to man!"

"Wrong again! You awake yet this morning, Kelly?"

"Yessir!"

"Good. What does that mean? Mano a mano?"

"Hand to hand, sir!"

"Very good, Kelly. You learn that in collich?"

85

I couldn't remember where I learned it. "Yessir!"

"Yessir, what?"

"Yessir! I learned it in college!"

"You men hear that? This is collich-level material this morning!" The Ghoul smiled at me.

"Aw right, on your feet and fix bayonets on those pieces," he instructed us. So much for the theory. "Sergeant Biller will now instruct you in the use of the bayonet."

For the rest of the morning, following Pusgut's surprisingly agile demonstrations, given his overhanging belly, we thrust and parried and butt stroked at one another in the open field, our bayonets shining in the sun, sweating dervishes, till our fatigues turned black and sodden with sweat.

ALL THROUGH THE DAY, the sun hung heavy in the sky, always, by some metaphysical chicanery, staying directly overhead, wherever Company G was. It was a total bitch.

After lunch at mail call, I was barely able to read Moira's letter before we fell in to go to the Ghoul's lecture but the last sentence had jumped out at me before I stuffed it in my pocket. "If my love can travel 1,000 miles, here it is." How could Moira write the rest of the letter and then write that?

"The M-1 is a gas-operated, air-cooled, clip-fed, semi-automatic shoulder weapon." The Ghoul's voice bored through the hot, humid air; he paused only to breathe, which was seldom. The Ghoul had a gas-operated, hot air, manual-fed, fully automatic mouth. Now there was a weapon.

He'd told us in Korea even the cooks of the Second Division Artillery were pressed into defending Divarty's perimeter and held their ground with a ninety-percent casualty rate. "You never know when you might have to use your M-1 to kill someone, a Gook or a Chink or maybe even a Roosky."

He stood on what looked like an upside down sandbox. On the table in front of him lay an M-1 Rifle. The only tree of any size for a hundred yards cast its shadow on him. We sat facing him on splinter-filled benches at long green picnic tables. There was no tree cover for us.

86

Each of us had our own M-1 disassembled on the table in front of us. When I touched the bolt it scorched my fingers. I slapped halfheartedly at the fly savaging the back of my neck and missed.

The Ghoul's voice bored on through the heat and humidity: "We will now ree-view the parts and nomenclature of the weapon."

Schlumberger's problems had a lot to do with his parts and nomenclature that really weren't his fault. He sat at the next table, his big eyes half-glazed, as sweat poured down his huge forehead. While the Ghoul talked on, Shapiro reached over and with the light-fingered touch of a shoplifter lifted the bolt from Schlumberger's piece right out from under his eyes while Schlumberger sat there, oblivious.

The Ghoul's voice droned around the edge of my consciousness like the flies. When my head snapped up, the way it does when you fall asleep in class he was standing there, seeing right through me, knowing my mind was wandering from his words of wisdom.

"Wake up, Kelly! This ain't collich! I'm tryin' to keep you from getting your ass shot off over in Kough-ree-ah!"

When the Ghoul said Kough-ree-ah he chanted the first syllable, pronouncing it to rhyme with dough, before going on to string out the second syllable, and then the third, which he snapped off like the crack of a whip. The Ghoul dragged out the syllables the same way Prof did when he railed against an in-sti-too-tion. Of course, they were different in about every other way.

The Ghoul took a perverse satisfaction that, college or no, this stuff didn't come easy to me. Next to Schlumberger, the Ghoul picked on me more than anyone else in class.

I waited for him to chew me out, but instead he said the magic words: "All right, men, take ten!" More Army poetry. The Ghoul reached into the starched pocket of his khakis. "If you got 'em, smoke 'em."

"Got a fuckin' cigarette?" Carl looked at me as if he hadn't asked me the same question at the last break.

"Yeah, sure." I had the pack of Camels in my jacket pocket, next to my body, trying to keep the sweat off my letter. I jammed the letter back into my pocket with my left hand while I shook a cigarette out of the pack with my right. Beads of moisture showed under the cellophane. A cigarette popped up, the end soggy and urine-colored from sweat. I pushed it toward Carl.

"Another fuckin' letter? You know what you fuckin' need, Kelly? Not a bitch whose daddy doesn't like ya to start with. Who writes you letters about some other guy."

In the evenings Carl and I had downed a few beers at the PX. I'd told him about getting the shaft from Moira, and he'd been really interested. When we were done, I'd bought most of the beer, and he knew a lot more about me than I did about him.

"Up yours, Carl."

The Ghoul's crisp voice interrupted our discussion. "All right, men, take your seats. We will resume with the reassembly of the weapon!"

Schlumberger's mouth moved soundlessly, and his eyes searched the table for the parts of his weapon. I took six short steps to Shapiro, reached in his fatigues and came out with Schlumberger's bolt, not to mention his operating rod spring and some other trinket and dumped the whole hardware store in front of Schlumberger.

"Are you ready to resume, Private Kelly? Or would you prefer to have a special class on the weapon this weekend? Because it's mox nix, Kelly, entirely mox nix to me."

"Yes, sir! No, sir!" I scrambled back to my bench.

THAT NIGHT WE SAT AROUND on our cots (steel, folding), and got our gear ready for inspection the next morning, shining and polishing everything leather and brass to gleaming in the dull light of the barracks.

At the same time, Walt Manley and I tested each other's memory of the general orders. We alternated back and forth till the words of number eleven marched out of Walt's mouth in close order drill: "To be especially watchful at night and, during the time for challenging, to challenge all persons on or near my post, and to allow no one to pass without proper authority." It was the *Baltimore Catechism* all over again.

Across the aisle Morrie grilled Schlumberger on them so he wouldn't screw up and cost us our pass. Schlumberger got them down while working on his boots and then, when he had his own gear ready, while he spit-shined Morrie's damn boots. Joe Nash looked over and shook his head and you could practically hear him, "Weird shit, man. Weird shit."

When Schlumberger finished with Morrie's boots, Morrie wasn't satisfied with having Schlumberger do the goddamn boots; he didn't like the job Schlumberger'd done. He glared at the boots and at Schlumberger and then without warning Morrie threw them across the bunk toward Schlumberger, and one boot hit him right in the face, and blood spurted out of his nostrils.

The rest of us stopped and watched. Schlumberger stood there. His chest rose and fell. His big hands opened and closed. He stabbed at his bleeding nose with one hand. He stared down at the blood on it, then up at Shapiro. He could have crushed Shapiro just by backing him up against a wall and leaning.

"Don't get hot and bothered, Schlumberger. Old Poppa is just kidding," Morrie said.

"Geez, Morrie, I'm bleeding."

Without thinking, I tossed him my handkerchief.

"Thanks, Tom," he said, pawing at his nose with it.

"Yeah, sure." There went that handkerchief.

The good news was the shoes were shined, the brass was polished, and the next morning the bunks were tight enough to bounce Sergeant Biller's tossed quarter high into the air, and we all passed inspection.

13

I said slow down, or I'll break your arms!" Gary suggested again.

"Okay, okay, Ol' Dad'll take it easy on you." The needle slowly dropped back to sixty-five, ten miles over the limit. We were driving up the highway toward Petersburg, where we had reservations at the Robert E. Lee Motor Court. We were going to live like civilians for two days.

The drab countryside slipped past the car. Wooden shacks stood along the road. Unpainted. No glass in the windows. Doors hung off frames; rusted screens with holes in them. Dogs sprawled wherever there was shade, their tongues lolling out, their ears twitching as flies landed. Black men and women sat on sagging porches and steps. Naked kids playing beside the road stopped to watch us with their hands over their eyes against the sun. The dust settled over them as we sped past.

Prof once told me his father was "dirt poor, and I mean dirt poor, Mister Kelly." Prof might have come from a place like this. He might have stood there, a little boy with dried snot under his nose and red clay caked on his little black fanny and waved as big cars coming from somewhere and going somewhere roared by. How had he found his road out? What had it meant to him to be on the faculty of a great state university? Was it the memory of a place like this that had pushed him to take the risks that cost him his job? And where was he now?

Morrie skidded the big Continental to a stop on the gravel driveway leading into the Robert E. Lee Motor Court. Schlumberger was supposed to have loaded the trunk with liquor from the PX before we left. He hadn't, but none of us was about to go back to the base. The rest of them dropped off Carl and me at the motel before going on in to town to pick up some booze and do whatever else they were up to. Carl lingered at the car, then returned.

"I ordered up a real live blonde for you," he smiled. "So you better go rest up."

There were two adjoining rooms with a bathroom in the middle. They were almost cool compared to the barracks. A large wooden-bladed fan on the ceiling turned slowly. The beds had white sheets and pillowcases and real springs and mattresses. Carl went in to take a shower with the entire bathroom all to himself.

I stripped down to my shorts and took one bed for myself. While the shower hummed, I got Moira's letter out to read again.

July 22, 1952
Tom dear,
You asked about me and Will.
Will is working on a paper to finish up one of his incompletes, recapping tires at Firestone, and to top it all off, he got a job as a busboy at Powers. It is absurd how he is falling into your pattern in so many ways. I am sure you wonder if I love him. That is a difficult question. Our whole relationship is so manic-depressive.

Last week the New Germany relatives came in to town and we had dinner at Lindeman's. We sat around the big dining room table, said our prayers, ate mashed potatoes and gravy, and laughed. After dinner we did the dishes in the kitchen, and the men went out in the yard and smoked. Will is so damn hearty. You know those argyle socks he wears all the time, atrocious looking. He's making me into a different person; I have to be a sturdy, Russian peasant woman, that sort of thing. He said, "You're going to scrub floors, and make graham cracker pie, and go to bed with me, and have parties for our friends, and after that you can do what you want."

But you see, I am never sure for more than a day at a time. He talks of getting married, and he works and saves money, but somehow

91

I feel that it will never be. I think of you often, always in comparison. Sometimes I think I want a synthesis of both of you, and that is impossible so I must choose. I cannot say that I loved you more than I love him or vice versa. Of course, it is primarily physical with Will, but you understand how strong the physical pull is and how it can obliterate other things. Then, too, there is the social life—the Club, parties, and gaiety—and Will is well liked.

I might be happy with Will, but I do not know if I could be satisfied. But don't ever count on having me back, nor even on my marrying Will. If you plan on things like that, reality hurts a little too much. I may love you that way again, or I may grow to feel that way about Will, or there may be someone else. I think it is a vicious bit of malice in me, which takes delight in hurting those whom I love the most.

But, Tom, do write to me, even if you have to get up at three a.m. like your friend Walt to do it. You have a hold on my heart which could not be loosened with a wrench no matter what I do. And a streak in me that keeps crying out for you not to get drunk or carried away, but stay safe and save money to go to Harvard and all the rest of it that we dreamed. If my love can travel 1000 miles, here it is—

Moira

Goddamn Moira. Moira from paragraph to paragraph: Moira, the peasant; Moira the socialite; and how about Moira the goddamn actress? But I kept seeing that one sentence: "Of course, it is primarily physical with Will." Of course. Of goddamn course.

"Hey Tom!" Morrie Shapiro's face loomed over me. I must have been asleep.

"Look what Poppa brought home for the kiddies." Morrie gestured toward the table crowded with fifths of Old Grand Dad, Jack Daniel's, Gordon's Gin, bottles of mix, a bowl of ice cubes, a bag of sugar, lemons, a box of crackers and glasses. "In another two minutes your Old Dad will have a batch of Seabreeze ready." He set about pouring a gurgling bottle with each hand.

Gary Kowalski plunked himself on one corner of the double bed and loosely shuffled a deck of cards; even Gary's hands were musclebound. "How about a little game of chance?"

The poker players made an unlikely garden around the bed, horseflies flitting from one of us to another, drawn by the sugary Seabreeze: a dark-blue nylon tee-shirt stretched over Gary's chest; Morrie in a cream-colored sport shirt with MS stitched in maroon above the pocket; me, still stripped to my shorts; Carl in a dark-red shirt, smoke hovering around him, and Schlumberger in a short-sleeved black seersucker shirt with red and pink and yellow flowers, a flower bed all by himself. Walt kibitzed and played banker—matches ripped from their books served as chips—from a chair off to the side. These guys were what I had for family and friends now.

Gary's worn red Bicycles went from hand to hand, shuffled noiselessly, sometimes sticking to one another, spinning out over the white bed. "Why don't you see if you can pick up the Senators' game, Tom?"

I fiddled with the Philco on the bed stand. Static. "The Democrats, desperately seeking a candidate to take the baton from a faltering President Truman, have chosen Adlai E. Stevenson. Stevenson told the delegates he had 'asked the merciful Father to let this cup pass from me,' but that he would accept the nomination."

"Yeah, yeah, Kelly," said Gary. "Can't you find the game?"

Gary took off on a streak that just got hotter as the game went along. He kept building his pile of matches and reselling them for cash; the pile reproduced itself, like angleworms, when Gary dealt.

Morrie finished pouring another fifth of Old Grand Dad, glared at the empty bottle and pitched it at the wastebasket next to Walt. The heavy bottom of the bottle banged against the cheap plaster of the wall.

"Hey, watch it," Walt glared at Morrie.

"Screw you." Morrie didn't look at anyone.

It was one of those moments that could go one way or another.

"It's too hot for that shit, you guys. How about tonight, Morrie?" Gary broke in. "Are the rest of us going to get laid or not?"

"Has Old Dad ever let you guys down? All we have to do is show up at Dot's Place. The Ghoul and Pusgut will be there with the girls."

The day faded into evening, and the game went on under lights.

Gary dealt the last hand—seven card stud, high-low, pig to win both ways—"to build a good pot for the last hand," he said.

"Lot of good that'll do anyone but you," Morrie said, pouring the last dregs of Seabreeze.

Through two down cards and three up, Morrie had kings and a jack up for high and bet the limit every time. Gary had a four and a three to go with his opening six for low and raised the limit every time. I matched Gary card for card that showed but had a crummy pair of nines in the hole, no good for high, and playing hell with my chances for low. Morrie was looking like a lock for high. I didn't know why Carl and Schlumberger were still hanging around, but then again, so was I.

"Tom. You in or out? Time to get the shoe clerks off the street," said Gary.

I looked at my last down card. A goddamn eight. A pair for low. Two crummy pairs for high. I was pissing away my whole stake but I was in too deep to fold. Everyone stayed.

When it was time to declare—high, low or pig with one, no or two match-sticks in closed fists put out in front of everyone simultaneously— Morrie opened his hand first and showed one match—high, the way he'd been going from the get-go. Carl opened his—one. Schlumberger—one. Gary opened his hand—one. One! Gary was going high too! I was alone for low and half of the best pot of the game.

"A goddamn lock! How's that for a shoe clerk, assholes?"

Carl turned over the five of spades. "Flush."

"Oh, Gawd," Schlumberger threw in his hand.

"Morrie," inquired Carl, "you got anything besides fuckin' bull-shit?"

"Read 'em and weep." Morrie turned them up. "A full boat. Kings over! Let's see yours."

Gary turned over a six first, pairing the six that was showing; then he turned over an ace, pairing the ace showing; he saved his third ace for last. "Full boat—aces over."

Morrie's face reddened and he lurched to his feet.

"Goddamn it, Gary. Every time you deal, you win!"

"You mean I been lucky, don't you?" Gary was so quiet that Morrie didn't say anything.

Morrie reached for his empty glass, stared at it, and threw it across the room, in the general direction of Gary. It shattered against the bureau and exploded in fragments. "I mean you're a goddamn cheater. Cocksucker!"

Gary's fist blurred through the smoke. He hit Morrie once, right in the face. Morrie's head jerked back and banged against the wall; he slumped forward as he slid to the floor. Gary leaned over and pulled him up against the wall.

Gary wasn't even breathing hard. "He's drunk. You guys understand, right?"

Carl answered, "Fuckin' little kike . . ."

Gary interrupted, "Walt knows I wasn't cheating."

There was a quiet second before Walt responded. "He had it coming."

"We might as well cash in," Gary began counting his matches.

When Morrie came to a few minutes later, he played it like he didn't have a clue as to what happened, and we all went along with it. We showered again and put on fresh shirts, except Schlumberger. He'd spent the whole time looking for his wallet, which he'd misplaced somewhere, till Morrie told him he'd stake him to dinner. Around eight, everyone but Walt and Carl loaded into Morrie's Lincoln.

DOT'S PLACE WAS OFF HIGHWAY ONE, down the road from the main gate of the Fort. It was a low stucco building with arches over a walkway like you'd picture a Spanish mission. Inside the air-conditioning washed over us. There was a hubbub of conversations and glasses clinking and guys milling around us. The crowd was mostly enlisted men. White enlisted men.

Down here the South had won the Civil War. It was a whole strange country. Down here black people got called "boy" and "nigger," and ate in their own restaurants, drank from separate fountains, and relieved them-

selves in restrooms, all labeled COLORED, like they were contagious animals. Some people in Fargo talked about "nigger heaven," when they meant
the balcony. Down here was where "nigger heaven" came from.

Even on the base. The official Army policy had been against discrimination, since an Executive Order President Truman promulgated
back in 1948, but some units remained all black, even in Korea, except
for the officers, who were mostly white. Early on, one of the barbers at
the Post Exchange, an old timer on the base, was hacking off my hair like
he was pissed off it would grow back. He told me that back in World War
II there'd been a shoot-out between white and black troops right on the
base. Some black soldiers had tried to use the white PX.

"Whole lot of them niggers got kilt that night," he'd said, glancing
around and gouging my neck with his clippers. "That put an end to it!"

Before Prof I might have let it pass. As little kids at the Fargo
Municipal Pool we'd holler "Last one in's a nigger baby" and we chose up
teams "Eenie, meanie, miney, moe, catch a nigger by the toe," and so on;
and even in my own family we called those big, black nuts at holiday din-
ners "nigger toes," without even thinking, but now I was thinking.

"How about you put an end to calling soldiers niggers," I'd suggested, and he'd nicked the back of my neck again in reply.

"Watch it, asshole," I commented. It was a good thing I hadn't
needed a shave.

The four of us pushed our way through the crowd of soldiers and
the smoke that hovered like thick fog in Dot's Place, but none of us saw
the Ghoul or Pusgut or the promised hookers.

We split up to get tables. Gary and I in the back; Morrie and
Schlumberger sat near the entrance, so they could keep watch. Gary
jerked his head at them, "Don't they make the darling couple? There's
something sick about those two."

We had the ribs. We could afford them. Afterward we sat back
and downed a couple of cold ones. When the waitress put the tray with
the bill in it on the tablecloth, Gary reached for it. "I'll get it."

"That's white of you," I said; but it was weird once you started
thinking about that shit.

"No sweat. Easy come, easy go."

"Just between you and me," I asked, "did you have that last hand wired?"

"Just between you and me, you'll never know. But Morrie can afford it. Him and his monogrammed fruit shirt."

"Well, shit!" Morrie's voice startled me, and there he was, Schlumberger trailing after, but no sign they'd heard anything. "They'd be here by now. They must have meant to meet us at the motel. Let's blow this joint."

14

Back at the Robert E. Lee, a dark-blue '48 Plymouth was parked in front.

Inside our room, a black woman, with tangled ringlets of blonde hair, sprawled on the bed. She wore a bathrobe-like purple dress, open at the top showing her breasts, and hiked up over thighs dark against the white sheet; she didn't have any stockings but wore a pair of red leather high-heeled shoes. The rim of her nearly empty glass was greased by a half-moon of dark red lipstick, and the end of her cigarette was the same dark red.

Carl was cradled in her left arm. For once he looked contented.

A GI, an older guy, late twenties or so, with a cigar in his mouth, stood poised on the edge of the bed. He wore starched khakis, with the paratroopers' insignia over one shirt pocket, and a blue, white and red airborne patch on one shoulder. His oxblood boots gleamed against the white sheet.

"Geroooonimo!" he yelled as he parachuted. He landed in half-crouch, knees bent, arms up holding imaginary lines. When he hit the floor, he did a sideways somersault on one shoulder, rolled to his feet, again in a half crouch, and hauled in the lines.

"That's the way you do it. Only you step out of the plane at three thousand feet with Krauts down there shooting at you like a slow, easy target in a shooting gallery. That's when you find out if you've got any balls," he panted. "If you're a man." He collapsed on the floor, lay on his back with his eyes closed, teeth still clenching the wet cigar.

"You got balls, honey," the woman said to Carl, nearly falling out of her dress as she turned to him.

Against the wall facing the bed, right under the dent Morrie's thrown bottle left this afternoon, Pusgut sat slumped forward, his legs drawn up toward his chest, a bottle of beer in his hand.

Walt sat against the wall across from the end of the bed, in civvies, his legs stretched out in front of him, and nursed a bottle of beer.

The Ghoul, in civvies too, didn't look like he'd had anything stronger than pop to drink. But the third fifth of Old Grand Dad was empty and one of the Jack Daniel's wasn't far behind.

"The men," Morrie surveyed the damage, "are here."

"How 'bout you, good-lookin'?" The woman looked straight at me. "You be the one lonesome for a blonde?" From her armpit, my buddy Carl waved at me.

"I guess." Sloppy seconds or thirds, or however many, weren't exactly what I had in mind.

Gary jumped in. "I'm Gary. I've always liked blondes. What's your name?"

"Rose, honey. Yellow Rose." Her laugh turned into a smoker's hack that shook her breasts. "You want a date with Rose, honey?"

"How much?" Gary romanced her.

"For you, honey, only twenty. On account you such a smooth talker!" Rose struggled to her feet and tossed her cigarette into her glass, where it hissed out.

Gary grabbed her hand and hauled her tripping into the other room. He didn't look back as he closed the door behind them. Almost immediately there was a yell from Rose and then it went quiet.

"Time for Ol' Dad to mix up more Seabreeze, before the booze is gone." Morrie set about his domestic chores again.

"You got a problem about the booze?" rumbled Pusgut from the floor.

"No sir, Sergeant. None at all," Morrie said, his voice clicking heels. "Schlumberger, what the hell are you doing?"

Schlumberger was rooting through a bureau drawer like a wart hog in heat. "Looking for my damn billfold!" He slammed the drawer shut and yanked open the next one down.

"You know, Kelly, you're the kind of boy I worry about." The Ghoul rubbed his hand over his flattop and held his glass out toward Shapiro, "Never mind that slop. Give me a cream soda."

"Thank you, Chief," I said.

"You mean Ghoul, don't you?"

"Sir?" I managed to get out.

"You think I don't know what you call me behind my back? Boy, I know everything that goes on in this company. And what I don't know, Pusgut does." The Ghoul laughed, and Sergeant Biller gave me a single-finger salute.

"Don't like to be called boy, do you, Kelly? Think I'll mistake you for one of the colored? You think I don't know how you got in trouble back home stickin' up for a Nee-gro commie professor?"

The pit of my stomach did a falling elevator drop. Just what the hell was in my personnel file, was the goddamn F, B and I bird-dogging me around the goddamn army, or what?

"Never mind, Kelly. You got other things you'd better worry about, boy. And I use the term ad-vis-ed-ly. You see him?" He pointed to the paratrooper who hadn't done anything but lie there ever since he gave his combat jump demonstration. "That's a man. You," the Ghoul pointed at me, "are a boy. Got that?"

"Yes, sir."

"That's good, Kelly. We can work with that. Like we can with what you call me behind my back. You know how I got that name, don't you? Hauling the bodies of dead boys off the battlefields in two wars, The Big One and Kough-ree-ah, that's how.

"They all thought they was men, but they was boys, Kelly, like you. My job was to go out on the battlefield and retrieve their bodies.

When they die from a single lucky shot, and they're all in one piece with their tags on, they look like they could have been you, a few minutes ago, an' now they're gonna be shipped home in a box. *Comprende?*"

"Yes, sir," I said, remembering Chick Belos closed up in that coffin.

Gary padded out of the next room, with his shirt on, zipping up his pants with one hand, his shoes and socks in the other. "Next," he said, looking at Morrie and me and jerking his thumb toward the partly open door. "Who's in the biggest hurry?"

"They aint in no hurry. Shapiro, stand easy. Kelly, you collich kids are the worst. You think you know everything, and you don't know nothin'.

"You don't listen to what's going to save your sorry asses when you get to Kough-reeah. That's what Sarge and I teach you. Quick, Kelly, there's a gook with a burp gun. Whadda ya do?

"Pop-pop-pop-pop-pop-pop! Too late, Kelly. The gook got you. The burp gun can make identifyin' your body a mess."

"Any more of you boys be comin' in?" Yellow Rose's voice drifted in from the other room. Her voice sounded odd.

"In a minute!" the Ghoul bellowed. "This is import'nt!"

He looked directly at me. "You think I don't see you sitting back there dreaming about North Dakota poon tang or whatever pissant shit you're thinking about instead of what you have to learn to stay alive!"

The Ghoul shifted his eyeballs to Morrie. "You think me and Sarge separate the men from the boys, Shapiro?"

"Yes sir."

"Wrong!" said the Ghoul. "The burp gun separates the men from the boys! Go on, Shapiro. Quit pretending you're listening and go dip your little circumcised wick."

Morrie headed swiftly for the other room and Yellow Rose and didn't look back as he closed the door behind him.

"Kelly. Unless you stop thinkin' so much, you're the kind of guy who gets yourself killed. There's only two ways to avoid that. One: don't get in the goddamn war. You're already in the goddamn war. That leaves number two. Do you know what number two is, Kelly?"

I laughed. I couldn't help it.

"Number two, Kelly, ain't nothin' to laugh about. What's the matter with you? Number two is to kill the other guy first! Remember that!"

"I will."

"Geez, you guys!" Schlumberger had combed the place and still hadn't found his wallet. "Who knows where my billfold is?" He stood there, his shirt hanging open, his eyes scanning from person to person. "I had twenty bucks from Morrie in there!"

"See the chaplain an' get your card punched," sympathized the paratrooper from the floor.

"It'll turn up," said Walt.

Schlumberger glanced at Walt, then glared down at the jumper.

The jumper sat up. His eyes were fastened on Schlumberger.

"The big buttface has the idea somebody stole his wallet. Is that what you think, Buttface?"

Schlumberger didn't say anything.

"Back off, Schlumberger. Walt and me was here the whole time. Nobody took your wallet." Carl leaned back.

"I ain't saying you or Walt took it."

The door to the next room opened, and Morrie waddled out. "Black bitch," he said. "I'm not paying for any blonde."

"Sounds like you're saying we did, private," Pusgut said to Schlumberger, ignoring Morrie. He stood up.

"It does," agreed the Ghoul from the chair.

"Just a minute, guys." Morrie was worried.

The jumper greeted Morrie, "If you know what's good for you, Fuckface, you'll leave this to your friend Buttface here."

Morrie didn't know exactly what was going on, but he immediately grasped the main point. "Schlumberger, you better apologize to the man."

Schlumberger's eyes flitted around the room.

"Well," he licked his lips. "I don't mean to accuse no one. I'm only askin'. I've looked all over."

"I guess that means you lost it, huh, Buttface?" The jumper wasn't satisfied.

"That's what Buttface means," Morrie intervened. "Hey, listen you guys, let's have a nightcap, you know?"

"So is that what you mean, Buttface?" asked the Ghoul.

"Yeah," Schlumberger mumbled. He might as well have sewed it over his shirt pocket, a new nametag: "Buttface."

"Aw right, Buttface," the Ghoul smiled. He waved at me. "Excused, Kelly. Go get laid."

My shoulders slumped, like I'd been holding myself rigidly at attention ever since we came back to the motel and the Ghoul had barked, "At ease!"

But when I went into the other room, I was not at ease. I didn't feel like a guy who was about to be laid ought to.

Yellow Rose sat on the bed with her yellow hair in one hand. Her own hair was tight against her head like a swimming cap. With her other hand she held a pillowcase to her mouth. She looked a lot younger than she did before.

She'd been crying. When she dropped the pillowcase on the bed there was blood on it and her upper lip was split. But she clamped her yellow hair back on her head like on a helmet.

"You next, goodlookin'?" When she smiled blood oozed from her lip and around her front teeth.

"What happened to you, Rose? Did one of those guys hit you or something?"

"Somethin'," she mumbled. "Yeah, somethin'." She laughed till her smoker's hack caught her. "I be fine." She patted the bed beside her. "How you like it?" She smiled again, and I saw the blood on her teeth again.

"No," I said. "Let me get you a wash cloth."

"No?" She looked hard at me. "Maybe you too goodlookin'. Maybe you a pussy boy?"

"Don't you worry about that."

"You say so. You don' want nothin' I best be leavin'." She stood up.
"You sure?"

She laughed and coughed at the same time. "Boy, you don' want
to do nothin' but worry 'bout me. You somethin' else, you know?"

"I guess." I was getting tired of being called boy. "How about
telling me how your lip got cut, Rose."

"And you gonna do what then?"

She didn't wait for an answer. "You want to help Yellow Rose?
You don' do nothin', you don' say nothin', okay?" She shook her head,
bouncing her yellow curls.

"Okay, if that's what you want," I said.

"Okay, tha's what then."

IT TOOK ME FOREVER TO FALL ASLEEP, and then I didn't. My feet developed
that prickly, asleep feeling, but the rest of me stayed awake. I tried to get
my brain to go numb too, but it kept replaying *pop, pop, pop*, and
remembering Chick Belos.

Finally I got up to go outside for a smoke. My legs let me know
they were still there with that feeling of a thousand pins being jabbed into
them. I hobbled around the dark room, found a crumpled pack of
Luckies and a book of matches on the dresser, edged past Carl's
stretched-out body, and shut the door and the screen door quietly.

I was surprised to find Schlumberger sitting there on the porch
bench, leaning forward, his elbows propped on his knees, his chin in his
hands; he was wearing only a pair of shorts, the same as me.

"Can't sleep," I said.

"Me either, I . . ." he stopped there.

It was restful to sit in the silence. The arc of the driveway fused
with the highway and the highway rolled away in a tapering ribbon until
it got lost in the darkness. The moon was someplace behind our cabin.
But a million stars clustered up there in front of us. There were no
sounds: no small animal scurryings, no whispers from jostled leaves.

"It's pretty out here, ain't it?" Schlumberger said.

"That's what I was thinking. Smoke?" I held the pack out to him.

"Naw. Thanks."

When I lit up, the scratch of the match was loud, and the sulfur was acrid in my nostrils. I missed seeing the twisting blue-gray of the smoke drifting from the end of the cigarette, but its tip glowed bright in the dark after the flare of the match.

"Geez," Schlumberger said, "I wish Marie was here."

"We'll get our thirty-day leaves in a few more weeks. You'll be able to see her then."

"We've only been married six months. It's tough being away from her, you know?"

"I bet."

Schlumberger sighed and sat back. His legs slid forward so his ankles and feet came in my line of sight; the knobs behind his big toes stuck out like a giant's knuckles.

"I used to get it every night, when I wasn't on the road."

"Yeah?"

In real life Schlumberger was an over-the-road trucker. He said driving was a tough job, taking bennies and dexies to keep from falling asleep at the wheel. At my old part-time job filling out bills of lading at Shortstop Trucking, I'd seen some drivers come in all wired on pills. Schlumberger claimed they weren't so bad, but the way his eyes flailed around, and then glazed over, sometimes made me wonder if he still used them.

"You know it," he said. "Every night." I could only see his ankles and feet out of the corner of my eye, and his voice seemed disembodied.

My cigarette burned down to a stub. I almost ground it out with my bare foot, but I remembered in time. I nearly burned myself picking it up, but I put it between my thumb and index finger, and catapulted it way out over the gravel driveway, spinning through the dark, a small, fiery pinwheel.

From way down the road we could hear the drone of a truck.

It roared past us and faded into the night. "Someone's driving truck all night," I said.

"That's how I met her," said Schlumberger. "I used to stop at a greasy spoon, in Elgin, outside Chicago. Get the noise of the cab-over outta my ears.

"Marie was a waitress there. I'd have the pecan pie a la mode. She always saved some for me. I used to kid her all the time about ridin' to Chicago with me. One night I ran into this big snowstorm—rigs in the ditch right an' left—but I kept drivin' for Elgin. Marie let me come up to her room that night."

He was silent, remembering, I supposed, and I remembered the Concord Bar and Fine Dining and Joan Hendrickson.

"It's funny, you know," I said, "the first girl I ever did it with was a waitress too." No point in telling him she was the only girl I'd done it with.

"A few trips after that," Schlumberger broke the long silence, "Marie tells me she's knocked up. She likes to do it bareback, ya know?"

Also no point in telling him how much I'd sweat worrying that I'd get Joan knocked up and wreck my whole life having to marry someone I didn't love.

"We went into Chicago for our honeymoon. Stayed at the Palmer House. Cost me a fortune." He paused. "But we must of done it ten times that night."

"Ten times? Come on."

"Anyways, a lot," Schlumberger said. "Gawd, I miss her." He went silent again.

"Maybe you could get her down here."

"Geez, we got the kid comin,' and I'm so far in hock to Morrie now. She better keep servin' pie."

"Yeah? Well, it was just an idea," I said. "I'm going to catch some shut-eye."

"Yeah, me too," he said, but he slumped forward again, with his chin in his hands, the same as when I had first come out, and didn't move.

I left him out there.

15

Sunday morning came early, misfiring and sputtering, with the gross frictions of six guys trying to use one bathroom at the same time.

"Morrie! How goddamn long can it take one guy to shave, shower and shit? Come on!" Gary yelled.

"Anybody else going to church?" Walt asked.

"If you can get Morrie out of the can, I'll go with you," Gary said. "What are you doing in there, Shapiro? Pounding off?"

"Hey! Look what I found behind the can!" Morrie's shrill shout came from the bathroom.

The room fell silent, and there was Morrie standing in the bathroom doorway, holding up a billfold.

"Your wallet, Buttface!" he glared at Schlumberger. "All that trouble with the Ghoul for nothing," he said. "Buttface is the right goddamn name for you!"

Morrie wheeled the Lincoln out of the driveway, the gravel crunching, in time for Walt and Gary to make it to twelve o'clock Mass in Richmond. Walt was no surprise; Gary must be one of those guys who'd screw his best friend's girl but wait till after midnight to avoid eating a hamburger on a Friday.

For a few minutes, we were all sharp in our fresh shirts. Except Schlumberger. He'd subdued his Hawaiian shirt again. Some competition to his aroma drifted in through the open car windows when we passed the Du Pont plant about halfway to town. The buildings and tanks, gray and silver, set back from the highway several hundred yards, spread sulfurous fumes over the highway, as if they were making poison gas in there.

We passed an artificial lake: bright blue water shimmered under the morning sun, and Walt suggested we cool off there after church. We sped on past a row of skeleton buildings, built low to the ground, LUCKY STRIKE painted on corrugated tin roofs, that sheltered stacks of dark tobacco leaves waiting to be shredded. On past a newly constructed state prison. In half an hour we reached town.

Richmond was Sunday morning pretty pictures for tourists. Leafy trees shaded quiet streets. Gracious homes. Green parks. University campuses. The old Confederate Capitol. Hollywood Cemetery where Jefferson Davis and 18,000 Confederate soldiers lay. My dad would have loved it.

We found a Catholic church, white-clapboard, with a stubby steeple and a plain cross, and dropped off Walt and Gary. Walt invited me again, "You'd better get back in the fold before they ship you to Koughree-ah to get your tail shot off."

After we dropped them off, the rest of us looked for some chow. Off the Jefferson Davis Highway we located a Walgreen's Drug with an orange sign blinking BREAKFAST. Inside double glass doors with Plexiglas handles was an air-conditioned heaven.

We picked up a *Richmond News Leader* and settled into a booth, Morrie and Schlumberger across from Carl and me. The waitress brought us glasses of water with ice cubes clinking in them and beads of water on the outside.

Walt and Gary would be hot in the little church. The priest would be saying the Latin with a Southern accent. At home it would be cool in St. Mary's, even on a hot summer day. Moira would be checking out my mother's hair to see how red it was today. Father Mahoney would be saying the same Latin as the priest in Richmond, but without an accent.

The big twenty-five-cent glass of orange juice was sweet and cold. The eggs were fluffy. The ham thick. The coffee hot in its heavy white mug. The good smell steamed above the dark surface.

Sections of the paper went from hand to hand.

"So what's the news, Kelly?" asked Carl.

I held up the headline: "HEAT CONTINUES BREAKS 10-YEAR MARK."

"Anything about the fucking war in theah?" Smoke curled around Carl's words.

"Yeah. Here we are," I read aloud:

NEW FIGHTING AT OLD BALDY.
UN OUTPOST OVERRUN.
(AP) Special from Chorwon, Korea.

Fierce fighting has erupted along the stalemated Korean front again as Chinese Communist Forces, after a merciless artillery barrage, at 2200 hours the day before yesterday swept in battalion strength over Old Baldy, a UN outpost at the farthest edge of its line in the war-ravaged area just west of Chorwon at the left corner of the Iron Triangle.

Counterattacks have been launched by several companies of the 23d Infantry Regiment and casualties are reported to be extremely heavy on both sides in ferocious hand-to-hand fighting. While some of the US troops have regained a position on the scarred slope, who will control the desolate hill when the attacks and counterattacks end remains in doubt.

Old Baldy, which senior officers say has no particular strategic value, was the scene of bloody conflict earlier in the war, with casualties in staggering numbers like those taken last fall at Heartbreak and Bloody ridges, where (continued on page 17, column 2)

"Wait right theah, Kelly." Carl blew off another cloud of smoke. "No particular strategic value, continue to page seven-fucking-teen."

Carl shook his head. "I don't want my ass shot off on the fuckin' front page, or on page seven-fucking-teen. No one gives a shit about this fuckin' war anymore. I'm seriously thinkin' of not going."

"Nobody wants their ass shot off," I said. "But we have to show them we're not going to give up now."

"If it wasn't for all those pinkos hanging around Washington, this war would be over! Take it from your ol' Dad."

"Morrie, do you have any clue what you're talking about?" I asked.

"The Bomb," he explained it all.

"The Bomb means we've got a bunch of pinkos in Washington?"

"Damn right! Or we'd use it, and the war would be over. Like last time."

"Pinkos my ass! Truman's the guy who dropped the bomb last time, and we're already bombing the bejesus out of Pyongyang. And if we start WWIII . . ."

"The Russians'd be crazy to come in," Morrie interrupted.

"If they did, we'd drop the Bomb on them and good-bye Rooskies!" said Schlumberger.

The Bobbsey Twins in Basic. "Good-bye Rooskies? How about goodbye Fargo, while you're at it?"

"Kelly, trust Old Poppa. Nobody wants to bomb Fargo. Why would anyone want to bomb Fargo?"

"Yeah? We'd all be better off if they nuked New Jersey and wiped out the mob," I said.

"Geez," Schlumberger said, peering at the rotogravure section.

"Look at that!" Morrie leaned over Schlumberger.

"What are you guys slobbering over?" Carl asked.

Schlumberger held up the paper: "HOW I HANDLE THE HOLLYWOOD WOLVES. By Marilyn Monroe."

We were back to the important stuff. There were several candid shots of the author. Her body reminded me of Moira's, although Marilyn looked softer, and there was a little more of her here and there. But

Marilyn gave the camera that "I'm just a dumb blonde who'd be fun to do it with" look; while Moira, on the other hand, looked as smart as she was.

Even the damn funnies reminded me of Moira this morning. Sad Sack was right out of F. Scott Fitzgerald. In the first panel, Sad Sack pled with a blonde; scorned as a pauper, he strode off, "I'll work day and night and be a success!" A year later, he returned, to tell her he was "RICH now!" She stretched out willing arms, but in the last panel Sad Sack was chauffeured away in a Cadillac, each arm draped around a redhead: "Phooey. Who NEEDS you now!"

"Kelly, you must have those fuckin' funnies memorized by now."

I passed them over to Carl.

In the churches the priests would conclude the masses and the altar boys would respond, "*Deo gratias.*" When I first served mass, I was a junior partner, assisting Father Mahoney in a magical enterprise, reliving Christ's suffering and death right there on the altar, but by the end I was glad it was over. After the mass, as his Holiness Pope Pius XI had requested, prayers would be offered for the conversion of Russia.

Walt and Gary should have bugged out of church by now.

"They're coming," Morrie pointed. You could see Gary's chartreuse tee shirt half a block away.

At LAKE CLIO (MAN-MADE LAKE), the sign proclaimed, we all changed into our swimming suits in the car, elbowing and kneeing each other, and jumped over the fence to the beach. Except Schlumberger. He had a headache and was going to sit in the car and watch for a while. It was only about a hundred degrees in the car.

When I paused on the diving tower overlooking the sparkling blue water below Gary and Walt a few steps behind me did a double take looking back down at the car, and Morrie's shoulders quivered like they did when he laughed that hyena laugh of his. All I could see in the car was Schlumberger with his head back and eyes closed, grimacing, his flowered shirt heaving up and down rhythmically.

I plunged into the cool water and came up bobbing for air in time to watch Gary spread his arms in a swan dive before bringing them back together to knife noiselessly into the water. We climbed out of the water and were joined by Morrie, hitting his head to knock the water out of his ears from his cannonball jump from the tower. He looked over at the car. "Guess what Buttface is up to now?"

"We all know," said Walt. "You selling tickets?"

"Tom, what say we just sit in the shade a spell and drink gin?" Carl proposed, producing a bottle of Gordon's, like Ashley Wilkes misplaced in a Hemingway story. We sat at a nearby park table under a forlorn tree, passing the bottle back and forth, till a family set up on the beach in front of us.

"This is a good spot. Ruthie, help Daddy. Grab that corner of the blanket," her dark-haired, still-voluptuous mother commanded. Ruthie, a ripe, teenage version of mother, sucked on a lime Popsicle.

"Ruthie! Don't let that drip all over the blanket," said her mother.

"Oh, all right, Mother!" Her even white teeth bit down over the rest of the Popsicle and she slid the whole thing off the stick and into her mouth. Lucky Popsicle.

"Don't pick on Ruthie, Mother."

"Oh, I get so tired of you always taking her side."

"Now, Mother . . ."

"Come on," Carl said. "Let's get out of here. I had fuckin' enough of these fuckin' people."

"Well, okay," I said. Good-bye, Ruthie. Eat all the Popsicles you want. Let them drip all over. Lime and cherry and grape and lemon and raspberry.

Carl and I walked up the stone pathway to the pavilion where Carl sat pulling on the Gordon's like he'd gotten his orders to Korea.

"So, what's your problem, Carl?" I asked and set him off into a long drunken story about his girlfriend, Elaine, Elaine Rosenker. Carl's good Lutheran mother and father hadn't wanted him to marry her. How would they raise the children? When he'd asked her anyway, she said he had to ask her daddy first. Daddy said no. She was going to college and meet a nice Jewish boy. Not some guy who worked in a refrigerator plant.

"So, Daddy's a kike and Elaine just fucking obeys him. Can you fucking believe it?"

"He wants her to marry a guy with money. Fathers feel that way. My girlfriend," I stumbled over the word, "my old girlfriend's father feels the same way."

"The blonde, huh? You ought to forget her, Tom. I'm not against Jews, only the kikes, like Morrie. Who's got all the fuckin' money in this outfit? If we wanna go anywhere, it's Ol' Poppa and his big Lincoln. If we need booze. If we need pussy . . . an' the way he leads Schlumberger around by the nose is enough to make me puke."

My brain was having trouble dealing with more than two or three of Carl's non-sequiturs at a time. How was it Gregory Peck handled bullshit like this in *Gentleman's Agreement*?

"We all leech off Morrie, and that makes him a kike? You know your problem, Carl? You're so fucking bigoted you don't know shit from Shinola."

Carl considered my argument.

"Let's go," I said.

THE GUYS HAD CHANGED and were outside the fence.

The car raked the fence with gravel as Morrie spun it out of the lot. "Nothing but jailbait and pigs around here," he said.

"Can't you guys ever meet a nice girl?" asked Walt.

"Speaking of which," I grabbed for the opportunity, "when are we going to meet these relatives of yours, Morrie?"

"Relatives schmelatives. You mean when do we meet my good-lookin' cousin."

"If we don't do it soon, this weekend will be over."

"All right, already." Morrie pulled into the next filling station and made the call. He emerged smiling.

16

Mrs. Abrams' house was a two-story brick Georgian set back from a quiet side street with a tall hedge across the front of the property and trees edging the driveway. Flowerbeds graced both sides of the steps.

Inside, we stepped into an open hallway facing a flight of broad, burnished stairs. The dining room, off to the left, was a room only women lived in. The chairs had legs that looked like they'd snap if anyone sat down hard. But the living room, where Mrs. Abrams had us sit down, had regular, comfortable furniture.

Mrs. Abrams had dark hair with a pretty gray washed through it. A nose like an eagle. Big brown eyes. She was dressed in black as if she was still in mourning, though her husband had been dead for a couple of years.

"So, you're Natalie's boy, Morrie! I haven't seen your mother since—I wouldn't want to admit since when."

"She often mentions you, Aunt Rachel. I was supposed to give you her regards right away, but they've kept us awfully busy." Morrie was a different Morrie, subdued.

"Have you boys been out on bivouac yet?" asked Mrs. Abrams's daughter, Natalie, named after Morrie's mother. She had her mother's brown eyes, hair more auburn than brown, and a belly like a basketball.

"Not yet," Walt answered.

"I certainly hope it cools down for you boys. I declare this heat is so awful!" Natalie's smile nearly made it all better.

"Natalie's Ralph is in Korea," Mrs. Abrams said. "He's just made captain in the Marines. Natalie's very proud of him." She smiled at Natalie. "We'll all be glad when he finishes his rotation. He's a fine boy."

"Of course, Mother's not prejudiced. In another five years we'll make major. By then this young man," Natalie pointed at the basketball, "will be starting kindergarten."

"You're sure it's going to be a boy?" asked Schlumberger.

"I hope so. There's already enough competition in this family," said Natalie.

"I hope we're going to have a boy, too," said Schlumberger.

"How nice," said Mrs. Abrams; her eyes lingered over his Hawaiian shirt.

"Is it only the two of you who live here, Mrs. Abrams?" I asked.

"Oh my, where are our manners?" Mrs. Abrams called in the direction of the stairs, "Annie! Annie Jones! Why don't you come down here and meet these boys?" Her polite summons ended in a lilted question mark.

When I looked up, suddenly there was Annie. Somber and beautiful, in a severe dark-blue dress, coming down the burnished stairs, she could have been making an entrance in a movie, except she was so quiet about it. Her hair was dark, like her mother's must have been before it grayed, and her eyes were deep-brown too. Only hers framed an Elizabeth Taylor nose, like she'd had one of those nose jobs the stars had.

But Annie could have been from another family. Her mother and her sister, Natalie, were Southern relaxed. They moved like they talked, with a drawl; she was quick, intense. Her hands seemed to be moving all the time, like she was lighting up a cigarette, or something. When her eyes first flashed over us I wanted them to stop on mine, and they did, for just a second, but I wasn't sure they paused enough to really see any of us.

"Why don't you fix these boys an iced tea?" Mrs. Abrams sounded annoyed at Annie's evident lack of enthusiasm for playing hostess to the troops.

Annie went off to the kitchen, and in a few minutes she returned carrying a silver tray that held a thick crystal pitcher, and glasses filled with ice and lemon slices. Her slim forearms and her slender neck were taut, her hands gripped the handles of the tray; and across the inside of each of her wrists was a faint, almost straight, line.

Annie Jones was older—at least thirty Morrie'd said—and up close she wasn't as perfect as Elizabeth Taylor, but she was beautiful. When she leaned toward me with the tray in front of her, her delicate musky scent made me want to touch her, and the vee of her dress opened a little and her skin was white and smooth against the dark blue. I took the pitcher off the tray to pour tea over the ice and sliced lemon in a glass. Her face was inches from mine, and she looked right in my eyes, and she smiled for the first time this afternoon.

"What's your name?" she asked.

"Annie Jones," I said, spilling the tea all over the rim of the glass, and feeling my cheeks redden.

"I don't think so," she laughed. She had a nice soft laugh.

We drank iced tea and talked. Schlumberger kept his shirt buttoned, and no one called him Buttface. Carl had sobered enough so he wasn't "fucking this" or "fucking that." And he didn't ask Mrs. Abrams if she was part of the International Jewish Conspiracy to Do in Lutherans. The Ghoul and Pusgut were nowhere to be seen. Rose didn't come tripping out of the next room ready for Morrie or Gary. Nobody put the make on Mrs. Abrams or Natalie. The Army ought to have hired Mrs. Abrams as our housemother.

But I didn't pay much attention to anyone but Annie, and it seemed like I was the only one she paid any attention to. Or maybe it was just every time she looked my way, I was staring into her brown eyes. Because of the unusual coincidence about our names.

We could have stayed longer, but the new Morrie developed this incredible attack of politeness, and he more or less hauled our butts out of there. By the time we left, Annie knew my name was Tom Kelly, and as I pled my case on my way out the door, she said she'd "think about" seeing me next weekend.

Before heading back to base, we decided to give the main drag a cruise in Morrie's Lincoln, but we didn't see any action. So we reconnoitered farther on foot. Off the main street, we saw a group of guys, mostly soldiers, standing in a circle on the sidewalk. From inside the circle, the sounds of a singer and a street band drifted up the street. We ambled over to check it out.

The singer, a black kid about twelve years old, stood in a doorway; a neon sign flickering CANDY in the store window beside him tinting his red silk shirt, and even his black, tiny-curled hair, an electric orange. Another black kid strummed a steel cable that ran from the bottom of an inverted washtub. A third, his fingers taped, beat a rectangular sardine can drum. They could all have been kids of an older guy who clicked battered tin mixing spoons castanets.

The singer finished his song and the castanet player took up a collection in a chipped white porcelain mug. When I threw a quarter in, a white guy next to me, all dressed up in a tie and a vanilla ice cream colored suit, looked at me like I was a sucker. The band played another song, coaxing gentle, sad music out of the bunch of junk they were playing. The singer hummed along, didn't even sing any words. When they finished, the clapping was tardy and mainly mine.

"Hey boy! Give us something lively, heah?" A big guy with a GI haircut and a lantern jaw called out from the rear.

Their next song throbbed like a morning pecker aching for release. The kid singer got into it, moving and sweating to his song:

"I got a ten-pound hammer, the women love to hear it sound.
They says 'Come on, Moses, go and drive it down.'"

He finished with a smile, then dropped his head forward on his chest, like he was exhausted.

"Yeah!" I hollered and clapped, but this time I was the only one, and I got that lonesome feeling you get when you applaud and discover the music isn't over yet.

117

"Hey, boy," hollered the big guy from the back, "What's that called? I'se gwine to sing ya'all a nigger song, all 'bout my big black dong?"

"How about shut my big fat mouth?" I turned partway around and entered the discussion. "Ever hear that one, asshole?"

The asshole's face reddened, and he came charging through the crowd. I turned the rest of the way around, with the store window behind me, crouched, and took a bead on his lantern jaw.

"What did you say?" the asshole asked.

Out of the corner of my eye, I saw Morrie moving toward me and heard Walt saying, "Take it easy there . . ." but I was engaged in the conversation with lantern jaw.

"I said . . ."

Without waiting for my answer, the asshole let fly at my face. I ducked and his fist grazed past me and slammed into the window behind me. He screamed like a damn orangutan, giving me enough time to swing at him, right in his gut, which turned out to be made of iron. When he swung again, his fist smashed into my face, right below my eye; I felt my skin tear, at the same instant the back of my head crashed against the plate glass window.

The doc in the Richmond General Hospital emergency room shot my cheek full of Novocaine. The guys bitched about the whole thing, and all of them, even Carl, had gotten a little banged up in the action that apparently took place with the big guy's friends and allies. I found out later that he was the base heavyweight-boxing champ, and he was wearing a silver ring made like a saddle; it was the saddle horn that tore open my face. But I was lucky. I got to keep my eye.

Back at the base the next few days the whole left side of my face felt like one giant toothache. Sleep was impossible. The Army's simulated food was hardly worth moving my jaws to chew. Even sucking on a beer at night was more painful than it was worth.

Sometime in the middle of the week, Joe Nash told me he'd heard a rumor that Prof Williams was teaching at East Wilberforce Methodist College, a small Negro college over the Carolina border.

"Methodist?" I asked. "Are you sure? That doesn't sound like Prof."

"Hey man, you asked. That's what I'm hearing. I'll try to run it down tight for you."

"Thanks, man," I said.

"Sure, man," he smiled his pixie smile that was almost a laugh. He was always doing that to me.

"Thanks," I said, without any "man" this time.

He started to turn away, paused. "The eye looks better," he said, before he left to rejoin his buddies.

It was toward the end of the week, that I called Annie.

"Hello," I said. "This is Annie Jones. Remember me?"

She laughed, "It sounds a lot like Tom Kelly. What made you think of me?"

"Your laugh," I lied, a little.

"Really?" She sounded skeptical.

"Really. You have the nicest laugh I've ever heard." At this point it wasn't even a little lie.

"So, you called to tell me about my laugh?"

"I called to tell you if you don't go out with me Saturday night, I can't be responsible for the consequences."

"You'll survive till the weekend after next. You've made it this far in life without," she hesitated, "dating me."

"True. But the situation's changed. Now I've met you."

"I can do it the weekend after next, not this weekend."

"Okay, let's compromise. What do you say to the weekend after next?"

17

Two weeks later I hitched a ride into town.

Annie had arranged for us to use Mrs. Abrams's car for a drive to Williamsburg, another of the places my dad had written me to be sure to see if I got a chance. There was a cream-colored Buick, long as a hearse, a four-holer with a ton of chrome, gleaming in the driveway.

Natalie met me at the door, even more pregnant than she was two weeks ago. I sat with her and Mrs. Abrams in the living room, drank iced tea and waited for Annie. Mrs. Abrams handed me the keys to the Buick and carefully explained one was for the motor and one was for the trunk and, by the way, the brakes were a bit balky.

"Hello." Annie's voice was soft as she came into the room. She wore a short-sleeved white dress. She looked younger than the first time I saw her and as beautiful. Her dark hair looked soft. And her brown eyes. And her pouty lips.

I stood up and Annie reached out her open hands toward me to shake hands. When I put out my right hand, she took it in both of hers, then quickly let go.

All the way out the door and until we reached the Buick, she didn't look at me again. "I know the way so well, I should drive," she said.

But I had the keys. "I'll drive." I went around the front of the car and held the passenger door open for her.

"So, fine." She shrugged her small shoulders, went around and got in.

I slid in the driver's side and managed to insert the right key into the ignition.

She looked directly at me as I was backing the car out the driveway. "You are very young, aren't you, Tom?" she said.

I was astonished at what came out when I opened my mouth. "I was. Until recently. Till my divorce." It was a way for me to be older, to somehow to have more in common with Annie. It was a truly stupid thing to say.

"You've been married?" She sounded even more surprised than I was. Her neck curved gracefully as she twisted in the seat to look at me again. I turned back to the road ahead, while I figured out what the hell I was going to say next.

"Yeah."

I didn't know whether Annie bought it; she laughed her nice laugh again.

"Take a right here. It's a pleasant drive to Williamsburg."

I relaxed my grip on the steering wheel. I'd been hanging onto to it so hard my fingers tingled when I eased up.

Williamsburg, this village restored to colonial days around the time of the Revolutionary War, was phony and staged. I picked up all the free brochures and bought a book of colored pictures to send to my dad, but it looked even phonier in the brochures.

James Fort was more interesting with its tiny thatched roof houses and a three-masted sailing ship in its harbor. The settlers had experimented with a common granary, each putting in grain according to his ability and withdrawing according to his need, but the whole deal flopped; everyone wanted to take out, and no one wanted to put in.

We had dinner in a fancy dining room in a restored colonial house. We sat at a little round table, so we were very close. I was a little uneasy about how much this was all going to cost, and that Annie would start asking questions about my marriage, that I was already wishing I hadn't invented. There had to be better ways to be older and sophisticated.

The waitress had us all wrapped up in big white bibs like barber towels. With her head sticking out of the bib, Annie looked like a pretty little girl at a birthday party. Her slender arms popped out the sides. Annie talked me into having my first lobster. I sucked every bit of meat I could out of the shells, gorging myself on it and the sweet, salty melted butter.

We split a long loaf of bread, a light fluffy white, with a honey brown crust. Annie tore off a piece for each of us. When she ate hers, she left a tiny crumb of white resting on her lower lip. I looked at it there, and I took the crumb from her lip with my finger, and licked it off my finger. I did it without thinking, but it startled Annie. She shivered for a second, like a cool draft had touched her through the summer heat, and drew into herself, before she shook it off and laughed.

While I paid the check, with the last cash I had, Annie went ahead to the car. I arrived to find her sitting in the driver's seat.

"We've been through this, remember?" I held up the keys and opened the driver's side door.

She slid over and let me in. I caught a trace of the musky scent I was drawn to the first time I'd met her and she'd bent close. I wanted to touch her, and I reached over and just put my hand on her arm, but she seemed to tremble then, almost as if she were afraid I might hurt her, and I quickly drew back. I was feeling my way near the edge of a cliff on a path I didn't know.

On the drive back Annie talked a little about herself. She'd been staying with her mother for months, but she was a New York girl now, and would be going back soon. As a matter of fact, she was expecting to hear about a new job any day. It was with a new marketing organization, but she couldn't tell me much more. "I'll let you know when I hear," she said when she ended, as casual as could be, but I stored it away.

"What makes you a New York girl?"

"You've never been there?"

"No."

"You should. It's an exciting place. You feel you're at the center of the world there."

I wanted to ask her about the guy in New York, but what I said was "I bet you do. I'd really like to see it sometime." Which was absolutely true.

As the miles and minutes slipped away, the sun eased into that magical time of day when it turns the green of leaves and grass into gold and the heat of its rays fades.

"Is there someplace we can sit and talk a little?" I asked as we pulled into town. I was dead broke, but reluctant for my time with her to end.

"All right. There's a place I like by the cemetery. I suppose you think I'm a strange one for that."

"No, I don't."

"Take a right at the next corner."

We drove a bit farther and she told me to park.

We got out and walked, not touching each other and not saying much. We wandered past statues of Robert E. Lee and Jeb Stuart and down cobblestone streets with shady trees and old brownstones. After a mile or so, we turned off on a side street that ended in a park that had green grass, trees with still leaves, and quiet lakes.

We sat on a bench and watched pigeons waddle down the gravel path. Half a football field away in the cemetery a half dozen boys were playing statue-maker. You couldn't see their faces; they were dark silhouettes against the sun. One took another and whipped him around, then let him fly, to freeze the way he landed.

"So, what do you want to do when you get out of the army?"

"I'm not sure. I really would like to see New York myself."

"Besides being a tourist."

"Oh, I don't know. Write."

"You want to write?"

We were both quiet for a moment. "Yes, write."

"What would you like to write about?"

"I don't know. You."

"Well that's a foolish thing to say."

"You think so?"

"You hardly know me. Certainly not well enough to write about me." Annie was quiet again for a while. "It's very flattering but you ought to write about what you know well."

English teachers were always saying that, but when Annie said it I could see for myself how true it was. I didn't know enough to write about her. I could write about how she looked, or feelings I had about her, but I couldn't really write about her.

"You should write about you and your wife."

"Well, she's not my wife."

"Ex-wife. Would you mind telling me about that, Tom? You seem so young to have gone through that," she said.

"Yeah. Well . . ." There was no place to go now but ahead. I told her Moira and I had grown up together in Fargo, and Moira had pursued me with poetry, sex, her hunter-green Ford convertible, and dreams. It sounded pretty good.

"Really?" Annie sounded skeptical. "What dreams?"

"Oh, the university, and Harvard Law School," I paused. "Secretary of State, stuff like that."

"My, my. Do you believe in 'stuff like that'?"

"Sometimes, I suppose. Moira is one persuasive and tenacious girl. When I got a scholarship to go away to the University of Minnesota, she followed me on down there, instead of going out East, like her daddy wanted her to."

One of the little black kids playing in the cemetery, wearing only a pair of ragged blue shorts, shouted as he was spun off into a swooping swan dive. Frozen there, he was a miniature, momentary version of Gary Kowalski, high over the artificial lake.

"Moira. That's an unusual name. So, she pursued you to Minnesota?" Annie prompted.

"Yeah." I was curious myself as to how I was going to get through all this. "And one thing led to another, and she said she was pregnant, and I married her. I didn't even mind so much when it turned out she wasn't. That bothered me, but I was glad too." I checked my nose to see if it was growing.

There was no way out of the stupid swamp now but to wade to the other side. "For a while after that, things were okay, but she hung onto me like crazy, and we fought all the time." At least that part was true. Annie nodded like she was accepting it. Hell, I believed it myself; now I was past the getting married part.

High-pitched laughter drifted across the cemetery as the kids went rolling and tumbling each other across the dark green among the white headstones. I wondered what the buried Confederate veterans would have thought of the game going on in the green grass that covered them, whether, as my mother would have said, they were turning over in their graves, or getting a kick out of it.

At the same time, I was working on just how to end my marriage. "Till one night," I began, increasingly curious as to what would come next, "Moira even tagged along to kibitz at a session of the only recreation I regularly engaged in without her, the North Dakotans to Save the World Poker and Beerdrinking Club and Debating Society, or NDTST-WPABCADS for short, and she got to talking—talking, hell, flirting—with, Will Lindeman, a friend of mine from Fargo, and . . ."

"Wait a minute," Annie broke in. "I love that. That NDTS North Dakotans to Save the World business. Can you say it again, the same way?" She laughed.

"Yes, but we're to the serious part and this isn't the time." I rushed ahead, "Yes, before you ask, Will is good-looking. And smart. And one thing led to another with Moira—again." By now I was surprised at the depth of my own outrage. "So," I finished the damn thing off in a rush, "I divorced her, got drunk and joined the Army."

"How sad for you." Annie was quiet.

"Yeah," I contemplated my plight with real sorrow myself. "But now I've met you, Annie."

"Yes," she said, "and it's hardly . . ."

"And I've lost the only thing I had left to lose—my broken heart, and good riddance to it. But, like the South, I'll rise again. So to speak."

"Not very funny, or appropriate," she said. "But very sad."

The kids, bored with their game of statues, ran off, twisting among the tombstones as they chased each other in a new game. The sun was falling and shadows moved among the graves in slow pursuit of the children.

"I know something about that. We have more in common than . . ." she trailed off and then was quiet again. She slipped one of her small hands into mine. She didn't squeeze, but let it rest in mine.

I turned to kiss her, but she put her finger on my lips and those soft brown eyes of hers were tearing up. My daydreams about the sophisticated lady from New York who'd done it and might like to do it again with a nice young soldier from Fargo felt so childish. I was going to go over the edge of the cliff and hurtle off into thin air toward I didn't know what jagged rocks below.

We sat silently a little longer. I wanted to kiss her, but she had her head burrowed into my neck so I brushed her hair with my lips. She felt relaxed against me. She was quiet, but it was a natural quiet, like she was resting, not like she was closing me out.

When we stopped at the gate so she could drop me at the base, I tried one more time to kiss her. And this time, when I kissed her, she kissed me back, and, strange as everything was, it felt as sacred as my first kiss with Louise Haberhorn, way back in grade school.

"Call me when you get back from bivouac," she said, like it was nothing, like oh, by the way.

When I entered the barracks, Carl and Walt were playing cribbage in Walt's room.

"Get your ashes hauled?" Carl asked through the open door as I tried to slip past.

"Fuck you, Carl! You met Annie."

"Touchy tonight, aren't we?" asked Walt.

"You ought to know better than to ask such a dumb question."

I had a tough time getting to sleep. I couldn't find anything around the empty barracks to read except the last thirty pages of *I the Jury*, which I wasn't in the mood for. I felt like talking to someone about Annie, but not to these guys. I got this urge to write about her, whether she and some English teacher approved or not, but I couldn't find any paper.

So I yanked one of last week's hundred and one notices from the bulletin board at the front of the barracks and, using the reverse side for paper, and Mickey Spillane for a desk, I started to write. Notes to myself, a letter to Annie, a diary, a story, an ode to horniness. I didn't even know what it was. After a few minutes, I tired and read what I'd scribbled. I tore the sheet four times making sixteen pieces out of it and flushed them down the can.

I could write Moira: "Dear, Moira, I've met this woman from New York named Annie Jones. She let me kiss her once, and she said to call her when we get back from bivouac, and I'm so excited I can't get to sleep. Ever yours, Tom."

WE SPENT THE NEXT WEEK on bivouac, which was so boring the high point of the week was an outbreak of crabs. I was sustained in the twenty-mile hike, the night problems, and endlessly scratching out and refilling slit trenches, not to mention scratching myself, by sudden, random thoughts of seeing Annie when we got back.

But when we got in Friday night, besides the usual from my mother, there was one other letter waiting for me. On the envelope my address and the return address were both typed. The return address was "A. Jones, 455 W. 34 St., #9D, NYC 1 NY." The envelope told me everything. She'd gone back to New York without seeing me, without any warning.

I was so tired I just lay there on my back in my dust-laden fatigues and sweat. I hadn't even reached down to take off my heavy, thick-soled combat boots; they were nailed to the floor with my feet in them.

Still lying flat on my back, I lifted the envelope up over my face. It was skinny; there couldn't be more than one small page in there. I smelled it. None of that musky scent of Annie that drove me nuts. I was getting it soggy and grimy turning it over and over in my hands.

I opened the letter and read it.

August 30, 1952
Dear Tom,
I'm so sorry to tell you this way.
Everything happened so fast.

I am working again—assistant sales promotion manager to a woman, you should forgive the expression. It's the job I told you I expected to hear about any day.

The organization is a new one—puts on shows at Grand Central Palace. The owner of the organization (Mr. Craig) has successfully promoted four home-furnishing shows, and now is expanding his operation to include another show on industrial design. The date is September 15th—which is too close for comfort!

I've been working since the plane landed and I don't know how we're going to get it ready. Margaret (my boss) has been out of town since showing me my office. I've been scrambling to make sense out of the chaos she's left me with. I can't say I'm overjoyed with the situation.

But there are three positive things, so far—-One: I'm employed. Two: I have a place to live. Three: I like Mr. Craig.

Please don't wait long to answer. I'm terribly rushed—but I look forward to hearing from you!

Affectionately,
Annie

P.S. My god, what an address!!! Hope I got it right.

I felt glad for Annie's sake, but it wasn't fair. I'd barely begun to know her, and she was gone. I was about to graduate from this finishing school. We'd all get thirty day leaves, whether our orders were for Korea or not, and she'd be off in New York.

I dropped the letter on my chest and let it sit there.

18

My family away from home showed some stresses and strains as we neared the end of basic. Carl and I still spoke to each other, usually when he was out of cigarettes, or when he passed the latest rumor about whether we were going to be shipped to Korea or whether there was a chance we might get sent to Europe instead. Every week he got new scuttlebutt—someone had talked to someone who'd seen a draft of the orders. We all worried about it, but Carl made it a full-time job. I wondered if he ever heard from his Elaine, but I didn't ask him.

Walt was made a squad leader. Walt had bossed a crew of guys building houses for his father-in-law, and he'd do a good job. If anybody would find out where we're being sent, you could bet it'd be Walt. But he'd keep his mouth shut to the end. His lofty new status enabled him to share a small room at the front of the barracks with the other squad leaders. Walt usually disappeared in there, writing his wife I supposed. It would be nice to have the room for writing.

JOE NASH LINED ME UP with the ride to Tollingham on the weekend, where I was able to catch the bus to Hamptonville, the site of East Wilberforce Methodist College, where Prof was supposed to be teaching, according to Joe. Tollingham Lines didn't make much on the trip. Apart from one elderly black man who rode on the back seat, I was the only passenger. Of course the bus didn't cost all that much either. They just stuck the engine up there where the oxen used to be.

The old man was dressed in a suit and tie, even though the bus was a rolling oven. On the floor, between his feet, was a tin bucket of water with a couple of the ugliest fish I'd ever seen, still alive and flopping around. All in all he looked like an interesting guy and I went to the back of the bus to ride with him and see what the story was on him. But when I tried to strike up a conversation, he barely answered. The back of the driver's neck was red even from where I sat. After a while I got the hint. When we stopped for a short piss call along side the road, we pissed side by side down a clay bank. But when we got back on the bus, I sat down near the middle of the bus, and everyone relaxed.

For another couple hours, the bus jolted along a rutted road that wound its way through scrub pines and around the edge of swamp, then broke for the low hills. The last hour or so should have been green, rolling countryside in an ordinary summer, but this year it was parched gray fields and dry, brown grass for miles. We passed an occasional town—a gas station and general store and a church.

When Hamptonville appeared around a bend in the road, there wasn't a whole lot to it. Signs CAFE and HOTEL hung over the sidewalk and the bus creaked to a stop right in front of the HOTEL.

I slapped dust off my pants, grabbed my ditty bag, and ventured into the lobby. The desk clerk had a sallow complexion, and yellowish eyes to match. When I asked for a room, even though I was the sole guest in sight, he made a big deal out of going through the register. He charged me a buck for the Presidential Suite, no doubt last occupied by Jefferson Davis.

"Business in town?" he asked, as I signed the card.

"At the college. Do you happen to know if a Professor Williams is there?"

A light went on behind his pale eyes. "You mean the nigger who got fired up North for being a communist. Yeah, he's out to the college." He punched the bell in front of him, dismissing me.

A bellboy took me up the rickety elevator to the third floor and down a worn carpet to the corner "suite." When I asked him about the college, he said "out to the college" was "jes a few blocks away." When we entered my "suite," which turned out to be a large corner bedroom with a small bathroom, he took me to the windows and pointed.

There were windows on both corner walls. One faced directly on the main street and the other up the street toward the college: a few two- and three-story buildings spaced around three sides of a quadrangle, the fourth side occupied by a narrow brick church with a white wooden steeple and cross.

I found a worn copy of the phonebook under a Bible with a faded cover in a veneered cabinet with its warped door ajar next to my sponge-soft bed. The phonebook was at least circumstantial evidence someone had occupied the suite subsequent to Jefferson Davis, but it listed no "Williams, Theodore R."

The operator had a new listing for Prof though. A young girl answered the number on the second ring. She said her father was at his new office. It was in the Booker T. Washington Building. On the Quadrangle—kitty corner from the Church. I couldn't miss it. Third floor.

The desk clerk stared at me when I left the key with him and set off.

The facade of the Booker T. Washington Building was of smooth stones set in crumbling tuck-pointing. The concrete front stairs were cracked and falling away from the building.

Inside, the building was cool after the broiling sun, but by the time I reached the third floor I was sweating again. The stairs were sway-backed, worn thin and gray in the center. The corridor floor was a dark clay tile, but over the years, a path had been worn down the middle of it, too, smooth and gray. There were cracks in the plaster intervals between the office doors on either side of the corridor. At the far end of the hall a rectangle of sunlight fell from a door open to the hallway.

Boxes of books surrounded Prof, the same as when I last saw him in his office at Minnesota, and he wore a T-shirt that said "Property of

Athletic Department" and "University of Minnesota" in a circle on the chest. His hands and forearms were dusty. The picture of his wife and their little girls was on his desk.

But Prof was different.

I always felt this vitality radiating from Prof whenever I was near him before, but now I didn't. I tried to figure out why. The answer was simple. When I saw it my gut jerked tight, and I exhaled a sudden, sharp burst of air.

Prof had turned gray.

Not his hair. Prof's skin had turned gray. It was as though he'd taken on the coloration of the trodden stairs, the worn path in the corridor, the smooth stones and crumbling mortar of the building itself, even of the dry, parched fields outside.

When Prof looked perplexed for a moment, I almost fled down the dark corridor without saying anything, not wanting him to even know I'd seen him this way.

"Mis-ter Kelly! Forgive me! I was so surprised to see you here!"

Prof took off his glasses and peered at me.

He reached down, and ran his hand over the top of my GI haircut. "Was this done to you by a licensed barber, Mr. Kelly? Can you sue?" He smiled before he looked closely at the purple welt the heavyweight asshole put under my eye. "And what is this?" he asked.

Prof's house was an easy walk from the campus. A small house. It would have been Lilliputian for the Prof I knew at Minnesota. The tiny front yard was burnt out, the sparse grass straw-like and matted against the dirt. There were bare patches across the front of the house, flowerbeds without flowers. The house shined with a fresh coat of white paint that made it more conspicuous. New front steps were freshly painted too.

Inside, the house was as immaculate as ours when it was about to be inspected by the relatives. Except for the books. Mrs. Williams had to be okay to let Prof's books overrun the house the way they did. They filled shelves in the living room on either side of the front window and a rack beside an easy chair. More in an oak bookcase in the dining room.

Prof's wife looked older than she did in the photograph in his office. Her eyes were dull and lines etched the corners of her mouth. Prof's daughter Lorraine was chubby and still in pigtails. She must have been the girl who answered the phone. His other daughter Lucy was out of pigtails—all long legs and bouncy little breasts.

We had iced tea with dinner. Iced tea seemed to be the adult Kool-Aid down here. It was okay, if you threw in enough lemon and sugar. Prof passed. "Methodist wine," he called it.

A spark came back into Mrs. Williams' eyes, and she said a little religion might not hurt Prof. "After all," she said, "you met me in church." The words could have been affectionate, but the way she said them they weren't. "Maybe," she said, the corners of her mouth drawn tight, "some religion would have kept you out of your troubles at Minnesota."

Lorraine and Lucy exchanged a glance, and Lucy's brown eyes went quickly to mine, before she looked down at her plate. Personally, I didn't see that religion had much to do with it.

"Leona," Prof sagged down in his chair, his elbows still on the table, "we've been over this a hundred times. And we have a guest."

Then she sagged too, as if she were a half-empty bag of flour, before she asked if I wanted more sweet potatoes.

"Yes, thanks. They're sure good." She'd cooked them with a brown sugar coating, like my mother did. The rest of the meal was good too. Some kind of flaky white fish with lemon. Peas.

With a prod from Prof, I retold an expurgated version of the story of my black eye. Prof said it was a shame my hands weren't as quick as my mouth. Mrs. Williams said I'd most likely cost the band some tips they could have used. Lucy thought I was butting in where I had no business. Lorraine only said it all sounded dumb, so she wasn't specifically critical of me.

Prof made me feel better by reminding Lorraine and Lucy that I'd gone down in flames, defending truth, justice, and their old man at Minnesota. Lucy's brown eyes lit up, and she turned their full voltage on me. But they flickered when she asked how come I was in the army. She understood about my getting thrown out of the university, but why did I have to go and enlist? Prof came to my defense, intervening to say after all I'd gotten kicked out of school over his right to speak out against the war. We disagreed about the war, that was all. But Lucy insisted, couldn't I have found anything better to do with my time? Didn't I have a girl-friend back home?

Mrs. Williams remembered. That was right. Didn't I have a girl? That Miss Moira Stacey who wrote that article? How come she had to put that story all over the front page of the *Minnesota Daily* anyhow? What kind of a person was she? Mrs. Williams paused and looked hard at me, like she was expecting answers.

I didn't know quite what to say. "I'm sure Moira didn't mean to get Prof fired."

"Humph, she could have thought of that before she wrote it."

"Someone was going to write it, Leona," said Prof. "I took that chance when I spoke out."

"And you could have thought of that before you spoke."

Mrs. Williams turned back to me. "And you. I'm sure your moth-er raised you to go off to war," she said. "And your father must be real happy you're not wasting any more time on school. You must be eighteen now."

It was none of her damn business.

"Nineteen," I said.

Silence fell over the table.

"Enough, Leona," said Prof. "Let's eat in peace."

Later, after Mrs. Williams and the girls had gone to bed, Prof broke out the bottle of Chianti from the kitchen cupboard and poured us each a glass.

He brought the bottle with him back into the living room and put it on the end table next to me on the sofa. He settled back in an easy chair in front of one of the bookcases flanking the front window. The floor lamp beside it cast his shadow on the floor.

"Leona and Lucy are right you know, Mr. Kelly. I do ap-pre-ciate your speaking out against what the university did to me. But I don't need it on my conscience you are in the army. You could have tried to get read-mitted to the university, or somewhere else. You didn't need to sign up to fight Mr. Truman's a-bom-in-able war!" He leaned toward me, his glass cupped in both of his hands. The lamplight burnished his skin, trans-forming the gray pallor I was so stunned to see a few hours ago.

"Prof, there's no way you're going to convince me President Truman wanted this war. Not with all the shit he and the Democrats have to take about 'losing China' and letting the Commies infiltrate the State Department and everything. "

"All the more reason, Mr. Kelly. But, never mind." He padded over to the couch in his stocking feet, filling my glass again. I felt a pleas-ant glow settling in. "I know when I'm wasting my breath." Prof sank back into the easy chair momentarily, then eased himself forward again, his eyes locking mine. "Yet, even if we assume, ar-gu-en-do," it popped into my head that the Ghoul would love that one, "the United Nations invaded Korea to stop North Korean 'aggression,' the United Nations—read United States—not only shoved the North Koreans back to the 38th parallel, it set out to conquer North Korea. And who said we intended to stop there—that we didn't see our chance to recapture your 'lost'—read 'seized by its own people,' —China."

"Prof, I can't waste a whole lot of sympathy on the Chinese. Maybe you're right about the Chinese people seizing power. I admire the Long March and all. Let's assume ar-gu-en-do," Jesus, it was contagious, "you're right about that. There's still no reason for the Chinese to get involved in Korea. We told the Chinese we weren't going to attack them."

"And your mama told you about Santa, I suppose!"

"Christ, Prof! What kind of an argument is that?" I got up and poured the remainder of Prof's Chianti into my glass. Prof reached to pour himself another only to stare at an empty bottle. He walked into the kitchen and returned with another. He raised the bottle toward my half-full glass and I nodded yes.

"Mr. Kelly," he stood over me, "we are the ones who should have ended this terr-i-ble war and all its fu-tile bloodshed months ago. We are the ones who take the position all of the issues in the peace talks have to be resolved before hos-til-i-ties end. We are the ones unwilling to implement a cease-fire along the 38th parallel. We are the ones who have kept the fighting going!"

Prof still packed a lot of contempt into a few syllables, I felt myself swept along as much by the power of his voice again as by his thoughts. The Chianti didn't hurt either.

"We both know if the war ends, the United States will have a difficult time keeping what it likes to call Red China out of the United Nations," he said, giving me credit for something that I hadn't thought about.

"That's stuff you and some newspaper columnists can bullshit about, Prof, but I'd bet everything I own it was nowhere near the president's mind when he committed American troops to stop the invasion. And that it's the farthest thing from his mind right now."

"And people in powerful places, Mr. Kelly," Prof went on, ignoring my comment, which told me he knew damn well I was right, "even cardinals in the Catholic Church, think we might as well fight a 'preventive' war against the Communists now as later. Tell me just how it is that a preventive war prevents war."

"A limited ground war may damn well prevent a worldwide nuclear one, that's how."

Prof turned away while I admired my point. He rummaged around the bookshelf till he found a book, *The Hidden History of the Korean War*, written by I.F. Stone.

"I don't know the book, but the title is paranoid as," I almost said 'you are' but caught myself, "hell if you ask me."

He began quoting numbers out of the book. "In the last six months of last year our battle casualties were 5,000 young men a month. Do you understand that? Five thousand boys like you dying or being wounded every month?" His voice boomed so loudly that he might have awakened his family.

"That's a terrible price, Prof." It was scary all right. Pretty like much the entire population of the whole town of Fargo killed or wounded in six months. Like a whole town of Chick Belos.

I still thought that we were right to stop the North Koreans and Chinese from taking over South Korea. How many people would they kill or ship off to the labor camps? If we just let them go ahead, where would it end? But a hell of a lot of Americans sure were dying to stop it. It shook me up.

"And nothing happened!"

"That's not true. The battle lines didn't move. We held fast. That happened. That means something."

"What it means, my young friend, is people, thousands of hu-man be-ings, being killed for nothing! And they aren't just the soldiers."

At the end, standing there, with the floor lamp behind him, he loomed like the Prof of old. He cradled the book in one big palm like a preacher and scanned the pages till he found a quote from a *New York Times* reporter named George Barrett who had entered a Korean village a few days after we had napalmed it. "And this is what he wrote," Prof's deep voice was soft but precise, etching every word into the night, as he read:

"A napalm raid hit the village three or four days ago when the Chinese were holding up the advance, and nowhere in the village have they buried the dead because there is nobody left to do so. This correspondent came across one old woman, the only one who seemed to be left alive, dazedly hanging up some clothes in a blackened courtyard filled with the bodies of four members of her family.

The inhabitants throughout the village and in the fields were caught and killed and kept the exact postures they had held when the napalm struck—a man about to get on his bicycle, fifty boys and girls playing in an orphanage, a page torn from a Sears-Roebuck catalogue crayoned at Mail Order No. 3,811,294 for a $2.98 'bewitching bed jacket—coral.' There must be almost two hundred dead in the tiny hamlet."

Prof choked up when he was reading it—it got to me, too—but it was strange when his voice broke. His voice caught as he read the long mail order number. When he finished, Prof looked down at me like thunder held in, like he was so mad he didn't trust himself to go on. "There's more," he said, and he, who treated all books like Holy Scripture, ripped out the pages and handed them to me.

Saying good-bye in the morning was like leaving family. Mrs. Williams was grumpy about Prof and me staying up half the night and keeping everyone else from getting any sleep. She fixed a big breakfast, pressing more gravy-laden biscuits on me than I needed. When I left she gave me a hug like I was one of her own kids. "Don't you get yourself killed now, son. Hear!"

19

The barracks were close with stale air from having been shut up all week. An oven stinking of sweat. The room was quiet with the bone weariness of all of us.

Only Morrie, on the bunk across the aisle from mine, was running his mouth. I marveled at where he got the energy. His body lived off its own fuel when mine was long since spent.

"The first thing this Ol' Dad's gonna do this weekend is get laid!"

Schlumberger, on the bunk next to Morrie's, stirred. "Geez. Me too, Morrie. If you'll stake me to some dough."

"Buttface, you couldn't get laid for free if you were the last man alive, and I'm out of spare cash." Morrie waited.

Schlumberger didn't reply.

"But there's gonna be some nice, juicy Virginia nookie for Ol' Poppa!" Morrie went on. "Beats you all to hell, Buttface."

Schlumberger sat up, "Whaddaya mean by that, Morrie?"

"You know what I mean, Buttface. How about a little of this?"

Morrie grabbed his crotch and jerked it, like he was waving it at Schlumberger.

Schlumberger sat up. "Gawd, Morrie! Gawd!" He looked around the barracks, his big eyes darting from man to man, stopping nowhere.

"How'd you ever get a woman to marry you, Buttface," Morrie said.

"Geez, Morrie. It ain't right to say that. My wife really loves me," he said, his eyes still flailing around, like he was looking for help.

"Well any woman who real-ly loves a buttface like you must not know what a buttface you are, or she must be a real beast. A r-e-a-l maggot."

It was one of those frozen moments, like they say happens in an accident, when you see the other car just drift toward you before it hits you. Even though it wasn't even a second before Schlumberger let out a cry, like a wounded, whimpering animal. If he hadn't cried out, or if he hadn't moved so ponderously, he might have gotten Morrie.

But Morrie, hearing the cry, and seeing Schlumberger falling at him, managed to roll off his bunk before Schlumberger landed on it.

Morrie scrambled to his feet. He hit the sprawling Schlumberger two or three times in the face, as fast and hard as he could, before Schlumberger grabbed at Morrie's arm.

Morrie leaped into the aisle. "You big bastard! You're crazy!" His voice was high-pitched, screeching.

Now everyone in the barracks was watching. Some guys near our bunks backed away, but other guys from the end of the room crowded closer so they could see better.

Carl was sitting on the edge of his bunk a few down, smoke curling around him. He had a bemused expression on his face. I could see him thinking: the little kike can fight.

Gary was standing up. He had a stupid grin on his face like he was watching trained animals perform.

Next to Gary a guy was standing on his bunk, bouncing on it, like he needed to go to the bathroom, yelling, "Let's see if Buttface can fight! Let's see if Buttface can fight!"

"Shiit," said somebody I couldn't see, "he can't fight no how! I b'lieve he a big white fairy."

Schlumberger stood at the end of his bunk, sweat pouring down his forehead and into his eyes, blood oozing from his nostrils, his chest heaving, facing Morrie like a weary bull ready to take it between the eyes.

140

Putting his hands in front of him, he made one more lumbering rush at Morrie.

Morrie, moving away, tripped him.

Schlumberger fell. His head cracked against a metal bunk post.

Morrie didn't waste a second. He kicked Schlumberger once as hard as he could in the ribs. Then he jumped down on Schlumberger and began beating his bloody face with a flurry of punches.

"Oh, Gawd" Schlumberger cried. "Oh, Gawd! I give! I give!"

Morrie rose to his feet. His pudgy face red and triumphant. "Talk about mano a mano!" he said. "There's your mano a mano!"

And, deliberately, he bent over and spit in Schlumberger's face.

"Anyone else?" He looked at the men crowded around. He meant anyone else to spit in Schlumberger's face.

I couldn't believe anyone would. I was wrong.

"Here, Buttface, let this drip off in your own soup!"

"Look this way, Buttface, look my way."

"Hey, you big faggot. Want to suck this?"

Even a couple of the black soldiers joined in.

I felt sick. My throat burned like I was going to throw up, and my body was hot like I had a fever. "Stop it! Knock it off!" I yelled, rising to my feet, and it wasn't even like it was me yelling, but someone inside of me with this hoarse voice breaking out, "Just knock it off!"

Maybe it was because my yelling at them surprised them, maybe they were ashamed, or maybe they'd just had enough of it, but they knocked it off. When it finally stopped, and Schlumberger walked down the aisle between the rows of bunks, he had his head down, but you could see blood and spittle on his face and sweat and tears.

Carl just looked down when Schlumberger went past him. Even Gary's shit-eating smirk was off his face.

Schlumberger kept going out of the barracks. When the screen door banged behind him the sound echoed down the aisle.

Some time after it was all over, Walt came through the barracks, reminding us we had infiltration course under live fire tomorrow morning.

The night before we were to go through the infiltration course, and it finally rained out there. Not just rain. A heavy downpour in a driving wind swept in a pelting staccato across the roof of the barracks. The fierce rain pounded into the hungry clay grounds between the buildings and ran along the tar walks in torrential haste. Then, abruptly as it had burst, the storm died, and it was cool enough to sleep.

But I lay in my bunk wondering what the hell went on between Morrie and Schlumberger. Morrie's taunts didn't make any sense. Maybe it was amazing that Schlumberger had gotten a woman to marry him, but he had, and whether or not he got it every night from his Marie, he was going to be a father. So he was no "big white fairy," nor any other kind of fairy. Morrie's vicious assault on him, and the sickening joining in by the other men, was explainable only by our human capacity for bullying and violence.

It was the middle of the night when Schlumberger came back in. He must have been soaked to the bone.

THE NEXT MORNING OUR SQUAD waited in the muddy ditch before crossing the course. The guys were scattered along the line. Walt, on my left, was supposed to be the final control on our squad going up and over the top. His helmet sat square on his head, like it was centered over his crew cut.

Down the line on my right Gary hunched over, cradling his M-1 in his arms, ready to go. Next to him, Morrie. Gary said something to him, and Morrie's shoulders shook with laughter like a heavy smoker's hack.

Schlumberger was next to Morrie, staring straight ahead, ignoring him. I didn't understand how Schlumberger ended up next to Morrie. Force of habit. A trick of the alphabet.

Farther down, Carl stood rooted in the mud. He looked ornery without a cigarette. Waiting for it to be over.

My boots sunk in mud every time I stood in place for a few moments. I dragged them out with a pop each time, only to sink right under again. I was waiting for it to be over, too.

We were all present and accounted for.

"Gentlemen! A few words of instruction that may save your lives!" The voice of the Ghoul through the bullhorn was practically polite this morning. He had to be glad it was about over too.

"The in-fil-tra-tion course consists of seventy-five yards. Less than a football field in length. But you will encounter wire en-tan-gle-ments, holes, logs, and concealed small charges!

"I guar-an-tee you men none of the concealed charges are of suf-ficient force to kill or severely wound you! Ir-re-gard-less of said charges, you will, at all times, keep your heads down!

"You will be crawling under live fire delivered by thirty caliber machine guns laying a field of fire over the entire course! Those will be real bullets going over your heads, and if you get in their way, they will kill you! How-ever, each said gun is contained by im-movable iron brack-ets set in concrete. If you keep your tail down, you will not be killed! If you do not, you will!

"There-fore, I repeat, you will keep your head and your butt down at all times!

"You will move on your squad leader's command! You will stop immediately on his command, and on my command.

"Sergeant Biller will inspect your weapon when you complete the course. If your piece is not ready to be fired when it is inspected, you have not passed the course.

"You will pass the course. If you do not pass the course the first time, you will take it again until you do pass it. It's mox nix to me how many times you take it, men, mox nix to me! Comprende?"

"Ready on the right? Ready on the left? Com-mence—firing!"

The fusillade of machine gun bullets whined through the air ahead of us. I knew I was safe if I just kept my tail down, but I was nervous.

"Move out!" Walt's voice rang around my steel helmet and right into my ears. I went over the top slowly and carefully.

I got one knee up over the bank. It was really scary at the begin-ning, getting the rest of my body up the muddy side, out of the trench, still staying close to the ground.

It was like taking the first step onto the ladder coming down from a roof. If the roof were only four feet high, you wouldn't even think about it. If there weren't the goddamn machine gun bullets over the course it would be no sweat going up and over.

I managed to bring my weapon and myself, with my helmet still on and my butt intact, over the top. If I took my time, I'd be okay.

The wet clay was slick. My elbows and knees kept sliding back when I crawled. It was a pain holding the M-1 across the vee of my arms, keeping the muzzle out of the mud, so it would look good for Pusgut.

The heavy, unforgiving steel helmet pressed down on the back of my neck. Every time one of the charges went off near me, spraying me with mud, I jerked my head, and the pot went sliding. Once or twice it nearly fell off. It wouldn't be all that much help against the thirty caliber rounds, but I wanted it on anyway. About the time I was starting to think I had it made, my elbows and knees began to ache, and I was still scared, but I was over halfway there.

So was Schlumberger.

It was just a freak that I had Schlumberger in my line of sight when he stood up.

He didn't make it all the way up.

I watched in horror as his pot went flying, and the side of his head, and holes appeared in the back of his fatigues, before he went down.

I wanted to go to him but if I stood up, the bullets would tear into me too.

"Cease fire! Cease fire!" the Ghoul was yelling, and the guns stopped.

I dropped my rifle and sprinted for Schlumberger, bent over while I ran, as though the bullets were whining over us yet, my boots slipping in the slick clay, pitching me forward.

By the time I reached Schlumberger, Morrie and a couple of other guys were already there.

There was a lot of blood flowing from the side of Schlumberger's head and dark circles spreading on his fatigues.

His M-1 was lying beside him. He must have been cradling the stupid thing when he stood up.

I was too late. We were all too late.

OF COURSE, THERE WAS AN INVESTIGATION. The Ghoul and Pusgut said it was an accident; something, maybe one of the explosions on the course, spooked Schlumberger into standing up. Having the Ghoul and Pusgut explain what happened was like asking a guy at the Pentagon to explain what a good deal the Army got when it paid twenty bucks for a screwdriver. Some of the guys backed them up. That was what they wanted to believe.

So did I, but I didn't. At first I blamed Morrie. I asked him what the hell he'd been talking about when he went after Schlumberger so mercilessly the night before we went through the course, but I never really got an answer. When I pressed him about whether he had said something like that again to Schlumberger right before Schlumberger stood up, Morrie said I was full of shit for trying to put all the blame on him.

He had a point. In a terrible way we were all responsible. We transformed Schlumberger into someone almost less than human by the way we treated him. Why? His physical repulsiveness, his clumsiness, his sweating, his stupidity—he couldn't do anything about that shit, God made him that way. His vacuous conversation, his semi-public masturbation, his disloyalty to his wife—all that couldn't be denied. Yet he was one of us, however much we disliked it.

And what no investigation, interviews, statements, or forms could capture was the hard, inescapable fact of Schlumberger's senseless death. Whoever he was, one moment he was alive like us, and the next his helmet was flying, and the side of his head, and blood flowing from his torn-apart skull, and growing circles of blood on his fatigue jacket where the thirty caliber rounds punched through, and he was dead. Leaving behind his pregnant Marie, serving pie.

WE GOT OUR ORDERS.

We were being shipped to Korea.

We had a thirty-day leave, and then Carl, Morrie, Gary, Walt and I—every one of us— was being shipped to Korea.

"Fuckin' A, I just knew it," Carl said. "Fuckin' A."

It was nearly our last night on base when he went over the hill.

He went AWOL without even a "So long, it's been good to know ya." Not a word.

He'd gotten moodier and moodier ever since he'd spilled his guts to me about his "obedient" Elaine. Maybe he'd gone after her.

What with our orders, the guys immediately figured he was running to save his butt from getting shot off in Korea.

"Your old Poppa knew he had a yellow streak!" Morrie gloated when we were sitting around the barracks waiting for our last inspection.

"Yeah," said Gary, "he didn't have much stomach for going to Korea."

Even Walt, when he came out of his private suite at the end of the barracks, put the knock on Carl. "When Schlumberger got mowed down, Carl was shook, real shook. And I never seen anybody worry so much about where he's goin' to be sent.

"This ain't just AWOL, now, this is desertion. In time of war. They'll throw his ass in the stockade."

We all fell quiet for a moment. I remembered in *From Here to Eternity*, where Fatso and his buddies beat the shit out of that soldier in the stockade, and they said he fell off a truck when he died. No stockade could be that bad anymore.

"Let his fucking ass rot there, the gutless wonder," said Morrie. "What if we all fucking said fuck you to our country? The fucking commies'd take over the world."

"You don't need to mock Carl," I said to Morrie. He might be right, but I wouldn't wish the stockade on anyone, especially a friend.

"I bet they ship his ass over to Korea anyway, soon's he finishes his time in the stockade!" Gary opined.

"Unless the war's over by then. It's got to end sometime," said Walt.

"Anyway, I don't think you guys know why Carl did it," I said. I didn't tell them about Carl's Elaine and how I'd bet he'd hauled his confused, sorry self after her, even if it didn't make a whole lot of sense.

Like I wanted to go after Annie.

Part III

20

I flew to New York.

The flight from Richmond was the first time I'd been higher than the big Ferris wheel at the state fair. It got my stomach when I watched the runway drop away from the plane's wheels and felt the plane rise into the night. My ears had just stopped ringing when all the lights of Washington, D.C., dotted the ground below us, like tiny bumpers on a great, dark pinball machine. My dad would have enjoyed seeing this.

In a few minutes the lady sitting next to me pointed out the lights of Philadelphia, and asked me whether I was going overseas. "In thirty days," I was surprised my throat was dry when I said it.

An hour and five minutes after we took off, the plane landed at La Guardia Field. The lady insisted on giving me a ride in the cab she got, and she was going right past Annie's place. So I lucked out. Even so, it took about as long to get to Annie's apartment on West 34th Street as it took to fly to New York. I was going to surprise her. If she wasn't happy to see me, I had no plan whatsoever.

"She's out of town, Jack," the caretaker who answered the door told me, squinting through the haze of his cigar smoke to check me out, making the same mistake about my name the cabby had. The caretaker didn't think well of me, or he expected to be paid; everyone in New York

149

apparently expected to be paid. "Said she'd be back later in the week," was his last word.

I stood in the hallway with the door shut in my face and my duffel bag beside me. With my daydreams about Annie kaput for the moment, as the Ghoul would put it, I needed a hotel room. I wanted to be where the action was—Times Square.

After I pounded on the door for half an hour, the superintendent came out again, and told me it was a couple of long blocks over and nine blocks up. I didn't pay him again, and he slammed the door shut in my face again.

I hoisted my bag up and trudged off. When I got to Times Square, or "Just 29 Steps West of Times Square," as the postcards at the desk put it, I checked into the Strand Hotel. First thing I mailed one of the postcards to Moira, just to let her know I was in New York, and one to my folks too. The Strand was only two bucks a night, and there was a scratched up typewriter for rent by the hour in the lobby.

From my room on the ninth floor, I could see the Paramount's marquee. The movie was *A Girl in Every Port*. The room was mangy. No rug. Weary blue wallpaper. Cracks in the ceiling. A dilapidated bed—I didn't even want to think about it—but I turned down the covers, and it looked clean. A beat-up dresser with a foggy mirror. A rickety wooden chair and coat tree. A sink in the corner with hot and cold running water, but all rusty in the bottom of the bowl. A shower and latrine down the hall needed a GI party.

It didn't matter. In ten minutes I was out where the bright lights were.

Times Square.

I was there. Where New York City counted down to the New Year with the whole world listening. Where during World War Two, skinny 4-F Frank Sinatra sent the bobby-soxers jumping and screaming and swooning at the Paramount Theater. Where at the end of the war a sailor kissed a nurse and in that moment they were immortalized by *Life* magazine. I bet there wouldn't even be any big celebration at the end of the

Korean War, if it ever ended. Everyone just ignored this war. It was so different from World War II that way, when the war was all we thought about.

I followed the flashing lights of a huge sign to "Lou Walter's World Famous Latin Quarter" and went in. I was seated with some other guy across a table that barely had room for our drinks. We each did our best to pretend we were the only one at the table, which was difficult with our knees practically touching. A band blared away while fifty beautiful girls threw high their long legs in black fishnet stockings, and I nursed my beer and wondered who got to go home with them. A waiter in a red jacket, like "Johnnie" who "Calls for Phil-ip Mor-ris!" kept circling, trying to get me to buy another beer, which apparently was brewed with gold. I left.

There was no way I was going to sleep. I walked a mile up and down Broadway, the Great White Way. It was nearly four in the morning, and the sidewalks were crowded. The people hustled along, jabbering at each other. One big guy, wearing a heavy coat, yelling "Praise be! Praise be!" over and over into thin air, nearly knocked me over and didn't even pause to see what damage he'd done. Finally I stopped for a beer at Gough's Bar, a couple of doors down from the Strand. The place was nothing special. The bar was worn smooth. Stools tottered under the early morning drinkers. But a bottle of Bud didn't cost a day's pay.

THE NEXT DAY, NO ANNIE. I left the number of the Strand with the super, but I worried about him giving it to her.

I took the subway down to the Village, where I fell in love with a girl from NYU who was working behind the bar at San Remo, and rode back all the way up to Columbus Circle, where I fell in love again, this time with the statue of Alma Mater. With her book open on her lap, she was big-breasted and noble and serene, despite the pigeon poop all over her. I wondered if I could use my high school transcript and register at Columbia as a freshman, ignore I ever went to the University of Minnesota. It was unlikely, but that night I wrote Moira and asked her to see if she could get my transcript and send it to me, in case.

Meanwhile, Annie hadn't shown up to invite me to move in with her and write the Great American Novel, but that night, sitting in the lobby of the Hotel Strand, watching the late night traffic of drunks and whores and their customers, I started to write. The rickety table with the typewriter bolted to it stood in a corner of the Strand lobby, under a dim yellow bulb hardly bright enough to cast a shadow. You got an hour's worth of the typewriter for a quarter, supplying your own paper, naturally. I was no big deal to any of the people who drifted in and out while I sat there in front of the typewriter; apparently they didn't appreciate how different I was from the usual kid who came to New York to be a writer.

I tried not to pay attention to anyone else either. In fact, when I was actually writing, my typing was so bad that it was hard to think of the sentence I was trying to squeeze out of my brain, at the same time I was searching for the S key or the R key or the comma. When I did stop and try to think, I could hear every conversation in the entire hotel—whether Myron, the night clerk would be in to work, if the new guy on the fourth floor was on the loose from Bellevue, when the toilet on eight would be unplugged—and everything sounded more interesting than my Great American Novel.

Of course it wasn't the Great American Novel. I was trying to write down what happened to Schlumberger. More than anything else, I hoped I might be able to exorcise his ghost. I vaguely planned to start with his rising up to his death, like a primordial beast from the slime, and flashback to why it happened. How he died. And, unless I followed Carl's lead over the hill, how I could die. I was going where the same goddamn thing could happen to me. Even if I didn't stand up. Even if I kept my steel pot on and burrowed into a hole in the ground like an animal. Worse than an animal because I was a man. But even thought itself would be nothing to me. I would feel nothing but fear, nothing but my body giving way to terror. Yet, if I died, wasn't I then nothing?

What was worth that? Not having to live with myself as a coward? Not shaming my father? Not doing the right thing for my country and freedom in Korea? Did my truth change because of Schlumberger's death?

"LUCKY TIMING, KELLY," the deskman other than Myron said when I came down the next morning as he handed me the desk phone, at the same time he gave me a pink slip with "Annie LO 4-8675," smudged on it in pencil. "Make it short," he said. "This is the house phone."

"Hello," I said, grabbing the phone.

"Hello, Tom." It was Moira. "I got your postcard, Tom. Did you get my letter yet?"

"No. What's going on? Is there something the matter with my mom or dad?"

"No. But I've been frantic trying to reach you. You have to come home. You just have to."

I looked down at the pink slip with Annie's number in my hand. "Why? What's going on?"

"I've made a terrible mistake. You'll have to read my letter."

"Has something happened to you?"

"You'll have to read the letter . . ."

"Clear the line, Kelly. I told you this is the house phone," the deskman's hand reached for the phone. It'd been a long time since he'd cleaned those fingernails.

"I have to go."

"Promise me first."

"I'll read it. I always do." With Moira it could be anything from someone dying to a hangnail, but it sounded more like the hangnail. I gave the guy back his precious phone.

I TRIED ANNIE FROM THE PAY PHONE in the lobby, leaning into the wall for privacy.

"Annie Jones please?"

"One moment," the girl said, and the line hummed.

"Hello, Annie Jones here."

"Hello, Annie Jones."

"Tom!" she sounded glad to see me. "You're here!" Her soft Southern voice turned here into he-ah. "I'm so sorry I wasn't home. We're doing a trade show next week, and I've been meeting with our reps from the plant in New Hampshire.

"God, it's good to hear you. Can you see me today?" Christ, I sounded like some "rep."

"I'd like to, Tom, but I'm just swamped."

"Sure. I know how it goes with a new job."

"Don't be that way."

"See, the thing is, I've only got thirty days, and they're already going fast. I have to head to the coast to ship out to Korea. The West Coast," I clarified.

There was a long pause. "Can you come for breakfast tomorrow at my place at eight? It'll have to be quick."

"Can I? That's why I'm here, Annie. To see you."

"Don't get the wrong idea. I have to be in the office by nine." I could hear someone in the background call her name.

"See you," she said, hanging up.

I rode the slow elevator to the ninth floor and went down the dimly lit hall with its peeling battleship gray paint to my room. I lit up a cigarette and lay back on the bed. It was so good to hear Annie's voice.

I DIDN'T EVEN WANT TO OPEN Moira's airmail special delivery mystery letter when it arrived. I knocked the ashes off my cigarette into the empty wastebasket beside the bed. Finally I opened the letter:

Tuesday, September 9, 1952
Dear Tom,
I have been frantic to reach you, but I didn't know where to send you this letter until I got your postcard. And you see I have written two others and destroyed them. This is the inevitable letter. When I began writing to you I thought: One day there will be a letter, a special letter which will either say "I must stop writing now, because I know I can never love you" or "I write this now because I know I love only you." This is that letter.

154

When you left I thought I loved Will Lindeman. I thought he could sit at a table at the Country Club with me and grin and pump a hand and make them love him. And we could have gaiety and laughter and parties. But there must be something more. You, Tom, are the only one who has ever understood the motivations for my complex actions; you comprehend this terrible schizophrenia, this driving ambition, the frightful loneliness.

I need you, Tom. I need the love which I have so ill-treated. I want to run, Tom, until I fall down exhausted. I want to know everything, see everything, do everything. I want Europe, and Asia, and Beekman Place, fifty-four-dollar gold shoes, and dirty bars, sex and misery, and quiet joy. But I do not want to run alone. I will wait for you, however long that must be. I will go anywhere with you. Just tell me you will take my hand and run with me.

I'm asking a lot of you. I'm asking you to swallow that mighty pride of yours, and come back to me before you leave for overseas. It's my one desperate plea. When you get out of the army you can write, or practice law, or walk a tight rope, and I'll love you to the depths if you'll just keep running, if you'll laugh and take my hand, and talk to me about metaphysics and Freud and writing.

I'm asking more of you than you know. I'm asking you not only to come back to a girl who's wild and scared and confused. But to a girl who has been dirty and unfaithful to you. I've sinned, Tom. I've loved Will like an animal. I loved him as a man would love—without thought of marriage, or vows, or morality. I could conceal it from you; but this is my attempt at honesty. I have told God and the man in the black box, and now I tell you—I'm sorry. It is wrong and I shall never forgive myself.

I do not know if you can forgive me, but you must remember I have forgiven you for the same thing. And there is no double standard; we are both human beings, we both loved for the same purpose, we both repented. But if you but stretch out your hand to me, I will grasp it tightly and we will run, you and I, across the world, together.

I love you, Tom.

Moira

It took her long enough to get to it, to the goddamn pain. Moira seemed to think the main point of her letter was she didn't love Will and she did love me. But what I couldn't get out of my mind was the thought of her going all the way with Will. Like an animal.

I remembered all the times I'd practically died I'd wanted Moira so much. The way we'd kissed until our mouths and tongues ached. How she'd put her pink nipples swollen and tender in my mouth and whimper when I touched her and kept on till she shuddered and came. How could she have wanted Will more than she wanted me? Why had she done it with him and not me?

I lay quietly for a while, not thinking at all, feeling the pain. When my contracted stomach began to hurt, I rolled over on my side and drew my knees under my chin. I closed my eyes but I wasn't sleepy. We should have done it. Jesus we should have done it.

21

The next morning, there was a lady selling roses right on Times Square. A few minutes after eight I was at Annie's door, clean, with roses, and light-headed with anticipation.

"Come in!"

Annie hugged me. She stood on tiptoe, and her cheek brushed mine. She felt tiny and soft in my arms. She drew back but left her hands behind my head and her body touching mine, and I was able to look at her.

We stood that way for a moment. She was in her stocking feet. Otherwise she was dressed for work with that combination of business-like competence and softness that put me a little off balance in dealing with her. I tried to take her in all at once: her dark-blue skirt gently clung to her; her pearl silk blouse had an open collar; I'd forgotten the curve of her neck—when I followed it to her face.

"Do I pass inspection, sir?" Her faint Southern drawl seemed to somehow curl around "inspection."

"You sure do." I bent toward her.

"Good!" She saw the bedraggled roses. "For me. How nice."

"They're pretty sorry looking. They seem to have gotten squashed in transit."

"It's the thought that counts!" She reached for them, brushing my cheek with hers again. She took a crystal vase from the cupboard and put the roses in water. "And you're sweet."

It was a small apartment, a tiny kitchenette and closet-sized bathroom, small living room and bedroom, all simply furnished, in woods of different tones. A big red couch with a door-sized coffee table in front of it strewn with magazines—*Harpers, Atlantic Monthly*, and the *Sunday Times Book Review* section. A couple of canvas chairs. A brick and board bookcase. A small table with a Smith-Corona she must have used to write me the letter. Prints, somber and violent, scattered on the walls, but sunshine pouring through her windows.

"Coffee's ready!" she gestured toward a chair at the tiny kitchen table. She poured expertly, with a flick of her slender wrist. Fluffy eggs and cheese with bits of bacon so it didn't seem like she was too much into being a Jew.

"So you're not very hungry?"

I rattled on and on about the breakfast like I was a food critic. It was like going out on a first date and getting into describing the last movie you saw, frame by frame, because you're afraid if you shut up you won't be able to think of another thing to say all night.

She was listening and laughing, but she was already looking at her watch.

I stopped. Here I was, with her for not even an hour, and I was boring her.

"Don't look that way. It's not you. My new boss, Margaret, is back in town, and she's such a bitch." Annie paused. "An opportunist. A liar. An egotist supreme. In other words, I don't like her," she smiled. "And I've got to be in early today after all."

She pushed her silk sleeves up over her small wrists and began gathering the dishes. I hardly even noticed the thin scars any more.

"Let me at least do that." I began scraping them and running hot water over them, while she disappeared into the bedroom. She emerged in shoes and with a big leather purse like a briefcase. "How about tonight?" I asked.

She frowned. "I'm invited to see the Balinese dancers tonight. If I don't have to work."

"You wouldn't want to miss the Balinese dancers. They might not be back in town for a long time. At this rate, I won't be seeing much of you in the few days I have either."

Her dark eyes studied me, tiny wrinkles appearing in her forehead. "Walk me to the subway."

When we hit the sidewalk, she moved right along, her bag swinging at her side; she slipped her other arm through mine and held my hand. At the subway entrance, she squeezed my hand to dismiss me before plunging down the hole like Alice off to Wonderland, her case bouncing off her thigh. She went down a couple of stairs full tilt.

She turned around.

"I'll tell my friend I'm working. Come by around seven. I'll make us a salad, and we'll have time to visit," she smiled.

"Great! That's great!"

I walked for blocks, aimlessly, in the crisp morning before I went back to the Strand.

I LAY ON MY BED IN MY ROOM and contemplated Moira's goddamn "inevitable" letter,

Inevitable at the moment.

When I'd left she "thought" she loved Will now she "knows" she loves "only" me. So how is it she knows that now? Will is great at getting along at the Country Club, as I wasn't and never would be, but there must be "something more," and that means she loves me? Maybe because she thinks there's a better chance that I'll make enough money to pay the dues to the damn club?

But no, it's because I am the only one who has understood the "motivations" for her "complex actions" and "comprehend" her "terrible schizophrenia," "driving ambition" and "frightful loneliness" and whatever other sophomoric shit is on her mind at the moment. Well, if "schizophrenia" meant making out because she wanted to but feeling guilty if she did, I'd had a lot of experience understanding that. I'd "understood" her "schizophrenia" too damn well.

Will had her figured right in the first place. She had screwed Will. Like an animal. All the rest of the total bullshit in her letter was so I'd "understand" that and forgive her that. She wanted me to just "swallow my pride" and come back to her. Well, I couldn't swallow what she did with Will. Enough, just fucking enough of her.

Annie was twice the person Moira was and just as damn beautiful. If there was anyone I wanted to stretch out my hand to, it was Annie.

I wrote Moira and told her where things stood.

ANNIE DIDN'T GET HOME TILL EIGHT THAT NIGHT. I paced up and down the block, watching for her. She arrived, hurrying up the street, still lugging her briefcase, and taking my arm again.

"Hi. I'm sorry. I had to do Margaret's work for tomorrow. The life of the working girl at the bottom of the heap. But I'm a free woman tomorrow! If you'd like, I'll show you around New York."

"If I'd like . . ."

"That's what I said," she laughed. "The best way is take a tour. That's the way I first saw New York, Tom, and I've never forgotten it. They leave right from Times Square every hour. At least they used to. That's settled. Come on up and let's eat."

In Annie's place I sipped wine and floated around on cloud nine while she tossed a salad and chattered away about what a bitch Margaret was, telling me a long, involved story about how Margaret had promoted a show that took her to Paris to present the mayor with a bouquet of flowers from the forty-eight states.

"Sit!" Annie commanded, handing me the big silver bowl brimming with delicate green lettuce, darker spinach, red and white radishes, slices of cucumbers and carrots, all crisp with tiny droplets of water sparkling in the soft light. Next to it she put a long loaf of French bread with a golden-brown crust. She filled two small glasses with a light red wine.

160

The wine was fragrant when I sipped it, carefully not gulping it, and it gently warmed me. Beneath its crust the bread was soft and warm. "Did anybody ever tell you, you make a great dinner?"

"Thank you, sir, the shy young maiden curtsied," Annie said, her fork poised in midair over her salad. "But she's a terrific promotion woman. And I can learn a lot—if I can stick it out!"

We moved into the living room for coffee.

"It's too bad Margaret's such a bitch," I said. Taking a chance, I added, "I'd think you might like working for a woman." I didn't say instead of how you got screwed by your last boss.

She stared at me. "You mean after last time? Is this what you're saying? My cousin Morrie told you all about me, did he?"

"I guess so. Not really." My cheeks grew red, as I remembered how it was Morrie's vague stories that made me so eager to meet Annie in the first place, and I thought about her wrists again. "I'd like to know all about you, and I know so little, that's all."

She was silent for a moment. I'd crossed a line she wasn't ready for yet.

"Sometimes Morrie's a real pisher," she said. "You know the word?"

"No," but it wasn't good.

"Let's just say it means what it sounds like, and he's still wet behind the ears, Tom." She might as well have told me I was too.

"I'm sorry I brought it up. I have no business saying something like that to you."

"No, you don't. It's time we call it a night."

"I'm sorry, Annie. We're still on for tomorrow?"

"Yes," she said, finally.

IN THE MORNING ANNIE WAS A GLOWING, petite goddess, in a bright yellow dress. Her dark hair was looser than I'd seen it before and smelled like lilacs, like she'd just shampooed it. I wanted to grab her, or at least touch her. She slipped her arm through mine, and I managed to brush against her now and then as we walked down the street.

Tours of the city left right from Times Square, it turned out, every half hour: Downtown Manhattan, the Statue of Liberty and the Financial District; Chinatown, Greenwich Village, and the Bowery; Uptown, the United Nations, the Fifth Avenue residential area, and Harlem. We took the Grand Tour: all of New York for five and a half bucks each, and we saw it all.

A noiseless elevator swished us up a thousand feet in sixty seconds to the top of the Empire State Building, where the tour guide informed us we were looking at "an area in which 15,000,000 people, one out of every ten Americans, live and work!"

We stood on the steps of the U.S. Courts Building where Senator Kefauver's committee had investigated organized crime before the entire country on television.

"My favorite was Bugsy Siegel's girlfriend, Virginia," said Annie, putting her hand on my arm. "Remember when she told the committee she hoped the 'atom bomb falls on every one of the goddamn bastards.' I liked that."

"So did I." I liked Annie's hand there, but it was a flighty bird and gone.

When we got to the Statue of Liberty we climbed all the way up the torch and caught our breath looking out over the boats and the skyline. Standing there, in the greatest symbol of freedom, in the greatest country in the whole damn world, having Annie so close beside me, all jumbled up inside me, and I choked up. Maybe because right behind all that, shipping out to Korea, the monster I didn't want to let out of the closet, kept knocking on the door, trying to get loose.

We went to Harlem, where ragtag little kids on the steps of rundown tenements stared at us as we walked past, and where Prof had said that even during the "Negro Renaissance" in the twenties, a giant like Langston Hughes was barely able to make a living.

When the tour stopped in the Rainbow Room, "high in the Rockefeller Center," and we looked down on Central Park, I remembered Prof telling me about Bayard Rustin, who had led a protest march

162

against the Korean War from Central Park to Times Square, and taught nonviolent resistance, until the cops busted him for being a homosexual.

The Bowery, "The Street of Forgotten Men!" was next. If you were a drunk and could write like F. Scott Fitzgerald and hang out with the rich, it might be exciting. Not if you were just a drunk your family kicked out on the street.

"Guys shouldn't have to live on the street, Annie. Not in America."

"No, not in America," she agreed.

The Dorothy Day Center had to be somewhere around there, but the guide wasn't familiar with it, nor was Annie.

On Fifth Avenue, the "Home of the Millionaires!" Moira, despite being such a fan of Dorothy Day, would have gone bonkers at Tiffanys, but I didn't need to worry about that anymore.

Still, "A piece of me wants to be able to afford that stuff," I confessed.

"Wouldn't we all," said Annie.

When the tour ended, it turned out she had to go to the office that night. So much for her being a free woman today. I'd been so swept away seeing the big city I hadn't noticed she looked tired. She left me with a hurried brush on the cheek, and a "Later."

THE NEXT DAY ANNIE WAS BUSY, and I lunched at the White Castle in midtown, where I turned into an immediate slider junkie. The flat square burgers had the consistency of sawdust, sandwiched between two chewy little buns like Wonder Bread leftovers, but their addicting semisweet taste made you want another as soon as you'd finished one. My dealer, Andy, an out of work actor who wore his dipshit cardboard White Castle cap like an overseas cap, told me there were White Castles scattered all over town.

With Annie tied up again the next day, I made a whirlwind tour of Castles. Down in the Village for breakfast. Intimate, only a few stools. The other customers were NYU students and free-lance intellectuals.

Great conversation. Up in Queens, a hellhole of Western civilization, where the help worked at killing speed, amidst noise and tumult, for lunch. Back at midtown for dinner, I helped Andy try to break up a fight between Greek sailors and some guys whose girls either misunderstood or understood the Greeks.

"They should never, ever give the goddamn Greeks shore leave," Andy said, but I had a job for life if I wanted it, starting at the new minimum wage of seventy-five cents an hour.

Later that night when she was finally free, I took Annie to Birdland to listen to Sarah Vaughan, the Divine Lady, sing "Tenderly," caressing every note, and still later we took the Staten Island Ferry and looked at the New York skyline from out on the water while I told her all about the New York of the White Castle. She laughed, so softly, I could have listened to it all night, but she wouldn't let me.

The next couple of days, whenever she could sneak away, we did things on the cheap, walking in Central Park, around the Rockefeller Center, checking out dead Egyptians in the Metropolitan Museum of Art. Annie tutored me around town, and we just hung out talking.

A few times Annie kissed me, light, fleeting kisses, sometimes when I wasn't even expecting it, but she shied away if I pressed her. It got me on edge, trying to figure out what would trigger one of her glancing kisses, wondering if we'd get past this grade-school love while my time with her was rocketing by and I was getting more and more frustrated. But mostly we talked.

One night back at Annie's, after we had gone through a New City Public Library exhibit about immigrants in New York City day, Annie told me about her grandmother, who had hidden in a loft in Kiev, trembling before a pogrom, then walked across the Armenian border all by herself, bundling her feet in rags when her shoes wore out. She'd met Annie's grandfather in a shelter, and they came to Richmond where Annie's grandfather had eventually done very well, in the carpet business.

Annie remembered her grandmother stocking her closets with shoes and shoes and shoes. That summer Annie's mother and father took her to

Europe, and at Auschwitz she saw a photograph of a huge pile of shoes taken from the Jews murdered by the Nazis, and she started crying, and it took her a long time to stop. She said it made her so aware of what it was to be a Jew, even though she said she didn't believe in any religion anymore. The very idea of God made her angry, and she was really angry at Christianity.

"You should go to Dachau," she said, her eyes fixed right on me. "The death camp is outside a quiet country town. Such lovely, charming countryside. You think the good churchgoing people didn't know when 200,000 Jews were transported there? The priests didn't know? They didn't smell the stink of burning Jews?" Her voice rose.

"I can't believe the people knew. It's not like Jews are so different or anything."

"Jews? Me, Tom, me! So how many Jews did you know in Fargo?"

"There are lots of Jews in Fargo." But I had a hard time trying to think of any I knew.

"Have you ever been to synagogue?"

"No, I've never been to a synagogue. I've never gone to a Lutheran church either. The Church says I might "give scandal," someone might think I believe in the heretics instead of the one, true, holy, and apostolic Catholic Church."

"Do you really believe that, Tom?"

"Not really, but I personally think the Jews make more sense than the Lutherans."

She paused, a puzzled look on her face. "The Jews make more sense than the Lutherans?"`

"Sure," I was happy to get off on a detour. "The Lutherans buy all the hard stuff, like there is a God, and Christ is God, but fudge on the junk about the pope. And all because Luther was a constipated monomaniac.

"Or take the Anglicans," I said, "A whole church because King Henry couldn't keep his pecker in his pants."

She shook her head but she laughed. "I'm talking to you about the death camps, and you give me Luther's constipation! And King Henry's pecker?"

But then she got serious again. "And I suppose you have no idea how Luther felt about the Jews? We're the Christ-killers. "

"Annie, I had a friend in basic—you met the guy, Carl Bergstrom—his Jewish girlfriend's parents stopped her from marrying him because he's Lutheran."

"So, what do you think about me being a Jew, Tom? Really?"

"Annie, if you think I think shit like that, you're crazy. I could care less if you're a Jew."

"Don't give me this 'shit like that.' What has your Catholic Church taught you about the Jews?"

"The Church teaches us to love everybody." But when I was a little kid, seeing the Good Friday play, the Jews had tried Christ. Spat upon Him. Struck Him. Reviled Him. At the big climax, as there was thunder and lightning, via cymbals and flashing lights, the curtain tore, and Christ had died in agony, we knew who the bad guys were.

"Do you think 'love everybody' is enough? To make up for all the pain and death your Church has caused?" Her voice quavered. "Does it even make sense there's a God, when such things go on?"

"No. It's not enough. I don't know about God," I added.

"For God's sake!" her eyes flashed. "Why are we fighting about this? Is this what you're going to remember in Korea? Am I going to think of you in my old age as that kid I argued about God with?"

She'd kicked me right in the balls when I hadn't done a damn thing.

"I'm not a kid!" I was pissed off now. "If you'd give us a chance, you'd see."

A strand of her dark hair fell down on her forehead before she pushed it aside, and said, totally unaccountably, "We're not all bitches, you know, whatever your wife was!"

Which had absolutely nothing to do with anything we'd been talking about. Not to mention I'd totally put out of my mind the cockamamie story I'd told Annie back in Richmond about my supposed wife and divorce.

"I don't think you're a bitch, Annie. I'm crazy about you, you know that"

"I'm sorry," she said. There were tears in her eyes. "But I just don't know if I'm ready to take on anyone that way, Tom. And you're going to be gone so soon. And I'll just be a girl you left behind."

"Annie, that's the . . ."

"It's late and I'm tired. Good night, Tom."

I stood up. "Tomorrow?"

"All right. Yes," she answered pushing me toward the door, her slender arms braced straight against my shoulders, backing me up. Then, as I went out the door she reached up and kissed me full on the mouth before she pushed me all the way out, closing the door behind me.

I caught the subway, and I rode all way to the end of the line and back. She drove me crazy. I'd take what she gave me, but not much longer. Every day we danced a little closer, and my time to leave for the war came a day nearer.

When I wasn't with Annie, I was banging away on the typewriter in the lobby down at the Strand. When she asked if I'd feel okay showing her what I was working on, I told her it didn't seem ready. But I brought it along.

"The man in the awful Hawaiian shirt," Annie said, when she read it.

"He committed suicide. Don't you think that's adequate atonement for bad taste?"

She drew back from me, as if I raised my hand to strike her. "Yes," she said, very quietly.

"I'm sorry. That was an asshole thing to say."

"Yes. It was."

She looked down at the pages. "There's promise in the story." She'd finished her sentence, but she hadn't.

"But . . ." I prompted. "I want to know what you think about the story, good and bad."

She hesitated. "So, you're trying to write it the way you think Hemingway might have?"

"I know I'm not Hemingway."

"'Truly, he said.'" She looked at me and reached across the pages between us on the couch and touched my hand. "And I don't think you should try to be. I'd like it better if you wrote it more like yourself. I want to know what you feel. Why are you writing the story?"

"I want to understand why Schlumberger died, and what part I had in it."

"Those are good reasons," she said, "but forgive me if I say you seem a lot more concerned about the effect of his death on you than you are about him. And if you make him so grotesque that he isn't a person like the rest of us, your reader won't care about him either.

"Tom, maybe you feel you contributed in some way that isn't clear to me to his death. Perhaps you ought to go back further in time to see how you came to feel that. But he committed suicide; he had that responsibility, not you. Believe me, I know what I'm speaking of." I could feel her draw into herself.

"Annie, I believe you, but how can I know you if you shut me out of the most important parts of yourself."

She looked down at the narrow watch on her small wrist. "I have to go. I'm sorry. We can talk more tomorrow."

"Can we have breakfast?" I asked.

She hesitated, not meeting my eyes.

"I've only got a couple of days left before I have to leave." I said it to get to her, but my time was about run out.

"I have an early meeting. You can come over tomorrow night, if you'd like." For a minute she contemplated what seemed like a bigger question than breakfast. At least she was looking at me. "Look, I know how much you want to finish what you're working on. If you get tired of that awful lobby of that awful hotel tomorrow, you can use my typewriter. I'll tell the super it's okay to let you in."

"How about Thomas Wolfe? Do you like Thomas Wolfe?"

"Out!" she said, but she smiled.

THE NEXT MORNING I COULDN'T WRITE. I could go over to Annie's and not write there, but that didn't seem right. Whatever I did next, I at least wanted to do it only if I thought it was right. That was one of the things my dad always said—be true to yourself—quoting Emerson or somebody like that. And it was one of the things Hemingway's stories showed you. Like one in the newest *Life* magazine, *The Old Man and the Sea*, about an old man teaching a young boy about fishing. You couldn't write better than that. But I was no Hemingway. And I wasn't even writing anything. Not jackshit. Period. I was just sitting, brooding in the lobby, when another letter from Moira arrived at the desk.

Sunday
September 23, 1952
Dear Thomas Stephen,

It is capital, dear Thomas, simply capital. Each letter becomes richer in conflict, pathos, tender emotion. Not only has this become a psychological (Oedipus complex, Jungian analyst) and economic (damned job/no time for love) struggle, but it has merged into a full-fledged religious conflict. However, I say to you "Convention be damned. Live your life to the hilt." What does it matter if your Annie Jones is twice your age?

What will bourgeois society say? Probably no more than you are a fugitive from Eugene O'Neill and who are you, young genius, to let the masses dictate your life? When one lives on the periphery, one ignores the judgments of the "center." The "center," to me, is conventional prosaic society—its mores, opinions, pattern of culture; the periphery, those who rebel against this, who draw away and build an aberrant society of their own. Okay?

Seriously, Thomas, I will even grant you a severe infatuation, but I cannot understand how a woman thirty??? could want to lead on a comparative boy such as you are. Have you told her how old you are? I should think the woman would have a queasy feeling at going out with you; walking arm in arm with you down Broadway; that is very "uncasual" in my circle. Such things may be done in New York, but I doubt if very frequently, and if they are, there is a nasty name for it.

I know you are serious. But I am afraid you will make a terrible mistake. It is a complete absurdity to think yourself in love with a woman twice your age. Perhaps you will say she is free of convention and ignores a little difference like age, but she must, not wishing to deride your erudition, sense some basic inequality between you. Why, good God, she'll be passing through menopause; she'll be incapable of child bearing. And you'll be a young man. Perhaps now you are thinking our having children would be too prosaic, detract from writing novels, but you will want children. Having children is an essential human function, not the sole prerogative of those in the "center."

I hate it that you ran away to the Army. But to think about staying in New York, hiding, it's just keeping it up. Yes, I deliberately haven't sent your transcript. It has passed through the proper channels and is now in the hands of your doting parents. Before you leave for overseas, please come home and see me. That's all I can say.

Please, come home.

Your Moira

P.S. Your "*pauvre mere*" will be white by the time you terminate this sojourn. (The emotional approach.) Please come home!

I was so angry my stomach churned as I read the letter. Moira knew right where to put the knife, attacking not only me but Annie. Math was never Moira's strong point; mean was, at least in this missive. I'd told her Annie was around thirty, which made her about ten years older than me, not "twice" my age, and it wasn't like she was in graduate school and I was in grade school or something. No reason for anyone to call Annie or me any nasty name, for walking arm in arm, or doing anything else together.

And Moira had all but told my parents I was thinking about staying here and going to school in New York. Her and her fancy French about my mother. My mother would be worried sick. I almost shredded the letter when I got to that P.S. And what would my dad think? The only way I could go to school in New York now would mean going AWOL. Whatever he thought about my being in the army, he would be angry, and heartsick, if I did that.

As angry as Moira's letter made me, it made me face up to the consequences of the half-formed options in my mind. It was time to think things out in some ordered sense. I took out a piece of paper and pencil and made two columns: Go Home and Stay, and started trying to list the pros and cons of each:

Go Home	Stay
Moira???	Annie
Family	Independence
Friends	Realization
Loneliness, hurt, normality	Loneliness, hurt, periphery

Shit, this was useless. I wasn't ready to decide the rest of my life and I didn't have enough time left to make it a real choice even for the rest of my leave. Unless I went over the hill, it didn't make much difference one way or the other. That was why I'd even asked Moira to send me a copy of my transcript. I knew the whole idea was crazy. I'd never do it. Now my mother and father would be wondering what the hell the transcript was all about. Damn Moira.

I might as well add it.

I added a third heading AWOL. I looked at it on the paper. It scared me just sitting there. That I'd even written it. I didn't put anything down under it.

I lay on the bed, smoking a lot of cigarettes, waiting for it to be night, so I could go see Annie. Tonight, I was going to hash things out with her.

"ALL RIGHT. YOU NEED TO KNOW about me so badly? I'll tell you."

I didn't say anything for fear it would be the wrong thing.

We were sitting on the couch for coffee, and she had her shoes off and her feet curled underneath her, but she hovered a moment before she leaned forward and went ahead.

"God, how far back do I have to go? In school, don't ask me when, I had a tough time even getting into the program for a business major. At the University of Virginia, nice girls were supposed to take Home Ec or Education. But New York was always my dream. When I finished school, I went job-hunting with a friend—you should pardon the expression—a goy. You know the word?"

"Sure. Some of my best friends are goys."

"Touché, Tom, and from Fargo, too."

Annie paused momentarily, then went on as though determined to get through a recital piece. "Anyway, I'd nailed better grades than my friend and was in every activity you could think of. But in the same offices my friend the goy would be invited in for an interview, I'd be sent a canned letter: 'We're pleased to know that you're interested in our organization, nothing open right now, blah, blah, and blah,' and mean-while." She paused. "Because I was Jewish, all right?"

I raised my hand palm out; I wasn't arguing.

"I thought my father's friends would help. They were his friends and they were Jews. Well, they were anxious to take me to lunch and give me loads of advice. Even a job. If I got my typing skills up.

"Finally I decided to go by Annie Jones instead of Annie Abrams." She shot a quick look at me, searching for disapproval. "Things were hard enough. It was like taking a stage name. My father wouldn't speak to me for a long time," she said softly. "And for a long time Annie Jones didn't have any more success than Annie Abrams had. Finally I was hired by an ad agency as an "administrative assistant," which meant glorified secretary to an account manager. But once they let me in, I made myself a real administrative assistant, all right? I worked my tail off. Every raise I got, I earned double, believe me."

"I believe you." I wondered if she was going to tell me about her affair.

"When my boss had a coronary and took early retirement, I thought I was going to get my big break. But the agency went outside, brought in a new man to head the accounts I should have had. I had been so sure I was going to get it, I'd even written the letter to my father. Not that I mailed it.

"Still, there was a silver lining. The new man knew I should have had his job. He respected me, relied on me. I was his indispens-able right-hand girl. And the more closely we worked together, the more attracted to him I was. It was only a matter of time before we became lovers."

The words came out slowly, then more rapidly, as if she had to rush to the end of this, or she wouldn't be able to finish. "There was only one problem: he was married. At first I didn't know, I didn't want to know, I wasn't sure. Then I couldn't deny it. I couldn't stop anyway."

I was a real asshole for pushing her to open all this up, but I wanted to hear it.

"So—one day his wife shows up at the office. Yelling and scream-ing at me: tramp, slut, whore. I find out how indispensable I am. I have my desk cleared by the end of the day.

"My friend, my lover, didn't help me find a new job. Even call me. I had disappeared. I had no salary coming in. My unemployment insur-ance wasn't enough to carry my apartment, and my savings ran out, and it was the holiday season, no less.

"So, I swallowed all the pills I had in the bathroom cabinet. But I had no confidence in them. I started the water running in the bathtub and lay there and slit my wrists that you're always staring at, like I was in a bad Joan Crawford movie." She said it like "I finished shopping."

"The building superintendent found me in the overflowing tub. I'd been bitching about how cold the place was the day before. Otherwise, I might not be here now. Or maybe I would. I botched it all up anyway. There's a moral in there among the clichés maybe?"

It was hard to listen to what Annie was saying. I wanted to hear only the music of her voice and ignore the harsh dissonance of the words. No, not ignore them, hear numbly, like I was asleep and this was a dream. I wanted her to be done with this and never have to talk about it again.

"At the hospital they pumped me out. But I'd messed up my insides pretty good, and left a series of gastric ulcers I had to nurse for a long time.

"I stayed out of the hospital for about a month. Then a bad ulcer attack put me back in the hospital for another week. Got the money from my mother, hating it.

"Incidentally, the hospital is where I was when I got word of my father's death. After that, I went home to heal. And the weeks turned into months.

"That's where things were when you met me."

She was quiet then, exhausted, but looked straight at me.

I felt so awkward that I looked away. When I looked back at her, she was crying, big tears rolling down the sides of her cheeks, and her lit-tle body shaking. I put my arms in a ring around her, barely touching her.

She held her breath for a second, then she leaned against me and let me hold her. After a while she nestled to me, her head against my cheek, the faint, lingering shampoo smell of her hair tightening my breath. I held her, feeling her breathe, feeling the tension easing out of her. After a long time I bent down and kissed her eyelids, first one then the other. She turned up to me, and I brushed her lips with mine. When I felt her respond, I kissed her full on the mouth, but she shook her head and said, "No. Please." She wouldn't let me do more than hold her. But she wanted me to do that.

23

In the morning, I took out my columns of pros and cons. I lay on the bed in my room staring at them, pondering what to do: whether to accept Annie's offer to use her place to write, my wishes aside that seemed the extent of her offer, and more importantly whether to head for home when it came down to it. The thing was, it was about down to it. In another few days my leave would be over, and I'd be AWOL unless I got my ass out to Camp Stoneman in California to take off for Korea.

"Hey, Kelly! You there?" It was Myron, the kid from the desk knocking on my door. What the hell was he doing here now?

I shook myself awake. "Yeah. What's up?"

"Telephone. It's long distance. Don't take all day, your old man said!"

I scrambled to my feet and charged out the door in my stocking feet. "Thanks Myron!" I headed down the stairwell.

"Aren't ya gonna wait for the . . ."

"I'll walk!" Jesus, there had to be something wrong at home or my dad would never call. It wasn't a holiday or anything. I ran down the stairs in my stocking feet and didn't stop for nine flights, until I skidded to a stop across the linoleum in the lobby to the phone.

"Dad?"

"Tom?" he yelled at me, like I might be somebody else.

"Yeah, Dad. It's me. What's wrong?"

"I thought it was you."

"Yeah. It's me. What's wrong?"

"Nothing," he yelled, like I couldn't hear him. He paused, "How's the weather there, son?"

"The weather's fine, Dad. If nothing's wrong, why are you calling long distance?"

Dad cleared his throat, which meant he was going to say what was on his mind that he didn't want to. "Are you coming home before you go overseas?"

His voice sounded old and tired, even yelling, and I remembered how worn he and my mother had both looked when we sat at the kitchen table the night before I left for basic training and our rushed good-byes at the train station the next morning and the stubble of my dad's unshaven whiskers against my face and my mother's half-nelson as I had to break free and board. Now, talking to my dad, I missed them both.

"You don't have to yell, Dad. It's a good connection."

"Are you coming home?"

"Listen, this must be costing you a fortune, Dad. Is everyone okay?"

"Your mother's worried sick."

He waited a second but I didn't know what to say. "I'm fine, Dad."

"I'm worried too, son. Moira was here about your transcript." He waited again. There was a long silence.

"Yeah, well, I was just checking out Columbia, Dad. I like it here." I tried to think of something else to fill the silence. "You would too."

"Your mother and I don't want you to do something that will ruin your whole life. We wish more than anything you didn't have to go to war. But we don't want you to be a deserter." He waited again. I kept thinking how much this was costing him.

"I'm not going to desert, Dad." That was it. So much for my lists.

A wave of sadness washed over me, drowning me in self-pity. My gut twisted, and goddamn tears welled up in my eyes, and I didn't even know why. But I knew, whatever else, I couldn't leave for Korea without seeing them and saying good-bye. Whatever my stupid screw-ups and wanderings they were always there with their love whatever I did.

"And I'll come home for sure before I ship out," I said.

My dad let his breath out, like he'd taken a big gulp to yell again, but didn't have to. "Good. That's good. We love you, son."

"Yeah. I love you, too, Dad," I choked out.

I rode the creaky elevator up to nine, put on my shoes, walked over to the Terminal and got my ticket to Fargo. Like Mike Hammer says, "It was easy." I walked around town with nothing in my pockets but a few dollars and change, all the way down to the Village and back, around midtown, all over. I wanted to take one last look around the big town, but it was no use, I wasn't even seeing anything. I decided to take Annie up on her offer and make one last effort to get some writing done at her place before I left. And let her know my news.

THE SUPER LET ME IN without any grief, but I prowled the apartment like a restless intruder. I'd just begun to get hold of Annie. Then one moment I was going over lists and carefully analyzing pros and cons, and the next moment, my dad called, and I was going home, and to Korea. Maybe somewhere in my gut I'd known all along that was what I was going to do. And all I felt was sad. I knew I was afraid; but I couldn't feel the fear, only this godforsaken sadness.

Schlumberger. I put the poor bastard in the typewriter again and stared at the forlorn piece of paper.

I should begin at the beginning, but what was the beginning?

I got up and walked around.

When I looked down at Annie's big red sofa, the imprints of where we sat last night were still in the soft cushions, like animal tracks in soft ground. I sat down in my imprint and looked at hers. I was tired.

Moira was right about one thing. I'd been running ever since I went down to the recruiting station. All through basic. Up here. After Annie. Thinking. Thinking in goddamn circles. Trying to figure everything out. Now my body wanted a rest and my brain wanted a rest, and instead of using my thirty days for that, I'd worn myself out trying to come to terms with Annie and gotten nowhere. I'd be the first guy ever to get to Korea and think it was relaxing.

I sat back and shut my eyes and let the warm September sun come through the window onto my face. I wanted to not think about Moira, to push all of the questions she raised about Annie and me out of my mind. I tried to conjure up Annie's kiss, to concentrate on her and what I felt for her.

Well, shit. Instead the questions that Annie had raised about us came after me like sharks after a weary swimmer. She raised the questions with the practicality that marked everything she did. She wasn't sure she wanted to take me on "that way." What the hell was that supposed to mean? Why not? Because I was leaving? Finally I dozed off, sitting on the red couch next to Annie's imprint, with the sun warm on my face and my thoughts going in circles, that ended in restless, fitful sleep.

When I woke up late in the afternoon, the sun had moved on. I was stiff from sleeping sitting up. It would be a while before Annie got home. I stretched and walked around the place, trying to get the kinks out.

I glanced at the naked sheet of paper I'd left in the typewriter. I sat down at the typewriter. I waited. Weren't words that had risen behind the dam while I slept supposed to come pouring out of me? Nothing poured. Maybe this wasn't the time to try to write this. I had too much on my mind. Too many things to sort through. Decisions to make. I didn't have any perspective yet. I walked around Annie's small apartment, looking for the answer in her kitchen, the living room, out the window, in her bedroom.

The phone rang. Thank God.

It was Annie, but she had to skip tonight. She had to work.

"Annie, I have to leave. Tomorrow. I've got my bus ticket. I have to go to Fargo and then to Korea and I don't know when I'll be back."

There was a pause on the other end of the line, "Oh," she said. She sounded as unsure as I was trying to be certain. She was silent for a moment, and a female voice ragged on her in the background. That goddamn everlasting Margaret. Annie said something to her.

"Stay there," she said. "I'll finish here and we're going out to dinner tonight. My choice, my treat, and no arguments."

"Good-bye," I said to the buzzing line.

I sat down at the typewriter again. The time to write this was right now, or else give it thirty years, and I might not have thirty years. Hemingway wrote a lot of his best stuff right from life, often a day or two behind the events he was living.

But I needed to break out of the trap I was in, at least to get the story out. Maybe go back further to understand what was happening to me. How I'd landed in this spot. Back to the university and Prof? Even earlier?

24

"Annie! Nice to see you!" The man bounded up to us in the line waiting for tables at the Blue Angel. Annie's treat.

"Max," Annie said, taking his hand. He owned the place.

We were seated right up front, a few tables away from a woman with raven hair, creamy smooth skin, and classic features I knew I'd seen before.

"Linda Darnell," Annie said. "I'm going to be sick."

She was even more beautiful than when she'd come into a saloon and stuck her leg up on the poker table in front of Henry Fonda in *My Darling Clementine.*

The steak set Annie back as much as my whole United States Army paycheck. I was on edge the whole time, afraid we'd get into a damn argument again, on my last night here.

Then Josh White sang for us.

He sat on a stool under a soft spotlight, his red silk shirt open on his brown chest, reminding me of that kid singer with the street band, cradling and caressing his guitar, singing with it, singing a cappella, holding us in his hands.

From standbys like "I Gave My Love a Cherry" and "God Bless the Child" to a new one called "The Ballad of Harry Moore" about an

NAACP organizer who was killed when his home was bombed. One moment White was tender, the next angry, and whatever he was, we were. He ended with "Strange Fruit":

> Southern trees bear strange fruit.
> Blood on the leaves, and blood at the root.
> Black bodies swingin' in the breeze,
> Strange fruit hangin' from the poplar trees.

He dropped his head to his chest when he finished with a harsh whisper, leaving all of us hushed, till we exploded with applause.

If White singing "Strange Fruit" told us where prejudice toward the black man ended, I told Annie that the kid with the street band and the crackers down in Richmond showed me where it began.

"Maybe," said Annie. "But you ignore so much if you think sexual fear is all there is to prejudice. There's all that religious 'shit' as you so elegantly put it once, Tom. And I think the very worst prejudice is because of what we fear in ourselves."

She glanced over at Linda Darnell. "Look at her," she said, quietly. "A woman who is as beautiful as it is possible to be. True? And never mind the gallantry."

"Sure."

"As well as rich and famous.

"But nonetheless," the way Annie said it reminded me of Prof, and of the Ghoul, "she struggles with alcohol and depression. She belongs to a deeply stigmatized group. Believe me, I know."

"Yeah? I wonder how real her problems can be? She spends more for dinner than most Americans make in a week, never mind the rest of the world."

"Don't you tell me she's without pain when you know nothing of it! Live a few more years. Have depression happen to someone you love, or you. Then come tell me about pain." I could hear the anger in her voice.

I loved being with Annie. When we kissed, sometimes her full lips were sweet as a first innocent love and other times seemed to promise everything. At the same time, I was aware of her vulnerability. Every time she showed me more of herself, she claimed more responsibility from me. I felt a need to protect and shelter her in a way I'd never felt toward anyone in my life. No matter how sophisticated she was.

She was hurting now, and she'd hurt me, sticking me with the unanswerable argument.

"It has happened to someone I love. You."

"It's happened to someone you're playing at loving."

She got me again, right in the gut. I'd laid it on the line, and she'd hit me with that.

"Hey, lady, it was a nice dinner. I'm not looking for a hand-out." I didn't know how damn mad I was till I said it. "So two of us can play the cheap shot game, can't we?"

I looked around for the waiter for the check, not knowing what I was going to do if I got it.

Annie stared at me like I was a new strain of disease and reached for her purse. I'd done it. I'd managed to say good-bye to her. A great way to say good-bye.

"I'm sorry," I said. "I didn't mean it that way."

Her dark eyes look troubled, and small creases nicked her forehead above her Elizabeth Taylor nose. "It's all right. It would be nice if you loved me."

"Godammit, Annie, don't patronize me, all right? I know what I feel about you even if you don't, and this is my last night, all right."

She reached a hand across the table for mine. She had tears in her eyes. "Oh, let's not do this your last night," she said.

"Would you like dessert?" One of the squad of waiters appeared.

"We don't want dessert," I said.

"Check please," she said to the waiter. "No more fighting," she said to me.

IN THE TAXI I PUT MY ARM around her, but I could feel the tension in her shoulders. Staring at the mug shot of the driver, who also stared back at us like an angry bank robber, didn't help. Outside her building, she paid the cabby. The super greeted her by name and waved with a smirk I wanted to wipe off his face. By the time we rode the elevator to her floor and Annie let us in, I was so steamed up I was ready to blow a valve.

But she moved away from me. She made coffee, padding about in her stocking feet, in a circle of light in the kitchen, her shadow gliding silently over the kitchen floor, while I sat on the couch. I loved watching her move, with a precision and grace I'd never known before, but now I wanted her to stop moving.

When she finally came over with the coffee, she curled up on the end of the sofa, her feet tucked under her, facing me.

"I'm going to miss you," she said.

"Will you? Or will you be glad to see me out of your life? With us never having been together. I mean making love," I said. That sounded bitter. I looked away. I was having trouble saying what I want to. Some of my problem was lugging around the stupid lie I'd told her about having been married. She'd figure I was just off the wall if I told her the truth now.

"You know I'll miss you, Tom. Where are you right now?"

"Thinking about you."

She stopped with her cup of coffee halfway between the saucer and her lips. "What are you thinking of me?"

I almost told her everything. I almost asked her everything, all the questions Moira's letter stung me with. But if I asked those questions, I'd answered them.

"How you drive me crazy. How pretty you are," I said.

She finished her coffee and put the cup and saucer on the floor out of sight behind the end of the sofa. "That's nice. What do you really think of me?"

"What do you mean?"

"What do you think of Annie who's slept with a married man and tried to commit suicide, and couldn't even get that right? Thirty-year-old

Annie going with a divorced soldier, who looks like a boy, my mother says." Her voice stumbled over "my mother." "A good-looking boy; but a boy." I leaned toward her, but she raised her hand like a traffic cop. "So, I wonder. In your eyes am I pathetic, damaged goods? What do you really think of me?"

"Christ," immediately I wished I'd started another way, any other way, "it never even occurred to me you'd think that. I'm worried all the time about what you think of me. I want you to let me love you."

"You think I wouldn't like to go to bed with you, Tom? You think you're the only one who wants that? Whatever you think of me, I don't do that just for fun. It means more than that to me. It means I might expect things from you that I don't know if you're really ready to give. And you're leaving, Tom, you're leaving me. As far as I know forever. You won't be here."

"I know all that, Annie. Does it ever occur to you that I might come back? That I'm not just looking for some sympathy fuck before I ship out. I love you, Annie," I said. "I love you."

Her face softened then, and it was like she had made a decision. She leaned over and kissed me, without reservation, without pulling back when I opened her soft lips with my tongue, but answering with hers, not stopping when I slipped my hand under her dress and inside her bra, feeling the warm smoothness of her breast under my fingertips and then her nipple growing erect under my touch.

When she stood up, she took my hand and I followed her lead into the bedroom.

She undressed quickly, but letting me look at her. She was so small and trim: below her lovely neck, graceful bones tapered toward her rounded shoulders; her little breasts stood out, firm and lovely, almost jaunty, with their pink nipples; her tight stomach curved gently downward; the delicate bones of her pelvis flanked her dark hair down there, above her smooth thighs.

"God, you're so beautiful, Annie," I said, my voice coming out strained, almost hoarse.

"Come here," she said softly.

When I slid in beside her, she asked, "Do you have anything? A condom?"

I was surprised she came right out and asked that.

"Yes," I said. I'd been carrying them around in my wallet ever since I got to New York.

"That's good," she said. "Let me help you?"

"Yes, God, yes," I said, although that almost got it over before we started.

I kissed her, still nervous and excited, nearly quivering. We held each other, and her body, tight against mine, felt tense too. I kissed her again and slid down with my face against her small breasts. I lay there against her and her hand went to the back of my head, and I could feel her whole body relax. For a while. I put my mouth on one of her nipples and then the other and put my hand below, first feeling her soft hair under my fingertips, and then loving the wet part of her.

She pulled at me then to come up and move over her, and I did. I almost came right away, but she lay still and held me still. "Don't move," she said, and, bad as I wanted to, I didn't. She was holding me inside and barely moving. I felt pleasure so intense it hurt to hold back, but she kept crooning not to move and to "Let me," and I did.

Her hands moved on my back, at first brushing me gently, slowly, then more firmly, and finally holding on as tight as she could, while her smooth-muscled thighs moved in rhythm, for a long time only a little, then in increasingly demanding tempo. Just before I died, her voice, soft against my ear instructed me, "All right! All right!" and I let loose.

Afterward I stayed there, close to her, resting against her. I felt peaceful and at rest; she and I were the whole world. We lay there breathing together and we didn't need words. Until I could feel myself getting heavy on her, and I moved off and lay beside her.

She brushed her fingertips gently across my forehead.

When I bent over and kissed one of her wrists and then the other she drew back and lay taut for a second.

"I love everything about you, Annie. Everything that is you."

186

She considered this, and she relaxed.

"You have such a nice young body, Tom." She raised herself up on one elbow and traced patterns on my chest with the other hand. "All tan and firm." Her fingers brushed lower. "No. A white tush and so smooth."

I was pleased but embarrassed at the same time.

"You don't like it that I say you have a nice body? You take care of it in Korea, hear me?"

"I will," I said, but my gut tightened.

As if she sensed it, she ran her palm over my stomach and then rested her head on it. "Nice flat tummy," she said. I couldn't see her face, only her dark hair and the gentle curves of her shoulders and on down her body. "So—you're sure you're not Jewish?" She looked up at me. "Oh, and you blush, too don't you?" she laughed.

For a second I wondered if she talked this way with the asshole who screwed her before. Then she was tickling me down there, only it wasn't exactly funny. That was all I could take without defending myself, and for quite some time we didn't do much talking. Afterward we lay there for a long time. I felt good right afterward, but then I started to feel sad.

As if she wanted to break the mood, whatever it was, Annie said a Yiddish phrase that sounded like and translated to something like "Pissin' you have none?"

"Annie, you are so practical, I can't stand it."

In the bathroom I couldn't get started, not wanting her to hear me. Hemingway never mentioned problems like this. I turned the water on in the sink and that helped. When I came back to bed, she popped out. But she was back in a minute.

She knelt beside me like the girl on the Rock Spring label, with her legs tucked underneath her. She bent over me and kissed me, and I caressed her breasts while she did. I loved the white smoothness of them, then pink and bumpy to my touch, then the nipples hardening again against my fingertips. I loved looking at them almost as much as touching them. She kept on kissing me and moving her hands all over me and we began again.

"Your wife was crazy," Annie said later, when I was lying there against her breasts, her hands resting on the back of my head. It was the nicest thing she could have said.

"I was never married, Annie. I lied." The words just came out of me before I had a chance to stop them. I held my breath waiting for her to let fly at me.

When I raised my head, her dark eyes were staring up at me, her cheeks red against the white pillow. "Really. I don't even know why I'm surprised."

"You sound angry. Are you mad at me?"

"More at myself. I think I already knew." She paused, "I'm glad you weren't."

I'd begun to breathe again, when she asked, "So—just how young are you, Tom Kelly—if that's your name?"

"Not as young as I used to be," I managed to get out.

25

The bus trip to Fargo was an around-the-clock drive. A candy bar in Pittsburgh. A bottle of Coke in Gary. Pancakes in La Crosse, courtesy of an old couple who told me I reminded them of their son and asked me to join them for breakfast at the counter in the bus depot.

When we left Wisconsin, the next stop was the Twin Cities. The skyline had dwindled to a few buildings rising up from beyond the Mississippi: pretty much the First National Bank Building with the big "1" on top in St. Paul and the Foshay Tower still ugly in Minneapolis. Beyond the Cities the low, rolling hills that carried us from Wisconsin tapered into the gentlest of slopes as we crossed Minnesota farmland and lake country. By the time we neared Fargo, the land was flat.

I'd tried to tell Annie about the claim North Dakota made on me when she had asked me, only partly kidding, how people could live out here, beyond one part of the civilized world and before the next. I'd searched and failed to find the language to describe it for her, so she would have a feel for it. Now, in this dreary season, with the grime and dust of twenty-four hours on a bus, and the land desolate and windswept outside the bus window, I didn't fully believe myself what I'd tried to tell her. But I knew I would again.

On the near side, Fargo was sheltered by the windbreak of Moorhead and downtown Fargo, but right outside town, in the winter, deep snow blew and drifted into white and gray ridges and rifts, piled along snow fences and against barns and silos and houses, in a barren beauty that would last for months.

In the spring, about the time we couldn't stand it any longer, or a little later, the snow and the last tenacious ice gave way to the sun. The earth came to life again. Roots drew water stored deep in the soil, and the trees and grass sought the warming sun. The farmers tilled the fields into rich black patterns and planted new seed.

The kids remembered how to whistle. They broke out their marbles: the clear moonies, the smooth steelies, and the trusted shooters. They flexed their shooting thumbs, ready to do battle in the circles scratched into the fresh soil of the playground and practiced lagging up against the school walls that had imprisoned them all winter.

In the summer, the grass grew green and the grain lifted higher and higher. The flat plains turned golden, endless waves rippling in the warm and gentle breezes. In the fields grasshoppers returned, an enemy to be feared, but in town boys caught them in vacant lots, held them till they spit brown tobacco juice, then mercilessly retaliated, dismembering them one leg and wing at a time. To write about this land you had to live on it, study it till you knew it.

When I first saw Fargo this time, the buildings looked like they were built low to the ground, so the winds that came sweeping in across the everlasting plains couldn't tumble them across the fields. There seemed to be only a few of them, huddled together for comfort, ringed by the little houses like settlers' wagons. The land was still enormous, but in town everything was small, so much smaller than when I was last home. I was Gulliver getting out of the bus. I half expected to hit my head on the roof of the bus station.

"Here, Tom!" My mother ran toward me across the wooden station platform, waving her hands like I'd miss her if she didn't. My mother's running and waving could be sort of embarrassing, but it felt so good to see her. She hadn't changed anyway. Her red hair was in curls that meant she'd spent half a morning at the beauty parlor, like she was going to the church ladies' luncheon, and the flowers on her hat were the only colors in a gray and brown world.

My dad strode along behind her, catching up. He'd have let her out of the car before he parked, and still gotten here at the same time, walking. He'd taken time off work, and my mother had him in his suit and tie, like I was a returning war hero, instead of his wandering kid finally stopping by for the last couple of days of his leave. He was sheepish about being all dressed up, but he looked sharp.

When my mother reached me, I bent down and hugged her and kissed her on the cheek, and nearly knocked her hat off. Dad and I shook hands. Then we hugged each other and pushed each other away at the same time, and I could smell his Old Spice skin bracer. He stepped back and looked at me real hard, to fix me in his mind again.

"It's good to have you back." Tears were welling in his eyes so he looked away, reached to grab my duffel bag.

"Even if it's just for a bit," he said, hefting the bag up over his shoulder. I reached to stop him. He'd shrunk too. A look from my mother stopped me.

"Moira was by about your Sacred Heart transcript," he said. "She seemed to think you were going AWOL to Columbia. That's why I called," he said, throwing a sharp glance over his shoulder at me. He must have been worried. He couldn't even let it wait until we get to the car.

"I know, Dad, you told me on the phone. She got it wrong. Maybe after I finish my hitch," I added, not quite looking at him.

"Good," he cleared a frog in his throat. "Good." He squared my bag on his shoulder, and stepped out ahead of me. "I thought she was crazy."

"There's nothing wrong with the Agricultural College," my mother said, hurrying along beside us. "Right here."

"Huh," said my dad, his favorite all-purpose response when he didn't see any point in discussing something further.

191

SATURDAY I WALKED DOWNTOWN. On the way, I stopped by St. Mary's School where one year a kid stole the used bicycle I got for my birthday. The cops found it and brought it back within the week. I couldn't understand how a kid could do that to another kid. My dad said he was a poor kid, but still.

I stepped into St. Mary's Church and stood at the back. The sunlight through the stained glass windows bathed the dark church with deep reds, greens, yellows, and blues. I was drawn in, past the Stations of the Cross I'd made so many times in Lents gone by, following Christ's footsteps on the way to his crucifixion, saying endless repetitions of the prayers that would get me out of purgatory faster if I died with sin on my soul. If there was a hereafter, it was a cinch I was going to need all those indulgences. Before the statue of Mary with Jesus in her arms at the front of the church, I knelt and lit one of the white wax holy candles.

I still felt safe in there. I could stick around and go to confession. Cover all the bets, like my dad would say. I was sorry for the bad shit I'd done, but I wouldn't be able to say I was sorry for some of the things I'd done that Father Mahoney had right up there as big sins, like making love with Annie. So, Father wouldn't be able to give me an absolution that would work right anyway. I felt bad about that, and I didn't want to hang around in there anymore.

Outside the sun poured down. I stopped by the drugstore where I'd read ten thousand comic books free, standing inconspicuously before the rack, tearing through Superman, Batman, Captain America, Captain Marvel and the Lone Ranger faster than a speeding bullet. Everything was clear and sharp. The good guys won every time with harmless cartoon violence of stars and x's hovering over the bad guys' heads. My mother hated them. When Classic Comics came out I'd brought home *Moby Dick* and *Ivanhoe* and the *Hunchback of Notre Dame*, but she threw them out too. Even the Bible turned out to be based on the King James Version, which I hadn't realized was the heretic version, and she tossed it too.

On across Broadway to the Broadway Donut Shop where Chick Belos had held up the paper with his picture on the front page. Where my mother and father had gotten me treats after church the Sunday I made my first communion. When I got older and quit going to church with my parents, most Sundays, I'd spend an hour reading at the drugstore and then go to the bakery, and spend the nickel I had for the collection. Till my mother noticed my nickels weren't going into the total our family gave as it was posted at the back of the church.

The sidewalks were dusty in the afternoon sun. The kids working for the downtown stores hadn't been out to sweep them since morning. Chick and I used to walk along the gutter, kicking up the dirt and rocks, watching for money someone might have dropped. Chick found five bucks one day, and we went to the movie and the doughnut shop and the drugstore and arrived home late and sick to our stomachs. When we got old enough to smoke, but not old enough to get away with buying them, we used to gather up cigarette butts and lie around and smoke down by the Red River. We worried about it, but we never saw it stunt our growth that you'd notice.

I wandered slowly past the low buildings that seemed so big in those days when I was a kid, the names carved into the stones as they were in my memory—the Bison, the Fargoan—I loved the way they sounded when I said them out loud.

At the Fargo Theater, *The Snows of Kilimanjaro*, starring Gregory Peck and Susan Hayward and Ava Gardner was playing, the same as in New York. Ava Gardner had to be just great casting, but the matinee was a crummy B Movie, *Charlie Chan Goes to Hollywood*.

The Black Building reflected the autumn sun, as white as ever. I poked into DeLendrecie's Department Store; it wasn't Macy's or Gimbels, but my mother loved that place. When I hit it big I'd open charge accounts for her in the stores downtown, every damn one, and let her loose to ransack and pillage. I poked into Herbst's Department Store to watch and listen to the pneumatic tubes send cardboard rockets like the tubes inside rolls of toilet paper, bearing sales slips with charges to be approved curled up inside, whooshing around the store and plunking to their destinations behind the cash registers. Something about the sound satisfied my soul.

193

I went into Woolworth's. My favorite birthday of all time was when my mother took me downtown with her and gave me a dollar to spend any way I wanted to. I'd spent hours arranging lead soldiers and cowboys and Indians, and thumbing the pages of Big Little Books, so the corners made moving cartoons, trying to make red and black Duncan yo-yos sleep and walk the dog, and flying tin planes, the same kind we were flying when we heard about Pearl Harbor, and taking aim with squirt guns, all spread out on the toy counters so immense then but so small now. I bought every toy dozens of times over, standing there with my incredible wealth stuffed in my corduroy pants pocket and held tightly in my fist, rechecked every thirty seconds. My palms tingled as I remembered it.

By the time I reached the Red River I was tired. I didn't know why, it wasn't that much of a walk, and it wasn't hot or anything. But it was like I'd been doing all those things I thought of from when I was a kid, all in one afternoon, just from remembering so much.

It was strange. Fargo was so much smaller than when I last left that it would never look the same. I could see why Annie felt New York was the center of the world, and from New York Fargo might seem another planet. But what was in Fargo I could see. It was right here, and it was real for me in a way New York never would be. I wasn't thinking I'd live in Fargo forever, but there was a lot more here than Annie realized.

The Red River was running slow and muddy. I stood on the bank watching it flow past. A hundred years ago, Moira and I had clung together here, watching the rain strike the water, thinking our separate thoughts. Sadness enfolded me, and I almost wanted to cry. This seemed to be happening to me a lot, and it was scary.

For quite a while I just stood there. I ought to at least see Moira once before I leave. Just for old times' sake. But I nearly wrenched my shoulder throwing a rock as far as I could into the river with all the anger I felt toward her.

AS IT HAPPENED I SAW WILL LINDEMAN. Not too surprising, since I stopped by Powers for pie and coffee, when I knew he was working. He came across the room, carrying the full tray of dishes he was busing, shaking his head sheepishly. He set the tray down on an empty table, his glasses sliding down his nose as he bent over.

"Hi!" He seized my right elbow with his left hand, grabbing my right hand with his and pumping it up and down, like a vacuum cleaner salesman. "It's great to see you! I heard you contemplated going AWOL in New York. Great move! Would it work though?" he laughed.

I didn't know how much of this I could handle without teeing off on his smiling face. Moira must have taken out an announcement in the *Fargo Forum* about my musings.

"Hi-i, Will," one of the waitresses lilted at him as she edged past, giving his butt a playful squeeze as she went by. "Who's your friend?"

He grinned at me. "So, are you back in the picture with our mutual friend?" he asked, his big, brown eyes looking innocently at me.

"No."

"Oh," he said. I might have killed him if he said anything more.

"So what do you say we have a brew when I get off work?" he asked. "Unless you've got something better to do."

"No," I decided, "I don't have anything better to do."

"Jesus, that's pitiful! We'll have to do something about that! How long do you have before you go over to get your ass shot off? You are still going over to get your ass shot off?"

"Monday morning. Democracy is safe. And your ass, Will."

"Not so," he shook his head slowly and sadly, "I can see you haven't gotten the word."

"What word is that?"

"I've been drafted."

"No shit?"

"No shit." From his face it was clear he wasn't joking. "A few lousy incompletes and I'm out of the university. It's because of you, and our mutual friend. You're bad influences." He smiled at the absurdity of it. "There's the record, of course," he added, dropping his voice, "back in New Germany."

"Ouch," he giggled again at the retreating waitress. This trip she'd pinched him, or grabbed some more tender part of his anatomy.

The son of a bitch wasn't breaking my heart.

"So, tonight, we'll do something special in honor of our patriotism. Should we call the blonde?" he asked. "Hell, no," he answered his own question. "Right?"

"Right."

Will picked up his tray. "No more about her. Agreed?"

"Agreed."

"We'd only get suicidal," he grinned, bouncing the tray nervously in front of him, the dishes rattling.

"Not me."

"Great! Be by at five!"

WILL WAS ALREADY CHANGED and waiting for me at five.

"Come on, we've got to hurry or they'll be closed," he said, striding over to an ancient Pontiac that should have been shot on the spot for glue. "I've got Joe's car, and we can catch Dinah Washington doing a set at the South of the Border. I love those women of color, and she is so great."

"Okay by me."

"But first we stop for the beer."

So we drank and bullshitted our way to Minneapolis.

I told Will about how Prof Williams, scornful to the bone of organized religion as we knew, had to take a job at a Methodist college to support his wife and kids.

"That's awful. To sell out to support a wife and kids. Agreed?"

"Yeah, well, it would be hard, you know."

But mostly we talked about how two nice young men like us ended up in the United States Army at a time when there was actual shooting going on.

"Jesus, I don't know," Will deftly popped another beer while keeping one hand on the duffer's knob. "They'll want me to shoot rifles and all that shit?" He sounded worried.

196

"Yeah, sure," I said.

"Jesus, you know where the only gun I ever shot hangs. I can't even remember shooting a BB gun." The car swerved as he drained his beer, pondering. "They might as well not send me to combat, because I'll run like hell. I mean, logically Socrates may have been right about a peaceful dreamless sleep. But there's all the girls I haven't made and all the vodka I haven't drunk. To say nothing of the hours of jacking off that lie ahead."

"The war will be over by the time you ever get there, Will."

"Yeah, well, you take care of it for me, okay? I'm not the kind of guy who's ready for this kill-or-be-killed bullshit."

"Sure, that's the kind of guy I am." I was ticked off and going to leave it there. But I started thinking about Schlumberger, and, with the beer and the two of us rolling through the darkness together in the rusty Pontiac, I found myself telling Will about the Ghoul, and Pusgut, and then about Schlumberger. And the death of Schlumberger. Will listened intently, grunting once or twice, "Christ! Jesus Christ!"

"Christ Almighty," he said when I finished, "it's perfect, don't you see? That's what they're trying to do," he tilted the can of Hamms back as far as he could, draining it dry. "Make you into a killer. The Ghoul! I love it!" Will paused, squinting at me. "By next year they'll incorporate the killing of Schlumberger into basic training throughout the entire army. I'm surprised the Pentagon didn't think of it long ago." Will hiccupped, and the big Pontiac swayed back and forth on the highway again.

"I wish you'd look at the road every once in a while to see if we're somewhere near it. At least let me live long enough to get to Korea to save your ass so you can share these persip . . . pers-pic," I was the sober one, but I couldn't seem to say it, so I slid over it, "thoughts for future genera-tions."

"Right." Will braked gently and rolled down the window on the driver's side.

I rolled down my window too, and the cool night air rushed against my face.

We were quiet as the old car rumbled through the night, the near harvest moon lighting the road beyond the reach of the ancient headlights.

We were there by ten o'clock, still alive and without getting a ticket.

The South of the Border—also known as The Key Club, a "club" that let in anyone who could pay and looked close to puberty—was on Washington Avenue, the Skid Row of Minneapolis.

We were funneled into the club by a couple of bouncers who looked like they could play tackle for the Chicago Bears, through a narrow entrance jammed with people trying to get in for Dinah Washington's next gig—college kids, some older guys, there for the music or some action, pimps, hookers, and onlookers.

Inside the place was a roar of sound and banks of blue smoke. Off to the right three black guys and a white guy were playing Hot Toddy as we came in. The white guy blowing into the trombone looked like his cheeks were about to burst and perspiration was streaming down them. Will and I were jammed together at a table, and we shut up and listened to the music while commencing some serious drinking.

After a while down what the Key Club no doubt tried to tell the fire marshal was an aisle, a big redhead in a bright red dress ready to come apart at the seams lurched over to our table. She had the idea Will knew her. When she asked him to dance with her, he couldn't refuse. Out on the floor, she glued herself right to him. This guy back at her table, who looked like a dentist from Milwaukee, kept glaring at them. When the band stopped, Will returned her.

"Jesus!" Will said when he got back. "That's nice stuff. Those big women, I love 'em," he grinned. "The guy with her is ready to kill me though. Do you want her? She looks pretty good to me. Hey, are you okay?"

"Yeah, sure." But waves of nausea were washing over me, and I was sweating worse than the guys in the band. "I've got to go to the can."

I made it to the men's room okay. I hovered over a urinal, ready to throw up, but nothing happened. I leaned my forehead up against the tile wall and stood there. It was smelly but the tile felt cool and comforting on my forehead and it was quiet. A still, sober voice somewhere in my head was telling me to just take it easy.

"Christ, I told the guy I don't want her. And that didn't help at all." It was Will at the next stall.

I was looking down and I saw him, and anger rose in me like sour vomit. The words popped out: "Jesus, Will, you've got a small prick, you know that."

Will didn't even look startled. "That's right, man! I hide it till the last minute!" He laughed, his Pepsodent teeth flashing white in the semi-darkness of the grungy can.

"But," the voice in my head sneered at me through the fumes of beer and urine, "you've been in Moira with it, haven't you, asshole?"

"Asshole." I said it out loud, and I grabbed Will's shirt and pushed him into the wall.

"What the . . ." He reached to grab me back.

I hit him in the face once and his glasses went flying. I wanted to smash his face and knock out all those white teeth and stomp his little prick into the dirty concrete and leave him lying there in his teeth, and I swung again. But he ducked, and my fist grazed off his cheek and into the wall behind him as his knee banged into my crotch.

I lunged at him and pulled him down with me as I went down in pain, and we both fell to the floor. We were rolling around and even in my pain I was aware this was one stinky floor.

"Hey, knock it off! Or take it outside!" A big paw yanked me away from Will.

Someone was pulling him away too. There seemed to be three or four of the Chicago Bears in here with us.

"Easy does it, now," one of them said, propping me up. "You okay?"

"Sure." Will was standing up. He had his glasses in his hand and was rubbing his jaw and shaking his head. Then the son of a bitch started to laugh.

I stood there and I couldn't believe it. Much as I hated the bastard, I couldn't help laughing myself.

"So, we're square? No hard feelings?" he asked.

"Yeah, sure, no hard feelings, asshole."

"All right, son," said one of the peacemakers. "Why don't you two shake hands?"

I was okay when we got back out in the smoke and din. The lady and the dentist were gone, and I was sober and Dinah Washington, wearing a tight white dress with a little girl big bow on it, that somehow reminded me of Annie, sang "It's Too Soon to Know." She was as great as my asshole friend said she was.

It was a long and quiet drive home. I handled the driving, and Will slept most of the way. He looked like an innocent farm kid with his glasses off, stuffed into his shirt pocket, and his shirt spilling out over his pants, and his red, black and yellow argyle socks. It would have been easy to break his damn ankles. Saint Christopher looked down on us from the dashboard all the way back and he must have done his job because we made it.

There was no way around going to church with my parents the next morning. It was bad enough that they prayed for me. Father Mahoney mentioned me from the altar for special intentions. God knew I could use all the help I could get, but it was embarrassing. I didn't go to communion.

On the way out after Mass, I thanked Father Mahoney for the prayers. He shook my hand and he proceeded to bless me again right there on the church steps, making me feel guilty for every unkind thought I'd ever had about him. After all, it wasn't his fault I was a sinner; he was just doing his job.

Things got worse while we were getting the Chevy.

Moira sailed toward me just as I was about to get in the car. Her gray-green eyes locked on mine, and when she reached me she took both of my hands in hers, without looking away from me at all. She was wearing one of her white sweaters, and she didn't have any makeup on and she was so pale, but Helen of Troy had nothing on her.

"Tom," she said, rolling one foot over on its edge, scuffing her fifty-dollar De Lisos or whatever they were this year, looking up at me, but speaking so softly I had to bend toward her to listen. "Please come over this afternoon. We have to talk."

"All right." It was the only polite thing to say.

Things were mighty quiet in the car on the way home.

"I'm having your favorite dinner. Roast beef and Yorkshire pudding," my mother said. "And I've invited your Aunt Mary and Uncle John and all of your cousins. I certainly hope you'll be staying for dinner."

"I wouldn't miss dinner for anything, Mom, but I want to stop over at Moira's this afternoon to say good-bye." I felt bad about not spending more time with them again in the last hours before I shipped out; I was always taking them for granted. But I didn't want to leave without seeing Moira.

TARA HAD SHRUNK TOO.

The summertime lush green of the lawn had faded to brown. The cottonwoods were barren of leaves and their bark a jaundiced gray. The lilacs had long since withered for this year. In the winter, when the snow drifted along the split rail fence and covered the brown, the white house would once again fit into the landscape. Now it was naked and exposed.

I rang and Moira swung open the heavy oak door and let me in. She reached up and kissed me.

"God, I'm glad you came, Tom," she said, stepping back, her white hands resting on my chest.

She took me by the hand and pulled me in. Her white anklets slipped along the tile in the entryway and across the white carpet to the white couch in the living room.

She sat at one end and patted for me to sit beside her. She tucked her feet up under her, like a little girl, in a movement that reminded me of Annie.

When I sat down beside her, she twisted toward me, her eyes intent on me. Her delicate collarbones were visible from the vee of the sweater, her breasts straining against it. "It's been so long," she said, reaching out to touch my face, then taking my hand and putting it against her cheek. "I'm so sorry."

"Yeah? Well, I suppose." I'd given a lot of thought to all the things I was going to say to her, right up to the time she opened the door, but I was having a hard time remembering what they were. I was still angry and wary.

"I know I've caused you suffering," she said, "but I'm as wretched as you ever could have been. This is my atonement, don't you see?"

"It's not that. I don't think you understand how I feel about Annie."

"Oh, Tom, when I'm thirty, or whatever she is . . ."

"Thirty. Not whatever."

"Never mind that. I don't want to talk about her. You're leaving, and I'm afraid you may be gone forever, and I'm desperate. God, sometimes I wish I was a man."

"Not much chance anyone will take you for a man."

"You know what I mean. I wish women could go after what they want like men can," she said, staring at me. "I want you, Tom, and I need you, and I love you. Oh, God, can't you see I'm begging?"

She reached out and pulled me toward her, her eyes boring into mine, and kissed me again, probing, probing. And she wasn't much on conversation anymore; I'd never seen her so quiet and intent. The house was so still I could hear her breath and my own like faint echoes of summer thunder.

She took my left hand and put it on her breast, outside her sweater. "There's no one home," she said, her lips against mine, and her tongue found mine.

I felt manipulated, and still angry, but my damn hand, still sore from bouncing off the Key Club men's room wall, didn't get the word and began caressing her breast through the sweater. She drew back and pulled her sweater over her head, her hair jouncing up and back into place. Her breasts were bound in a plain white bra. She reached both hands behind her, undid it, and shucked it to the floor, then reached to pull my head against her breasts. I knew better, but I let her. After a while she took my aching hand again and placed it under the plaid skirt. I stroked her thighs, higher and higher, and I kissed her again.

"Touch me," she said, still against my mouth, against my lips that were getting swollen and sore. "Here." She put my hand on her cotton panties. "No," she said, muffled, "underneath."

I touched what I was looking for, as she wanted. She was wet and flowing to my touch, and I wanted more too. She lifted to me and pulled free as I pulled down the panties, and she went after my zipper, and we didn't even get the rest of our clothes off before I was inside her pumping furiously, and we came.

We lay there then, tangled up. After all that time, it wasn't like it was all so goddamn great. I felt depleted but more like I'd gotten even than I'd made love with Moira. And angry. Still angry.

"Goddamn you!" Mr. Stacey's voice burst in my ear like an explosive, the same time his hands grabbed me, one clutching my shirt collar, the other the front of my shirt, tearing at me.

"You keep your goddamn hands," he jerked me up to my feet, "off," and shoved me toward the door, one hand digging into the small of my back, the other still choking me at the collar.

"Daddy," Moira cried. "Stop it! Please stop it!"

He didn't until I was out the front door and it banged shut behind me. I could hear the hollering going on inside behind me, and the door opened and Moira stuck her head out, holding her sweater in front of her.

"Come back," she yelled. "You love me. You know you do!" She was crying when her father grabbed her and pulled her back in again and the door banged shut.

I stood there for a minute on her front porch catching my breath. I straightened out my shirt as best I could and tucked it in my pants.

The door opened once more. "If you're not off my property, now," Mr. Stacey said, "I'm calling the police." He was quiet when he said it, scarier than when he was yelling. But when I looked at him, he looked more scared of me than I was of him. He'd gotten older, and he'd shrunk too.

"I'm leaving."

IT SHOULD HAVE BEEN GREAT to stuff my face with my mother's Sunday dinner, her special of roast beef and Yorkshire pudding, and visit with her and my dad. But I felt guilty in the first place that I hadn't spent more of my leave with my parents. I had a gut ache from getting yanked off Moira by Mr. Stacey, and I also couldn't help wondering if she hadn't known her dad was going to show up. So, I had a hard time enjoying the dinner and the time I did have with my folks.

Besides which, my mother had to have all the relatives over. Uncle John told me to be careful over there and that got him to remembering his days in the New Hebrides in World War II. He was a nice guy, and I'd always been fascinated at how he and the other Americans controlled the island for most of the war, but still had Japs hiding there in the backcountry the whole time. But my parents and I didn't really get to talk, like we might have if it had been only us.

I never said it to them, sometimes to my mother, but I loved them both. They couldn't have any idea how many times I thought of them, of what they'd think about something I saw or did, what they'd say. I tried to tell them, but it got all mixed up with getting the dishes done after the relatives left, in case one of them dropped back for a midnight inspection.

Before we went to bed, my mother put her arms around me like she wasn't going to let go.

"I hate so to see you go. We've had so little time. I shouldn't have had everyone over," she said. It surprised me how she felt strong, even though she was crying.

"No. No. It was great to see everyone, Mom. It's my stupid fault we didn't have more time before."

"Yes, it is," my father practically yelled. He'd never do it, but he looked like he wanted to take a swing at me, and I didn't blame him. Then all the steam went out of him. "But there's no use in crying over it now." He put his arms around my mother and me both for a moment, and then tugged at her and walked her into their bedroom.

The next morning, my father took off work again to drive me to the train station, but it was a big rush with none of us saying anything but the stupid stuff you say when you can't say what you want to. I gave my mother a quick hug, and stepped back before she could get her hammerlock on me. Dad threw my duffel bag up the train steps and looked away so I wouldn't see his tears as I climbed on board. I got to the grimy window in time to look out at them as the train rolled out of the station. We all smiled and waved at each other till I couldn't see them anymore.

27

The Military Air Transport Service DC-6 that was to carry us to Korea struggled skyward over the Bay area. In the last week I'd traveled across the whole country of America from the Statue of Liberty to the Golden Gate Bridge below us, and when I looked down at the cables and spans, like a great harp stretched over the shimmering water, from back in the first-grade words surged to my consciousness:

> America, America,
> God shed His grace on thee
> And crown thy good
> With brotherhood
> From sea to shining to sea.

But when the plane got out over the ocean, and the coast receded, and I looked down at the endless water below, the whole plane with all of us in it was an insignificant fly in the vastness of the sea and sky.

We were all boxed up in the ancient MATS plane, dressed in khakis, like we were going to a parade, with our little group jammed back in the tail. I never thought I'd be glad to see those turkeys, but I was. Gary Kowalski grinned his choirboy grin and bruised me with a friendly

206

punch to the arm before trying unsuccessfully to start up a little game of chance. Morrie Shapiro told us about the great nookie Old Dad got on his leave in New Jersey. He knew I went up to New York and wanted to know if I "got any" from Annie, and I told him it was none of his goddamn business. Walt Manley was a dad now—an eight-pound baby boy, Walt Jr.— born just before Walt made it home on leave. He showed us pictures but then was quiet.

It was Walt who finally brought up Schlumberger. Walt's wife's father had staked them to a second honeymoon down to Chicago, and they went to see Schlumberger's widow, Marie, in Elgin. Marie had a boy too, a big nine pounder, John, Jr., I'd forgotten that John was Schlumberger's first name. Marie showed them the letter the Army sent her about how, even though he died in a tragic accident in training for combat, her husband perished in the defense of his country as surely as if he made it to Korea. Gary wondered if she was getting the same benefits though.

Later I asked through the smoke that enshrouded us if anyone had any scuttlebutt on Carl Bergstrom, but no one did. If Carl didn't get back and square things away, I hoped he was out there, on the loose, with his Elaine.

We didn't talk about the main thing on everyone's mind—that we were winging our way to Korea. I kept pushing our destination out of my thoughts, but it wouldn't leave me alone. While we droned on over the Pacific, we hit some turbulence, and I felt the decrepit MATS plane shudder. It wasn't reassuring when they made us move from the rear of the plane up toward the center because they were worried about the weight distribution.

The flight was interrupted by a layover in the middle of the night in Hawaii, where the Japs had stabbed us in the back at Pearl Harbor. Chick and I had been playing airplanes when my mother called me into the house. President Roosevelt's voice, scornful in his indignation, had come over the Philco as we crowded around: "Yesterday, December 7, 1941—a date which will live in infamy—the United States of America was suddenly and deliberately attacked by the naval and air forces of the Empire of Japan." Later at the Fargo Theater I'd seen the newsreels of our ships listing in the harbor and our planes burning on the ground.

They let us out of the plane at the airport. We had a balmy, unreal miniature vacation. For twenty minutes, we sat on a terrace, drinking pineapple juice, basking in the warm breezes and watching the silhouettes of trees swaying in the darkness while the plane was refueled. Somewhere out there in the darkness was the ocean and under its surface lay the battleship *Arizona* and the other ships American sailors died on.

That was it for Hawaii. Join the Army and see the world. On to Wake Island.

From a distance, Wake was a speck that made the Pacific even more immense, a tiny piece of coral, rock, and sand barely large enough to land on. It was so small and indefensible, it was no wonder Brian Donlevy and William Bendix couldn't hold it against the Japanese. The Second World War still lingered over Wake. All around the perimeter of the island and on out into the water there were long abandoned vehicles and weapons, burnt orange and black, peeling and flaking, with jagged holes rusted all the way through the metal. It was funny, on our way to the war in Korea; it was the Second World War we all talked about. As though that was still "the war," and Korea didn't count, even to us, just like the rest of the country.

It wasn't until we were airborne again that Walt looked back and said, "Well, that's where Truman and MacArthur met."

"Yeah," said Morrie. "That twerp Truman. If Truman didn't fire MacArthur, this war would be long gone over."

"A damn good thing Truman fired him or he'd be emperor by now," I said.

"Well, we know the war's not over now, don't we?" Gary threw into the pot.

"Why don't you guys can it? There ain't no sense arguing about this shit," said Walt, running his hand over his crew cut.

HANEDA AIRPORT OUTSIDE TOKYO with planes from all over the world parked on the runways was one long way from the Hector International Airport at Fargo. Tokyo itself was a mixture of big modern buildings that reminded me of New York, and small wooden structures you'd have thought a strong wind would blow apart. I wanted to see more of it, but it was "offload" the plane, and "onload" a GI bus, in the United States Army's relentless war on the English language.

The bus took us to the processing point at Camp Drake. All of Camp Drake was painted the colors of the First Cavalry Division, yellow, with a black horse's head in the upper right, and a diagonal black stripe below the horse. To separate the horseshit from the chickenshit. Inside the fieldhouse there were hundreds of wooden stands to lean on and fill out forms for our next of kin, which wasn't very comforting.

After that, they gave us the serious stuff. We all lined up for short arm inspection, followed by an inspirational message and colorful slides about VD from a captain who was a doc. He explained the incubation period for Asian varieties of VD was the worst and told a story about a girl yelling to a savvy GI, "Hey, GI! Come here! I give you somethin' you no habe before!" to which the vet replied, "What you got? Leprosy?" No one laughed, which either was a compliment to the troops or showed how tired we were.

We were so punchy from thirty-four hours of flying it was hard to stay awake for any of it. Gary, next to me, kept nodding off. He flopped like a life-size Raggedy Andy from one side of his folding chair to the other, and I had to keep pushing him off me. On the other side of Gary, Morrie caught up on his sleep. Even Walt's eyes were bleary and glazed.

We woke up briefly for chow. A grumbling sergeant who looked like he'd arrived sometime around the Spanish-American War pushed us through a serving line open around the clock. The "local nationals," Army for Japanese, sweat up a storm as they manned the serving lines and rattled around doing the KP work. I didn't even know what meal it was, much less what the Army's mystery food of the day was.

After chow it was off to the base theater for a talk about where things were with the war now. Our lecturer droned on about the peace talks that had been going on, first at Kaesong, and then at Panmunjom. There was stalemate along the front, while the negotiators argued. The big issue was whether prisoners of war we had taken would be forcibly "repatriated." Although I was practically to Korea, all of it still seemed unreal and far away.

We moved on to more down-to-earth matters. How to tell the friendly Koreans, the Republic of Korea or "ROKs," from the North Korean People's Army or "NKPA" or from the Chinese. The lecturer threw up slides of different faces and told us which ones were Korean and which were Chinese. The Koreans' faces looked flat, compared to the Chinese, who seemed rounder, but that might have been these particular slides. And of course the Koreans north of the 38th parallel must not look a lot different than those south of it. They told us that sometimes the NKPA had been known to infiltrate refugee columns of South Koreans and cause no end of havoc, which had also resulted in some casualties among the refugees on occasion.

The different uniforms were of more help. The ROK Army and the KATUSAs (Koreans Attached to United States Army) had uniforms like ours. The NKPA uniforms had a squarer look, like I imagined Russians wore, and our lecturer kept referring to Kim Il Sung as "Stalin's Stooge." The Chinese uniforms were more padded or quilted looking. Of course, if the guy was shooting at you, he was either an enemy or making a mistake, but you would shoot back without inquiring further.

WE TOOK A TRAIN DOWN THE LENGTH of the coast of the big island, Honshu, to Sasebo, Kyushu. All along the ride we saw terraced hillsides with every inch of land being farmed. The shore was dotted with fishermen setting out nets and monitoring long poles thrust into the sand.

Sasebo was Japan's big sub pen during the war. Banked all around and behind it were high hills used to store supplies and ammunition during the war. Or so I was told by one of the "indigenous personnel"—another of the Army names for the Japanese that sounded like we were just putting up with them—when we were killing time at the PX drinking and waiting for our turn on the landing ships to Pusan.

This indigenous person said the caves in the hills had been stocked to last for months. The Japanese had everybody, even first grade-school kids, drilling with spears. She made it sound like they'd still be fighting us if the emperor hadn't surrendered after we dropped the A-bombs. A lot of the guys thought we should drop the bomb in Korea or lob in a few atomic rounds with the big 280mm artillery that we had now but hadn't been using.

This indigenous Japanese person also kept telling me the Koreans were "Number fucking ten!" (the worst) ignorant, lazy and shiftless, and Korea was "big honeybucket." I wasn't sure what honeybucket meant, and she just laughed at me when I asked her.

THE SEA WAS CHOPPY, and the ride over to Pusan on the gray, flat-bottomed troop landing ship was a little rough. Morrie from seaside in New Jersey tossed his cookies all over himself, and for once he didn't have much to say. But for North Dakota sailors like Gary and Walt and me, there was nothing to it.

Pusan was a busy, bustling port. We were greeted at the dock by a Korean band playing, "If I'd a known you were comin', I'd a baked a cake!" A bunch of schoolgirls decked out in bright red silk tops and flowing white skirts handed us flowers, like you heard they did in Hawaii (but not to MATS flights in the middle of the night). Things might not be too bad after all in Korea.

It was when they loaded us on the train to go north to the Replacement Depot that I began to change my mind. The train down the coast in Japan was streamlined and modern, clean as could be; the Korean train was a twenty-year-old Lionel by comparison. It was rusting and as many windows were broken as not. No one had even cleaned out the jagged glass. Inside, the cars were so dirty that it smudged off the seats and window ledges onto your uniform when you sat down or put an arm on the windowsill.

The weather was cold, and when the train started up it just got colder.

All along the way, every time we neared a station or a small town, even though we didn't stop, mobs of dirty, ragged kids came running after the train. "Hey, GI! Candy bar? Cigarette? C-Rations?" When we threw candy or cigarettes out the window, the kids scrambled like a pack of hungry dogs, pushing and shoving and fighting each other for it. Gary threw candy out just to watch the fights. The kids wanted the stuff, but it was so damn degrading.

We "detrained," as opposed to "offloaded," at a place called Yongdungpo. Mud huts with clay walls and thatched roofs and dirt streets crawling with kids and beggars. The "dung" part was right. The place smelled to high heaven. I found out what honeybuckets were—buckets of shit they collected in carts to use for fertilizer to grow their food.

From Yongdungpo, we went by truck north to the Replacement Depot.

28
Fall 1952

We were in the Replacement Depot, not twenty-four hours into Korea. We were supposed to get fixed up with all the winter gear we needed, have a combat orientation and be sent to units. Those guys would be glad to see us; our arrival here meant some of them would be rotating home.

I sat in the back of a covered deuce-and-a-half. It rained a cold steady drizzle, and the tarp at least kept the rain off. I contemplated just how it was I ended up here. How worried my mother and father would be. How far away Annie and Moira and Will, all of them, had become so suddenly. What Prof Williams would think of all this.

But the shouted command broke into my thoughts: "Everybody out of the trucks!"

I scrambled out, and I was soggy in about thirty seconds. They lined us up in the rain and started throwing rifles and cartridge belts at us. Everybody was saying that the Chinese were attacking all along the line in front of us. They'd taken a hill—right near a destroyed city named Chorwon. Hell, that's what the sign said at the Replacement Depot.

Stories came down the line like diarrhea through the tubes. "The ROKs are bugging out," one GI said, "throwing their weapons down, turning tail and running. We got to load up and go save their asses again."

215

"It ain't the ROKs," said another guy. "It's a colored outfit. Like them jigs from the Triple Nickels who turned tail and ran. This time, it's some Rum and Coca Cola outfit. A bunch of spics. If they can't do it to you in an alley from behind, they ain't worth shit."

One of the black GIs heard this, "Bull*shiiit*. Our guys didn't run. They got butchered up tryin' to push the Chinks back off the hill. That's why they need us. Ask the sergeant. Fresh meat, that's what we are."

They started loading us back into the deuce-and-a-halfs. Walt and Gary were in one truck, and Morrie and I were in a truck behind them. We pulled out and bounced down the road. But we reached a Y in the road and some trucks went one way and some the other. The truck Walt and Gary were in careened to the left.

A second lieutenant stood there yelling at Walt and Gary's truck as it pulled away. "Where the fuck are you going?"

Our truck took off down the other road. Shit. From the sound of the lieutenant, those lucky bastards would end up safe and sound somewhere we weren't going.

Our truck jolted along, jarring my kidneys. I could smell the guy next to me. He'd crapped in his pants. But I was okay. I was light-headed, almost like I had a mild concussion. My hair was standing out. The back of my neck tingled. My whole body tingled. I had a hard time breathing. But I felt good; it was like I had this glorious buzz on.

The truck stopped and someone dropped the gate, and we jumped out. We were in the middle of the countryside. Paddies all around us. A couple of farmhouses off across the paddies. Probably deserted. We were way north of the No-Farm Line—the line civilians were to stay south of, to keep them from harm, and so no North Koreans could infiltrate our lines among them. Farther on across the paddies, off to the right, high hills were visible through the misting sleet.

A captain, a couple of lieutenants, and some sergeants stood by the side of the road. They were grim-faced, and they looked real tired. The officers started directing us, like kids picking teams in a sandlot game. "You, here!" "You, there!"

"You!" the captain was talking to me, pointing. "Fall in behind Sergeant Brown." Sergeant Brown was brown, I couldn't help but notice. Sergeant Brown took a handful of us. Morrie was the only other guy from our group, and I wasn't sure I liked that. Schlumberger was the last guy I saw next to Morrie going under fire. I heard the trucks leaving behind us. I didn't like that either.

We marched route step down the side of the road behind Sergeant Brown for a couple hundred yards. Then he went off the road and started leading us across the paddies, along the mud dikes that rose up from the paddies, like they were paths. The dikes were slippery, but Sarge was running, bent over from the waist, his rifle swinging in his right hand. I was right behind him, staying as close as I could, breathing hard and sweating.

Sarge slid down the bank, and all of a sudden right in front of me was a dead GI, lying on his back with his eyes open, staring up. I just about stepped right on him, but I went down the bank around him, too. Now there was mud up over my boots and it was slippery coming back up the little slope.

"Move it! Move it! Goddamn it!" Sergeant Brown had opened up a few yards on me, and somehow he knew I wasn't there behind him. I ran even harder. I didn't want to lose sight of him.

Ahead of us, maybe fifty, maybe a hundred feet, a small rise folded below another, larger hill. There was nothing growing on the rise but a few splintered gray stumps. It was pockmarked with holes and littered with ammo boxes and packs. Among the debris a bunch of our troops were leaning into the rise. Somebody saw us coming and hollered, "Come on, Brownie! Come on, man!"

Brownie, still running, yelled back, "Give me cover, man! Give me cover!" I heard whining sounds over my head and to the side, and there were little splashes in the paddy beside me. I ran faster and made it to the little hill behind the sergeant. He was already talking to some corporal.

Morrie arrived behind me. He was breathing hard, his face red from the exertion, and he looked at me and he winked! The guy was nuts.

217

I wanted to ask him, "Did you wink at Schlumberger, Morrie?" But I didn't.

We were better off tucked against the little rise than trying to run up the big hill in front of us. The air hummed over our heads, and small sprays of dirt went up around us, but I didn't see anybody get hit. I was torn between wanting to watch to the front of us, so I could see if any Chinks headed down the hill, and wanting to eat dirt. It was giving me a headache.

A lieutenant came running, crouched down behind the rise. He was built like Ichabod Crane, lanky, with his skin drawn tight on his cheeks and a bobbing Adams apple. I couldn't tell where he even came from, and that bothered me. The lieutenant yelled at Brownie and the corporal. The lieutenant had a map, and he pointed at the hill ahead, and then at the map, and back and forth. There was the goddamn hill in front of us. Either we stayed here, or we went up it. How complicated could it be?

"Lieutenant Winton says we're going up," said Brownie. He laid it out for us. "When we see the first red flares, we go up to that small knoll to our right. We regroup there with the other platoons and Divarty's gonna blow the top right off the fucking hill. When the barrage lifts and the second red flares go off, we move out and up the hill. Got it?"

"Yeah, Sarge, but what's the name of this goddamn hill?" Morrie asked.

Brownie looked at him like Morrie was out of his head. "The hill doesn't have any name. Okay?"

"Okay," said Morrie. Like, "Thank you very much, asshole."

"Put your bayonets on those pieces," Brownie said to us.

Brownie moved along the rise, spreading the word. I fixed my bayonet but I was still thinking about what he said about "the other platoons." What we had here was more like a squad.

There were *pop! pop! pops!*, like the Fourth of July, and the red flares burst ahead of us.

When the sergeant said move out, we started up the rise slowly, but when I got to the top I went over the crest of the rise as fast and low as I could.

Over the rise was the rest of our platoon. One guy just ahead of me lay face down with his helmet cradled by his hand next to his head and his weapon lying in the mud beside him. Another guy next to him, face up, his hand outstretched, like he was grabbing for air. Another couple of guys lay with their heads next to boulders that were hardly bigger than rocks, their hands digging into the ground, trying to claw holes for themselves.

I looked up and I could see guys on the top of the hill shooting at us. They were trying to stay behind stumps and rocks and in little creases they'd found or dug, but you could see the bastards. I pulled the trigger of my weapon, not even aiming, and ran like hell for the first knoll up on our right. All I could think about was making it to the knoll.

When I was almost there, I went past another guy. He didn't have a head. Vomit rose in my throat, but I choked it back and swallowed it, and kept on running. I made it to the knoll and there was a body there, too, and this guy must have been there a while, and the smell of him got to me and I did puke, leaning to the side, trying to keep it off myself but still stay burrowed into the hill.

I heard the whistling sound of artillery shells coming from behind us and the whole hill rumbled. They were going to blow the whole top of the hill right off. Then, as abruptly as the artillery started, it stopped, and the mountain was still for a minute. Then the red flares exploded all over the face of the hill. And Brownie was yelling "Move out! Move out!"

I wasn't shooting, just running for the next rock to hide behind, but Morrie stopped and squeezed one off at someone up the hill, before he dropped his piece and doubled over like someone hit him in the stomach. When I got to him blood was flowing from somewhere on his head into his eyes and his intestines were sticking out through his fatigues. This goddamn line from a training film came into my head: "Do not bruise the protruding gut." We used to laugh about it. I didn't know what to do. I hollered for a medic.

"Leave him," I heard. "He's bought it. Get up the hill!" yelled Brownie.

219

I ran up the hill, gasping for breath. I stopped and fired a couple of times not even sure what I was shooting at. There wasn't much firing as I reached the top of the hill. I didn't even know how anybody could be alive up there. There were bodies, in Chink mustard-colored padded jackets, sprawled all over the top.

Out of the corner of my eye I saw one of the Chink bodies a few yards away move. He didn't have a helmet on. His head was shaved, but he was a kid, staring right at me. He reached inside his jacket with one hand. I went crazy. I ran at him, firing what was left of the clip into him, and still running right at him. When I got to him I pushed the bayonet forward with both arms as hard as I could, and dove at him. The bayonet went through the padding and into him. I pulled the bayonet out, and he was still staring at me. I stood there looking at him, and I almost lost my footing I was so weak. I managed to walk away so I couldn't see him anymore.

"God," some guy said, to no one in particular, "it's colder 'n' a witch's tit up here. Where in the hell are we?"

That's when I started to shiver. I couldn't stop shivering.

I was still shivering but I made myself go back and look at the guy I killed.

His head was shaved, and he had heavy black eyebrows, but he was just a kid. He'd died with his black eyes wide with fear. I didn't want to touch him, but I closed his eyes so they'd quit staring into space like that. There was a dark stain on the front of his mustard-colored jacket, where he'd bled out.

In the inside pocket of the jacket, he had a small cotton bag with some papers in there, and a brownish, worn picture of an unsmiling man and woman; she had on a long white dress, and he was wearing a smock over sort of puffed-out pants, standing in front of what looked like an adobe hut. I guessed they were his parents. They'd wonder what happened to their son, just like my mother and father would if it was me. I would have liked to get his stuff to his mom and dad, but of course there was no way to do that.

I asked Brownie what he thought I should do with it, and he said there was no point in worrying about it. I could keep it like a souvenir or throw it or leave it with him. I didn't want any goddamn souvenirs.

We got a runner back to company, and the next day we got some replacements for the guys who were killed taking the hill back. Kids right out of the Replacement Depot like I was a hundred years ago, two days ago. By now even in this bitter weather, the Tit was starting to stink the nauseating stink of death. The Graves Registration guys showed up and started hauling the bodies of the GIs away. I half expected to see the Ghoul; this was how he earned his commission.

If the goddamn Chinks would just come and bury their own, I'd say let them do it, you know, but no one showed up. I supposed they figured we'd kill them if they did, and they'd be right about that. When nobody bothered to get the Chinese bodies, I dragged my kid off to one side and back down the hill. I bundled him up in a poncho from another body and scraped out a hole for him. I left his stuff in the hole with him inside the poncho, and I covered him up with dirt from the hole. It didn't seem right to just leave him like that so I stuck a big rock over his grave. I didn't even know why. I thought maybe someone would find him and his stuff after the war.

The rest of the Chinese bodies were turning putrid. When the wind was right, the rotten smell seeped right into you. I wasn't scared. I just felt like throwing up. When someone got worried we'd get the plague or something from the bodies, they told us to dig a big hole down on the side of the Tit. I lucked out because I was one of the guys keeping watch on the perimeter instead of digging.

But I wasn't so lucky, because I ended up on the detail dragging the Chink bodies into the hole. That was not great duty. The goddamn bodies had started to decompose, and I was never sure the hand or foot I grabbed wouldn't fall off the son of a bitch I was trying to lift. On one body, I interrupted rats having dinner on someone's hands and what used to be his face.

I hadn't eaten much in the last couple of days, but I did a lot of throwing up before we were done tossing the Chinks into the pit. I couldn't figure out where all the vomit came from. Even when I ran out of vomit, I kept heaving the dry heaves.

I WROTE SITTING IN A MUDDY HOLE on the safe side of the Witch's Tit. I had the hole covered by my poncho on a couple of sticks, making a tent over it.

I was using my helmet as a seat to keep my butt out of the mud, and my pack as a desk. But the rain came in the front, where I had the poncho propped up, so I could see, and around the edges and tunneled down the sides of the hole. The water started to collect in the bottom again, so it might have been a lost cause. And I might have been interrupted at any moment, by circumstances beyond our control, as they say on the radio.

But at least it was quiet for the moment, and I was trying to get down what had happened in the past couple of weeks. One thing, the main thing, I made it. I was alive. I still couldn't believe the rest of this shit. I couldn't believe it about Morrie. But it was not going to happen to me: we were digging our asses into this goddamn hill. The Corps of Engineers was here digging us one humongous hole and shoring it up with logs and sandbags till hell wouldn't have it, which was why I was temporarily evicted. Construction duty wasn't all it might be. When one of the engineers, I didn't know his name, got careless, he got picked off by one of the Chink snipers across the way.

I was staying on line instead of going to the rear like Walt and Gary had, through no great choosing on their part or mine. My four points a month toward rotation out of here were better than their two; that was about all you could say for it. Lieutenant Winton thought he talked me into it with all his bullshit about this was where the real war was, how it was my chance to make a difference, but I'd killed enough to last me a lifetime and more.

The lieutenant was a West Pointer. He told me classmates of his, platoon leaders, were getting killed quicker in this war than any West Point class had since the Civil War. He felt really bad about that, but you could see it was also like this was his big chance to get started toward general, and he ate this shit up. He hadn't been here much longer than I had. I found out from Sergeant Brown that Winton wouldn't be Company Commander if the captain who was here before him hadn't gotten killed first thing when the Chinks pushed the company off the Tit. To most of us Brownie was the real company commander.

THE LIEUTENANT NOT ONLY KNEW I'd spent time in college; when I made the mistake of starting to tell him about Prof and how I got expelled, it turned out he knew about that too. Whatever the hell was in my file seemed to follow me everywhere. Winton thought I was a misguided radical. But he was going to straighten me out.

In the meantime, we weren't doing anything, and I took up letter writing in a big way. I wrote my mother and father to tell them I was here and okay, and that was about all, not about what had been going on. I didn't even tell my dad that he didn't miss anything by missing his war. He'd want to know why I said that. I wrote Annie. Will. Even Moira. I sent Prof Williams a letter mostly about Brownie. It didn't come back as not received or anything, but I didn't hear back from Prof. I wondered if he'd moved on again. I was surprised, and hurt, that he didn't even write me if he got the letter. In a way he'd had more to do with my ending up over here than I was sure he was comfortable with, what with the way he hated the war. Of course, nobody made me do anything.

We heard that the truce talks at Panmunjom had broken down and were recessed indefinitely over the question of what to do with the prisoners of war we'd taken who didn't want to go back to North Korea or China. If they didn't want to go, they shouldn't have to, but I didn't see why our guys had to get killed for them. And they were, every day. It was stalemated trench warfare, cautious patrols, and shelling, shelling like they say World War One was, with nobody going anywhere. Except the guys who were wounded or killed.

BIG DAY.

I got some mail. Wouldn't you know it, the first letters I got from anyone, except my mother, were from Lindeman. The poor son of a bitch was in the Army. He was breaking my heart.

Fort Ord, California
October 15, 1952

Tom:
What do you say, kid?
I feel like bitching and you're the most likely.

I'm sitting here on my finger waiting for a big inspection. We are supposed to be firing today, but there is a tanker in the bay, and they are afraid a stray bullet might hit it. So for lack of anything else today, these chickenshit R.O.T.C. (pardon the truth, I know you used to be a member of the organization) officers have called a big inspection. So I'm cleaning my rifle. Incidentally, I'm not doing too bad for never shooting before.

Oh, get this—

The very first day we got our rifles they were sitting in our racks and S-4 came through our company with an inspection. They inspected 2 rifles, mine and another kid's. Well, somebody had to pay, so I got Article 15 and 14 days hard labor. I about shit. We went to see the C.O. and he scared the other kid out, but I was too scared to even leave. So I went on and saw the Battalion Commander. He said it is too severe, and I would be let off early, but I wasn't. Well, It's all over now—

I had a wet dream last night—they don't even give you a chance to jack off, & I'm getting so horny I'd jump a snake. There ought to be a young damsel somewhere in Korea willing to offer 3 or 4 hours to your happiness. If so, I know you'll find her.

Speaking of happiness, I just finished Wilde's *Dorian Gray*. Have you read it? If you have, write and tell me what you think of Lord Henry. If you haven't, do so at the first opportunity.

Goddamnit, I admire your writing over there under all of the circumstances. If you have an extra copy of your efforts to date lying around your foxhole, for Christ sake—please send it back here.

Whatever you do—you S.O.B.—stay in your hole for an afternoon and make epistolary remuneration.

Will

P.S. Say hello to your poor mixed up friend Annie.

LINDEMAN'S FOURTEEN DAYS HARD LABOR might well have been "too severe," but I didn't have too much sympathy for him. The so-called "Uniform Code of Military Justice" as meted out at the company level was pretty damn arbitrary. If he thought he'd seen chickenshit ROTC officers, he ought to meet one from the Point. Lieutenant Winton, for instance.

Also the dumbshit thought I was over here with a bookmobile.

October 26, 1952
Fort Ord, California

Tom:

It's 9:30 on Sunday morning, and all the "Catholics" are at church, so I have a little time.

I got transferred to my new co. this week and it's an 8-week cycle, instead of the normal 16 weeks of basic, so it looks like I stand a pretty good chance of going to Adjutant General school, which I think is a better deal than going to Officers Candidate School, which would mean an extra year like we talked about.

At first I didn't mind this outfit too much. But Friday night we had a GI party for inspection Saturday, and this one kid is really sick, so I put him in my bed up in my room. The next morning he went to the hospital, and I came down with it. Well, last night I was so bad I coughed till I choked and threw up, and the sergeant got a cab (first ride in a car for three weeks) but they wouldn't let me in the hospital. They gave me some codeine & sent me back. The Bastards!

I finished *Crime and Punishment*. How morbid & depressing can you get? Now I think something by Steinbeck.

Well I have to wash my clothes. Be sure to write when you get a chance.

      Will

IT WAS FUNNY, AS PISSED OFF AT HIM AS I GOT, and as annoyed as I was with his petty bellyaching, the fact was, I felt closer to Will than to anyone else back home when I got these letters from him.

A LETTER ARRIVED FROM MOIRA that must have been sent over by Wells Fargo pony express.

"Hey, Kelly. Mail, huh? From some pussy back home?" grinned one of the guys.

"You bet. Eat your heart out."

Moira wrote about three kids in a car accident out by Black Duck getting more of the front page of the *Fargo Forum* than all of the guys over here. I got mad reading that what we were doing here was being ignored at home, but I knew it was true. And I knew I wouldn't be able to begin to tell Moira what it was like over here. No more than

I could tell my folks. Who I'd become, what I'd done, I couldn't even understand or accept about myself. It was not her fault I didn't want her to know. I just didn't.

Even Annie I didn't tell much. But the plumbing had come unplugged in the mail line. At the next mail call, I got one from Annie; this was my lucky week. I went off to a corner of the bunker with my letter to open it.

> November 1, 1952
> New York City
> Tom dear,
> It is so good to receive your letter and learn you are alive and well. It is so terrible to learn of Morrie's death. His father and mother are devastated. There is nothing we can say to them. Nor do I know what to write you, Tom. I feel I know very little of what's happening to you. I hope you are able to work out what worries you so very much in a way, even if troubling to you, you can accept and live with. I know you can come to terms with all that you must.
> As for us, I feel more for you than you might imagine. You must know our last night together is special for me, as is our friendship. Believe me, I don't enter into such a relationship on a lark. I am very fond of you. I know you think you love me, and I'm certain that in a way you do. You were very sweet to me at a most difficult time in my life, and for that I'll be forever grateful.
> But I have to be honest. You say the years between us don't bother you, and I believe you mean what you say now. How long you will go into raptures about me is yet another question. I don't know what will happen—whether we will even see each other when you return. A year seems such a long time to you, I know, but a year can go very quickly. We will just have to see. I am only being realistic.
> My social life has been rather limited to things political, to me very interesting, trivial compared with what you are experiencing, but it is all I have to write you about. My itinerary did include the Stevenson rally at Madison Square Garden on Tuesday. I know how much you would have liked to be here for that. I don't know how much you've heard about Nixon's "slush fund," some shady money from fat cats that he's trying to explain. He gave a ridiculous speech about his wife's cloth coat and his dog Checkers on television that apparently has gone over with the voters as well as General Eisenhower. It's enough to make you wonder, even though I can't

agree with you that I'd move to Canada if Nixon ever became President!

That's about the extent of my activities, and you can see I'm doing fine. Be very careful, Tom. And write when you can.

With love,
Annie

When I read her letter, it was hard to believe I shared her life even briefly. It would be stupid to expect her life then to be different from what it was before I left. Her life was as real as it had been before, and as real as mine was. But our lives were just so different. God knew I wouldn't want her ever to experience anything like this. But her world was so far away, and she was so distant.

Later, I read just part of Annie's letter—the part about that asshole Nixon—to the guys. I couldn't believe Eisenhower for buying into Nixon, after all the shit Nixon'd pulled, right from the get-go. Eisenhower had to be getting senile. A lot of the guys here did "like Ike" and his "let Asians fight Asians" and "I will go to Korea" though.

The election came and went, and my heart broke when Stevenson lost. I bet my family came out different ways on this one. Of course, I couldn't vote. My mother would never forgive Stevenson for being divorced. But I had this awful feeling even my dad voted for Ike. I could see him in the voting booth, standing there for a long time, thinking Ike might get me and the other guys home quicker, and voting for a Republican for the first time in his life. But he wrote me about staying up to listen to the returns on the radio, and hearing Stevenson's voice barely break when he told Lincoln's story about the little boy who stubbed his toe in the dark and was "too old to cry but it hurt too much to laugh."

Eisenhower did "go to Korea," so the *Stars and Stripes* said. I didn't see him and I hadn't talked with anyone who did, but I believed he was here, like Kilroy. Big hairy deal. I guessed he listened to the Marine band and saw his kid, who was an officer but in the Fifteenth Infantry, so he couldn't be all bad. Everyone said you could trust Eisenhower, and I figured if there was any reason to, it was because he had a kid of his own here.

Ike got home for Christmas, but we didn't. They got us cold turkey and cranberries and that was about it. Otherwise Santa couldn't find us. We were actually in North Korea. The front line jutted into the north with the Tit being the northern most part of the front. We were about sixty miles north of Seoul and a few hundred yards south of a lot of Chinks. Not the greatest of Christmases, but I was alive.

30

It was the middle of the night, but I couldn't sleep and I was sitting around shooting the shit with Robbie, our forward observer—the guy from the Artillery assigned to the Infantry to spot fire missions and radio them back to the Fire Direction Center. The only job with a higher casualty rate than infantry platoon leader was forward observer; usually you were out there moving around right on the point with the infantry. It should have been better in this bunker we were in on the Tit. At least it felt safer. Anyway, Robbie was all set up to FO away, but there was nothing going on.

Robbie was a Second Lieutenant—by way of ROTC at Texas Tech and Basic Artillery School, at Fort Sill, Oklahoma. If Lieutenant Winton looked like, as my mother would put it, "death warmed over," Robbie was just the opposite. He had a chunky face, that reminded me of Hans Brinker, and Robbie was a beefy guy, filled out his parka. He told me, after I did some asking, he played "a little tackle" for Texas Tech. I found out later he was everybody's pick for All American.

If Robbie wanted to, he'd be playing for a service team and setting himself up to play for the pros after the war. But he didn't want to; he said those guys got their brains beat out and didn't make as much as a truck driver. He'd rather be a veterinarian, and that was what he was going to pursue when he got back to the real world. He was not a half bad guy. It felt good to be making a new friend, now that none of the guys I knew were here.

It wasn't supposed to be as cold when there was a cloud layer as on a clear night, but it was dark and so cold my breath curled right out of my mouth and nose, and I could feel it making frost on my face. The only thing warm was my feet—I had my Mickey Mouse boots on, rubberized boots that made my feet sweat pools of water on the bottom no matter how cold it was.

Robbie let me take a squint through the glasses, but I couldn't see a damn thing, and he took the scope back. So Robbie was going through the charade of looking through the glasses, but I could tell he wasn't seeing shit either, not a tank in sight, and no movement. He and I were the only guys awake in the bunker. It was so quiet I could hear the sweat slop around inside my boots when I moved.

Till I heard a whishing sound, real quiet like, *whish*, and a second later, bam! There was an explosion right in front of us. It hurt my eardrums so bad I let out an involuntary whimper and fell back. At the same instant Robbie's head jerked back, his face all covered with blood, and he fell too, bleeding all over me. I pushed Robbie to the side, and his blood squirted all over the front of my parka. He was moaning something, but I couldn't make out any words, just a god-awful animal moan.

There was a split second of silence and another explosion, right outside the bunker. This one was followed by a scream in the corner of the bunker. Before I could even think, the explosions started coming one right after another—*whish bam! whish bam! whish bam!* and they kept coming.

A guy over in the corner was screaming: "Pisshitfuckpisshitfuckpisshitfuckpisshitfuck!" It was like there was a cracked record somewhere in his brain and the needle kept bumping away and the scream kept coming out. His screaming went on for what seemed like an hour before something happened in there, and the needle skipped a track to "Ohgodohgodohgodohgodshootmeshootmeshootmeshootme!" Then I heard the muffled sound of an M-1 going off in the bunker, and I didn't hear the screaming anymore.

I started to stand up, but I didn't. I wanted to know what was going on out there, but I was afraid I'd get my head blown off if I looked. The shells were still falling outside. They must have been mortar shells, from the way they sounded coming in, but I didn't see how the Chinks could get them off so fast and at such a sustained rate of fire. There had to have been a hell of a lot of them out there.

I looked at Robbie. What was left of his face that wasn't covered with blood was as pale as gray snow. He didn't have any eyes or nose, and I couldn't see his chest move. He was dead, and he was better off dead.

But we were not better off because he was our artillery support.

I might have been able to call in artillery fire of our own. I couldn't get anything at all on the field phone. I tried to get Robbie's radio to work. But I couldn't raise the FDC.

The Chink shells kept bursting, all over the hill it had to be, and I wondered how long they'd keep this up, how long before the Chinks came at us. The shelling went on for a long time, but I didn't know if it was ten minutes or half an hour. Just the shells but no one coming. I yelled for the other guys, but no one answered, and I wondered for a minute if everyone was dead except me.

The shelling stopped. Stillness fell on the hill. The Chinese had to be coming and I stood up and looked out. I saw nothing but the dark at first, but then I saw some of our guys in their holes starting to stand up too.

The quiet didn't last more than a minute before we heard all these high-pitched yells followed by goddamn bugles and whistles. It was like the Fourth of July in hell.

I looked out, straining my eyes so hard they ached, and the back of my head felt like my brain was going to burst right out of my skull if something didn't happen, and I saw all these weird shadows coming toward us up the hill in the dark. It was the Chinese in their winter gear, running like humped up turtles, close to the slope, yelling like crazy. They didn't seem to be shooting, just running toward us.

232

I got my rifle up and tried to track one, and I'd have gotten him, but I couldn't pull the trigger. I still had my goddamn mittens on, and the trigger finger was stuffing up the trigger guard so I couldn't pull a shot off. I ripped the mitten off, and the trigger was so cold it burned my finger. But I began firing as fast as I could, and the Chink went down. I didn't know if I got him or someone else did. I was trembling, and the goddamn rifle was wobbling, and I was jerking the shots off.

I could hear a lot of firing now, popping and whining through the air, and it had to be ours. Chinks were falling down all over the hill. I put another clip in. I was beginning to settle down a little. I had yet to see any of the Chinese firing at us. Then one dropped to his knees, and I saw a flash of fire from him. I emptied my rifle at him, but he kept on firing. I needed another clip. While I fumbled with the clip, I took my eye away, and when I looked back he was gone. But right ahead of me, another form moved out of the dark, and I could see it was a Chink too, and I opened up on him dead on.

Jesus! They were right on us. I was going to die.

I could feel myself flinch, like someone was going to hit me and there was nothing I could do about it.

But it fell quiet again.

For a long time, I didn't hear anything.

"Hey, Jimmy, you there?" An American voice.

There was no answer. But I could see some of our guys poking their heads up out of their holes. It was over.

Whoosh—Bam! Whoosh—Bam! Bam! Bam! Bam! It wasn't over. It started again. This time the shells screamed and whistled at us. They had to have called in artillery or it was the goddamn tanks Robbie pointed out the other day, and this time it went on and on endlessly.

I crouched down in the hole. My right hand was numb, and I looked around in the dark for the mitten that I tore off what seemed like hours ago. I found it and put it on before I tried to lay Robbie's body down. He was stiff now. Just a stiff. I wanted to cry, but not even for him, really, for me. He could just as well have been me.

I didn't even try to look out while the shells were falling. I hunkered down next to Robbie and waited for the shells to kill me or stop.

Sometime around dawn, silence fell over the Tit again. I was cold and I needed to take a leak. I didn't want to stand up outside the bunker, and I didn't want to piss all over myself or Robbie, and I didn't want to foul this bunker we were in together.

There were a few other GIs in the bunker with me. There was another guy lying in the corner of the bunker, dead, with his eyes all clouded over and his face looking like it was frozen stiff. His mouth was twisted. He had to be the guy who was yelling the obscenities. I wonder if the guy next to him, who was still alive, shot him.

I eased over and got a helmet lying next to the live guy. I took my leak in it. My dink felt cold and shriveled in my numb fingers, like when you'd been swimming in real cold water, but my urine steamed and hissed into the bottom of the helmet liner, yellow and strong and powerful, and I was alive.

"Pass me that helmet man," the guy said.

"Yeah, sure," I said. I was alive. Nobody else in the world seemed to care, but I was alive.

The day dawned gray over the brown of the hill.

I could see bodies now, strewn everywhere. Most of the ones I could see were Chinks.

Slowly, our guys started to stick their heads up.

"Jimmy? You all right, man?" That guy was yelling for his friend again.

I wished I had a friend to yell for, or to be hollering for me—"Hey, Tom. You all right, man?" I'd at least know there was somebody here who gave a shit whether I was alive or dead. But the only guy I could think of was Brownie, and I couldn't yell for him; it'd be like yelling for my mother.

I picked up Robbie's radio, but I still couldn't raise anyone on it. All the firepower in the world behind us and it wasn't doing us any good. Why the Chinks didn't come again I'd never know. All they had to do was walk up the hill and kill a few more of us and it'd be theirs.

But they didn't.

And in a few days, the Diggers showed up.

Robbie's hands had started to turn a greenish black and he was bloated under his parka before the Diggers bagged him up and carried him away somewhere. Home? I wondered if they sent him home in this shape. A closed coffin like Chick's and no one knew.

IT FELT GOOD TO GET A LETTER FROM ANNIE. It was a thin, small envelope. It would be a short letter, I knew. She always said less than I wanted. But her letters never got any longer by my leaving them in the envelope. I opened it, tearing the envelope as little as I could.

> February 10, 1953
> New York City
>
> Tom dear,
>
> It is so good to get your letter and learn you are well.
>
> I can tell how difficult it must be for you, even though there is no way for me to fully understand what you are going through. I'm glad it helps you some to write.
>
> Of course, I don't mind if you think of me in the way you wrote. In fact I find it flattering. Now Natalie isn't the only one in our family with a handsome young serviceman in Korea writing her love letters! But you mustn't worry about writing to me about what it is really like over there, if it helps even a bit in your difficult times. Or worry about how often you write. I'll understand, even if I worry about you.
>
> I still have the job I had when you were in New York, but to tell you the truth I'm not enjoying it too much. My boss Margaret continues to be an absolute terror, and Mr. Craig isn't being as helpful as he might be. Enough! You asked about jobs in NY when you return. I have no specific suggestion for you. Except that when the time comes you pick up copies of the N.Y. Times and Herald Tribune, particularly the Sunday editions. Ad agencies are always looking for trainees. You might find it difficult to do that and write though; at least a friend of mine has. If you complete your book and decide to submit it, I might be able to help you. My friend in publishing might be of use.
>
> My life other than work has involved some things to me very interesting, trivial compared with what you are experiencing, but it is all I have to write you about. Was invited to the UN General Assembly last

Saturday. The new building is certainly impressive—the general assembly hall is interesting—although I don't approve of the color combinations or so-called modernistic murals. Had lunch there, and met Rev. Scott, the man from So. Africa who is trying to get the assembly to do something about the situation there. It is quite exciting.

Take care, Tom. And yes, I look forward very much to hearing from you.

Love,

Annie

In all the talking and arguing with Annie, I thought I had begun to know her over the brief days and nights we had. But now Annie's world was not only so far away, but so different from mine that it seemed like I hardly knew her. I still couldn't bring myself to write her honestly about some of the things that went on here. I could tell Will more about this shit than anyone.

31

We left the hill except for a skeleton force and took off by truck with the rest of the Division at night. It was a moonlit night and our breath curled delicate patterns in the winter air, but nobody seemed to know what we were doing. The column moved out with the jeeps and three-quarter-ton trucks leading the way. We drove in blackout. No headlights on any vehicle, just the small red "cat-eyes" that could be seen from up close. The lead jeep relied on moonlight and luck, and each following vehicle clung to the cat-eyes ahead of it. The vehicles rumbled over the rutted roads so slowly the worst jolts were softened. The whole column was serpentine and beautiful in the stillness. You were in the belly of the beast, but the beast was loving and protective. You wanted only to stay close to the cat-eyes ahead of you and behind you.

You bounced on the hard bench of the deuce-and-ahalf, somebody groaned, "Oh, my achin' kidneys. Let me off this son of a bitch at the next stop!" But it didn't even bother me. While we were riding, we were safe. We were not doing anything. You thought you were crazy for enjoying the ride like it was a sleigh ride under a harvest moon at home. But then another GI responded, "We ain't shootin' at no one, and no one's shootin' at us. Shit, man, I kin ride forever!"

It stayed that way for a while; after that, quiet; yet I felt connected to the rest of the men in the trucks snaking ahead of us, and behind us. I still didn't feel close to any individual, I didn't do that any-more, but I felt close to the whole damn convoy.

But we left the "main road," and began driving on what could hardly be called a road; it seemed to go for miles right across the fields, and some stream crossings, and still in blackout. It was not long before one of the big deuce-and-a-halfs ahead of us slid off the "road" and lurched right over on its side, smack in the middle of a damn paddy. One guy got lucky and broke his arm, that might get him home, but no one else was even hurt. The rest of the troops came climbing out of the muck, swearing and stinking of shit. We loaded them into the rest of the trucks. They were not well received. We left the truck for scavengers, ROKs or KATUSAs or whoever; I'd give odds it'd end up on the back streets of Seoul.

Before we covered the next couple of miles, two more deuce-and-a-halfs and one three-quarter-ton truck turned over. By a series of mir-acles no one else was even hurt. But when the last truck ended up in the muck battalion decided we were not leaving any more trucks in any more goddamn paddies, period. Well fine, but it took all of us till near six a.m. to get the truck upright and moving again, by which time all of us stank like we'd been wading around in a honeybucket.

Everything was so screwed up by then even the army realized we were going to have to change the plan. We were told we would get some rest. So right out there in the midst of the stinking paddies we broke out our sleeping bags. We got to spend about three hours in our fart sacks trying to get some sleep. It smelt awful in there, and the bag was picking up an aroma that would last a long time, but it was nice and warm, and I was ready to stay there for the rest of the war.

After a few hours we got routed out for a feast of C rations. The dried prunes were particularly delicious this morning. They rounded us up to continue the mission.

We rode a little farther and hooked up with some Greeks we were going to go the rest of the way with on foot. The Greeks were great guys, but hardly any of them spoke any English at all, which was a lot more than the

Greek we spoke. They were also great hikers. They walked us what felt like endless more miles to get into position for a joint attack at dawn.

We were choggying through the paddies, about as quiet as a large body of troops carrying all their gear was when they thought they were on safe ground, when these guys with mustaches like Pancho Villa silently appeared, steam hissing out from their nostrils like smoke, bandoleers crisscrossing their chests, and bayonets at the ready! Scared the shit out of us.

"It's the fawking Turks!" a Greek guy hissed at me.

One of the Turks said something and I guessed they were asking us for the password, in Turkish, which wasn't too surprising, but didn't exactly help. Well one of the Greek officers knew Turkish apparently, so he went up and started jabbering away at the Turk, his arms waving around like he'd been attacked by bees, but that was almost worse than no one knowing it. It was one scary moment, but these allies finally let us pass.

To celebrate making it through our own lines alive, we drank cognac out of canteen cups and ate cheese with the Greeks until about three a.m. the next morning. A guy named Andreas, about four feet tall and with a fantastic mustache of his own that twirled in two waxed hoops on either side of his nose, told me the Greeks and the "fawking Turks" hated each other worse than the Japanese and the Koreans did.

Another of the ten thousand things about this "United Nations police action" they never taught us in Troop Information & Education. I wondered what it was about drawing these lines on the map, and everybody behind one line being so sure their shit didn't stink and the guy on the other side of it was nothing but a turd incarnate. Peace was worth fighting for, but countries? What the hell were they anyway? What was the point? I was beginning to think it was stupid to fight about countries, any of them.

I asked Andreas if he'd ever been to America and told him about doing battle with some of his compatriots who had been tearing up Andy's White Castle in New York.

"No," he laughed, "but I weesh I was there."

Andreas kept telling me how great Greece was. He said "the son-beeetching hills" here were nothing compared to his hills at home in Greece. I had to come visit him in Athens when "theese shit" was all done.

"I'd like that, see where Homer and Aristotle and those guys hung out and started everything."

"Sure," he agreed, and, there was "really fine pooosy home."

"Sure," I said, when I got what he was saying. "For sure I'll come to Athens. No shit now, Andreas."

"No sheet, Tomas!" He kept pouring cognac into my canteen cup and laughing while I drank it. His teeth were small, like a puppy's, and they flashed white in the darkness when he lit a cigarette and handed it to me, grinning, before another Greek tore into his ass for lighting the match in blackout. I took a drag and handed it back to Andreas. He took another quick hit himself before he giggled and ground it out under his boot. But not quick enough—the other Greek was a noncom, and he stepped over and smashed Andreas right in the mouth and yelled at him. If there was anyone that could see the match they'd long since have heard the noncom yelling anyway. But the warm glow of the cognac in my belly had made me invincible. We curled up in the fart sacks to grab a little shut-eye.

They woke us for the attack at five a.m. The moon was still up, and we could even see stars fading into the gray-blue sky. We had to double time on the attack, but the paddies were frozen that morning so it wasn't so bad. The problem came when we found ourselves climbing a ridge in full gear after doing all that running. As we slipped and scrambled up what wasn't even really a path, and the cognac started to sweat out of me, my battle pack kept tugging me backwards. Why were we carrying all this gear?

But I looked around and saw something crazier—there were a couple of guys from the signal corps scrambling along with us, dirty, wet and unshaven, carrying this huge movie camera, and filming us. I wondered what in the hell was going on. Something to show this was a real United Nations effort, not just Americans, I supposed. But it sure seemed goofy.

My foot struck a rock, and I almost fell, but I looked down and it was no rock that had tripped me It was a head, attached to a uniform sprawled just off the path; it looked like it'd been there a long time, to the point where it was more like a skull than a head. A Greek was swearing beside me; he had stepped on what was left of another body.

The whole goddamn side of the ridge was like an open graveyard. There were dried up bodies and shredded remnants of uniforms worn into the rocks, and rusted rifles lying everywhere. The bodies were intact, with the arms and legs still attached to the trunks, so they had to have been killed by small arms fire, or hand to hand, not blown apart by artillery. God knew how long they'd been there—-they didn't even stink anymore. We clanked our way among the corpses and debris all over the goddamn ridge with a lot of swearing in English, and I could tell the Greek I was hearing was more of the same, a true United Nations effort. But I hadn't heard a shot fired.

Just as I pondered this, the sound of artillery whistled overhead, way overhead, and there was a dull thud from somewhere over the ridge, and another and another as the shells impacted. What the hell was our forward observer doing? As if in answer, the next rounds came whistling in, right over our heads, and landed right ahead of us. Dirt and pieces of bodies went flying all over the place. It was like blasting up a damn cemetery—Christ, the FO must have called in drop five hundred and fire for effect!

"Yeeahoo!" one of our guys yelled, and our guys were just standing there watching the bodies fly around. So were the Greeks. Two or three of them on my right were pounding each other on the back and laughing like crazy. We were capturing a goddamn graveyard with the most magnificent artillery support one could imagine.

A moment later I was nearly knocked off my feet by a blow to my back. I turned around, startled, and there was Andreas, pounding me on the back, laughing like a wild man. He thrust his canteen at me, grinning, "Dreenk theese!" he yelled up at me.

I tipped the canteen, and the cognac backed up into my nose before it burned all the way to my belly.

241

Andreas laughed. "Thees is the way to fight a fawking war, hey? Drinking cognac and blowing the sheeet out of dead men, hey!"

"Thees is!" I was Ernest fawking Hemingway.

"Closer! You fawkers!" Andreas yelled, his teeth flashing below his loop-the-loop mustache.

Closer it was. Our own artillery nearly got us. I didn't know what the problem was, except like they always say, communication. The Greek company commander and our forward observer walked those artillery rounds right down the ridge to us. The last firing for effect wasn't twenty-five yards in front of us. It was a good thing we were all drunk or we might have been scared. Even drunk, it started to get to me, seeing all the damn bodies flying around under our barrage, for nothing but the movies so far as I could tell.

"Thees is just sheeet, Tom." Andreas had stopped laughing and looked at me as he handed me the canteen again. He shook his head. "Just sheeet."

Later, after we'd blown the shit out of everything in sight but ourselves, we moved back down the hill. Mission accomplished, I guessed.

We drove back in daylight, passing the trucks we'd lost on the way. They were lying on their sides in the paddies, like huge fallen beasts, waiting for their bones to be picked clean.

AFTER NO MAIL FOREVER FROM ANYONE but my folks, I got a couple of letters from Will Lindeman. It was funny how big a deal it was to get letters here. If none came for a while I began to think no one but my mother and father even knew I was alive anymore, or cared. When they did come, they proved the real world was still out there. Even from Lindeman and his pissing and moaning about how tough he had it in sunny California.

I opened my letters by postmark dates, that way it was more like I was hearing about things as they happened. I didn't bother to even find a private spot in the bunker to read these.

Fort Ord, California
March 8, 1953

Tom:

So Stalin is dead. Have you noticed any change over there?

Here it is Sunday and I am on post trying to catch up on my letter writing. Today I have perhaps overly ambitious intentions of writing five letters, but if I don't start making out better with this typewriter I'm going to give it all up and go drink beer.

I've got it pretty nice. I'm going to clerk's school and not doing too bad. However, you know I have a tendency to fuck everything up by getting drunk or getting caught bugging out or with whiskey in my room. I do have a room now and it is much better, only three of us in the room. They made me squad leader. Three of us have a room with no lights out and we don't pull any details. Of course the rest of the boys are out in the barracks but I don't give a shit about them anyhow.

Actually the school is pretty good. We had a solid week on Mil. Justice, which as we both know is a misnomer. At least from everything I have seen, while it may be military, it is anything but just. I used to wonder how the Army wasted four years at the Point. Now I wonder how they learn all this in four years, if they do. I can get off from five every night to five-thirty the next morning, and every weekend, so it isn't so bad.

Incidentally, my appreciation for classical music has been enriched considerably every night three or four of us come over to the Library, which has a record room and quite a collection. I don't know a goddamn thing about music, but I do enjoy it and I am learning—I will be the only Gandy Dancer on the whole Great Northern railroad line that has a true appreciation of Beethoven.

Christ, I wish we could go out and get drunk some night. I have gained ever more appreciation of women of the other color, and you should see some of the nice stuff that frequents the clubs around here. Of course, I suppose you are surrounded with it there. They played Hot Toddy at one of the clubs Fri. night and I experienced quite a nostalgic feeling in the pit of my stomach. Remember the Key Club.

Write soon—
Will

No, I hadn't noticed any change over here since Uncle Joe's death. But I was hoping.

Mainly we stayed hunkered down, but some nights the Chinks came and we killed some of them, and sometimes they killed some of us. It went on and on.

That damn Lindeman had it knocked. Sometimes I thought he did all the pissing and moaning just to make me feel better by getting me mad at him. The perverse bastard had to know how cushy he had it. I was getting tired of hearing about all those beautiful girls, and what hurt was I was sure it was true. You could say a lot of things about Will, but one of them wasn't that he was a liar. I was a lot more likely to lie than he was.

But I didn't know what it was with Lindeman and his fixation on "women of the other color." I had nothing against women of the other color, whatever the "other color" was, or any color, white was fine too, but this preoccupation of his was a little weird. And he hadn't got the foggiest idea of what it was like over here, no matter how many times I told him—"surrounded with it there"—I was getting so horny I could die and he gave me that.

> Fort Ord, California
> March 15, 1953

Tom:

Well, I hope you get to the drinking and fucking in Korea soon? So far it still doesn't sound too great over there.

Did I tell you I am reading a critique of philosophy by Durant that's kind of shabby? He doesn't even mention the Scholastics. The other day in the library I picked up *Problems of Philosophy* by Ewing from Cambridge, which has at least two very good chapters "Cause" and "Freedom." Sometimes I can't tell whether he's all fucked up or I'm just too dense. For instance, he attempts to prove the possibility of a synthetic *a priori* proposition which, while not a logical contradiction, is at least completely foreign to my way of thinking.

Well, now for some moaning—today I am depressed beyond all depression (I would go jack off but these bastards have got everything figured out so we never have any privacy goddamnit). I wound up 3d in the class with a 94 average and they want to keep me as an instructor. It isn't a bad deal for somebody living out here 'cause they live like kings, but this is the last place in the world I want to spend my time. I refused, I threatened, and when that didn't work I whined, but I'm fucked. I told the O.I.C. I'll be the worst instructor he'll ever have and he laughed saying, "You'll work out fine."

I'm going to enroll in USAE for six courses, get a job in the PX seven nights a week so I can save money and go to Harvard, and turn to dope. Tom, the more I think about getting drunk together the more I think of it. Get transferred back here, Goddammit!

Write immediately—-
   Will
P.S. I found $5 in the Co. street yesterday.

A synthetic *a priori* proposition, which while not a logical contradiction, was at least completely foreign to my way of thinking? Christ almighty. Mine too.

I was never going to get to the drinking and whoring in Korea. Now and then women straggled up across the No-Farm Line to service the troops. The last ones were operating out of the back of a deuce-and-a-half with a couple of fart sacks they'd scrounged up somewhere. Lieutenant Winton got wind of it and volunteered a few of us to send them on their way back south. Eddie Kvard was fired up about this particular "mission," but when we dragged them out like frightened animals and our flashlights shined on their greasy hair, and filthy faces and hands, even he lost his enthusiasm.

"Meece" the troops called them—Meece being the plural of Moose—and the troops used them like animals; they were human dregs of this war. I couldn't even begin to understand what their lives must have been like. Yet as we turned them loose on the dark road south, one of the women's breasts swung free, and underneath my feelings of pity, sadness, disgust, anger, I felt a sudden flash of desire. God, this was pitiful; I was worse than goddamn Eddie Kvard. I took a vow of chastity while on Korean soil. Not to anyone, just to myself.

I opened the next letter from Will, and it was very short:

THE GRASS

Fort Ord, California
March 16, 1953

Tom:

Just a line, to send you word I received from home that you may not have heard. Our friend Moira is supposed to be hot for that Art Ramsted. The guy's so flush he can drive a Plymouth and everyone still knows he's rich. She's going skiing with him and his family out West somewhere. Next thing we'll be invited for the wedding. Or did you get invited already? If so, I feel insulted, after all I did for that girl. After all I practically made her!

You know the guy don't you? What the hell do you make of this development?

I start teaching Monday Goddammit.

How's Korea?

Write soon.

Will

P.S. I've been thinking of suicide, can you think of any good reason not to?

P.P.S. I'm serious about your book! Send me a copy immediately!

I read and reread his letter, and I got so damn mad that it didn't make any sense. What did I care anyway? Ramsted. The guy was nothing more than a rich pantywaist. I couldn't believe Moira would marry him. Not after all her bullshit about how she could love only me. No, I could believe it. What pissed me off was how it made me feel.

I was mad at Lindeman. I was mad at Ramsted. I was mad at Moira. And most of all, I was mad at myself for the way it got to me. And the feeling I found under all my anger and didn't want to admit. I had another thing to be scared of. Coming home and being alone; no Annie, no Moira, just me and Lindeman to get drunk and argue and sniff around "society girls" forever.

For quite a while I sat there in my corner of the bunker, contemplating. In fact after a while one of the guys in the bunker leaned over and asked if I was okay. I told him yes. But God, I had to get out of this place before I went crazy. Lindeman ought to be somewhere he might get killed; maybe then he wouldn't be so damn glib about suicide.

A WEEK LATER I GOT MY NEXT LETTER from Moira. After Lindeman's last letter, I looked at it a minute before I began to open it, but then I just tore it open. Moira wrote about her "reduced social life" but she'd been with Arthur Ramsted to see Les Brown and dance to *Slaughter on Tenth Avenue* and *American in Paris*, and to a buffet supper at the SAE house with him, but she didn't love Arthur. He was only "the Country Club and a fetid laugh on the still spring air," she said, but she seemed to get along okay with the social life, whether reduced or not. It was a bullshit letter and I just tore it up and threw it away.

Christ, that was a good way to drive myself crazy. It was just easier to brood about that shit than to remember where I was. A little more of this and I'd be ready to put in for a Section 8 discharge as a psycho. I'd have a lot of company. Sometimes I wondered if most of us here weren't candidates.

The other morning as we were coming back from Division, with the sun not even up over the frozen tundra, we heard voices in cadence coming from the other side of a hill. When we eased over the rise, there they were, the United States Marines, double timing along the sides of the road their breath vaporing in the air, no shirts on, slapping their guts with open hands in time as they jogged—chanting it out:

> If I die in a combat zone,
> Box me up and ship me home.
> Sound off—
> Hut two
> Sound off
> Three four
> One two three four!

Shades of basic. My mother always said God loved the crazy. If there was a God, those gyrenes would be in good shape.

32

A lot of fighting went on in the "Iron Triangle" area but none right here on our part of the line for a while. The negotiators were talking again and we'd made a proposal to exchange sick and wounded prisoners. The best and worst thing was that there was nothing to do but sit here, counting days till I came up for R&R, Rest and Relaxation, or I&I, Intercourse and Inebriation, as the troops called it. But I had time on my hands to work on my book, and I was getting a lot done.

The Republicans were helping us out with their "New Look." Supposedly, they were going to get a lot more bang for the buck out of the taxpayers' defense dollars, mostly, it seemed, by relying on the threat of nuclear retaliation to scare the piss out of everyone. We wouldn't have to go to all the trouble and expense of maintaining large conventional forces, i.e. us. What it meant to us so far was that battalion gas supply had been cut a flat twenty-five percent this month. Economy. It also meant little inconveniences like one batch of men instead of two getting back each week to battalion to get a shower.

We hadn't had a can of beer or a candy bar for weeks. We were going to have to start draining gas out of the trucks to run the kitchen. And the army as usual had to make a terrible situation worse by making us take three deuce-and-a-halfs all the way back to the Division Motor

Pool for maintenance. Some clown in S-4 thought it was a good idea. There was one hope left for the whole state of affairs—that the great Nobodaddy Eisenhower got beer to us. Or we went dickering for some from the Koreans.

You couldn't figure the Koreans. The few I'd gotten to know at all seemed okay. But I didn't know. We had choggy boys who helped out. They did whatever was asked of them, from scrounging up equipment to carrying gear in the middle of combat. They seemed to like you, and want to be friends, but sometimes they were slickee boys who cut through a tent wall in the middle of the night, reached inside, and stole you blind.

There were even stories of ROK units attacking our units in platoon-sized groups to steal GI equipment. Hell, we supplied the ROKs with uniforms, equipment, ammunition, everything; and nobody ever got enough. Including us. And they turned around and stole from us. Brownie said we'd steal from the Koreans if the situation was the reverse. He just might have been right, and that pissed me off more.

Of course, when we needed to get winterizing kits for our jeeps— canvas doors and a top to keep rain and snow out of the otherwise open vehicle—we couldn't get them through regular channels. No way. How did we end up getting them? Brownie and me and Picasso and good old Gary Kowalski, that's how.

Picasso was our supply sergeant, a guy who worked in an art museum in Boston when he was back in the real world. Sergeant Kowalski had wound up running a GI laundry in Inchon, where the GIs got clean uniforms to go home in. Picasso heard somehow that Gary, or I should say Gary's lieutenant, was short about ten thousand pillowcases. Pillowcases the dumbshit lieutenant had signed for, but that were nowhere to be found. Brownie had an idea about how to turn the missing pillowcases into jeep kits.

If Brownie were running this war, we'd all have been home months ago. Brownie and Picasso and I got Lieutenant Winton's permission to go off line to try to do some business with Gary. I went purely and simply because I'd told Brownie how Gary was a buddy of mine, and if anyone could enlist him in the wheeling and dealing it would take to get the winterizing kits for our jeeps, I was the guy.

So we got a junket to Inchon.

The laundry was as immense as an airplane hanger, with a high curving metal roof like an oversize Quonset hut, grounded in a concrete floor the size of a couple of football fields. There were rows of huge drums to launder the filth of war out of uniforms worn by the guys coming off line and preparing to go stateside, and line after line of cumbersome presses.

There was a clean smell to the whole place, like a fresh basket of laundry my mother had taken down from the clothesline. I hadn't smelled anything like it since coming to Korea; it smelled so good it was intoxicating.

Except for Gary, and the lieutenant he theoretically reported to but never saw, Koreans, all of them women, ran the place. There had to be a hundred of them. They wore white cotton work clothes, splashed with colorful silk, like flowers amid the heavy equipment.

The building was filled with the pleasant murmur of their voices chatting with each other heightened by an occasional yell to a friend across the building. The giant presses hissd and steam rose from them as they opened and closed.

One of the women looked at me as we walked past. She was young, with a smooth, delicately boned face. Her eyes were dark, and her lips somehow reminded me of sweet, ripe plums, and I had this crazy urge to bend down and kiss her. I smiled at her, and for a second she smiled back at me, her lips parting. But then she grimaced, as though she was in pain. I was so struck by her face that it was only then it fully entered my consciousness she was very pregnant. Her belly was so large she seemed to have trouble reaching over it to the handle of the press. She might have been about to have her baby.

But Gary shepherded us back to his office, in the rear of the building, to confer.

The office, naturally, was the Taj Mahal of South Korea. It was furnished in lacquered black and whore-house red.

"So, Sergeant Kowalski," asked Picasso, "how is it you're short ten thousand pillow cases?"

"Come on, you know why! Because the women who work here steal! All the time!" Gary grinned. He was hiding his choirboy face behind a bushy, drooping mustache, and even grinning, he looked sinister back there.

Gary sat behind a desk about the size of a Ping-Pong table. He could be running the biggest poker game in the Far East; the desk had piles of Korean currency, *won*, stacked on it. It had to be payday for the Koreans.

The won was Monopoly money, hardly worth shit, even to the Koreans, but Gary's .45, with which he couldn't be depended on to hit his pecker, was on the table at his right hand. Two trusty retainers, Military Police, were at Gary's side to assist him in guarding the won. Gary still had those big pecs he had when I last saw him riding off to the south from the Replacement Depot, but the beefy MPs made him look scrawny. They each wore a .45 in a dark brown leather holster.

"They hide stuff. Under their clothes. Between their boobs. In their crotches!" Gary laughed. "The GIs can't search them, only Korean women police. So they just bribe each other and split the take!"

If Gary was running things the way he used to play poker, the Koreans were not the only ones splitting the take. Gary had come a long way from Williston.

Gary's lieutenant who'd signed for all the pillow cases was getting short; he was due to go back to the world more *sukoshi*, and he didn't know whether to shit or go blind about the missing ten thousand pillow cases. He was going to have to turn them over to the next guy who signed for the laundry, or he was afraid he was going to be an indentured servant to the army the rest of his natural life.

This was where we came to the rescue.

Brownie, who personally controlled much of South Korea, had a favor coming from a supply sergeant down at Pusan. Brownie's Pusan connection just so happened to have squirreled away about two thousand pairs of combat boots that weren't on his books. The trick was to change the two thousand pairs of boots into ten thousand pillowcases and winterizing kits for our jeeps, thereby making Lieutenant Winton a big hero with battalion.

"No problem," smiled Brownie at Gary, a fellow man of the world, bemused by the intricacy of it all. "My man down at Pusan ships the boots on the next British ship to Hong Kong and we get *takusan* sheets. Enough for you to make over into twenty thousand pillow cases, all the pillow cases your lieutenant will ever need." Brownie also knew an MP First Sergeant down in Seoul, one of these Regular Army thirty year guys, who knew where he could winterize every jeep we had, for the other half of the pillow cases. "You dig?" Brownie's voice came out smooth as molasses.

"I dig," said Gary, the dude from North Dakota.

The final leg of the great trade was to take place back in Seoul City. Once Brownie got the two thousand boots sent to Hong Kong for enough sheets to make twenty thousand pillow cases, and Gary had delivered the extra ten thousand to Brownie, who would deliver them to the First Sergeant for the winterizing kits, minus a slight spiff along the way to the British forces for arranging the Hong Kong transport.

Before we left, Gary pulled me aside and asked me if I wanted any light reading material to take back to the line. In the corner of his office Gary had his library and memorabilia, in two fifty-five gallon drums. Each drum brimmed over with books and pamphlets and photographs and drawings and statues and carvings all confiscated from our boys before they returned home to mom and pop or the wife and kids or the girl next door.

Comic books like *Tillie the Toiler* and *Popeye the Sailorman* that never made it to the drugstore in Fargo. Photographs and drawings showing women and men, and women and women, women and various animals engaged in every sexual activity imaginable, and some not imaginable, at least previously by me. Carvings of sexual organs of immense size and diversity challenging all preconceptions of human anatomy. Playing cards with fifty-two different positions on the backs. Any of these artistic efforts might have touched a chord in me, if seen singly and under other circumstances, but taken together in one big dose, the stuff made you want to barf. I told Gary thanks but no thanks.

A Korean woman came in from the floor, jabbering away and motioning for Gary to come. One of the MPs started to give her the heave-ho, but Gary stopped him.

"Goddamn! I'll go take a look," he said.

We went with him, and there was a cluster of women around the press where the pregnant girl had been working. She was lying on her back in a bunch of white sheets on the floor of the laundry. She was up on her elbows, with a pillow behind her back, and one of the other women holding a pillow behind. Her head was tilted back, and her eyes were closed, and her face scrunched up in pain. Her skirt was hiked way up, and her legs were bent, and there was an old woman kneeling on the floor between the girl's legs.

The old woman had this bloody little head in her hands. Then right while we were standing there, the rest of the baby came out, all slippery and bloody. Another woman handed the old woman big scissors to cut the cord connecting the baby to the girl. The baby was a boy. The little guy hollered like hell, and I wondered if that was regular at this point or if he felt his cord being cut, which you would think would sure hurt.

They laid the baby up by the mother's face while they cleaned him up. She was all sweaty, but she smiled and cupped the little guy's head in her hands and smiled at him. She looked so tired and beautiful. I felt like I was in church. I relaxed. It was like all the air went out of me and I deflated. I was tired from doing nothing but watch her have the baby. I couldn't tell if the baby looked anything like her, but at least he didn't look like Gary.

"All right," Gary said. "Let's get this mess cleaned up. Somebody has to take her and the kid home. On their own time. Tell 'em," he said to the Korean guy standing next to him.

Before we left, Gary and I made plans to try to hook up for R&R shortly. Sergeant Kowalski had a line on how to get hold of Sergeant

Manley so what was left of the gang could get together for old time's sake and tear Tokyo apart. With my lowly single stripe, I might be at the bottom of our class but while Gary and Walt were still serving their sentences in Korea, I would be on my way home.

THE GREAT TRIANGULAR TRADE MADE everybody happy, especially Lieutenant Winton. Everybody except the poor supply officer somewhere in the Far East Command—FECOM— who'd signed on the dotted line for two thousand pairs of combat boots that had vanished. Brownie and Picasso and I got to Seoul to celebrate the consummation of the trade, and, more importantly, Brownie's last day before returning to the World, by getting drunk with him and the British.

Seoul in springtime was not the place you might pick to go sightseeing. But Seoul was a place everyone ought to see. Syngman Rhee had seen it, I'd give him that, and yet he talked of South Korea "going it alone" in the war if the UN settled it in a way not to his liking. Rhee at least knew what he was talking about doing to his own people; I'd give him that too. But Seoul needed to be seen by all the old guys who made the wars and by all the young guys who thought they wanted to fight them.

The city was totally shot up. Many of the buildings were destroyed, and the rubble was as the guns left it. Some buildings were standing, but even in those the windows often were out. The steps to the City Hall, where MacArthur made the big deal out of turning the city back to Rhee when the UN recaptured it the first time, had tank tracks crunched straight up the middle of them. The buildings that were being used reeked of the food the Koreans ate. The big favorite was *kimchi*, a kind of sauerkraut that could have anything in it from all kinds of vegetables to dog meat. It smelled like cooked cabbage, but that was one inadequate description. In a crowded lobby it'd knock you right over.

The people left in the city were women and kids. The Korean men in Seoul were mostly papasans with long white beards carrying a ton of stuff on A-frames on their backs, or guys in uniforms like ours, so I supposed they were okay. The rest were either off in the ROK army or the

Korean Attached Troops United States Army—KATUSA—or dead. Maybe some of them had gone north to join up with the communists, I supposed, but not likely.

But mostly Seoul was a city of children. Hundreds, maybe thousands of kids, roamed the streets of Seoul. They were drawn and dirty, scabrous, and with open sores, dressed in castoffs and rags. They begged pitiably from you and then grabbed for your wallet if you took it out. They hustled you with "Hey, GI! Want number one shoe-shine?" fighting to get your foot on their box, and "Hey, GI! Want to fuckee, fuckee, my sister? Number fucking one girlsan!" There were so many of them, and they were often in packs, so it was hard to see them as kids.

But I saw one.

One little girl, hardly older than ten, who had to have been caught in a fire. Her face was covered with stretched ridges of brown and reddish and white scar tissue and these big scared eyes staring out at me from all the scar tissue. I wondered for a second whether it was napalm or a round of white phosphorous? Whether it was one of theirs or one of ours? But what the hell difference did it make what it was, or whether it was theirs or ours?

I wanted to hug her and make it feel better, and at the same time it was so hard to look at her. I was ashamed I was even part of the human race. I tried to give her a handful of Military Payment Currency, but when I held it out to her, another kid plucked it out of her hand. He ran down the street and she scurried after him, running like her feet hurt. She called after him, "*Oppa! Oppa!*" but he left her behind by the time he turned a corner.

I followed them to the corner, but they were gone.

I felt this heavy sadness push down on me, and my damn shoulders shook, and I stood there crying. Thank God none of the guys were with me. I wondered how these kids survived, and what kind of a future they'd have. No matter who won this war, these kids had already lost it.

THE OPPORTUNITY TO ATTEND A PARTY with the Brits was part of the benefits of the triangular trade. After seeing the town, Brownie, Picasso, a couple of the Brits and I got hold of in the neighborhood of thirty quarts of champagne. Over the course of an all-nighter we managed to finish them off, every bloody one—a new world's record—we all went screaming through the sound barrier. We got drunk was the short of it.

After the first few quarts, the Bloody Tories, as Picasso called them, started singing this song to the tune of "On Top of Old Smokey":

> Way down in Seoul City
> I met a Miss Lee
> She said for a short time
> Oh come sleep with me
> Her breath smelled of kimchi
> Her chest it was flat
> No hair on her pussy
> Now how about that!

"'On Top of Old Smokey' is our song," I said. "Why don't you put words to one of your own damn songs. All right?"

"Listen, lad," said one Tory, like he was humoring me.

"Listen, lad, yourself," I started, but Brownie interrupted me.

"Easy, Tom, easy." He turned to the Tory. "Listen, man. You ain't been usin' your eyes, you know?" Next thing he was telling them how the Korean ladies of the night were better endowed than their Japanese counterparts. Shortly before morning he determined to show Picasso and me the astuteness of his powers of observation by seeking out some such ladies.

For once I didn't follow Brownie's lead. However weakened my resolve, I left alone, determined to maintain my vow of chastity while on Korean soil. I was walking along thinking about that girl having her baby. But as I walked on a still dark street, down a steep hill with a slippery surface, like cobblestones slick with rain, I went past some hooches, Korean houses made of mud and straw, all crowded together. One had a door open onto a front porch. The porch was strung with lines like clotheslines draped with dripping seaweed and with fish.

As I came past, three Korean women started yelling at me: "Hey! GI! Lucky GI! How about a short time!" I could hardly see the women through the weeds and the fish, and I had a hunch they were staying in the dark for a reason. The thought went through my head that I might even get rolled, but still I got this impulse to forget about my stupid vow. No one would ever know, and any day back on line I might die, miserably horny.

I gave one of the women all the MPC I had left in my pocket. I figured we'd go inside. But no, she pulled down my pants right there on the spot. Next thing I knew she was on her knees fishing in my shorts and hauled me out. Her teeth were right on me and I had this flash of fear— she was going to bite it off! I jumped back, almost doing serious harm to myself, and took off down the hill. As I staggered away, holding my pants up and trying to get dressed as I went, the women hooted and laughed behind me. The whole experience was not too great and I was glad no one was there with me.

The next day Picasso told me he and Brownie ended up in a hooch, on the outskirts of Seoul occupied by amicable Korean damsels, as Will Lindeman would put it. Picasso accused me of just not liking dark meat, and said his girl was really nice. He claimed he felt the best he'd felt in months, despite the catastrophe that ensued after I left. Due to the champagne, they made love only more or less, his performance not winning any medals, even by his own admission, but she was so soft and loving it didn't make any difference. She liked it better, so he claimed. Maybe. Maybe not. He didn't even know her name and he wasn't sure if he'd recognize her if he saw her again. They lay there, with him against her ass, while she held him between her legs and he was drifting off to sleep, when disaster struck.

The Gestapo arrived in the guise of several MPs who caught him in the whorehouse and practically in the whore. When the MPs burst in, he just burrowed under the covers, like he was going to be invisible under there while the MPs yelled at him to come out. He admitted he was lucky he didn't get his equipment shot off when he emerged. As it was, it was going to cost him a fifty-dollar fine and a reprimand.

Meanwhile Brownie got off totally free. The MPs, like half of the United States Army in FECOM, most likely owed him for one thing or another. The guy should consider a career in politics when he got home. He was on his way home, and I envied him. I'd missed him. I also thought I had to get out of here myself. At least I had R&R coming up in a couple of weeks.

THINGS WERE QUIET IN FRONT of the Witch's Tit, but all kinds of shit went on along the line. We heard about the Marines storming up hills named Carson, and Vegas and Reno, fighting their way up through murderous fire, and I wondered if any of them were those gyrenes we saw jogging back at Division in the dead of winter with their damn shirts off. They'd be crazy enough to do it. And there was supposed to be bloody, bloody fighting going on at a place called Pork Chop Hill where a handful of isolated GIs stood off a goddamn horde of Chinese. I guessed it was all supposed to show we hadn't lost our will to fight, but whether or not we were right to intervene here, you had to wonder if all the killing was really accomplishing anything now. At least the damn armistice negotiations were going again. If we fought as well as they negotiated we'd be pushed back to the Red River Valley yet.

THE DAY BEFORE I LEFT FOR R&R I got a letter from Annie.

It had a return address I recognized—Mrs. Abrams house. A visit home, I figured, as I opened it.

> Richmond, Virginia
> April 30, 1953
> Tom dear,
> I'm the one who has been remiss about answering letters, and I'm sure you've been wondering what's happened to me.
> However—I've had me a spell of lousy luck, and am still trying to find my equilibrium. The job I had when you were in NY, I never made it a secret, I didn't enjoy too much—but stuck with it until the pressure became too much. So I quit—and came back to Virginia where I'm going to stay for a few months—if not permanently.

I'm staying with Mother and Natalie here until my nerves settle down—then I am going to try and find an apartment and a job. I broke down, if you must know. I'm seeing a psychiatrist. I feel ashamed, and I wasn't going to tell you at all, but now I have. Enough! I don't want you to dwell on any of this.

Natalie is in tough shape too, but for good reason. She has a fine new son—Adam—but her Ralph is reported missing somewhere in that godforsaken place you're in. Very difficult for her.

Speaking of which—you take very good care of yourself, Tom. You have your whole life ahead of you, and I know it is going to be a happy and successful one, no matter what you decide to do. Mother and Natalie both send you their best.

Now that you know why I've been remiss I hope you'll forgive me and not think too badly of me. Your letters are more of a comfort than you know.

Love,
Annie

I felt so sad for Annie. There was something about her I just couldn't understand. A weakness that she couldn't understand herself and couldn't do anything about. She seemed to have so much shit in her life. I wished that I could be there to put my arms around her, hold her the way I did when she told me about the asshole.

"I'm seeing a psychiatrist," she wrote. I remembered McAndrews' lectures to us in Basic Pysch. I liked his stuff about Joe McCarthy's sleazy tricks, but when McAndrews got into "mental illness" with all his mumbojumbo about "personality deviations," "organic disorders," "delusions," "paranoia," "hysteria," "manic-depressive insanity," and "schizophrenia," it seemed like he got into a bag of tricks of his own. A bunch of labels, not for real people.

None of them described the Annie I knew. "I broke down"—what did that mean? What happened inside her when she "broke down?" It sounded like an old car wearing out, needing new parts, or perhaps beyond fixing. I knew it was not like that with Annie, but I didn't know what it was like, and that scared me. I wanted to be able to fix her. Yet, if this had happened twice to her, it could happen again, whether I was there to hold her or not. This time Annie told me more than I wanted to hear. More about me. And wanting to fix her wasn't the way I wanted to love her.

Christ, that was awful about Natalie's husband. He could be dead and had never even seen his son, and she was left hanging, not knowing, to raise the kid all by herself. I hardly knew Natalie, and I never met her husband. For all I knew he could have been one of the officers for the crazy bunch of gyrenes I saw last winter. Of course, their son, Adam, was just a basketball when I met him. The news about Ralph missing in action spooked me.

I sat with Annie's letter in my hand, and I felt sad, and scared. This place was messing me up. It was a good thing I was getting out of here for some R&R.

33

I caught a drop to Fukuoka and a C47 to Tokyo where I was going to meet Walt Manley and Gary Kowalski.

The trip gave me a chance to digest official pamphlet "AFFE PAM 12-7 Rest and Recuperation JAPAN." This told me Japan had one of the world's highest VD rates. In addition to gonorrhea and syphilis, it offered chancroid, immune to penicillin—all of which might send me home "physically crippled, unable to marry safely, and a sufferer throughout life." "Liquor, prostitution and narcotics go hand in hand through the Far East." "WATCH OUT! SMOKE YOUR OWN CIGARETTES AND NO ONE ELSE'S."

"Japan is one of the 'have-not' countries, and its economy is essentially weak." The reason for its weakness was summed up as "too many people per square mile, 853 as compared to 51 in the U.S." With my first walk down a Japanese street, I would be "impressed immediately by three things" concerning the people: "first, in stature, they are small; second, there are so many of them; and third, they are formal and seemingly polite." I noted the seemingly. "The Japanese have always been taught to conceal their feelings, to show neither pain nor pleasure. They are so poker-faced it often seems impossible to tell what is going on in their minds."

Nightclubbing was an expensive luxury. "Such things as cover charges, tips for the ever-present hostesses, and other charges are not mentioned beforehand, but are included in the bill."

Sergeants Manley and Kowalski were already there and waiting for me in the bar in the hotel in Tokyo. It was a wonder they were willing to be seen in public with a peon corporal like me. It was one of the few times I wished Lieutenant Winton had given me a third stripe. Brownie got Winton to give me the second one, right after the great triangular trade, but since Winton didn't like my attitude, I didn't get a third stripe, although he knew damn well I was entitled to it. Gary looked his same new self with his mustache that went so well with his body-builder physique. Walt didn't look so hot. He was very sharp in his khakis, you could cut a steak on the crease, and he was still wearing that wire-brush haircut, but he looked older, tired.

After a minimum amount of pounding each other around about how good it was to see each other, we went forth into the falling dusk in search of the nightclubs, and the chance to ruin ourselves for life, including, it seemed, Walt. So Walt might be not so much tired as prematurely guilty. When we hit the streets it turned out everybody in Japan was hustling all the time. We went down the Ginza and everybody was bouncing off each other like the balls coming down in *pachinko*, their version of pinball. I could feel the energy in the air. It reminded me of the going-to-work crowd in New York. Except it also was kind of scary. Even though there were Americans all over the place, when we walked down the crowded sidewalk, it seemed like a torrent of Japanese flowed around us, and we were small boats that could be washed downstream at any second.

The Japanese didn't appear to pay much attention to us, but we ran up against a bunch of young Japanese guys, crossing a small footbridge. They jabbered at us, glaring as they stood in front of us on the narrow bridge, like they were angry at us for being there. I supposed because we kicked the shit out of them in the war, even if they more than had it coming, after the way they stabbed us in the back. When they deliberately bumped against us, they were picking the wrong GIs to hassle.

Under the bridge stagnated the foulest smelling water I'd ever encountered, in Korea, there, or stateside. Gary looked at one of the punks and then he looked at Walt and me, and then below. He picked up one of the wise-ass punks right off his feet and did an airplane spin with the kid draped over his wide shoulders, like Gary was the French Angel, and the kid was going out of the ring. Only this time it was into the sewage.

Inspired, and taking advantage of a certain element of surprise, I picked up another Jap and hiked him over my shoulder. Walt picked up a third Son of Nippon. I didn't make a full spin with my guy, but I got him up and over the rail the same time Walt let his guy fly. The Japs fell through the air, their hair flying out like they were in a Disney movie, their arms flailing as they hit the water. We laughed our asses off, watching them sputter out of the sewage, till they all took off.

We stopped for a few more drinks in a joint off the Ginza. We decided that since we had chucked the guys into the sewage, we needed a bath. We were not drunk, at least I wasn't, but we were like a bunch of kids at recess. Before we did get drunk, we went in search of hot baths and massages. We found a place practically next door. It seemed innocent enough; there was that thing about mixed bathing in Japan, whole families did it together. But there were only these two Japanese girls in there, and us, no families.

Shortly Gary was lying on a big table beside the bath, trying to communicate in pidgin English his admiration, even need, for one of the girls. Next thing she jumped up on the table with him and pummeled his back and giggled "Big GI! You big GI!" and then she walked barefoot all over his acne-scarred back and shoulders. Till he turned over and dumped her off and grabbed at her towel. She had startlingly big breasts for such a tiny girl. I wondered if she wanted Gary to lay off, but she didn't mind. Next thing Walt was fooling around with her friend. I had the same thing in mind myself, but I didn't like to see Walt do that. It pissed me off. At the same time, I was so horny I couldn't stand it, and there was no girl in sight for me. Still pissed, I got dressed and left alone. The two sergeants, my buddies, hardly even said good-bye.

I EMERGED TO FIGHT MY WAY through Traffic Hell, as I later found Tokyo was described by the English language *Nippon Times*, thinking I'd just as soon not run into the kids we threw off the bridge, now that I was alone. I didn't see them, but the streets were clogged with pedestrians, some dressed in Western clothes, some in kimonos, all bustling along.

Bicycles darted in and out among the stream of cars, big cars, small cars, taxis—the most popular seemed to be 1934 four-door Fords— all driven by angry kamikaze pilots put out of work by the end of World War II, and driving with what the *Times* described as "the unprecedented discourtesy of Tokyo drivers," beside which New York cabbies were like nannies pushing baby carriages around Central Park.

I made my way alive to the World Famous Ginbasha Club on Ryokan Avenue between Tenth and Fifteenth streets. Don't ask me what happened to Eleventh, Twelfth, Thirteenth and Fourteenth streets. This place could teach Lou Walters' World Famous Latin Quarter a few tricks. Inside was a dance floor with tiers of tables rising from it, a bar, indoor flower gardens, and a thirteen-piece band playing "Managua, Nicaragua." Two skinny blondes, wearing Spanish ruffled shirts and mesh stockings shook castanets and belted it out, off key:

"Managua, Nicaragua, is a beautiful spot,
There's coffee and bananas and the temperature's hot!
So take a trip, and on a ship go sailing away,
Across the agua to Managua, Nicaragua, Ole!"

Seated at tables girls chatted and giggled with each other like high school girls at the prom, but dressed like mother never saw them. They were wrapped up and on display, like fancy presents, red silk dresses slashed down to the navel and way up the side, showing off bosoms on top and thighs below.

"Hey! GI! Sit down! Buy me a drink! Come on." One of the girls patted the seat beside her and slid over. She wasn't what I had in mind. Not that she wasn't pretty. A round face and a short hairdo, I guessed bangs would be the right word, dark hair and dark eyes. A red dress held up by a couple of thin straps left her shoulders and back bare. I could just see the tops of her small breasts, but when she bent over and laughed I could see more. But it was funny, she looked just like she might live down the block—except she was Japanese—and the girl who lived down the block was not what I had in mind.

"You like me, GI. I talk you like a machine gun, smoke like a locomotive and fuck like hell!" She laughed so hard she was about to have a fit, her Sunday-school face, round, pug nose, breaking up at whatever she saw when she looked up at me. She had one gold filling back in her little pink mouth.

I sat down. Then, almost by accident it seemed, she got me out on the dance floor. She glided, real light in my arms, smiling up at me from around chest high, as she maneuvered me into steering her around the floor.

She asked my name and I told her "Tom—Tom Kelly" but she said, "Thomas, I like Thomas."

I asked her what her name was.

"Mickey," she looked up at me.

"Mickey what?"

"Mouse."

She was totally straight faced till she completely cracked up, she liked her joke so well. I could feel her back quiver under my hand, and she leaned back against my arm, and I felt her against me down on my leg, and I saw almost all of her small breasts before she snuggled against me, still laughing. She must have pulled this on all the GIs, she was so pleased with herself.

After we danced, we sat and drank and I watched her make little paper birds and animals out of scraps of paper and tinfoil—*origami* she called it. Her arms were thin, birdlike themselves; her hands were nimble and precise; her dark eyes were rapt as she worked, shy as she glanced at me to see if I approved. Altogether that was what she was like, a small bird come to rest beside me.

A half-bombed GI stopped by the table. "Hey, girl-san, you dance with me tonight?" he said.

I was about to coldcock the asshole, but Mickey smiled and put her hand on my arm, and told him, "No. I with Thomas."

Without wanting to, I hated the idea of her leaving. It made me furious because there were all these beautiful women all around me, and they wouldn't do me any good because of this Mickey Mouse. There didn't seem to be anything I could do about it. I kept buying her phony drinks she hardly touched, she was so busy making the little paper toys. I was sampling all the beer in the place, Ashai, Kirin, Nippon, and it was good beer.

Mickey asked me what one of her little paper sculptures was. When I said the bird was a dog, she broke into a fit of the giggles—"A dog! How you say a dog?" and punched my arm hard with her tiny fist. I caught her fist in my hand and held it in mine, and she didn't move it for a moment. Her arm was slender, and there were delicate hairs, barely visible, like fine filaments on it. It was not like any other arm, yet it reminded me of some other woman's arm, but I couldn't tell if it was Moira's or Annie's or whether it was someone else's altogether, and I wondered how drunk I was getting.

"Dog! You a country boy? It's a bird. Same same Picasso!" She startled me with that and laughed at me, pulled away and punched me again. "Whatsa matta? You can't talk, Kelly-san? You look like a goldfish—mouth moving but not saying anything."

The imitation Xavier Cugat band again struck up, this time with that Latin favorite, the "Hokey Pokey," and Mickey was on her feet, tugging at my hands, "Come on, honey-chile. We dance. Cha-cha-cha-cha-cha. Okay?"

Next thing we were putting our left foot in and our left foot out and we were shaking it all about. Mickey jumped up and down, her small breasts bouncing under her red dress, beads of sweat on her forehead and arms. "Shake it—no break it, Kelly-san!"

I was back in the eighth grade. Younger even. When I was a real little kid, and I met this girl in first grade, and we liked each other, but we didn't know what to do about it but giggle and punch each other on the arm. Mickey and I were having a hard time talking to each other, except like Bud Abbott and Lou Costello doing a bit in pidgin English, but we were laughing all the time.

I wanted to forget Mickey was a business girl and I was a GI. I wanted her to be just a girl, and me to just be a guy she'd met and liked a lot right away, and I was getting more and more pissed off at myself. I was here on a mission, to drink and screw my brains out till I didn't think about anything but drinking and screwing. Till I ran out of money and had to go back to Korea and get shot at. I was not in Japan to meet a nice girl for Christ's sake. But all the while I was sitting there playing little games with a whore who didn't look like she should be out this late on a school night, who wouldn't even tell me her damn name. For a while, I didn't say much of anything and that must have bothered her.

"Meiko," she said, after we'd both been quiet for a while.

"What?" I asked, but I knew right away.

"My name. Meiko."

"It's a nice name." It was, the way she said it, it had a musical ripple in the middle of it.

"You got money to stay with me?"

"Yeah. I have money, Meiko." It was the first time I said her name, and it pissed me off that's what I had to say.

"You leave some for old mamasan," she said, reaching in my pocket for money, and encountering something else. "We go home," she said, picking up her little silver purse, leaving her colored water untouched.

I WONDERED HOW A BAR GIRL came by a house so nice. A wooden frame with a tile roof; sliding doors on the porch. Meiko didn't let me get past the front door with my shoes on. While she was showing me around her house, she was alternately shy and giddy. One minute she was carefully explaining something, the next she was punching me and giggling. Even while she was telling me the Japanese word for something, she was just like a regular girl. But with her stupid little joke I could tell she thought me some kind of rube and she was from the big city. I didn't know why the hell I chose her. While she was showing me around and giving me a beer, I kept getting simultaneously madder and madder, and hornier and hornier.

267

When she offered me a bath from a basin of hot water and hot towels, I was dying, and I told her no, I'd already had a bath. Things were crazy, then. She read my mind and she was mad at me because I was mad at myself for going with her. I saw it in her eyes. She stopped the tour.

"Okay. Thomas. We make love now." Her chin quivered, and she said it like, "If you think you can find better than me, you're crazy GI. I'll show you."

So we began. She could have been any woman. I didn't care. I was not even thinking of her as a person. I was pulling my clothes off and pushing her down on the futon on the floor and she was falling back and pulling me down at the same time she was twisting and turning and slipping out of her dress. She pushed and struggled underneath me, and she opened herself wide, rising upward to meet me. I plunged into her again and again, in and out, and over and over. We were sweating, angry animals, our bodies slap-slapping together, until I exploded inside her.

In a few minutes we started again, and she fucked me every way possible. She knelt astride me, taking me all the way up inside her, deeper and deeper. She sat squatting above me, grabbing me inside of her, moving in tight little circles, grinding down on me. I could have been any man, not even a man, an animal. If she was nothing more than her sex to me, I was nothing more than a cock to her. Or goddamn money. I pushed harder.

Once when I looked up at her she was glaring down at me, and she was as angry as I was. Another time, later, I looked up and saw her with this calculating expression on her face. I didn't know if she was trying to figure out how much more I could take before I died and how she'd get rid of the body. Weird as it seemed, for a second I was almost scared of her. She'd break me off, or wear me away to nothing, so I'd never have anything for another woman, and I bucked and writhed back at her, hard.

One minute I was a sweating, stinking animal screwing without thought, only feeling, not emotion, only feeling. The next minute I was on top of her, and in her I was immortal and we were going to do this forever. In my euphoria, I wanted her with me on the top of the world, and I wanted her to feel everything I felt. But much of the time I didn't know what she was thinking or feeling, and a lot of the time I didn't even care. We had at each other, angry beyond words, angry at each other, even at ourselves, in intermittent furies, without thought or care or tenderness. As though we could kill each other. Could kill each other without guilt. We didn't stop till I was raw and she was so sore she could hardly stand up.

When we stopped and she fixed us rice and fish and crackers and the last couple of bottles of beer, she moved around the house slowly, with the shuffle of an old woman. She approached me warily, thrusting the plate and chopsticks and the bottle of Ahsai at me and backing away as from a lion she was feeding through imaginary bars. We stuffed the food down, I was not even sure of what I was eating, hardly talking, like we were resting for another ten rounds.

"*Biro?*" Meiko asked. She giggled and showered me with the beer, pouring it over my head, giggling again like when we first met forever ago, and I got her back and we forgot about eating, and we were doing it again. But it was different this time; we were different. It was as if we'd screwed every last ounce of anger out of ourselves, and now we wanted to play, tickling and giggling like silly schoolchildren.

When we were exhausted, or at least I was, everything changed again. It was hard to explain, even to myself. It was not that the sex stopped, but it was very different. We lay together, still, resting. Meiko reached down and put me next to her. She just touched me for a while, barely moved against me. She put me inside her so gently it was like I hadn't even moved, I'd just flowed into her, merged my body into hers. We lay there together, and I felt her breathing against me, holding me, and I was sleepy and contented and safe.

After a long time, she murmured against my chest: "*Mizo mo, Morasanu naka da.*" It was a Japanese saying, she told me. "It means he she so tight together even water would not leak out between them. Like us, Thomas," she added, and I felt her lips move against my chest as she said the last words.

I didn't understand what happened next. She began to cry and so did I. We had gone on a perilous journey together and made it home and we were so relieved that we were crying for joy, yet at the same time we'd suffered a grievous loss together and we were mourning together. And so we lay there together crying and holding onto each other. After a while, the sexual feelings still there under the tears, in the tears, were transformed, not into love, but into something like love, just caring. Somehow in our tears and clinging together all of the differences between us, even though they were still there, and maybe even important, must be important, didn't make any difference.

Even that she was a woman and I was a man. It wasn't that I stopped being aware of my sex. I was so aware of myself in her that I ached—and I could feel her feeling me—but it wasn't so much I was a man and Meiko was a woman, as we had melded together, and our sexes had flowed into each other. And then it was like, without letting go of the animal part of me, I rose above that part of me. I was a kite riding an endless gentle breeze, yet all the while tethered to the earth by my body and Meiko's. I had this feeling of tranquility and freedom so strong, for a moment I'd risen above anger and fear, and even death. At the outer edge of my world, I was at peace, for those few moments in the arms of, in the body of, that woman.

LATER THE NEXT DAY, MEIKO STARTED to tell me about herself. It sounded like an old story: a poor family in the country, and all of her money going home to support them. An officer in the First Cav who got killed early on in the war gave the house to her. They had a kid, and the kid was with her parents in the country, so her house in Tokyo was no good because her child wasn't there. I wanted to believe her but I was not sure I did.

She told me about her friend Yuko, who had a house, too. Yuko's GI Bill-san was "no handsome like Thomas, no sharp—a white pig with big gut"—borrowed *takusan* yen for Yuko to fix her teeth, she said, laughing, and I see her gold filling. She was hinting around about money, so I went over to my pants and got all the yen I had, I didn't know how much it even was, and threw it on the floor. "Here! Don't talk money anymore!" I yelled.

She looked startled, and her lips quivered, but she knelt to pick the money up, and I had the whole thing right. But then, crying and staring at me, she stuffed the money back into my pants pocket, the yen and the MPC flying everywhere, falling on the floor again. "You no give me like that. Stupid Kelly-san," she said.

"Right. I'm sorry."

She stared at me. "Okay. Let's have big time. Spend it all, Thomas-san. Okay?"

"Okay."

So we set off.

I wanted to see the Imperial Hotel designed by Frank Lloyd Wright, but it was disappointing. From the outside it was a low, crumbling gingerbread building. Inside it was full of people like me, who might not belong there but were trying to look cosmopolitan. We went through the banquet entrance to the main bar in a new wing. The bar was plain brick columns, triangular tables scattered around.

A bunch of Marines and some French soldiers sat at a table near us watching a Japanese baseball game on the TV and arguing about Indochina. The argument was whether the Americans should go help the French in the war they were fighting there. The French soldiers were saying, after all, that they were helping in Korea; but one of the Marines said, "You lousy frogs have a couple hundred guys, max, in Korea, and you prob'ly want thous'nds of us!" I didn't want to think about that shit right then, and when someone came by offering a tour of the hotel for 700 yen, Meiko and I left.

We rambled all around town, the way I saw New York. Only Tokyo, in a whole different way, was a more beautiful city than New York; for one thing New York could use Mount Fuji as background. Everywhere there were Japanese taking pictures of other Japanese. I didn't get a camera because if I did I wouldn't look at things themselves, just how they looked in a picture, so I tried to get it all down in my mind. The pictures that stayed in my mind didn't have any names, like this is the Empire State Building, and those that did, that Meiko told me, I could hardly learn.

271

Dead branches of a withered tree framed a music pavilion with curved white arches. A schoolboy and schoolgirl peered through a latticed iron fence at a cemetery. A young boy intent on fixing the flat tire on his bicycle pumped away, ignoring the crowd that swirled by him and occasionally shrilly cursed at him. Gardens and flowers were everywhere: delicate pink and white apple blossoms, cherry blossoms, flowering almond trees, carefully stunted and shaped in their growth, rock gardens, each rock positioned just so. Miniature bridges and shrines, tranquil in the midst of Tokyo turmoil all around them. Young students in dark blue uniforms and knee-high socks walked under the stern eyes of elderly proctors who looked like they taught school in Boston, their hair drawn tight in buns.

A beautiful woman in a white silk kimono covered with elegantly stitched trees and shrubbery and flowers stood taking a picture of her young daughter in a flower-covered kimono in the sunlight and shadows near a shrine.

"God, she's beautiful!"

"No ugly like me you mean?"

I looked down for Meiko's smile. Instead her face was a disc with slits for eyes and a mouth.

"No. Beautiful like you."

"Bullshit, GI! No bullshit me!"

"No bullshit," I said. She tugged away from me, but in a little while she slipped her arm under mine and guided me away.

That night we went to the Kabuki Theater. The play was set against vivid scenery that somehow reminded me of Good Friday plays. The actors wore rainbow-colored costumes and painted faces and played both men and women. They leaped fiercely around the big stage, thrusting and parrying with immense curved swords while off-stage choruses chanted. Meiko tried futilely to translate for me. You didn't need to be a genius to figure out guys flailing away at each other with swords were fighting. Even the lovers' suicides were easy to follow.

The audience reminded me of Americans at a baseball game. We were in the upper deck and people had brought all kinds of food with them to last through the hours-long performance, apples and bread and fish and rice. They were like rapt children, oohing and aahing and crying, all the while chowing down. Nothing like the stoic Japanese the Army had told me to expect.

From nowhere, like an unexpected jab in the back with a sharp stick, I thought of Moira, and how she would lap this stuff up. Less a thought than a picture: of Moira leaning forward, her elbows on her knees, her gray-green eyes devouring the actors, taking in everything, storing it away to use in her own acting or writing or dancing someday. I never saw Moira pray any more fervently than when we saw *The Red Shoes* at the Fargo Fine Arts. "She's so beautiful, and she's got my name!" That was the way she put it, not that she had the same name as the star but that the star had the same name she did. "Why can't I dance like that? God, please, God!" Moira had said, clenching her fists, like she wanted to pummel the world in front of her.

"You like Kabuki?" Meiko asked. My reveries must have made me sad, and Meiko reached over and squeezed my hand.

"Very much." I said, "*takusan*," inexplicably close to crying.

She squeezed my hand again. She had to think I was going native. I was putting together the small collection of phrases the GIs used to pretend we were learning the language. *Takusan. Dozo. Ah so deska. Moshi moshi. Domo arigato. An na tobi. Gomen—nasai. Hai. Doitashamoshti. Sayonara.* She giggled, delighted with my pitiful efforts.

Toward the end of my week we went to the PX and I blew what I had left on gifts. Meiko tugged at my hand to show me a glass-encased porcelain doll of a Japanese woman in a flowered kimono, and I bought it for her. I got a good Nikon camera for my dad, in case he ever went to any place he wanted to take pictures again. A camera was one thing the Japanese could make better than we could and not just copycat us. For my mother, I got a yellow *kimono* I hoped she'd like; it should go good with her red hair. I picked out woodprints for Annie in pale pinks, blues, and oranges; stuff more cheerful than her entire somber collection.

I picked out an inexpensive single pearl ring to send to Moira.

While Meiko and I were at the counter, she kept asking me about who that was for, even after I told her it was just for a friend.

"Sure, honey-chile," Meiko sulked.

"Here," I said, on impulse. "Let's see if it fits." I slipped it on her finger, and it slid on just right. "So, I guess it's for you."

"I'm friend, Thomas?"

"Yes. Sure."

Meiko studied the pearl, looking from every angle, even though it was just a round little pearl that looked the same however you looked at it as far as I could see.

"Thank you, Thomas."

After we were done at the PX, Meiko teased me to take her to a place called the Ginza Swing. A small pale green building with a sloped roof and a couple of windows. Outside a sign on the door said, "SWING," and one on the walk said, "JAZZ." Inside were green velvet chairs and coffee tables. A large brown-skinned Christ hung on one wall there and underneath it a banner wished us HAPPY EASTER! Behind the bar was a picture of Dave Brubeck and from somewhere came Earl Bostic's "Flamingo."

The only customers were a student in his uniform and cap reading a book, another young Japanese who looked like he was from the Mafia, wearing a pink button-down shirt and a pink knit tie—*Stars and Stripes* said some guys were actually wearing pink shirts back home, and of course the Japanese wanted to copy everything American; and this German that Meiko knew from way back somewhere.

In my imagination, Germans tended to be steely-eyed guys with stiff gray hair and with a dueling scar on one cheek, from the days before they took up killing Jews and trying to conquer the world. This German was gray-haired all right, like a grandfather, with a round face, and wrinkles from the corners of his eyes. He ended up buying us a few beers even though it was still morning. After prodding by Meiko, he told me his story, using better English than a lot of us, in a soft, hesitant, school- teacher's voice, worrying the slower kids wouldn't be able to get it.

Though he was German, he was in Tokyo all during the Second World War and survived the firebombing. When the American planes darkened the sky, and the bombs began falling, the fires were everywhere, destroying the tinderbox buildings, roaring through entire neighborhoods, walling off streets with flames, especially in the residential areas. Only scattered concrete and steel structures were left standing.

He ran from his office, a handkerchief over his nose and mouth, billowing fires singeing his hair, smoke and ashes burning his eyes. Ignoring shrieks he heard coming from all sides, he dodged through cracks in the fire, searching for his house, his wife and his three-year-old daughter. What he came home to, and his face reddened and his voice choked as he told me, was the stench of burning flesh. He was able to identify their bodies.

I didn't know what to say, and stumbled out with, "You'd never know it now. This would be a nice city to live in now."

"Yah? I have been to Hiroshima and to Nagasaki," he said, looking straight at me, "and they were no more devastated than Tokyo was by the firebombing! No more!"

What could I say to a guy whose wife and kid were killed by our bombs? I'm sorry? You guys shouldn't have started the damn war? If we hadn't dropped those bombs, a lot more GIs would have died, or just a lot more people, period? I sat there like a dumbshit and mumbled about how stupid war was, how stupid for people to kill each other for "countries."

"We'd be better off if there wasn't any Germany or America, or Japan or Korea, or Greece or Turkey for that damn matter, and we didn't do this shit to each other," I said.

"Yah?" he said again, still looking straight at me. "Maybe we do it anyway."

"You think so?"

"I think so, Thomas-san!" all of a sudden Meiko said, loudly. "People number fucking ten!" The worst she meant. She said it like she wanted to kill me again.

"You're wrong, Meiko," I said, startled by her anger. "You're people. You're not number ten."

"No?"

"No."

"Yah. No. He is right about you," the German said to Meiko.

THE DAY I LEFT, MEIKO'S KID was there when I woke up, sitting next to me, staring at me. He had to have been about four or five years old; compact and solid as a rock, dark hair in a bowl cut. Otherwise he looked a lot like an American. Meiko told me his name was Keijoro. He reminded me of Eeyore, from *Winnie the Pooh*, maybe because of his solemn, almost sad eyes. Meiko hadn't heard of the book.

Keijoro wasn't old enough to read the sports pages, but he could speak English and knew quite a bit about baseball for such a squirt. He had a real baseball and a big mitt. There wasn't a real field nearby. We went out in the cemetery and threw the ball around for a while in the middle of all the tombstones with Japanese writing on them. He had no fear of the ball at all and got right down on it, but his big mitt kept sliding off his little hand. "Oh, man!" he said, real disgusted, and pounded the mitt with his fist, like he'd been doing it for years.

He was really a trusting kid. After we'd played for a while, right there in the middle of the cemetery, he crawled into my lap and sat there the longest time, before he got restless and went zooming around the park after the butterflies with one of those nets all the Japanese kids carried on their backpacks when they went to school. It would be neat to have a kid of my own like him. Moira had me figured right when it came to kids.

Meiko cried when I left her and Keijoro at her house to go back to the hotel to join up with Walt and Gary for my flight back to Korea. I started to say maybe I'd come back someday, but she got mad at me, and kept saying, "Never happen! You no come back, Thomas. You no take me to America! You same same Keijoro father!" and hit me on my chest till I held her tiny wrists and stopped her. I was sorry Keijoro was there when that happened; he stood there looking at us with his eyes wide and his face real serious. I felt like such an asshole. I'd never even thought of taking her home. Stuff like that didn't happen in real life.

"You're right, I'm not thinking of taking you home with me," I told her. "I was just thinking about staying here awhile. Seeing your country. Finishing a book I'm writing. Then going home. I promise you one thing, I won't forget you as long as I live."

"All same same, Thomas! All same same to me," she was crying while she said it. And at first she wouldn't let me kiss her good-bye, and when she did she pushed herself against me real hard, still angry, making sure I wouldn't forget. She stepped back and gave me a sad smile, "*Sayonara*, honey-chile."

Keijoro stood there, with his face solemn, and waved good-bye by just holding one hand up and moving his fingers up and down like he was making a shadow duck on a wall. When I ruffled his bowl haircut he bobbed and smiled at me.

WHEN I MET GARY AND WALT BACK at the hotel, Gary looked satisfied and rested. Walt looked guilty as sin. I started to tell them a little about Meiko on the bus out to the airport. About how I was thinking of coming back to stay in Japan a while when I was discharged, but I discovered I didn't want to talk about her with them.

"Going native, huh Tom? "

"No, but she's a nice girl, whatever you guys think. At least I wasn't screwing around behind my wife's back and with a kid at home." I was surprised at how pissed I was at Walt. It was none of my business.

Walt's face got red, but he didn't say anything.

It was a quiet flight back after that.

But as the plane neared the airbase at Kimpo, Gary looked out the window. "Here we are, back in the armpit of the world," he said.

I didn't say anything. I was sweating like I was breaking a night fever. Scared again already. Back in Korea again.

Winton decided we were going to stage a raid on the Chinese that night, supposedly catch them off guard. "Give the peace talks a little push, huh?" he said.

I tried to argue with him, but he didn't want to hear from a peon like me, and, knowing Winton, he had the okay at least as high as battalion before he ever let us in on it anyway.

Things started out okay as we slipped out through our own wire under cover of a pitch black night. They began to go wrong when we reached the enemy wire and flares went off all over the place. When Chink mortar rounds came lobbing down on us, Winton had a new forward observer call in for fire support, but the goddamn FO took forever to call it in, and then he fucked up. I didn't know if he was confused about our position or just rattled; he called our artillery fire right down on us.

Winton was calling the FO every name in the book while half of our guys panicked and got snarled up in the wire they were in such a hurry to bug out. A guy off to my left exploded, parts of him, arms and legs, went flying off him. Another guy just ahead of me let out a scream as a round of phosphorus came in and left one of his eyes hanging out of his face. A couple of guys near him stood up and immediately pitched forward without any shells going off. They must have been hit with small arms fire. I was so scared, I just lay low and hugged the ground, hoping nothing hit me.

"Fall back! Fall back!" Winton shouted.

I wanted to get the hell out of there. But the Chinese had to be firing into us with machine guns now, too; I heard whining right over my head, and I was not about to stand up. I stayed flat to the ground and started crawling back, praying I didn't get trapped in the wire.

I almost crawled smack into Jimmy Hickok lying on his back, moaning. One arm was a ragged stump and blood was pouring out of where the rest of it should be. His fatigues were torn and blood-soaked. I managed to tear a strip off and wrap what was left of his arm to try to stop the bleeding.

I got his good arm pulled over my back and held onto his wrist as I crawled a slow circle, dragging him out as I went. He kept sliding off of me and I kept hauling him back on. The whole thing was awkward as hell and he was screaming all the while. For a second it seemed like the rounds had stopped coming in, and his screams were the loudest noise I heard. Then I heard more machine gun fire whistling over our heads. I lay still for a moment, and Jimmy stopped screaming.

I heard gear rattling as guys around me were crawling for safety too. When one of our guys stood up in a crouch to make a run for it, a burst of machine gun fire cut him right in half, and the top half just fell off to the ground. Then it was quiet except for grunts from our guys hauling themselves slowly back, and the groans of our wounded.

I inched my way forward through a field full of rocks and debris, till I was so tired that even with all of my fear I could hardly move. When I neared our lines I yelled for our guys to hold their fire, and off to the side I heard Lieutenant Winton yelling the same thing. As I was sliding back into our trench I hollered for a medic, and one was there right away.

"Jesus Christ!" the medic said. "Jesus Fucking H. Christ. He's alive," while he put a real bandage on him and got him on a stretcher.

Half of us didn't make it back. I wished Winton was one of them. There were a lot of men who would have been a lot better off if he'd bought it that first day on the Tit.

Things fell into a monotonous routine of the Chinks and us watching each other across the hills. We made as few patrols as we could get away with—even Winton seemed to be learning—and waited for the war to go away. We were bombing the shit out of North Korea, especially Pyongyang, but it didn't seem to be ending the war. Now the hot scuttlebutt was when we were done here, we were all going to be sent to Indochina. I didn't understand what was going on in Indochina, but, whatever it was, it was the French's problem. I didn't need anymore government-sponsored travel.

But I was playing with the idea of some traveling on my own. I'd applied to Columbia. Not just because I promised my dad; I owed it to myself to finish school. But before I went back to New York, I was thinking of getting discharged in Japan, seeing Meiko. Going home by way of India and the Middle East and Europe and Ireland. I was getting all these travel brochures with pictures of the Taj Mahal and the Pyramids and the Parthenon and St. Peters and Notre Dame and Trafalgar Square and the Dublin Horse Show. Even the moronic copy—TRAVEL IS EDUCATION IN ITS MOST ENJOYABLE FORM and ODYSSEY TO ADVENTURE!—couldn't take away from the pictures.

Meantime I kept working on my never-ending book. Courtesy of Walt, who seemed to have forgiven me for seeing him go after that Japanese girl, I was getting all the paper I wanted. Some of it was even fancy, had the Division crest on it, like we were out here at a country club. Had to have been for the chickenshit officers back at Division to write to their wives back home and lie about how tough they've had it, all the shrines they visited on R&R.

The only question at the moment was whether I got out of there before a truce, as to which it seemed there was a new rumor every day, or after. It would be good to sleep between clean white sheets, have hot and cold running water for showers, steak, Jack Daniel's, women.

> May 10, 1953
> Fort Ord, California

Tom:
Well, you bastard, it's about time you come across with a letter.

I've forgotten everything military I ever learned. I honestly think it would scare the shit out of me to fire an M-1, just like it did the first time. Believe me, it did scare me, as you know what the only gun I ever fired uses for ammunition. Sometimes I'm scared of the target, but I never get gun-shy.

Well, I'm enjoying teaching more than I thought I would, but I still haven't given up the idea of suicide. Self-preservation is an instinct, but we have reason and therefore must have a reason to live. If not why not go to a "dreamless sleep"?

Last weekend I had a three-day pass so I went to S.F. and stayed at the home of one of my friends. I had a pretty good time drinking up his money and eating his mother's food. Incidentally she's a devout Catholic so I attended church Sunday for the first time in 7 or 8 months. What do you think about religion these days? Is it true there are no agnostics in foxholes or are you the first? Write and advise, dammit!

Did I tell you about that broad that I met in S.F.? I went to see her Monday with visions of eight hours of unadulterated sin. When she came to the door, she was much more beautiful than I had remembered her, so I limped into the apt. with a huge hard-on. However, it all came to naught, and I left, the epitome of frustration. She said, "I did it before because I loved you and now you think you can just drop in and (I quote) 'knock off a piece.'" She also said she used to have trouble coming but now she has a middle-aged capitalist (I saw the picture) who satisfies her. So I guess I'll have to go back to jacking off with my lusty 2½-incher.

As far as reading goes, I am still working on *Anna Karenina*, just as good as *War and Peace*. But I wasn't aware of what a socialist Tolstoi is or at least so it seems from this work.

Got to close

Will

PS Where the hell is your book?

WILL WANTED TO KNOW if there were no agnostics in foxholes, or if I was the first.

Damn Will and his glib, smartass questions.

I wanted to believe in God the way I did when I was a kid and I knew He was there listening to me when I prayed. Prof argued the odds were that sometimes you'd get what you wanted anyway, like daily praying, "May this house be safe from tigers," and, sure enough, no tiger arrived at the front door.

Prof had something about religion being comforting. It might even have been a way to keep my sanity over here. The fact was, when I was scared enough, I still tried to pray, no matter what I thought. And when I thought about stuff like that baby born on the floor of the laundry, it almost seemed there might actually be a God. We didn't seem able to make anything that perfect by ourselves.

If there was a God, and I got my butt shot off before I got out of here, I was going to be pissed off about the whole thing. But God was getting tougher and tougher for me. He just seemed so unlikely, what with all the shit that went on. That we did. Prof argued religion was a way to escape responsibility for what we did and not face the fact we were there alone. No set of rules handed down from a Great Being. Just all the damn choices we had to make for ourselves. He just might have been right about that.

Lieutenant Winton was on my case to see the chaplain. Not because he had concerns about the state of my soul. I made the mistake of idly mentioning to him I might like to take my discharge in Japan. He thought maybe I'd decided to go native, and the good Father would talk me out of any such foolishness. I hated to admit it, but sometimes I wouldn't mind talking to the right padre, but not about Meiko.

35

I was up before five every day on patrols for a week. We didn't go out so far that we encountered serious trouble. Not that there weren't sweaty moments. We'd seen several Tojo tanks and a lot of movement behind their lines in the past few days, and the night before there'd been random shooting; but nothing happened, no one was hit.

A lousy thing happened one night. Returning from patrol, we came upon one of our guys sleeping on perimeter. The one time this week Lieutenant Winton decided to go out with us. It was a clear night, and as we approached our lines coming back in, we could see one of our guys on perimeter, sitting there with his head slumped down and his rifle off to the side of the hole. I wondered at first if he'd been killed, but right away the lieutenant put up his hand to stop us all.

"Kelly," he beckoned me forward with a choppy, urgent movement of his arm, like he was directing a goddamn assault. He pointed toward the guard and whispered in my ear, "That soldier's asleep. I want you to come up on him easy. Take his piece before you wake him. All right?"

"Yes, sir," I whispered back, too loudly to suit Winton.

"Quiet!" the lieutenant hissed, his skin drawn tight over his cheekbones. "I want that man on his way to the stockade in the next two minutes. You got that, Kelly?"

"Yes, sir, but—"

The lieutenant put his hand up in front of my face, almost touching my mouth. I didn't like his hand there, that close.

"But nothing."

"Yes, sir!" I whispered.

I crept up on the guy. I wanted to wake him up before the lieutenant got to him if I could, but I didn't want to startle him and get shot. I could feel the sweat running down from my armpits by the time I got to him. When I got up close I recognized the guy. He was Sam Warren, a black guy from Dearborn, Michigan, near Detroit. Sam and I had shot the shit about the Tigers a little, and that was about it. He was an okay guy.

Sam's eyes were closed, and I could see the quiet rhythm of his breathing. He was damn near snoring he was so sound asleep. His rifle was lying against the rim of the hole next to me. I inched up, nearly shitting in my pants for fear he'd jerk awake and shoot me before he saw who I was. Carefully, I reached out and lifted the M-1 out by its barrel and set it to the side. I slid into the hole noisier than hell, ready to defend myself if Sam came at me. He didn't even move.

To wake the guy up, I slapped him across the face as hard as I could without really taking a swing at him, so that the lieutenant didn't see what I was up to.

"Hey, man!" Sam said, his head snapping up, his arms flailing. "What the . . ."

I hit him again, this time with my fist, right in his gut, and he retched and put his hand up over his mouth.

"What in the hell is going on?" I heard the barked whisper over my shoulder and twisted to look.

Lieutenant Winton was crouching over us, dark silhouetted against darkness. He leaned forward, and I could see his pale eyes glistening.

"Nothing, sir! This man is sick. Sir." I looked at Sam. "Isn't that right?"

I must have split Sam's lip. He was wiping blood off his chin and looking up at the lieutenant. For a second I feared what Sam was going to say.

"Thas' no shit, man. I'm real sick, sir."

"Sick my ass," said the lieutenant. "I won't forget this," he said, looking right at me. It was like he was more pissed off at me than at Sam.

"What's the matter with you?" the lieutenant asked me.

"Nothing, sir. The man's sick. Can't you smell him?"

"I smell something all right, Kelly, and it's not this man."

The lieutenant walked away, not waiting for an answer. He'd forgotten all about patrol. He walked straight up and down like he was on parade; the arrogant son of a bitch must think he was invulnerable. I figured, what good did it do us if Sam got written up. It'd be a general court martial and he'd get up to five years and a Dishonorable Discharge for it. He didn't need that much help to remember it next time.

But the lieutenant wrote it up, and the next night he hauled me in front of him, and he was all over my case about it.

"How the hell could you do that, Kelly? You know Warren's falling asleep could cost good men their lives. You and I have been here long enough not to risk lives that way."

"Sir, I don't understand what you mean by 'do that.' None of our men were killed last night," I stood at attention in front of the lieutenant, looking straight ahead and avoiding looking at his eyes. "And, sir," I plunged ahead, not to defy him, just tired of it all, "if PFC Warren is court-martialed, we know that will ruin his life."

The lieutenant pulled out one of the long, skinny stogies he smoked, like a prop; I felt his pale blue eyes appraising me. He scratched a match on the bottom of his boot and lit up.

"At ease, Kelly," he said.

I went to at-ease. I didn't relax.

"You know why we're here, Kelly. A lot of good men have died here to stop Communism, and by God, we've stopped it. Haven't we?"

The lieutenant looked at me through a cloud of blue smoke rising under a hooded kerosene lantern. It was not meant as a question, and whatever it used to mean to me had gotten worn out somehow. I didn't answer.

"That's what you're scribbling about all the time, isn't it? What we're doing here?" he leaned forward.

"I'm trying to write about what we're doing here, yes, sir."

"All right, Tom," he'd decided to be friends again. "You know, a hundred years from now people will look back to Korea, and say this is where Communism was stopped. We can't jeopardize the men fighting here just to be softhearted about one Negro PFC. You know that, don't you?"

He thought because he went to West Point he was the second coming of General MacArthur, but he wouldn't talk that way about "one Negro PFC" if Brownie were still around.

"Lieutenant, with all due respect, I don't know any more that what we're doing here is worth spending one more life for—black or white or brown or yellow. I don't know if it's worth it, or if anyone else will know or care in a hundred years." I hadn't realized how I had come to feel, until I said it.

Eyes turned to blue ice, he looked at me over his stogie, and he spoke real quietly, but with an edge to his voice, like he was having a hard time not yelling at me. "Get out of here, Kelly," he said, like I'd contracted a loathsome disease. "And don't come back until you do know."

Afterwards, alone, I thought about it. It'd taken all this while, from the time that poor bastard Schlumberger bought it till then, but at least I knew how I felt. Prof was wrong about a lot of things about this war, but he was right on the big thing, the main thing. We shouldn't be over here killing people. I wondered again where he was then—whether he was drinking Methodist wine and still taking shit from his wife for having said out loud he thought the war was bullshit.

I didn't want the lieutenant pissed off at me, and I was scared he would find some way to stick it to me. He was even more of a pompous jerk than I thought, but I was going to be out of here in thirty-six days. And counting.

SAM'S COURT MARTIAL DIDN'T TAKE LONG. In two weeks he was in front of a Court Martial. A General Court Martial, meaning bad shit could happen to Sam. The Court Martial was held in a big tent back at Division. It was another world back there, where smart or lucky GIs like Walt and Gary were fighting their war. A goddamn country club, with a huge painted sign over the dirt road into the area that said, "Welcome to the Rock!" The tents were all laid out like a little city, and white-painted rocks marked the paths. A big American flag flew over the mess hall.

It was a dry day with the sun blazing down so hot the air shimmered over the dusty roads. I was half expecting to see Walt Manley around the Division Area, and I'd have liked to talk with him and get his advice. But I had to wait outside the tent while the lieutenant testified. I was trying to keep cool. I didn't want to sit on the dirty deck that underlay the tent, and there was nowhere else to sit. I was also hoping I could hear what was going on inside the tent. So I stood around in the sun with my throat feeling like cotton. I couldn't hear a damn thing coming from inside the tent.

Sam's appointed defense counsel, Lieutenant Simms, was a bright-eyed Judge Advocate General second lieutenant fresh out of law school, and scared shitless to be here. We had shot the bull a little about the merits of law school, and he liked being a lawyer so far, which was a good sign. He seemed to be a nice guy, for what that was worth, and he was excited because he thought he might win this case. I gathered that was a rarity in his brief legal career.

I'd told Simms that Sam was awake but sick, bent over and heaving when I came up on him in the hole. Sam had told him the same thing. Lieutenant Winton hadn't had much to say to me at all since we last talked about Sam. Just went around looking pissed off and giving me every shit detail he could think of. He apparently had a statement from Eddie Kvard, one of the other guys on patrol that night, backing him up. The lieutenant was in there testifying, so I was a little nervous about what was going on in the tent.

When the lieutenant came out, he looked like he'd been assigned to guard the Unknown Soldier at Arlington. He was in khakis with creases like razors; his brass was burnished; his boots shone like buffed rubies; and he'd got on every possible piece of lettuce, from his Combat Infantryman's Badge, to his Good Conduct medal, to his Sharpshooter's Medal, to the blue and white Korean service ribbon we all got just for being here. It was pitiful.

He glared at me when he went past, but he didn't say anything to me.

"You're next, Corporal." It was Lieutenant Simms, equally decked out. I was not. Simms had told me to come just in clean fatigues. I'd always heard you should wear every medal you could put on, like Lieutenant Winton's display. But me in fatigues fit his "theory of the case" Simms told me, and whatever that was supposed to mean, he was the lawyer.

Going into the tent was like going into a bar in the middle of the day. It wasn't cool like a bar; it was a canvas oven, hot and stifling, without a murmur of a breeze, but it was kind of dark in there, and it took my eyes a minute to adjust.

I was sworn in, and they sat me down on a folding chair, all by myself in the middle of the tent. It was awkward sitting there, but at least the rigid chair digging into my back kept me in the right position, sitting at attention.

There was a big table a few yards in front of me, about the size of a couple of doors laid on sawhorses, with an American flag at one end, the division colors at the other, and a bunch of officers in between. I could see Sam out of the corner of my eye. He was sitting like a ramrod off to the side. I marveled he could still be sitting so straight.

Simms was looking pretty cool despite the heat. He got it established that I'd been in combat off and on ever since I got to Korea and asked me about my medals that I was not wearing and everything. He was even smooth about how come I'd stayed a corporal but I saw a funny look on one of the officer's faces about that.

Simms got to "the night in question," as he put it. He asked me to "tell my story in my own words," like he did when we talked earlier; it was a routine he had. I didn't have anyone else's words, so I used my own. Simms seemed content with what I said, though I was getting nervous about sitting there all by myself, in front of those officers scowling at me in the gloom.

When Simms was done, another lieutenant, this one overweight, took over. The prosecutor. Simms had told me the prosecutor was going to cross-examine the shit out of me, but he started out all friendly, leaning in so close that I could smell that he had breath like a cigar butt.

"Corporal Kelly, you have been in Korea for nearly a full tour of duty. In fact, you're about to go home, is that correct?"

"Yes, sir. In twenty-one days, sir." Sam's lieutenant had told me just to answer the questions, but it couldn't hurt to try to look like I was being cooperative.

"In fact, you've known the defendant in this case, PFC Sam Warren for some time, haven't you?"

"Not real well, sir, but yes, sir."

"Well enough to talk some baseball with him? That sort of thing?"

"Yes, sir, a little."

"Now PFC Warren is a Negro? Isn't that correct?"

"Yes, sir." Didn't the dumbshit know about the Constitution or what?

"Your best friend in the platoon was a Sergeant William Brown, was it not?"

Brownie. "Yeah. Yes, sir. I'm sorry." For the yeah, I meant, not that Brownie was my best friend, but it was too late to explain.

"Several of your friends in the platoon are Negroes, aren't they, Corporal Kelly?"

"I guess, sir. We have a number of Negro men in our outfit. More of them than white." What the hell was I explaining this for?

"Corporal Kelly, no offense intended, but haven't you been particularly friendly with Negro troops, even more than white?"

"Not particularly so. No, sir."

"Isn't it a fact, Corporal Kelly, you have been called a 'nigger lover' by some of the white troops?"

"Not that I know of." This guy was a real asshole. I wondered what was with Simms not objecting to this shit. If he was as dumbfounded by it as I was.

"Not that you know of." While Cigarbreath walked back and forth a couple of times, I sneaked a look at the panel of officers listening to all this bullshit. I was happy to see that one of them, a major, looked as uncomfortable as I felt.

"How do you happen to be in this man's army, Corporal Kelly?"

"Now hold up a minute, Lieutenant. Where is all of this going? What is its relevance?" The major was apparently tired of waiting for Simms to object. He sounded unhappy.

"I'm nearly done, sir, and I believe you will see."

"All right, Lieutenant. You'd better be. Corporal Kelly, answer the question."

"Yes, sir. I enlisted, sir." I felt the back of my fatigues sticking to the back of the chair.

"In fact," Cigarbreath leaned at me like he was Mr. District Attorney himself, confronting the guilty with a bloody shirt, "didn't you enlist after you were expelled from the University of Minnesota?"

I saw where he was going. "Yes, sir," I said, not very loudly.

"And you were expelled for organizing a rally for a Negro professor who happened to be a communist, and who opposed our actions in Korea! Isn't that right, Corporal Kelly?"

Well, shit. It would be funny even if the asshole wasn't so proud of it. Simms practically had a heart attack. I did my best to explain it, but I could see the whole thing was going down the tubes, even with the major.

By the time I got half-way organized, Cigarbreath was asking me if it wasn't true that within the past few days I'd told my company commander I didn't think what the United Nations Forces were doing in Korea justified killing the enemy. The fine hand of Winton, a meaner shit than I ever imagined.

Finally, Cigarbreath came back to my "story," as he put it, of coming up on Sam in his hole that night. He asked me if I knew the lieutenant had testified, and Eddie would testify, they saw me wake Sam up by hitting him.

At this point Simms got into some mumbo jumbo about hearsay and facts not in evidence. It all sounded like bullshit. An officer sitting on the side, called the law officer, told Cigarbreath he'd better be careful.

Even if Cigarbreath was telling me the truth about what the lieutenant and Eddie said, they couldn't see anything that night, and they were lying as bad as I was. Anyway, whatever anyone else said, I'd told my story and my best bet was to stick to it, and I did.

The thing was, when I was all done, Cigarbreath asked me, "Corporal Kelly, if you didn't hit PFC Warren as your company commander and another soldier on patrol with you have stated, would you please tell the panel how is it that PFC Warren's lip was split and bleeding profusely that night?"

Now, when I needed him, Simms didn't say anything. I sat there in a pile of shit. I hadn't talked to Simms, who thought he was such a Clarence Darrow, about how Sam's lip did get cut and bleeding if I didn't hit him like the lieutenant and Eddie testified. It was the kind of question Clarence Darrow was supposed to think of before we got to this point, a real good, simple question.

I didn't know what answer Sam had given. I tried to catch Simms's eye, but he wouldn't look at me. I'd look guilty as hell, even though I was not the one on trial, if I delayed any longer. So I just said, "I don't know, sir."

As soon as I did, I could hear Simms breathe this big sigh of relief. I didn't know what the hell he was so relieved about.

Lieutenant Cigarbreath waited for a long time. Then he asked me again if it was my testimony that Sam was awake when I first approached him.

I said, "Yes, sir," again.

Cigarbreath got red in the face, a bright red, like he was going to have apoplexy, and leaned right into my face and asked me, "Do you know the penalties for perjury, soldier?"

"No, sir," but, because at this point I was damn curious, it popped out, "What are they, sir?"

Apparently, Cigarbreath didn't expect to be asked to provide the answer because he got even redder in the face, and said, "Very severe, soldier. Very severe."

He got me to say guard duty was important, and guys could get killed if one of their comrades messed up, which I had to admit or sound like I was ready for a section 8. I fleetingly considered commenting on his choice of "comrades," but naturally I thought better of it.

After Cigarbreath was done, Sam's guy asked me a couple of questions, stuff like whether I was telling the truth or not, which was an interesting question, when you thought about it.

That was all for me. I was dismissed without immediate prosecution for perjury. I noticed one of the big honchos at the head table shaking his head as I left.

As it happened, Sam didn't get off. The court found Lieutenant Winton and chickenshit bucking-for-corporal Eddie Kvard more convincing than Sam and me. Not too surprising, since I was such a fellow-traveling, pinko, perjurer, nigger-lover. I tried to remind myself what I'd put to one side amid all the bullshit: Sam was asleep on guard duty.

Even though justice prevailed and Sam was shipped off to the stockade, the lieutenant didn't appreciate my testimony. He took each and every available opportunity after the trial to let me know that he did not. When I asked him what stockade Sam had been sent to, he just glared at me and didn't even answer.

Screw him. I was out of here more skosh now. I was getting short, real short.

36

Up and down the line there was ferocious fighting while the truce talks at Panmunjom dragged on. The word was they agreed on what to do about the prisoners, but then Syngman Rhee on his own just let thousands of the poor bastard North Korean prisoners go, why God only knew, but probably to sabotage any truce. Rhee seemingly didn't want this war to end and kept talking about going it alone. We heard that the Chinese attacked and slaughtered thousands of ROK troops, wiping out a whole division, near someplace called Kumsong, till our guys shifted down the line and bailed them out. It was all crazy but at least they were talking again.

A BONANZA AT MAIL CALL. Two letters, one from Annie and one from Lindeman. I started with Will's. I saved Annie's for last.

> July 4, 1953
> Fort Ord, California
> Dear Tom:
> Happy Fourth of July—if I can still count you will soon be liberated! However the Secretary of the Army is coming through this post, so we have to stay in the office. As I have nothing to do, I will condescend to write to you, even though, as I remember, you are in debt to me for the sum of more than one epistolary offering.

Two of the other instructors are also writing letters this morning, but they are writing to their respective Congressmen. The school here is wonderful, however they have teams of officers come around and inspect the classes while they are in session. These officers don't know the subject at all, and cannot, therefore, offer anything in the line of constructive criticism but only note petty things: "Instructor is too pleasant." "Students were neat but two needed a haircut" "Subject is covered well (I don't know how he would know), but the instructor didn't offer any humor" (We do mix humor with our lecture, but since much of it has these inspectors as the butt of the joke, their presence in the class of course cramps our style). These are actual quotes, so you can see what we are up against.

I am enjoying teaching more all the time. I definitely think I will follow something like this in life—a teacher, or maybe a lawyer. However the way to make money in the legal profession is to become a tax expert or a corporation lawyer working over books eight or ten hours a day, and that doesn't quite appeal to me. I have been thinking of requesting a grant from Ford or Rockefeller (or one of those bastards that avoid taxes by "giving" money away) and starting a debating tour challenging all the Jesuits in the world to a debate on the validity of Christianity. Would you like to tour the country with me?

There is one of the instructors here who is very much in love with an apparently devout yet intelligent Catholic girl. However, compromise is impossible on his part. He wrote a letter to her last week suggesting what a boon to society it would be if somebody "cut the liver out of the Pope." He has gone home this weekend to try to patch things up. I told him to try to reach her on a rational ground. But he looks at the Church as a horrible monster, which should be shown for what it is, and then stoned to death in the street.

Well, I am 21 now. All of these guys took me in town and bought me the first ten or twelve legal drinks. We wound up drinking straight Vodka. Don't try it; it's treacherous, but we had a hell of a good time. Sex life is at a low ebb. If it wasn't for occasional jacking off, I would go crazy. About that society climbing, there's an N.G. cpl. who wants me to go home to San Francisco with him and meet more of his "beautiful society girls." That's what he calls them. Well, you know I have nothing against marrying rich, but I couldn't take any "Country Club" bullshit now.

What are you going to do when you get out? I can't decide where to go to school, what to take or anything. I don't even know what I want to be in life. If we get home to Fargo together, we could get drunk and convert the whole place. Stacey said to me one time her friend Arlene got into the car and said to you, "Hi, how is Communism, atheism, and all the other isms?" Write and advise what you're up to, dammit! And where is your damn book. I won't show it to anyone if you don't want me to. Never mind! You'll be home before the book is. Stop by San Francisco when you arrive in the States, and we will get drunk and figure out what you should do when you're a free man!

Will

What do you hear from your friend Annie?

Right, Will. I was not a circuit rider for or against the Jesuits. Otherwise reading a lot of his letter was like looking in a mirror. Will. Me.

I'd wondered about many of the same things, and it was nearing time to decide. I remembered my conversations with Moira about going to Harvard Law School as a ticket to fame, fortune, and becoming secretary of state. Even after I decided I didn't want to spend my days making the world safe for General Motors, I still thought about law as a way to make a living, do some good, and later go into politics.

But somewhere along the line, maybe just because I kept doing it, it had become clear to me I wanted to be a writer. This scared the shit out of me. You had to get very lucky to even earn a living at it, much less a good living. I tried to tell myself that I could do a lot of good in this world by writing, but deep down I just wanted to write well, whether it did anyone any good or not. This was even scarier because nothing I wrote was ever anywhere near even satisfactory.

I read Lindeman's litany of the grief religion was causing his buddy. The Church caused nothing but pain for Moira and me. To hear Carl Bergstrom tell it, the Jews and the Lutherans wrecked his and his obedient Elaine's love life. Annie worried like crazy about the Jews and the goyim. I wondered idly what Meiko was—Shinto, Hindu, or Bantu. Whatever the deal was on religion, I just couldn't take very seriously any more the idea any God who was worth bothering about could give much of a damn about anyone's religion.

I had Annie's letter to read. I opened it.

THE GRASS

June 28, 1953
Richmond, Virginia

Tom dear,

I was really thrilled to get your letter, thrilled you've decided to go back to school and that Columbia has accepted you! What exciting news! You are doing the right thing to finish school, Tom, whether you stay with your dream of writing or take some other path. I was quite amused by the part saying you were loafing! You've certainly more than made up for that in the past—if it's true—and the writing you've been doing hardly qualifies as loafing even if it isn't being done for the Army.

But how close you are to coming home! I'm very happy you are being so careful—-and that things are working out well. With just a little more good luck you ought to be safely out of Korea. If I were a praying sort of person, I would certainly pray for you, but you know you are in my thoughts, and that I wish you all the good luck possible.

There's nothing much new with me. I'm feeling much better—both mentally and physically. I'm even eating a few fresh vegetables and some fruit, which, believe me, I appreciate. Of course being limited is a pain in the derriere—but I'm grateful for small favors.

I'm looking for a job—which seems to be as difficult to find in Richmond as it is in N.Y.—however, as you see, I'm still staying with Mother and Natalie—and Adam!—so my overhead is not too high. Incidentally, Mother and Natalie send their best. The baby keeps Natalie very busy but she still holds onto the hope that her Ralph is alive somewhere in that dreadful place you are in.

As soon as I find a job, I will get a place of my own, which will be better living circumstances, although having company has its merits. You complicate things with your decision to go to New York. You don't say clearly that you want me to return there to be with you. I don't know that I'm ready to return there myself, Tom, not just yet.

I don't know how to answer all your questions, Tom. You said to me in one of our arguments, about your friend Schlumberger, that everything you did or didn't do had consequences. Of course! I said. Remember? I'm afraid that's true, whether or not I said you could tell me anything, and whether or not you "confess." I wouldn't write these things to you, but you asked for honesty. So honesty you get!

I feel something has changed in you. You say that I can scarcely comprehend the things you've been through in Korea, and that may be true. I sometimes wish I hadn't encouraged you to tell me everything, or that you'd lied to me anyway. But there is no room for lies or half truths between us, is there?

Some of what's happened to you has changed you, and my knowing of it, may change the way I will feel about you. I don't think so, but I honestly don't know. But you once chided me for closing you out of the most painful part of my life, and you were right to do so. I can only ask that you not do that to me now.

I sometimes sense that your feelings toward me have changed. I hope not. Yet if they have I ask that you tell me honestly. Whatever the truth is, no lies between us. Having said all this, and faced more disapproval from my mother than you have any idea of, I give you fair warning, don't say anything more to me you're not prepared for me to take seriously. So how do you feel about that? You'd better be careful. I might just take you up on what you say!

But this is much too serious for such a time. You are coming home! Come home!

With love,

Annie

I read her letter again.

Right then a lot of me wished I'd never told her about all that was gone on over here. Not all that had "gone on"; all I'd done. I loved Annie, and I was going to see her when I returned, wherever she was. But the truth was, if I was honest with her, and I owed her that, and with myself, which I might as well be, I didn't know if I was ready, as she once said about me, to "take her on." Her breaking down again had scared me, and I was going to be moving on, and I didn't know if she'd be ready to move on with me. We'd have to see who we both were now. I didn't want to turn out to be just another asshole in Annie's life.

ON THE TIT THERE WAS BOREDOM, tedium, and apathy, for everybody but me. One more week and I was going off line for good. I was not bored. Someone got killed in our sector just often enough to remind us there was a war going on. It was hard to figure out. Sometimes we could see the Chinese through the glasses. Just the other day we watched a bunch of them right behind their position, playing volleyball, laughing and slamming the ball over the net. A jerk forward observer wanted to call it in to the fire direction center for an artillery fire mission. But most of us figured why do that, and draw fire in response, so he didn't. We even got to rooting for different sides and some of us started taking bets. Bets on the same guys who still tried to kill us every now and then, and might try to kill us tomorrow if it fit into the great scheme of things.

That morning one of the Chinese crept into our lines to surrender. He came in clutching a white hankie. His hand trembled as he waved the hankie, and his wide eyes looked frantically around from one of us to another. He was so young I couldn't help but think of the kid I killed our first day on the Tit, the time I killed someone and knew I'd killed someone.

Of course this kid didn't speak any English, and we didn't speak any Chinese. When shithead Eddie Kvard laughed and pointed his piece at him like he was about to shoot him, the poor kid shook like he had the chills and shit in his pants he was so scared. I pointed my piece right at Eddie and yelled at Eddie that if he blew the kid away, I'd blow him away. Fortunately Eddie said he was just kidding. It turned out the kid didn't even have a weapon, just rice and dried apples in a pouch.

IT WAS NICE TO GET A LETTER AND CAKE from my mother, and a note from my dad, for my twentieth birthday. And a book, *Moby Dick*, and another letter from Moira. It all got to me for my b-day. I was surprised all the way around.

After I'd read my folks' letters, and my bunkmates demolished the cake in about thirty seconds flat, I read the letter from Moira.

> July 6, 1953
> Fargo, North Dakota
>
> Dear Tom,
>
> I'm at the breakfast table, which is still piled high with dirty dishes. Daddy has dashed off to play golf and Mother is no doubt on her third Bloody Mary by now. It is hot and I am so alone. I have gone through a period of tremendous religious doubt. None of what I had been taught seemed to be true in my life. I felt I had no opinion, that I am amoral, passive, confused. But I went to confession to Father Mahoney, and I felt so much better. Of course, you'll just say that I resolved it in the usual way—I believe in God, therefore—

Writing has always been in a way like talking to you. But now you are so far away, and your world so different from mine. So many of these letters have passed between us in the past months—all beginning and ending the same, all containing much the same thing—that you have become to me a name scrawled on the bottom of a page. I am afraid you have become lost to me, without my ever realizing it. Sometimes I'm not sure I know you anymore.

Even so I haven't ever admitted you were lost to me; rather, I thought one day you would call and say you were home, and I would see you again and know you were real. But suddenly the other morning, I woke up and I felt a vacuum, a frightening void in my whole life, and I cried, Tom. And I remembered what you said that time we broke up over that bar girl you slept with: "I'll lie down in your doorway until you come and lie beside me—" And at that time, I thought it was momentary and we would both forget and go our separate ways. But the other morning I cried, because I had lost the one, the only big important thing in my life—you.

I can't fight for you with thousands of miles between us; this is the best I can do. With all that has gone on between us, you must know I can't explain every word, every action, every thought of the past months. I can't understand myself, why I did some of what I've done. But I know, this I really know, I have made mistakes. I have been misled and deluded, more than I can tell you. But, Tom, you've made mistakes, too, and it's not fair there's a double standard.

I may not be the person your Annie Jones is, but I am young, Thomas, like you, naive and selfish and inexperienced. I have tried before to be self-sacrificing and compassionate and at times I have succeeded. And we would have a whole life together, we could have children and all the things that belong to youth. Isn't that worth some consideration? Grant me that I can grow, that I will become a woman.

When you come home, Tom, and you must, you'll have to give us just one more chance. You saw us as inevitable once, and I believe you will again, if you will but look honestly within yourself. I have prayed to God like never before that He would send you back to me. And if there is a God, He will. If you will only come back, I will prove to you nothing can come between us again. I love you without reservation, without condition. When you return I will take up any life you choose, if you will only take me with you.

If you don't come back, I will take my money and come after you. Wherever you go, I will stay and make you support me, I will plead and

cry, until you have to "come and lie beside me." Please, my Tom, come
home soon.

All of my love, always,
Your Moira

I could see Moira alone at the breakfast table with the dishes
piled high, writing earnestly, putting herself right on the line. I could still
see her so clearly, touch her image in my mind, and still want her so badly
sometimes. I felt sadness, and a terrible, surprising loneliness.

She'd "made mistakes." Ramsted. I'd always known Moira didn't
give a rat's ass about him, though she wouldn't mind the money, and I
didn't give a rat's ass about him either. Will was another story. Will still
hurt. I'd made mistakes too. After our stupid fight about Joan, I did tell
Moira that I'd lie down in her doorway till she lay down beside me. Joan
was a mistake. But Joan wasn't the same as Will.

Gary Kowalski, one night sitting around the barracks, had said
that, with a guy, unless you were in love with the girl, it was like you put
your dipstick in, and you just wiped it off, the image of metal sliding into
metal making me wince despite the truth in it. Yet somehow with a girl it
seemed like this Holy Grail had been defiled, by somebody else, and
could never be the same for you. Of course, I knew Moira was no grail,
nor Annie, and I didn't really want them to be.

It was a wonder how women had the capacity to give and receive
so much happiness, and so much pain. Somewhere in *From Here to
Eternity* I read a line about how God dealt the women all the cards
between their legs. But after all of Moira's and my crazy ups and downs,
what the hell was the point in keeping score anyway. In my gut I knew she
was right about the double standard. They needed us as much as we
needed them.

With Moira putting it all on the line one more time, one last time,
as hurt and angry as I'd been so many times, my gut got tight. I hated all
the ways Moira was right about herself and me and Annie. Annie. Annie
wasn't a mistake. Moira was right that she wasn't the person Annie was;
she was a girl and Annie was a woman. But maybe Moira could grow and

she would become a woman, and she and I could have a whole life together and children and the "all the things that belong to youth."

The first time I told Moira I loved her, we were just kids, hanging around her house, listening to records. When she bent over to put a new record on, the ridge of her spine was outlined against the light-blue oxford cloth man's shirt she was wearing on top of her leotards, and then Lena Horne's cool voice singing "Where or When" filled the room:

> Some things that happen for the first time
> Seem to be happening again . . .

Moira had beckoned for me to dance with her, and we barely moved to the music, and I felt her breasts soft against me, and she made the words against my neck, "I love you, Tom. I've always loved you, and I always will." I felt her breath against my neck, and her lips brush me there, and her hair was fragrant as if she'd just stepped out of the shower. "You love me, too, Tom. You know you do. Tell me you do."

"Yes," I'd said, "I do."

"Tell me, Tom."

"I love you, Moira," I'd said then, and I did.

But I just didn't any more. There was no point in going through all this shit in my head. Remembering things that happened or didn't between Moira and me. What each of us thought about God or getting rich. Figuring out this or that. It was all bullshit. Either you loved someone or you didn't, and I just didn't love Moira anymore. And then I almost physically felt what I once felt for Moira recede, the way the ripple of the tide on the beach feels when it washes over your feet and then recedes. I felt free.

I didn't know what would happen with Annie, and for a second I felt scared about that and lonesome as hell, but I loved Annie. Whatever I thought about her and me, that was how I felt. That might be all I knew, but I knew that.

37

My last week in Korea.

I was sitting on this treeless hill, looking out over the Chorwon Valley, writing in my notebook. A huge white moon lit everything like an enormous floodlight and I could see the paths for miles along the floor of the valley. Paddies shimmered inside the remnants of dikes, still silver ponds. In its way Korea was beautiful, with its rugged mountain ranges and rolling valleys and miles of the paddies. When the early sun burned the mist off the hills, I could see why they called it "The Land of the Morning Calm."

But the war had devastated the land itself. Up close, ridges that should be green were cratered and desolate, devoid of trees, shrubbery, even grass. And otherwise barren high ground was littered with equipment and sometimes with bodies. I had to go over to the ROK position on White Horse Mountain the other day. There'd been heavy fighting going on there, and the whole hillside was strewn with decaying corpses and rotting uniforms. I didn't see how the survivors could even stay in position with all the bodies putrefying around them.

Lieutenant Winton kept telling me we were at the hinge point of history, that a hundred years from now people would say this was where and when we stopped the spread of communism. I wondered how those poor peasants who got killed in the Thirty Years War felt about the whole thing.

Whether one of their officers told them they were at a hinge point in history. I doubted those Koreans on White Horse felt any better for stopping communism.

When an old mamasan with a bundle on her head trudged along the road, the same as a mamasan did two hundred or two thousand years ago, or an old papasan, in his stovepipe hat, with an A-frame piled high on his back, I wondered if all of us made a bit of difference to them. Other than to have ripped up their lives by moving them off their farms and down to someplace they didn't want to be, except it was better than being killed by artillery shells, didn't matter whose.

The Chinese weren't likely to come at us here tonight, not with this moon. They hadn't come in force for a while, but they could come in close with a few guys and lob in mortar rounds, till we got them or they faded back into the night. One of the odd rounds they fired a couple of nights ago killed the newest guy on line: a big, awkward kid by the name of Smitty, who reminded me of a little of Schlumberger.

I was counting the days and the hours and I was edgy tonight. I kept hearing something moving. One of our guys, or just the rats that had decided to call this bunker home, but I worried that it was a Chinese guy out there on patrol, scared, just like me, just wanting to get out of Korea alive. Scuttlebutt had it a truce might be signed real soon. None of us wanted to die just so some politician could cut a little better deal.

The politicians. Why was it so often the guy with power turned out to be such an asshole? And it was funny the turns things took when you went against the assholes. I was on Winton's shit list for trying to help out the sad case of Sam Warren. Hell, I wouldn't even be here in the first place if I hadn't stood up against the university for Prof Williams when Werrecker caved in to the politicians. I'd be hanging around school, drinking coffee and writing about young love, not counting down the days writing about killing in Korea. I couldn't help but wonder if all my scribbling was a real book. Enough of a book to get it published.

I wished I had someone to talk to about it. Will Lindeman kept writing that he wanted to read it; and he might even understand. I'd show it to Annie, when I got back home. Some of it would hurt her, but, still, if we were going to be together, she'd have to know what I'd written. I could imagine the pain it would cause my folks to read it. The killing I'd seen. The killing I'd done.

Maybe I should stash it away for thirty or forty years till they'd died untroubled deaths. I wondered if Hemingway ever worried about what his parents might think of his writing? I didn't know at what point in Hemingway's life his father committed suicide. Well, shit, I was just getting morbid.

Screw it, I'd figure it out after we planted the damn grass seed tomorrow. Our new Division Commander toured the sector by helicopter yesterday. He was upset that the paths to our bunkers were so worn the Chinese could see them. So somewhere in FECOM he'd found some damn grass seed, and by nightfall tomorrow, "it will, repeat, it will" be planted on the paths. Only in the Army. If Brownie were still around he'd find a place to plant it all right.

But Lieutenant Winton would have us out there at dawn, spreading seed. I was surprised he didn't have us out there doing it by moonlight tonight. Whether it was because he was still pissed off about Sam Warren or because I was not going to re-up for another tour to save the world from communism, or all of the above, naturally, since it was this week's shit duty, the lieutenant had volunteered me for the seed detail.

The only thing I had to give the son of a bitch was he was just as short as I was, and he'd be out there tomorrow leading us. I'd like to think Winton, despite still having such a hard on for me about Sam Warren's court martial, was okay, but he wasn't. He'd "won," but I still couldn't see the use in ruining the next five years of Sam's life because the kid fell asleep. No one could see White Horse and say the Koreans were not ready to die for their country. And the Chinese must think they were dying for something. I just didn't think it was Sam's war.

For myself, I didn't think anything was worth this war any more. Or maybe anything ever had been worth any war, period. Like the song went: "Fuck 'em all, Fuck 'em all, the long and the short and the tall"—

all the countries and all the isms—capitalism and communism and nationalism and patriotism, and all the other isms. None of 'em was worth killing anyone for, not one human being. Well, shit. Much more of this and I would be going home as a damn section 8 case.

Time to hit the sack before tomorrow's chickenshit mission.

WE WERE UP BEFORE DAWN but it was already hot.

The Division Engineers had left all of the hundred-pound gunnysacks of grass seed on pallets outside our bunker during the night. The sons of bitches could have at least put the bags along the trails, but that would have been too much work, and it wouldn't do for the engineers to risk getting shot at while engaged in such a lunatic enterprise.

So the first thing our detail had to do was haul the bags by hand to intervals along the trails under the watchful eye of Lieutenant Winton. A few of the detail had weapons, and made a loose moving perimeter, mostly to make the rest of us feel better. But most of us were just grunt laborers this morning: throwing sacks awkwardly over our shoulders, picking our way down the steep, worn paths, as the bags slid around on our backs and dug into our shoulders.

I was already sweating as the sun cleared the mist off the distant ridges, and Winton started telling us to "Hurry up, men! Move it!" Of course he was too busy officering to carry any of the sacks. But when we looped back to the sacks to start spreading the grass seed along the trails, he was right there.

We had shovels, also courtesy of the engineers. Mine, left over from the First World War, splintery, dug into my palms as I changed it from hand to hand, to sprinkle the seed on the path. I tried to hug the hill, keeping my shovel and my ass as low to the ground as possible and still spray the seed around, and I was not too particular about how the seed actually covered the trail.

"Come on, Kelly. You can do better than that. Here!" Winton said to me. The stupid asshole grabbed my shovel, pushed it into the bag, and stood up to spread the shovel full of seed.

He was a black silhouette against the pale morning sky, when I heard a single rifle shot, and he crumpled over and fell. He lay motionless, my shovel across his chest.

Then I heard the thud of a mortar coming in near me, and another, before something slammed into my right arm, spinning me around and knocking me to the ground. I couldn't hear any more, but my ears were ringing. At first I didn't even feel any pain because of the shock. But that didn't last long and then my arm felt like it was burning up.

I looked down and I was bleeding and I tried to make a tourniquet out of the cloth hanging off the arm, but the blood was soaking my fatigues to it, and my fingers were numb and clumsy, and I panicked. I started screaming for a medic then, before I passed out.

I WOKE UP FLAT ON MY BACK in the Field Hospital with one hell of a headache, my ears still ringing against the hum of a generator pulsing somewhere near by, and an IV sticking in my good arm, but I was alive.

A young, balding medic—maybe a doc—his surgical mask loose above his sweat-soaked OD tee shirt and stethoscope hanging from his neck, hovered over me, his thick glasses glinting as he peered down at me and reached for my wrist.

"We're awake, are we?" he said. "Can you move your right arm?"

I winced as I lifted the bandaged arm from the pillow.

"Great. Now, make a fist."

I curled my fingers slowly into a fist and then extended them again.

"Good. No nerve damage. You're very lucky, soldier. A little concussion and a flesh wound. You lost some blood, but that's all. Your head-'ll feel like hell for a few more days, and you'll be a bit wobbly when you get up. Ask the nurses for some more pain meds when you need them. But you'll be going home soon."

I was too doped up to tell him I was going home anyway.

"Good as new," he said, lightly patting my shoulder.

"Good as new," he said again, before he moved on to the next man.

Spring 2007

Ben and I, along with twenty or so tourists, mainly other Americans, a couple of Brits and Australians, waited on the sidewalk outside the Westin Chosun Hotel in downtown Seoul.

Seoul had become a city of concrete, steel, glass, and chrome, complete with a TGIF and an Outback Steakhouse. The sidewalks were filled with crowds of well-dressed teenagers chattering into cell phones. Three purposeful men in double-breasted suits strode past us down the sidewalk, eyeing appreciatively, without breaking pace, two young women in short denim skirts who passed them without glancing back. Unending heavy traffic clogged the streets with cars, most of them Hyundais and KIAs but an old silver Mercedes rounded the corner. The traffic filled the air with exhaust and a number of older passersby wore small white masks.

The smog filtered unimpeded into my lungs, which had never fully recovered from years of smoking, even though I quit years back, when Annie had her first bout with cancer.

"Are you okay, Grandpa?" Ben asked when I coughed the second or third time.

"Yeah, thanks. Just the damn smog, you know."

"I know. My eyes are stinging," he said.

Ben was only fifteen. We'd come to Korea to see what Ben could learn about his birth parents. We had an appointment with the Seoul office of the Lutheran Social Services agency this afternoon. Ben's mother, I thought of her as his mother anyway, my daughter Elizabeth, had sent me to accompany him on this journey because, while she understood Ben's wish and had always thought this day would come, she "just couldn't deal with it now." With all of the trips Annie and I took over the years, even as close as China, we never came here. Maybe I just never wanted to deal with it either.

When the tour bus, more like a van, that would take us to the Demilitarized Zone arrived, there was a slight delay while I explained to the tour guide, as no Koreans were allowed on this tour, that Ben was American.

"Yes, yes," said Shinhee, her nametag in white on blue plastic. She was slender and businesslike in a white blouse and red blazer, and very pretty, with her smooth brown skin, dark eyes and full lips. "May I see your passport, please?" she asked Ben directly. Apparently the situation was familiar to her, and, satisfied, she handed the passport back.

We rode some thirty-five miles north of Seoul on a four-lane highway, flanked on our left by barbed wire and, now and then, wooden guard towers on stilts; and, beyond them, the slow moving Han River; endless paddies stretched off to our right. While we rode, Shinhee gave us, in excellent English, a Cliff Note history of Korea.

She skimmed through the country's occupation by the Japanese, its division after World War II, and the Korean War, saying that over four million people—men, women and children—died in the war.

When I asked how many GIs were killed or wounded, she handed me a pamphlet showing the flags of all of the UN participants in the war and listing all of the casualties by country. For America it showed 54,246 died, 33,269 on the battlefields, and that 103,284 had been wounded.

Ben commented on what a small portion of all of those who died in the war were American.

"Well, it was their country, not ours," I pointed out. "And I don't know the exact numbers, but I think we took almost as many casualties here in three years as we did in ten years in Vietnam. We had as many Americans killed in a day or two in some battles as we've lost in the whole war in Iraq, and no one at home cares about them, Ben. They're all forgotten."

"Well, okay," he said.

"You may keep the pamphlet, if you wish," Shinhee said to us.

We presented our passports for collection at a checkpoint that reminded me of Checkpoint Charlie, where Annie and I had passed through between West and East Berlin before the wall came down, the year before her cancer first recurred.

Our tour bus parked in the parking lot of Imjingak Park, which had a monument built to honor the sacrifice of the Americans in the war. Shinhee told us the park memorialized the "sadness and pain left by the war and the wish for reunification."

We transfered into a shuttle bus and paused at the Freedom Bridge built for the return of POWs after the war, for picture taking—strictly forbidden for much of the tour—and for popcorn and lattes, before we proceeded on to Tunnel 3. One of several the North Koreans dug in secret after the ceasefire, the tunnel was discovered in 1978. We donned safety helmets and rode a small monorail into the tunnel, where a few of us bumped our heads on the walls and ceilings.

Afterwards, before going on to the DMZ, we saw a mini-movie, a mini-museum and a sculpture of a divided but hopefully titled "Uniting Globe." President Eisenhower, when the Korean ceasefire was signed, quoted from the biblical language of the final paragraph of Lincoln's Second Inaugural Address, "With malice toward none; with charity for all . . ." and from what Shinhee told us families on both sides would like nothing more than "to bind up the nation's wounds." But that remained elusive. The South was trying to pursue a policy of "sunshine and openness," not always with American approval, while the North's Kim Jong Il sporadically threatened to go about his father's business, sometimes invoking possible North Korean nuclear weaponry.

At the Dora Observatory, located within the DMZ itself, pictures were allowed only from behind a painted yellow line set back fifteen feet behind a concrete wall. Behind us a group of Americans held up cameras to shoot the DMZ. Along the wall were binoculars for us, not unlike those on the Empire State Building. About one hundred yards out from the wall were guard towers. The Imjin River ran through the floor of the DMZ. A factory was being built on the other side of the brown valley.

The southern side of the zone was green and grassy and forested. Shinhee told us the northern side was brown and barren because the trees had been cut down for fuel for the North Koreans. Like the earlier checkpoint, the green hills and the brown reminded me of East and West Berlin before the fall, when the West was vibrant, colorful and thriving, and the East a world of drab, sullen gray. I wondered, mawkishly, just how many generations of grass had sprouted—since our last mission spreading grass seed in these hills when Lieutenant Winton—God, how many times had I wanted him dead?—gave his last full measure.

I remembered my father telling me years ago that he had stood on the high ground overlooking the grassy fields of Gettysburg and recited silently to himself the well-remembered words of Lincoln's address there. This ground before Ben and me was just as hallowed and consecrated with deaths. But, so far as America was concerned today, or even then, these were largely ignored or forgotten deaths. Despite a long delayed monument, and the occasional Veteran's Day mention, not many at home really gave a damn about these deaths. Not to mention those who came home but with shattered or wounded bodies. Or minds.

The one right and true thing I'd done with my life was to marry Annie, because I loved her, and I was lucky enough that she loved me. But there was an irony in our marriage that, with all we shared, I hoped she was never aware of. I had been so worried. Worried that taking care of her wasn't the right kind of love. As it turned out, Annie was the one who took care of me.

She couldn't heal me, but she gave me sense and strength to go ahead with my life when what I had experienced in these hills had pulled me into the deep slew of unreasoning depression that had threatened me in ways I didn't fully understand myself. It wasn't my fault that I'd lived. The killing that I'd done was not only what my country called for from me, those I killed had been trying to kill me. To this moment, I didn't know how many I killed. Many times I had fired into the darkness and at shadowy, moving figures that I didn't know for sure if I'd hit, and they had no faces.

After my first day in Korea, I never saw another face of anyone I knew I'd killed. But to this moment that kid haunted me. I wondered if his parents ever found out what happened to him. How painful it would have been for them not to even know. I'd tried to get rid of him. I knew that he was why, all elaborate arguments to the side, I wound up on the streets with the kids and peaceniks protesting the Vietnam War and on the streets again with the anonymous protestors when we invaded Iraq. But there was no point in getting maudlin about him now, a half century later.

I was surprised by Ben's arm around me.

"Are you okay, Grandpa?" he asked. "Are you crying?" He was still not as tall as I was, but he was stronger, his shoulders like a square T under his black tee shirt.

"No, of course not," I said. "Just thinking about when I was here before."

We went on to the Dorasan Station, visited with some publicity by President Bush in 2002, where the high speed train built by the South, with hopes of linking up through North Korea and all the way on to the main continent of Asia ended for now. Outside the station was a wall engraved with the names of Koreans who donated funds to build parts of the railroad. Shinhee said this was where the future of Korea was, waiting to be realized.

At a stop on the way back, I declined an opportunity to buy amethysts at a thirty-percent discount but purchased a piece of rusted barbed-wire fence, Serial No. 008193, removed from the DMZ and mounted on a plaque "on the occasion of the fiftieth anniversary of

Korean War with the dearest wish of Peace for Mankind." My Visa card was accepted for the costs of the tour, $47.84 American, each, and we got our passports back.

We'd look for Ben's birth mother that afternoon.

We'd already been told at the Lutheran Social Services at home that finding her would be problematic. Ben wanted to find her, though, meet her, and I would too if I were Ben. He knew that was his past, and that his future was at home. But he felt a need to learn what he could, and he had confidence.

"You being old and all," Ben said, and it no longer surprised me how direct he was at fifteen, "people listen to you, Grandpa. You can talk 'em into it."

"It doesn't always work that way, Ben," I said. "But we'll try."

ACKNOWLEDGMENTS

Early help with *The Grass* came from Mary Francois Rockcastle and writing classes at The Loft and from Will Weaver at Split Rock. Individual writing groups with Loren Taylor, Roger Barr, and Melissa Wright and others, and many writers from the Minneapolis Writers Workshop, contributed to the shaping and reshaping of the book; as did a careful read by editor and journalist Jeremy Stratton.

In writing *The Grass*, apart from my own experience, I drew inspiration from photographs, newsreels, magazines, movies, and from some actual events of the 1950s. I also shaped letters from that time to fit fictional events occuring to the entirely fictional characters in the novel. I was helped by comments from many combat veterans, including most notably Tom Chisholm.

In researching *The Grass*, I read far too many books to list in full, but those I found particularly useful include: *The Fifties* by David Halberstam; *No Ivory Tower, McCathyism and the Universities*, Ellen W. Schrecker, *The Hidden History of the Korean War*, I.F. Stone; *This Kind of War*, T.R. Fehrenbach; *The Forgotten War: America in Korea, 1950-1953*, Clay Blair; more helpful than anything else published on the war, *The Korean War, An Oral History*, two volumes, Donald Knox, with additional text by Alfred Coppel; and *Many Lives Intertwined: A Memoir*, Hyun Sook Han.

The Grass benefited from reading and comments along the way from my wife, Betts, and our daughter, Anne, sons Matthew and Paul, and son Steven's wife, Joanne Tobey. Thanks are also due to my brother Mike and his wife, Judy, and my sister Susan for their support.

In its final stages, *The Grass* owed great credit, and no blame, to the careful editing and suggestions of Paulette Bates Alden.

I also owe thanks to Corinne and Seal Dwyer of North Star Press for taking a chance on my book.

Finally, this novel would never have been written without the loving and patient support over many years of Betts.